# F

Case Number One

## THE MISSING
# ANGELA HOSSACK

Copyright
All rights reserved
This book is a work of fiction and any resemblance to individuals, either alive or dead, or any resemblance to past or current events are purely coincidental.
© Copyright Angela Hossack 2021
The right of Angela Hossack to be identified as author of this work has been asserted in accordance with the Copyright, Designs and Patents Act 1988

# Prologue
# Kevin

THEY NEVER TURNED OFF the lights, so he never knew if it was day or night. The incessant hum of the fluorescent tubes on the high ceiling was often the only sound in the room, but – more often than not – screams rent the air.

Sometimes, those screams were his.

They wanted to take his eyes. He'd heard them talking about it. They thought he was asleep, but the drugs had worn off and he was wide awake. He had the sense to remain perfectly still. He was good at feigning sleep. He'd learned how to do it during the years he'd lived with his mom. Sometimes, it had been the only way to stave off the advances of the men she'd brought to the apartment for sex. Other times, it allowed him to close himself against what he heard in his mom's room. He'd never heard anything nice coming from that room.

Now - strapped to a strange bed, helpless, alone, and terrified – he wished for something he never, in his wildest dreams, imagined he would want.

He wished he was back in the apartment with his mom.

Wishing didn't work, so he tried silently praying.

*Dear God... help me. I'll be good, I promise. Please... please...*

Even as the words to God swirled around in his head, he knew they were a waste of time. God had never helped him before – not once in the whole of his thirteen years. It wasn't that He never had ample reasons or opportunities to intervene in his life. There had been plenty of those. He just never seemed to pay any heed to him or his troubles.

The day he left home for good, he pretty much gave up on God, but – now that he was *really* in the shit – he thought to give Him one more chance. After all, he had nothing to lose.

*Lord God, you know me, don't you? I'm Kevin Murphy. I don't go to church, or anything like that, but I hope you won't hold that against me. I'm not a bad boy. You see everything, so I know that you know that. You know I only stole those things so I could get money to eat. I'm not sorry, so I guess I won't ask for forgiveness, but there is something I really do need to ask you. Will you to help me get outta this place? Please... before they take my eyes. I promise that, no matter how hungry I get, I'll do my best not to steal anything ever again. Amen.*

He waited. He wasn't sure whether to expect some sort of sign from above – a bright light, a burning bush, or something along those lines.

They were poking at him. He dared to open his eyes, hoping to see one of God's angels poised to free him.

There was only *them*. He blinked and let out a small groan.

"Ah, you're awake," the man said, leaning over and peering down at him. "Excellent."

"His clinical observations are all normal," the woman at the man's side said. "He's a healthy little fucker. Do you want me to feed him?"

The man nodded. "I don't see why not. We won't operate for a few days yet. Best to keep him hydrated and nourished."

"Very good, doctor. What about the others? Shall I feed them, too?"

He shook his head. "Nil by mouth for them."

Kevin Murphy – thirteen-year-old, street kid, scrawny but as smart as a whip – gave up on God for the final time in his life.

# Friar and Tuck

# 1

TUCK FROWNED AND GLANCED at her watch. He was late – *again*. She wished that she could break him of the habit of rolling in whenever he damned well pleased, but there was no way to control anything that Detective Bolton Friar did. He simply wasn't a man that anyone could control. Puffed up by his own self-importance, and not giving a damn about keeping her waiting, he wasn't the partner best suited to her. The problem was – there was no one else prepared to work with her.

She wasn't hurt by that fact. Such things as not being liked, or being thought of as a weirdo, didn't affect her. What affected her was the asshole thinking that he could run late on her again.

It smacked of disrespect and it pissed her off.

He didn't seem to piss anyone else off. There were officers around the precinct who were naïve enough to be taken in by his easy smile, and the clever way he had of nodding his head, and saying, *yeah, yeah*, as if he agreed with everything they said, and then went right off and did exactly what he wanted. They didn't seem to notice or care that he was never on time for anything.

Well, *she* noticed, and *she* cared. One of these days, she'd swing for him.

She glanced at her watch once more. *Damn him to Hell and back.* Today was not the day to fuck about. She'd give him five more minutes.

She felt their eyes on her – her colleagues, her peers, her antagonists, her fellow detectives. She knew that they were looking at her with bemused expressions on their faces, wondering when she was going to erupt. She knew that they were already laying bets on how long it would take her to lose her shit.

*Ten minutes past fucking ten.* She'd give him until a quarter past, and then she'd leave without him – and, she'd do it without making a fuss. Now, wouldn't that surprise the hell out of everyone in the room – her walking out without raising the roof? It would give them something to talk about – Tuck keeping hold of her temper.

She silently fumed. She wouldn't forgive him for this. She'd left messages. She'd emphasized the importance of being on time, and he'd still fucked her over.

The ability to forgive wasn't written into Tuck's DNA. Some genetic twist of fate had rendered her quite incapable of the tolerance required to pardon anyone for anything. As far as her uptight and anally meticulous mind was concerned, there was never *any* reason to either excuse or exonerate bad behaviour.

Some would say – her parents especially – that Detective Josephine Tuck wasn't cut out for law enforcement. They would say that she didn't have what it took to work as part of a team. They believed that she was nowhere near capable of engaging appropriately with people. The fact that they were most probably right hadn't stopped her from pursuing her dream. When she considered the obstacles she would be forced to overcome in applying to the academy, she'd developed a *fuck it* attitude, and just went for it.

She had more than met the minimum academic qualifications. She not only had a Batchelor's degree, but also earned a Master's degree in Law Enforcement from Georgetown University. The entrance exam for the police academy was a piece of piss to pass. Her knowledge of criminal investigations, interviewing techniques, and all relevant case law, meant that passing the detective exam was also a piece of piss.

She was a damned good detective, but it seemed that Friar was the only one with a skin thick enough to tolerate working with her. Unfortunately, it was that thick skin that riled her the most. She couldn't pierce through it and that meant there was nothing she could do to bring him into line.

Once, he'd told her that *her* line wasn't *his* line and she could draw *her* line in the sand as often as she damned well pleased, but he would ignore it, or walk across it whenever he chose.

Fucking Friar. She really would swing for him.

Someone sniggered at her back. She didn't turn to look. Whoever it was, probably Baxter, wanted her to do just that - look. He wanted to goad some reaction out of her. They were always doing that – trying to rile her. They loved watching the show that stirring her up would cause.

Over the space of six years she'd successfully kept her weirdness to a minimum and literally forced herself to assimilate. However, despite all of her attempts to conform to what was expected of her, her colleagues all knew that she was different, and they didn't like her for it.

She didn't give a shit about not being liked. She was used to it. What she *did* mind was the perpetual requests for transfer by those detectives forced to partner with her. She hated that they virtually begged for reassignment after mere weeks of working directly with her. *Bunch of pussies.*

In the six months, since moving to New York, and joining the 76$^{th}$ precinct in Brooklyn she'd gone through two partners. Bolton Friar was currently her third.

She didn't have high hopes of him lasting much longer than the others an, at that moment she didn't much care. As far as she was concerned, the sooner he fucked off, the better.

So far he seemed to be tolerating her foibles. Her eccentricities didn't make him nervous, and her fits of temper were water off a duck's back. Where the others would choose to be locked-in with a murderous sociopath - armed to the teeth and foaming at the mouth – rather than be in a room alone with her, Friar could sit in a car for hours on stake-out, or share an interview room all day with her, and not bat an eyelid.

He was no pussy. If it wasn't for *his* foibles and *his* eccentricities – like his unpunctuality, his nonchalant attitude to crime, and his habit of hoovering up anything with sugar on it - she might actually have a grudging respect for him.

*Fifteen minutes past ten.* She really ought to go. Time, and crime, waited for no one.

She stood and grabbed her jacket off the back of her chair, then reached into the desk drawer and removed her gold shield and her weapon.

When the door swung open and he walked through, there was a collective sigh around the room. It was almost as if everyone was disappointed to see him arrive.

Friar entered the squad room on a saunter and headed straight for the coffee machine. He greeted no one, and kept his mind tightly focussed on grabbing the first cup of java of the morning.

Many would describe Friar as striking. He wasn't handsome in the traditional sense, but he had a charismatic and appealing look that drew the eye.

Close-cropped hair, a morning shadow, and wearing clothes that looked as if he'd slept in them, Bolton Friar owned the room. He was well aware of the daggers being shot from Tuck's eyes, but he paid them no heed. All he was interested in was the coffee.

She wasted no time in marching right on over to him.

"Where the fuck have you been?" she said. "It's gone a quarter past ten."

"Good morning to you, too," he returned. "You want a cup of coffee?"

"No, I don't want a fucking cup of coffee. I want to get out of here."

His eyes were warm. He wasn't in the least perturbed by his partner's potty mouth. He was fast becoming used to it. Anyway, she'd caught him in a good mood. After the wonderful night he'd just shared with the woman of his dreams, nothing could sour his disposition.

"Sorry I'm late," he said.

She wasn't impressed by his apology. She knew he didn't mean it. "I was expecting you an hour ago."

He shrugged. "Things to do, Tuck. You know how it is."

Yes, she knew. She wondered what particular *thing* had kept him in bed way past time - probably a blonde *thing* with a tight ass and big boobs. It usually was.

She huffed in a sigh, willing herself to calm down. There was no fucking way that she was going to put on the spectacle of a show for all the assholes in the room to witness – not that morning.

"Well, you're here now," she conceded. "So, let's roll."

"Not without coffee, Tuck. Give me a minute."

"A minute? You want another minute?" Her foot tapped out on the floor. "You're joking, right?"

"I never joke about coffee." He placed a paper cup into the machine, pressed one of the array of buttons, and waited as the antiquated machine began to splutter and fill the cup with brown sludge.

He felt her eyes on him. He wished, for her sake, that she would learn how to chill. She was doing herself no favours by being so uptight and self-righteous. Others weren't quite as understanding as he was. Her fundamental lack of manners, her weird quirks, and her propensity to get right up their noses, meant that she was being increasingly ostracized. Okay, so she had some sort of psychological problem, but who *wasn't* fucked-up in some way? Having a screw loose was no excuse for bad manners.

He smiled to himself, recalling the age-old saying – *you don't have to be mad to work here, but it helps.* That sure was true of the 76$^{th}$ precinct. A bigger bunch of misfits you'd never hope to meet. But, they all did their job and tried to keep their individual peculiarities to themselves. Not Tuck, though. She rammed her issues right down their throats, and then wondered why nobody liked her.

Although he understood and sympathized, there was only so much of her crap that he could take. When the lieutenant literally begged him to partner with her, he agreed only on the understanding that he be allowed to ditch her - no questions asked – as, and when, he'd had enough. Well, he was reaching that point and – if she didn't allow him to have his coffee in peace – that point would be immediately reached.

He removed the cup from its little slot, turned, and said, "Don't be so impatient, Tuck. Another minute won't hurt. There's no fire to be put out, so what's the big deal?"

He searched the basket for sugar. There wasn't any, just those little pink sachets of sweetener. His good mood suddenly soured. He hated coffee without sugar. He wondered if Tuck would agree to stop at the Starbucks on Union Street. Starbucks would definitely have sugar, and, anyway, he preferred their coffee to the disgusting concoction spewed out by the machine in front of him.

"What's the big deal?" She dragged in another breath. "I've got a lead on the Murphy boy."

Friar took a sip of the unsweetened mud and glanced at her over the top of the cup.

"The Murphy boy?"

She nodded. "I've arranged for us to go talk to someone."

"And, what *someone* would that be?"

She looked down at her feet. She knew that he wasn't going to be pleased with the name.

"Well?" he prompted.

"Natalie Bridgman," she said.

"The hooker?"

Tuck flushed. "She's an escort... not a hooker."

He took another mouthful of coffee, and immediately spat it back into the cup, earning himself a look of disgust from her.

"A rose by any other name..." he said, throwing the cup into the trash can. "She has sex with men for money, and that makes her a hooker. Dress it up any way you want, but that's what she is."

"Whatever... Look, can we just go?"

Friar hated missing kid cases. They often morphed into homicide cases, and there was nothing worse than dead children. Tuck recently told him that *missing* kids were much worse than *dead* kids. He'd asked her to go ahead and explain that little pearl of wisdom, and she'd said that dead kids were past all the pain and terror. All the unspeakable things had ceased, and they were now at peace. She had a point, but it wasn't one he wholly agreed with - and one that the parents certainly didn't sympathize with. They all wanted their kids back alive – no matter how broken they were.

He believed that the Murphy kid was dead, and being dragged out to speak to some hooker wasn't going to alter that fact. He told her as much and watched as the colour flared across her face.

She was about to go nuclear. She never hovered much below Defcon Four and it didn't take much to catapult her into Defcon Five.

Before she could blow, he put up his hands in surrender. With no caffeine in his system, he wasn't capable of surviving one of their epic blow-ups. For the sake of peace, he'd let her have her own way.

"Okay, okay..." he said. "We'll go see her, but were stopping at Starbucks on the way."

# 2

They didn't stop at Starbucks. Despite it only being a stone's throw from the precinct, Tuck drove straight on by. Friar was speechless with fury.

"I promise to buy you a double helping of expresso later," Tuck said, glancing at him and raising a brow at the sight of his expression. "We'll only be an hour."

Another hour without coffee wasn't something he relished, but there were no other coffee shops on the way and – unless he forced her to turn back – he was forced to suck it up.

They didn't stop until the car pulled up in front of one of the brownstone buildings on Cobble Hill.

"We're here," Tuck said, shutting off the engine and turning to look at him. "An hour late, but were here."

He was impressed. To afford an apartment in such a building meant that Natalie Bridgman must charge a great deal for the use of her body.

He hiked a brow. "Are you sure you've got the right address?"

"Absolutely sure."

"So, perhaps you could explain what we're doing here? The hooker had nothing to say when she was questioned before. What makes you so sure she has something to say to us now?"

"That's not true... about her having nothing to say before. She had plenty to tell us."

He mentally flipped through the files in his mind, bringing up a picture of the prostitute on the night the Murphy boy went missing. He recalled questioning her, recalled her belligerence, and perfectly remembered her refusal to give them any information.

"I don't recall her saying much more than her name, rank, and serial number."

"Very amusing."

"Well, you must admit that she hardly said a word that night."

"We made the mistake of questioning her in front of her date."

"Her *date*?" He let out a small chortle. "That's one way of describing him, I suppose."

"Whatever you want to call him, his presence intimidated her into silence."

"It didn't seem like that at the time. They were witnesses... no more and no less. There was no need to haul either of them back to the precinct to carry out formal interviews in separate rooms."

"I know, but..."

"Look, Tuck – just tell me what we're doing here. It was pretty clear that neither she, nor her *date*, saw anything that can help us."

She adjusted her position in the seat, so she was looking him full in the face, and asked, "Don't you think her behaviour that night rather odd?"

He shook his head and shrugged.

"She was agitated. I would go so far as to say she was afraid."

"Of what... her *John*?"

"Maybe."

"Bullshit." He said the word softly, already re-examining his memory of that night. Now that he thought about it – she had seemed a little afraid.

"You gonna explain to me why we're here, or do I have to guess?"

"No, you don't have to guess. She rang and left a message for me. I rang her back. She suggested a few things..."

"What things?"

"That she might know what happened to the boy." She watched for a reaction. None was forthcoming, so she said, "I tried to persuade her to come down to the precinct and make a statement, but she wouldn't hear of it."

"Surprise, surprise."

"She didn't want anyone to know that she was about to act the rat."

"*Act the rat*? She actually said that?"

"They were her exact words."

"You shouldn't have given her a choice. You should've hauled her ass in for questioning."

She bristled at the implied criticism. "If I'd attempted to do that, she would've bolted."

He nodded. There was some truth in that.

Ignoring her pained look, he opened the car door, and said, "We'd best get in there, then, and listen to what she has to say."

The brownstone was a smart townhouse that – like most of the others in that part of town - had been turned into swanky apartments.

Her name was etched on one of the small brass plates to the left of the door. There were brass buzzers next to each name. Friar counted six, which – judging by the size of the house – suggested that each apartment was on the larger side of huge.

Friar pressed the one next to Natalie's name. There was no responding chime or buzz. Obviously, it rang in the actual apartment, which made sense.

A full minute passed with no response.

"You said she was expecting us an hour ago?"

Tuck made a point of looking at her watch. "An hour and twenty minutes, to be exact."

He pressed the buzzer a second time, leaving his finger on it until Tuck elbowed him in the ribs.

"Doesn't seem like anyone is at home."

"Just give her another minute," she returned.

He narrowed his eyes at her. "That's not like you... to be patient. You're the least patient person I know."

She ignored him. "Try the door."

"What for? No one is stupid enough to leave a door unlocked around here... not if they don't want to be robbed or raped."

"Just try the fucking door, Friar."

He eyed her a moment longer, not in the least surprised by her flare of temper. Tuck was never able to keep a lid on her anger. He liked his partners calm and unaffected by whatever situation they found themselves in, and it was another reason he didn't like working with her.

"Take a chill pill," he said. "She probably just got fed up of waiting. Try phoning her."

She hauled in a breath, took out her phone, and scrolled until she found Natalie's number. She stabbed the call button with an angry finger, and listened as the phone rang out and then went to voicemail.

"Now, will you try the fucking door?" she ground out, thrusting her phone back into her pocket and glowering up at him. "Something's obviously wrong."

"Don't jump to conclusions." He reached out and pushed on the door. To his surprise, it creaked open.

For Tuck, it was the hairs on the back of her neck. For Friar, it was a tingling sensation down his spine. Cop radar was never ignored. Ignoring it could cost someone their life.

Tuck was right – something was definitely wrong. There was no way that door should've been unlocked.

A look passed between them, and they both simultaneously drew their weapons.

Neither of them made a sound. They held their guns - two-handed, elbows bent tight against their chests - and simply listened.

Silence.

Friar leaned against the door, holding it open, and Tuck stepped inside, then Friar made a sharp gesture with his head and they both moved further into the lobby.

Their arms were now extended and their guns were swinging in slow arcs in front of them.

A long lobby, stairs to the right, doors to the left. Friar went automatically to the bottom of the stairs and looked up, gun pointing to the top. Tuck eased along the wall and listened outside the first of the doors – the door to Natalie's apartment. She shook her head She heard nothing.

Friar joined her. He nodded and Tuck dropped her gun to her side, raised her other hand, and knocked loudly.

No response.

"Natalie... it's the police." Tuck knocked a second time. "Open the door, Natalie."

Still, no response.

"Try it," Friar said.

The handle dropped without any resistance. Tuck pushed it open a crack.

Friar put his forefinger to his lips then held up three fingers. Tuck took up a stance that would propel her through the door. She eyed him with a concentrated urgency as he counted down on his fingers. When he made a closed fist, they both rushed inside.

They moved from room to room without speaking - each searching opposite ends and opposite corners with critical eyes and without the need to confer.

The first three rooms were cleared quickly, then, as one, they moved to the door that was standing closed at the very bottom end of the long hallway.

Friar's expression was hard and edgy, his eyes like slitted grey flint. He knew what they were going to find behind that closed door.

# FRIAR AND TUCK CASE NUMBER ONE: THE MISSING

Call it instinct, call it pessimism but, whatever it was, it made his belly clutch.

He nodded at Tuck. She pushed the door open.

She was lying on her back on the tiled floor, a bloom of blood mushrooming out from beneath her. Sunshine cascaded through the window and Tuck noticed how it made the blood glisten. It was obviously still wet, probably not even tacky, and that meant the kill was recent.

Neither of them stepped over the threshold. They both stood in the open doorway, arms locked and guns presented, and surveyed the scene.

Friar's eyes panned the room. They took in everything. Then, Tuck - on a nod from Friar - dropped her arms so the muzzle of her weapon pointed to the floor, and inched her way towards the prone figure.

She was mindful that she was walking across a crime scene, so, she skirted the periphery and avoided the blood. Her only goal was to ensure that there was no need to send for the EMT's.

Natalie Bridgman's throat lay open. Tuck could see cartilage beneath the still oozing blood. Whoever had cut her throat had certainly meant to do serious damage. The ooze told her that Natalie was beyond help. If she still had circulation – if her heart had still been pumping – the arterial blood would be spurting out of the gaping wound.

She threw a look across at Friar and shook her head, just once. Friar narrowed his eyes, turned, and made his way back out of the kitchen and along the hallway. Every few steps, he stopped, cocked his head, and listened. There was no way to determine if the killer was still in the building – except by going door to door and searching every corner of every apartment. They would do that, of course, but not until he sent for back-up.

In the kitchen, Tuck holstered her weapon and snapped on a pair of lurid purple latex gloves. She stepped around the body and eased over to the door that led to a small outside yard. It was locked. The key was still on the inside. Both windows were closed and secured, so, if the killer was gone, he hadn't escaped through the kitchen.

She turned her attention back to the body. It didn't look as if it had been posed, yet it was a gruesome sight. Natalie looked as if she'd been tossed and discarded. Once killed, the body had simply been thrown to the floor, as if of no regard. Apart from the slash across her throat, that had nearly decapitated her, Tuck saw no other visible signs of injury. So, she thought, likely not a sexual deviant, or a run of the mill nutter. No, this was a professional hit. There was usually something immediately recognizable about a murder that suggested an execution by someone who knew what they were doing. Natalie's body screamed that was the case.

She was both fascinated and intrigued. She wasn't offended by either the sight or the smell of the body. Death didn't repulse her - although she was careful not to let that be known. Natalie Bridgman's murder didn't move her, except towards frustration because she would never now get to know what she'd wanted to tell her. It meant they would be no further forward in finding the Murphy boy.

She took in the fact that Natalie was fully clothed. She had expensive tastes. Her outfit certainly wasn't off the rack and her jewellery – fingers covered with large-stoned rings – attested to that.

One shoe lay a few feet away from the body, probably kicked off in the struggle with her assailant.

Her pocketbook was lying open on the table. Cash was visible – a great deal of it.

So, not robbery either.

Satisfied that there was nothing else to observe, she moved to follow Friar.

She found him on the stairs.

"There are three apartments above us," he said. "I don't know about you, but I don't believe we'll find our killer in any of them.

"I agree. He's most definitely gone."

"I'll get the ball rolling." He holstered his weapon, and pulled out his phone. "You see if any of her neighbours are at home. Tell them to stay indoors."

She nodded and turned back for the downstairs apartments. There was soon going to be an almighty commotion in the building, and they had to ensure that no one left until they'd been questioned. After his phone call, summoning the troops and CSI, Friar would secure the above apartments and their occupants.

# 3

"Are you *very* pissed at me?"

Tuck tuned him out. Ever since the medical examiner had arrived with his forensic crew, he'd been attempting to downplay the fact that they'd been an hour and twenty minutes late to see Natalie. He adamantly refused to acknowledge that, had they arrived on time, she might still be alive.

She couldn't be arsed arguing with him. The woman was dead. Period. There was no point in crying over spilled milk.

She kept her eye on the comings and goings, and every so often, she swept the crowd of onlookers and rubber-neckers with a regard that was both shrewd and penetrating.

"You *do* know that she's probably been dead for longer than an hour, don't you?"

*Jesus, Friar. Shut the fuck up about it.*

"She was probably killed hours before we arrived."

"We weren't just late by an hour," she said, finally pushed to speak. 'We were late by an hour and twenty minutes."

He hiked a brow. "Are you sure it wasn't an hour and twenty-*one* minutes?"

She turned to look up at him. "Don't be facetious."

"Well, get a grip, Tuck. It makes no fucking difference."

"That remains to be seen. The blood was still wet."

"Tacky. It was tacky... nearly dry."

She sighed and glanced back over at the small crowd of onlookers being held back behind the barrier erected by the two uniformed officers at the scene. She scanned their faces, looking for anyone who appeared suspicious. It was a well-known fact that the *Unsub'* – the unidentified subject - tended, more times than not, to return to the scene to get an eyeful of the action. Tuck didn't think that she'd spot him. It wasn't that sort of kill, and it wasn't that sort of killer.

It didn't stop her looking. That was the obsessive-compulsive part of her personality taking over. She'd look and look until either the crowd dispersed, or until her attention was demanded elsewhere.

"He's not here," Friar said, matter of fact. 'You're wasting your time searching for him.'

"I know that," she said. "You don't have to state the obvious."

"He's long gone."

"I'm aware of that. I 'm also aware that it wasn't your usual perverted whack-job homicide."

"*Whack-job homicide*? I know I shouldn't ask, but – what exactly does that mean?"

"You don't know?"

"Well, I know what I would mean, if I said it, but..." He shrugged. "Beats me what you mean."

'Probably the same as you."

"I seriously doubt that."

That was meant as a swipe at her peculiar way of thinking, but she chose to treat the question as a serious one. 'It means the taking of a life by a deviant predator who has shit for brains and more than one screw loose.'

'Ah.'

It was her turn to hike a brow. 'Not that different to how you would describe it?"

He shook his head. 'No, not that different."

A smile of satisfaction, and a knowing look, was meant to put him in his place, but Friar wasn't easily wrong-footed. "I guess I'm rubbing off on you."

"What?"

"You're learning, is all."

She ignored that, and said, "This was a professional hit. Nothing whack-job about it."

"I agree. So, do you want to hand it over to homicide?"

"Hell, no."

"Technically..."

"I don't give a shit, Friar. This is our case."

"The lieutenant might not see it that way."

"He will... if you tell him to."

He mulled that over. "There *is* precedent, I suppose."

"There's a lot more than *precedent*," she said. "The Governor's instructions are pretty clear – this new task force of ours is allowed to pursue any lead, make any investigation, and follow-up on any case, that seems linked to a missing person... particularly, but not limited to, a missing child."

"You memorized the protocol?"

"Of course." She looked shocked that he even doubted it. "Haven't you?"

He looked at her askance. "I've better things to do with my time."

"It would be better if you took the job a little more seriously, Friar. We're on trial... being scrutinized. Everyone wants it to go tits-up."

"All the more reason not to take on a homicide case... not this early on, and not when we have a caseload that is growing by the day."

"We have leeway to prioritize. That's also in the protocol - as laid out by the Governor. If you'd read..."

Friar threw up his hands. "Okay. Enough, already."

"Then, she's ours?"

He gave a grim smile. "If you want her... she's yours."

"Ours."

"Okay... *ours*."

"Where do we start?"

"You tell me."

"You're the one with all the homicide experience."

"So, what? It doesn't mean I have to do your thinking for you."

His eyes roamed absently over her face. He wondered why he wasn't attracted to her. She was pretty enough, with lashings of blonde hair – just his type – but he couldn't muster the least interest in her. Anyway – quite apart from the fact that he never got romantically involved with anyone he worked with - she was too intense, and he hated the fact that she saw right through him.

"If we knew what she wanted to tell us, then we'd have an idea of who wanted her dead." She looked at him expectantly. "Don't you think?"

He rolled his eyes. "But, we don't know what she wanted to tell us."

"We could find out."

"A Ouija board, you mean?"

She frowned. Sometimes, his words confused her. Her brain didn't work the same way as his, and some remarks went right over her head.

"Divining the spirit of the dead," he said. "It's the only way to know anything for certain."

"Is that a joke?"

He shrugged. "Maybe."

She looked at him, sideways.

"Yes, Tuck... it was a joke." He shook his head. "Jeeze."

She felt herself flush. Not getting jokes was her main kryptonite.

He said, "There's always the possibility that her murder was nothing more than a coincidence. I mean – she *was* a hooker. I'm sure that some of her clients had violent tendencies. One of them could be her killer."

It was Tuck's turn to shake her head. "I don't believe in coincidences. She was killed to keep her quiet."

"That would do it. No surer way to shut someone up."

They both stepped off the sidewalk to allow the crime scene investigators to pass on their way back to their vehicles.

The onlookers craned their necks in an attempt to get a good look at what they were carrying. A few held up their phones and took pictures. Most were disappointed that the body was still a no-show.

"'Someone needs to move that lot along,' Friar said. 'Nosy bastards.'" He rolled his shoulders. "Guess they're finished inside. If we're taking this on, we'd best go and have a chat with the medical examiner."

"I was thinking," Tuck said as they climbed the steps. "If we try and find out what she wanted to tell us, it would kill two birds with one stone."

"You're thinking we still need the information to help find the Murphy boy?"

She nodded.

"What if it's bullshit?"

"What if it's not?"

"Okay." He shouldered the door open and stepped through. "I'll bite... we'll open it as a line of enquiry."

Back in the kitchen of Natalie's apartment, they saw that the body was already bagged and tagged. The medical examiner – the acerbic Doctor Ralph Simms – gestured them forward with a curt nod of his head.

He was a great bear of a man, much taller and wider than Friar, so he absolutely dwarfed Tuck. She had to bend her head way back to look anywhere up near his face.

"Who's your friend, Friar?" he asked, cutting his eyes down at Tuck.

"This is Detective Tuck. I'm surprised you haven't heard about her being my new partner. Had her a few weeks. Still breaking her in."

"Ah... yes, detective Tuck. I think I've heard that name mentioned in passing. Pleased to meet you, detective." He crooked an elbow and pointed it at her.

Tuck looked at it and then at Friar, a quizzical expression on her face.

"Elbow bump," he explained. "No shaking of hands allowed."

She shook her head. "I'd rather not."

"Suit yourself," Simms said, turning his full attention on Friar and giving him a similar look that everyone else tended to give whenever they first made Tuck's acquaintance. It was a look that asked, *is she for real?*

Friar stared back at him blankly, giving nothing away. There was such a thing as loyalty between partners – deserved, or not.

"Nasty business," Simms said, taking the hint and moving on from the look. "The head was very nearly separated from the body."

"You mean, decapitated?"

Simms ignored her, obviously stung by her refusal to elbow-bump.

"The spine seems to have been almost severed at C2."

'I guess that was the cause of death?"

"Well, a near *decapitation* would do it, but I'm giving no firm opinion - not until I dice and slice."

"It doesn't take a genius to determine that having your head almost cut off was probably what killed you," Tuck put in. "Why can't you simply say it?"

Simms looked at Friar and spoke the *look* aloud. "Is she for real?"

Friar shrugged. "Afraid so."

Simms dragged in an impatient breath. It made his huge chest expand to giant proportions and nearly popped the zipper on his white jumpsuit.

He said – in as patient a voice as he could muster – "The slash to the throat could have been peri or post-mortem. She could have a stab wound to the heart, or be pumped full of narcotics. Either could be the cause of death, and not the injury to her neck. It's not my job to make assumptions, or give ill-informed opinions, Detective Tuck. And, it's not *your* job to attempt to do *mine* for me."

"So," Friar interjected, avoiding Tuck's glare. "Anything useful for us?"

Simms appeared as if he was about to refuse to answer, thought better of it, and said, "I would say you were looking for a man... probably right-handed. It could be a woman, I suppose, but she would have to have been an extremely strong female. As far as I can determine, there was only one brutal slash. It cut all the way to the spine, so would've taken phenomenal strength."

"Any obvious forensics?"

"Maybe on the body, but..."

"I know..." Friar waved a hand. "You'll have to examine her first."

"Obviously." He screwed up his nose and sniffed. It was a disgusting sound and Tuck grimaced. He turned away and did a final sweep of the kitchen with his eyes. "We've bagged a few items for examination. No sign of the murder weapon, but let's see what you stumble across."

"Was she raped?" Tuck asked.

He turned and dropped his eyes to look at her. "No obvious sign of that, but you can never be sure. I'll begin the autopsy later this afternoon." He eyed them both speculatively. "Will I have the honour of both of your presence?"

"I'll be there," Tuck said.

"Fantastic' Simms said, a little too exuberantly.

Friar looked away. "I'll be otherwise engaged."

He always tried to avoid autopsies. They gave him the willies. Luckily, Tuck was fascinated by them and didn't mind attending. Most of the previous autopsies had been on those missing people whose corpses had been discovered. Natalie Bridgman was a fresh corpse. The others weren't. Even so, Friar preferred to sit it out.

"See you around four o'clock then, Detective Tuck. Don't be late, or I'll begin without you."

"I'm never late," she returned.

"Why am I not surprised?"

Simms gave one final sniff, collected his bag, and left them in the kitchen. The body was placed on a trolley by two of his colleagues, and it soon trundled out after him.

"Why do you always turn down the chance to observe the autopsy?"

"Why do *you* always jump at the chance?"

She looked at him as if he was half mad. "It's part of the job."

"Even if it wasn't – *you'd* be there. Admit it - you're a ghoul, Tuck, pure and simple."

She visibly jerked at his words. She was used to being called all sorts of names. She'd been labelled as weird almost since she could talk, but it was the first time she'd been called a ghoul. It was just one more stupid attempt to define her as something she most certainly was not.

Friar could see that he'd stung her. He hadn't meant to. It was supposed to be a joke, but he'd quite forgotten that Tuck had no comprehension of humour.

"Sorry," he said. "I didn't mean that. I know you enjoy the science of the autopsy. I didn't intend to suggest..."

"Just forget it," she said, blinking back her anger. "Let's just get on with our search."

He nodded. "Where shall we start?"

Tuck appeared to consider the question before saying, "I'll do the bedroom. It's better if I'm the one going through her frilly knicker drawers."

Now, *he* could take that statement as an insult. She'd implied that he couldn't be trusted with Natalie's underwear, but he let it go... just as he let go of almost everything she ever said that was below the belt. *One rule for her, and one for me*, he thought wryly.

"Suits me. I'll make a start in the sitting room."

There was an awkward pause. It seemed as if they both had something more to say. Then, Tuck moved away.

He waited until she'd exited the kitchen before he followed.

An hour later, they were finished.

"Anything?" Friar asked.

She shook her head.

"CSI already took her laptop and iPhone."

"They left most of her sex toys."

"She has sex toys?"

Tuck gave a wry half-smile. "Dozens of them. It seems she invited her clients back here for fun and games."

"That's not good. Forensics will have their work cut out with the amount of different fingerprints and DNA. Jesus, can you imagine what sort of DNA they're going to find?"

"That's Simms's problem."

"And, ours."

"I've been thinking about that."

"What?"

"I think we should pay a visit to Potter."

"Potter... the other witness?" An image of Potter appeared in his mind. He remembered him as a slimy toad.

She nodded. "Stands to reason that he might know exactly what Natalie knew. They were both there that night. They both saw the kid being dragged into the van."

"We promised him a degree of anonymity. We can't simply arrive at his house. His wife will wonder why we're there."

"Am I supposed to care about that?"

"You *could* care a little. It's not the wife's fault that she's married to someone who likes screwing hookers."

"He's our only lead."

He took a deep breath. She was right about Potter being their only lead, but he had no intention of alienating him by dragging his poor wife into the mix.

He flipped open the file in his mind. He ran through all the questions and answers from their previous, brief, interview with him.

It was carried out on the street where the Murphy kid had been abducted. There had been no need to take him, or Natalie Bridgman, back to the precinct. They'd seen very little and there was no suspicion that they were in any way involved.

Both he and Tuck had arrived within twenty minutes of the abduction. That was one of the most successful aspects of their unique partnership – their quick response time.

*Despatch* had to prioritise child abductions. Friar and Tuck - or one of the other two partnerships based in the Bronx and Staten Island – had an obligation to drop everything and arrive on the scene as soon as possible. Usually, the child's disappearance occurred hours, or even days before, but, the Murphy case was different. His abduction was observed in real time, and Potter had immediately called it in.

"Why do you think Natalie told us so little on the night?" he asked. "I mean, Potter was a little more forthcoming, but – looking back – I can now see that she actually went out of her way to say less than nothing."

"I'm pleased that you're finally seeing it my way."

"I hardly think..."

"You didn't see it before I mentioned it."

"I'm not admitting to thinking that she seemed frightened," he returned, a tad defensively.

She jerked up her chin. "Well, she was, and – it seems – for good reason.

"That remains to be seen."

"That's one of the things we can ask him when we go visit... what she was afraid of."

"You're determined to rock that boat, aren't you?"

She shrugged.

"Why don't we ask him to come see us at the precinct instead?"

"Because, I want him wrong-footed."

"Well, I don't. It's not the right way to play it."

"I'm not playing, Friar."

"Jesus, Tuck. Do you have to take everything so literally?"

She flushed, realizing her mistake. Of course, he didn't mean playing, as in *playing*. She really had to try harder at interpreting the meaning behind such sayings. Unfortunately, her brain took things much too exactly. She found it impossible to associate some sayings with people's intended meaning. She *did* take things too literally. It was one of the reasons she'd lost her previous two partners. They got sick of having to explain themselves to her.

Now that she'd taken the necessary few moments to understand, she felt she could ask - "So, how do you want to play it?"

"I want him relaxed and co-operative. We might only have one shot at him, and I don't want his wife's histrionics screwing it up for us."

"Fair enough."

He did a double-take. "You're agreeing?"

"Of course, I am. You made a good argument."

"Well, thank the Lord for that."

"What has God got to do with it?"

"Nothing, Tuck. It was..."

"Just a figure of speech?"

"Exactly."

"I wish people would simply say what they mean."

"You mean – you wish I would stop using euphemisms?"

"Is that what you're doing?"

"For want of a better description... yes."

"Then, yes – I wish you *would* stop."

"I don't think I can. Nearly everyone does it. It's as if it's ingrained in our DNA."

"Not in mine."

He sighed. "No."

"I'm sorry."

He didn't want her to be sorry. It wasn't her fault that her wiring was all screwed up.

"No need for that," he said. "No need to be sorry."

"It's just..."

"I'm not going to dump you, Tuck. I'm not like the others." Yes, he was, but was determined to deny it. "Those assholes made a big mistake in requesting new partners."

"You're humouring me."

"No." He shook his head. "I mean it." And, suddenly, he did actually mean it. Despite her weirdness, she was a great detective. If they could get used to one another, he was sure they'd end up being a great team.

*If they could get used to one another.*

# 4

The Governor of New York State was a progressive, and a man who had a reputation for thinking out of the box, but – where law enforcement was concerned – he had a history of non-interference. He left the individual mayors to determine how best to police their cities. He supported their decisions and kept no more than a weather-eye on the overall picture across the state. Shortly after his nephew was abducted and murdered, that had changed.

The boy had been eleven years old. There was no Amber Alert, no real investigation into his disappearance, and there had been an overall assumption that he was a merely a runaway. The boy was of an age to get himself into trouble. He had absconded from home once before, and – in spite of his family's insistence that he was a good boy, and despite him being the Governor's nephew - his disappearance wasn't considered a priority. Very little resource was turned over to the case. With over thirteen thousand people going missing every year across New York, there simply wasn't the resources to spare to find one boy, no matter his pedigree.

When his body was discovered – battered, bruised, and badly used – it motivated the Governor to seek, and win, federal funding for an experiment.

Friar and Tuck were part of that experiment.

Based at the 76$^{th}$ Precinct, in Brooklyn, Friar and Tuck were two of the six detectives recruited to the governor's special task force. This task force was, in effect, a cross-precinct resource to increase the chances of finding missing persons where there was some evidence of a crime. The governor was realistic. He didn't expect six officers to make much of an impact, but he did expect that some of the robust investigation into these crimes would result in missing people being found, or some families receiving closure and justice. To that end, he funded the recruitment of two detectives in the $76^{th}$, a further two at the $40^{th}$ in the Bronx, and a final two at the $122^{nd}$ at Staten Island.

Their fellow officers at the $76^{th}$ believed that Friar and Tuck had it easy. They had cart-blanche over what cases they accepted, could - more or less - come and go as they pleased, and often didn't have the lieutenant breathing down their necks.

But, neither Friar, nor Tuck, felt they were being given an easy ride. Their caseloads far exceeded any of the other detectives, they were on call twenty-four-seven, and – to top it all off - they didn't have the same level of administrative support as their peers. Although their cases were usually more complex, because their *victims* were – more often than not – the dregs of society, their efforts were frequently dismissed as being a total waste of time. That didn't mean to say - when there was a serious crime involved, like a homicide – that their fellow officers would be happy to see them work it. Where such crimes were involved, there was too much of a rigid hierarchy to ensure that any blurring of responsibilities would go unchallenged.

So, Friar in particular, knew that there was going to be resentment when it became known that they'd grabbed the Natalie Bridgman homicide for themselves. He knew that, despite every one of the homicide detectives being extremely busy, they sure as hell didn't want something they considered as their case being stolen from right under their noses. They didn't understand about the new protocol and, quite frankly, they didn't give a shit. What was theirs was theirs... simple.

Up until recently – before he'd been persuaded to transfer across to work with Tuck – Friar had worked homicide, so he was under no illusions as to how deep the resentment would go. He knew exactly just how territorial those homicide detectives were.

Knowing all of that, as they entered the precinct building, he said, "Brace yourself, Tuck. We're in for a bumpy ride."

Tuck knew all about bumpy rides. Ever since she'd entered the department, her whole journey had been a bumpy one. Some of it was down to her, but not all of it. There simply wasn't a culture of give and take, and no one was prepared to cut her any slack. It didn't help that – before Friar arrived on the scene to temper her more abrasive behaviour, or to have her back when he couldn't – she'd trod on so many toes that no one would now give her so much as the time of day.

It didn't matter that she was competent, and it didn't matter that she worked damned hard. She was different, but being different in a multi-cultural, multi-faceted police department wasn't what excluded her, or what made her subject to cruel ostracism. No, that was more to do with the fact that she came across as believing she was better than everyone else. No one liked a know-it-all, especially one who seemed to go out of her way to antagonise and infuriate, and – because of that – she would never be one of them.

Friar knew that Tuck was right about the homicide of Natalie Bridgman being theirs. The protocols were clear. He believed that, if his partner had been anyone other than her, his colleagues would've accepted the situation more readily and probably without any fuss. After all, *he* was one of *them*. He had no axe to grind. He had no enemies within the precinct, and no one thought that he was a fucked-up asshole.

He would have to deflect some of the ensuing hostility towards Tuck his way. He was going to have to stand up for her, and their right to the case.

The door swung open and they both stepped aside as several uniformed offices filed through. There had been a change of shift, and the precinct was heaving during the handover period. They made their way upstairs, Friar acknowledging with a nod some people he knew, whilst Tuck kept her head down, acknowledging no one.

At the top of the stairs, he turned to her, and said, "I'll interview Potter on my own. You've got the autopsy to attend, so it's best if I arrange for him to come in then."

She didn't immediately respond, but Friar felt the enmity coming off her in waves.

"That all right with you?"

"We should do it together," she returned. "You'll need me in there with you."

"It's not necessary."

"I think that it is." She looked up at him defiantly. "You need me."

"I *was* a homicide detective, Tuck. I think I can manage perfectly well on my own with one co-operative witness."

She shook her head. "You might think that you can, but I beg to differ."

His lips thinned. "Oh, really? Why is that?"

"I see and hear things."

"You mean like that little boy out of *The Sixth Sense*?"

"What?" Her confusion was palpable.

"You see ghosts?"

"No, of course not. I don't believe in ghosts."

"It was a joke, Tuck."

"Well, I don't get it."

"Haven't you ever seen that movie with Bruce Willis? It scared the shit out of me."

"I don't watch movies."

"No, I bet you don't."

She ignored the barb. "Will you arrange a time when I can be there, or not?"

"If you insist."

"I *do* insist."

"Because I need you? Because you see and hear things?"

"Precisely."

"Things I might miss?"

"That's why we work in pairs... because one sees and hears what the other one doesn't."

"Whatever."

He turned his back on her and strode along the corridor, counting slowly from one to ten under his breath as he walked. He still hadn't had that cup of coffee and, before he said another word to her, he thought he'd better find one.

Tuck watched him go. She bit down on her lip and silently admonished herself, yet again, for inadvertently alienating him.

She turned and caught sight of the lieutenant standing just inside his office door, staring at her. She wasn't sure about him yet. As far as she was concerned, the jury was still out about whether, or not, he was good at his job.

Tuck rated detectives, and particularly those senior to her, dependent upon three things – their investigative skills, their work ethic, and their leadership. She didn't much care about their character, and cared even less if they liked her. Anyway, the leadership aspect of her rating took the character aspect into consideration and – even if they didn't like her – again, the leadership aspect covered that. To her mind, it was okay not to like her, but a good leader didn't allow that to influence his professional judgement, or allow the team to be influenced by it.

She knew lieutenant Mitch Mitchel to be a thirty-year veteran. He came from a family of police officers and had a stellar reputation. The reason the jury was still out on him was because Tuck wasn't sure that he was doing everything he could to show true leadership. He'd been railroaded into accepting her at the precinct, and he'd made it very clear – right from day one – that he didn't want her there. He'd allowed her previous two partners to give up on her, and made no objections to their requests for a transfer. His actions spoke volumes, and the other officers at the precinct followed his lead and treated her as an outsider, and as an unworthy colleague.

But, Mitchel had given her Friar. She was beginning to think that went in his favour. They had worked well together that day, and she was pleased to note that he'd listened to her, and – at times - almost seemed to respect her. Yes, he was still an asshole, but much less of one than she'd thought him that morning.

She thought it was a sound leadership decision on the lieutenant's part, and she was veering towards rating him highly. She hoped that he wasn't about to say something to her that would jeopardise her change of opinion.

"Where's Friar?" he asked.

"Gone looking for coffee, I think," she replied warily.

"Then, you'll do. Step inside my office, Tuck."

She nodded and followed him. He sat behind his desk and she stood in front, like an errant schoolgirl facing her headmaster.

"How are you getting on with him?"

"Friar?"

"Who else would I be referring to?"

"Fine. I'm getting on with him fine."

"Would *he* say the same?"

She shrugged. She couldn't read his expression, so thought it wise to play dumb.

"No comment, Tuck?"

"No, sir. Detective Friar should speak for himself."

He considered her for a moment, choosing his next words carefully.

"There might be a problem looming with this recent homicide," he said. 'The victim is known to you, I hear?"

"She was one of our witnesses in the Murphy case. Why is there a problem?"

He shrugged her question off. "Remind me about the Murphy case."

"Young street kid... grabbed and hauled off in a van a few nights ago."

"Street kid?"

"Mother is a junkie. Father unknown. He's been living on the streets for about a year."

"How old?"

"Thirteen."

"What's he selling?" Mitchel knew that – to survive on the streets – you had to be selling something.

"Himself, we think."

"Not drugs?"

"No evidence of that."

"This witness..?"

"Natalie Bridgman. She was a high-end hooker. Someone tried to cut her head off in her kitchen."

"Nasty."

"Very."

"And, you think her murder has something to do with your missing kid?"

"*We* do, sir, and that's why we want to investigate, and not hand the case over to homicide."

"And, therein lies the problem. It'll cause ructions."

She made no response to that. Ructions were his business, not hers.

"What other cases are you both working on?"

She understood the reason behind the question. He was trying to find an excuse to take the homicide from them. If they had a caseload that bordered on unmanageable, he would have reason enough to refuse his permission to keep hold of it.

"Only three others, sir. We recently cleared two."

"So, four with the Murphy kid?"

"Yes, sir."

"And, the other three?"

"In hand."

"Any of them children?"

She shook her head.

"Tell me about them."

"A forty-two year old banker... happily married... no financial difficulties, didn't arrive for work ten days ago. Not been seen since. A sixty-two year old woman who went out on a blind-date with someone she met on an internet dating site. First time for her, apparently. She's been missing for two days. We picked that case up almost simultaneously with the Murphy case."

"And, the third one?"

"A prostitute, sir."

He hiked a brow. "A prostitute?"

"She has two children. She wouldn't just up and leave them."

"That's debatable."

Again, she made no response. She didn't dare.

"Okay." He let out a slow breath. "I'm going to allow it, Tuck - but only because Friar is on the case. He knows his way around a homicide."

"Thank you, sir."

He grimaced. "Don't fuck it up."

# 5

Doctor Ralph Simms stood with a deadpan expression and cast his eyes over the naked woman on the slab. It wasn't really a slab. It was a stainless steel autopsy table with removable grids, power points, and a sink with a wide drain.

All of the blood had already been sluiced from Natalie Bridgman's body. With the exception of the beginning of purple livor mortis across her shoulders, her underarms, and buttocks, most of the colour had leached from her skin.

She had a mole on her left breast, and a yellow bruise just inside her right wrist. Both stood out under the harsh overhead light.

To Tuck, she looked ghastly. To her mind – unlike some bodies she'd observed - Natalie was one person that certainly didn't look as if she'd simply drifted off to sleep. The diabolical injury to her throat and neck denied her that kindness.

"I'm ready to make a start," Simms said. "She's been examined and photographed externally, and all trace evidence has been bagged and tagged. The mole is the only identifying mark, and the old bruise on her wrist the only injury to suggest possible prior abuse. There are no scars and no tattoos. She is a well-nourished Caucasian female, weighting fifty-point-eight kilogrammes, aged in her late twenties to early thirties with trauma to the neck probably caused by a sharp instrument. There is no evidence of any defensive wounds." He took a breath. "I will begin with the Y incision."

The two long arms of the Y ran from both shoulder joints down the torso and then curved under the breasts before meeting to form the stem. He sliced all the way down to the pubic region. Her skin parted bloodlessly.

Tuck appreciated the artistry and proficiency of his work. When she thought about the extent of his ability, she didn't believe it was incongruous to apply the word *talented*. He was truly endowed with the gifts bestowed on the greatest of surgeons, and she appreciated the cool detachment in which he deployed those gifts so as to ensure the victim related a true story of their death.

The cause of death seemed absolute, but Tuck didn't question – even in her own mind – why it was necessary to remove and weigh the organs and carry out every other aspect of a forensic autopsy. Knowing how someone died wasn't the only question a detective required. A good detective required to know everything.

There was much to be discovered from a dead body. You could learn a great deal about a person just by looking at their cadaver. Tuck could tell that Natalie Bridgman took care of herself. She didn't seem to have an ounce of excess fat, however she didn't show the emaciation of the anorexic or the bulimic. Her muscles, although somewhat flabby in death, were well defined, her teeth pearly white, and her tongue unfurred. She had been someone who appreciated a good diet, and Tuck was interested to eventually see what her stomach contained.

Simms didn't use a rib cutter to cut along the edge of the ribs and their connecting cartilage. Instead, he used a large pair of shears to cut the sides of Natalie's chest cavity, leaving the ribs attached to her breastbone, and then lifted the whole thing out as one wide chest plate. It was the first time that Tuck had seen it done that way and she thought it was a much cleaner and much more effective method of gaining access to the now exposed organs.

First, he removed the chest organs – the heart, the thoracic aorta and the lungs. Normally he would have removed the trachea, the thyroid gland, the parathyroid glands, and the oesophagus at that point, however – due to the damage to her throat and neck – he left them until after he'd dissected the abdominal organs.

Once the chest and abdominal organs had been removed, weighed and examined, and once the stomach contents had been scrutinised – Tuck was not surprised to see the evidence of oats, fruit and nuts, suggesting muesli - and the intestines flushed, Simms turned his attention to the neck and to the thyroid organs.

"The weapon cut deep above the thyroid cartilage, leaving an extensive, gaping wound," Simms said into the overhead microphone. "It appears to be a single cut, with clean edges, administered with such force that it severed C2 and C3 vertebrae. The head remains in place by skin flaps to the back and sides of the neck. I'm now removing the windpipe."

He took measurements and requested additional photographs of everything.

There was a strong smell in the room – an aroma that the overhead fans refused to completely disperse – that increased as time passed. She caught Simms looking at her, expecting her to be affected, and then covering his surprise by blinking and dipping his eyes back to the body.

Once, he invited her to take a break, saying that it would be perfectly understandable if she wanted to finish her observation from the viewing room. She declined with a curt shake of her head. Again, he hid his surprise, but not well enough for her not to notice it.

When it was all done, and Natalie's remains were rolled into one of the refrigeration units, Tuck stripped off her gown and mask, and joined Simms in his office for a debrief.

She liked his office. It was a clinically stark room with no frippery or family photographs imposing on his workspace. She took a seat in front of his desk and let her eyes travel over the framed evidence of his qualifications on the wall opposite. They were impressive.

"Considering her line of employment, she was in excellent health," he said, right off the bat. "She kept herself fit and, when the tox screens come back, I wouldn't be surprised to find that she wasn't a drug user. She wasn't raped, and there were no signs of recent penetration. One thing, though..."

Tuck raised a brow and leaned forward in her chair.

"She's had at least one child."

"Oh?"

"There is evidence of bone impressions - a series of little markings along the inside of the pelvic bone – that point explicitly to the tearing of ligaments during childbirth. These markings are a permanent record of that event."

"Can you tell how many children she gave birth to?"

He shook his head. "Unfortunately, not."

"There was no evidence of a child at her apartment."

"I can only determine that she gave birth, not what happened to the child thereafter."

"No, of course not."

"Maybe she didn't keep it?"

"That's a possibility, I suppose."

"Or, she farms it out when she's working?"

"If that was the case, I would've seen evidence of the child."

"Yes, I guess you would have."

"Is there any way to tell how long ago she gave birth?"

"I could tell you if it was recent. There would be strong evidence of that, but..."

"Not if it was some time ago?"

"I'm afraid not with any degree of certainty. I wouldn't like to guess."

"But, it wasn't recent?"

"No."

"I'll look into it. There will be records."

"There's sure to be."

"What else can you tell me?"

"Well, you're looking for a really strong man, who knew exactly what he was doing. This was an execution... no doubt about it."

"How do you know that?"

"One slash? A clean, professional kill? No fuss and no drama? That's the picture her body painted for me."

"What else?"

"Tall, right-handed... the cut was left to right."

"So, a tall, strong, right-handed man? That certainly narrows the suspects down."

"Perhaps the fibres we found in her hair will help. They most likely came from whatever he was wearing – transfer from when he pulled her back against his chest. There would've been blood on his clothing... lots of it."

"No one reported seeing a man covered in blood fleeing the scene."

"The fibres are dark, so his clothing was, too. You wouldn't necessarily spot blood on a dark sweater or jacket."

"I know that. You're stating the obvious."

He sucked on his teeth, then said, "You're rather forthright. I'd heard that about you."

"So? Is there something wrong with being forthright?" She recognised the hint of defensiveness in her tone, and swallowed it back.

"Maybe... sometimes." He stood up from behind his desk, his huge body unfolding from the chair like a giant accordion. He leaned forward, splaying his hands on the desk.

She'd noticed his hands before, and her eyes were drawn to them. For such a large man, they were delicately beautiful – a surgeon's hands.

"Why haven't we met before now?" he asked. "By all accounts, you spend a great deal of time hanging around the autopsy suite."

"I don't *hang around* anywhere."

"No? Well, that's not what I'd heard."

"People talk about me?"

"You're the sort of person everyone talks about."

"Now, who's being forthright?"

"You must know how true that is?"

"At the precinct... yes."

"And, here." He saw her frown. "It's mostly good things," he added, hastily. "What they say... it's mostly positive."

She wondered why he was lying.

"Usually, the detectives avoid us like the plague. According to my colleagues, you seek us out... want to observe as many autopsies as they'll allow, and, in your own time."

She recalled how he'd acted towards her at the crime scene, and how he was now behaving. He suddenly seemed to respect her, and she found that extremely disconcerting.

She turned the conversation back to the case, asking, "What about the murder weapon?"

"What about it?"

She rolled her eyes. "What was it?"

He pushed back from the desk. She had to crane her neck to look up at him.

"It was a clean, straight blade," he said, buttoning his jacket and flicking a hand over some fluff on his shoulder. "A large hunting knife, at least eight inches from tip to hilt... but one with no serration. There were no jagged edges on the wound."

"He came armed," she mused aloud.

"No one keeps a knife like that in their kitchen so, yes, I'd say he arrived armed and ready."

"She didn't fight?"

"No. The bruise on the inside of her wrist was at least a week old."

"Anything under her fingernails?"

"Plenty, but we'll have to wait to determine what. I don't think there is any skin, if that's what you're hoping for?"

"Skin would be good."

He smiled. "Agreed."

She pressed herself out of the chair, nodded, and turned to leave.

"No time for a coffee?" he asked, hopefully.

She turned and looked over her shoulder. "No thanks. I don't drink coffee."

"Tea, then?"

She wanted to smile at him. She wanted to do that one socially acceptable thing, but her lips were frozen. She had no idea if he was hitting on her, and - if he was - she wondered what the correct response would be.

She hesitated, turned back to face him, and said, "I only drink chamomile. Do you have chamomile?"

"Um... I don't think so. I think we might have some green stuff somewhere."

"Green tea? I only drink chamomile."

"Yes, you said. Oh, well... perhaps next time?"

"Sure." She waited until she was positive that he wasn't going to say anything more, then turned, and briskly left.

She glanced at her watch. She hoped that Friar hadn't started the interview without her, but thought that he probably had. He didn't think he needed her. He thought that she was worse than useless. She knew that she wasn't and wished that he could see past her personality to the competent detective beneath.

The sky was overcast. She'd be lucky to get back to her car before it opened up in a deluge. There was a rumble of distant thunder and she quickened her pace, her heels clacking on the tarmac as she made her way across the parking lot.

Some idiot had double-parked, hemming her in. She glanced at her watch again and silently cursed as the first drops of rain fell.

She climbed into the car and rang Friar. His phone went straight to voicemail.

"Friar," she said into the phone. "I'm running late. Some stupid prick's blocked my car and I'm stuck for the duration. I'll understand if you start without me." She felt it was the right thing to say. "I'll get there as soon as I can."

The time spent stuck in her car turned out to be over an hour. She'd wanted to verbally eviscerate the driver of the errant car, but it was a bereaved father visiting the morgue to identify his son, so she was forced to bite her lip and accept his tearful apology.

She wasn't good with grief. She wasn't good with any visceral emotion, except anger. Anger she could deal with, mainly because she'd been brought up in an angry family, in an angry house, by angry parents. Any other primitive emotion left her bewildered and at a loss as to how to respond.

She tried not to be curt and irritated by the grieving man's inability to put his car into reverse and get the fuck out of her way. It took every ounce of self-control not to haul him out from behind the wheel and move the damned thing herself.

What was it with people, she wondered, that made them turn to mush just because they'd lost something? Okay, it was a son – and she did feel for the families of all those she worked with who's child was missing – but at least this particular man knew where his son was. He would at least have a grave to visit.

She held herself in check, and was eventually rewarded when, at last, she was able to manoeuvre her car out of the tight space and point it in the direction of the precinct. By the time she arrived, the rain was pelting down and it was growing dark.

She wore a linen pantsuit that was now extremely creased and she wished that she was one of those women who cared enough about their appearance to keep a spare set of clothes in her locker.

Usually, she wasn't preoccupied with how she looked. She liked to play down, rather than play up, her appearance - hence the pantsuit – but she was astute enough to know that it was important to make an impression. She tended to be careful of what that impression was, especially when facing a potentially hostile witness, or a suspect, across an interview table.

Anyway, she had no flair for fashion. Even if she'd wanted to look attractive, or even pretty, she would have no clue what clothes would help her achieve it. Clothes were a functional necessity. She much preferred her own skin to anything that covered it.

But, damp, rumpled, and grubby, she was anything *but* presentable. She was about to show herself at a disadvantage, and that gave her pause for thought.

Why did she care? Because, no one – least of all a witness being questioned under an element of duress – ever had respect for the creased and the grubby. The only exception would be if her name happened to be Columbo.

She thought about turning around and leaving Friar to it. He wouldn't care. In fact, he would probably be pleased.

*Fuck it!*

She smoothed her hands down her trouser legs, attempting to iron out a few of the creases. Of course, it was a waste of time. Those creases were there for the duration.

She swerved towards the ladies' room and shouldered her way through the door. The overhead fluorescent light automatically turned on as soon as the door opened and she squinted at the seizure-invoking flick, flick, flicker.

The mirror over the sink reflected a sorry image. Her hair – naturally curly and prone to frizz – horrified her. She hated her hair. One day she would shave it all off. She ran her fingers through it, then searched in her pocket for something to tie it back with. The contents of her pockets resembled those of a six-year-old schoolboy's.

# FRIAR AND TUCK CASE NUMBER ONE: THE MISSING

The only thing that was missing was a toad. She seemed to remember her six-year old schoolfriends - the boys, that was - producing the odd toad or two and waving them in her face, hoping to frighten her.

She wasn't that easily frightened.

She yanked out a pen, an eraser, a stick of mushy chewing gum, two crumpled pieces of notepaper, and – at last – an elastic band.

It would tear up her hair, but needs must. Grabbing handfuls of her wild mane, she gathered it into a thick ponytail and secured it with the band.

She then turned her attention to her face. There was nothing she could do with it. There was no lipstick in her pockets and, as she didn't carry a purse, she had no cosmetics to hand.

She had to accept how she looked, and just get on with it.

# 6

Friar put on a pair of reading glasses and picked up the buff folder. He hated spectacles and, whenever he could, he avoided the wearing of them. It wasn't vanity that raised his antithesis, but the fact that they gave him a headache. Tuck had suggested that perhaps his prescription was too strong. He thought he might actually agree with her assessment, but had done nothing about getting his eyes retested and the prescription changed, preferring to suffer the pain of the headache rather than going through all that hassle.

The writing was small, the letters crammed together so that the words became almost illegible. The original notes were supposed to be typed up within twenty-four hours of a statement being taken, however – days later – they were still in Tuck's original hand.

He knew why, and he groaned inwardly. Her request to have the notes transcribed had either fallen on deaf ears, or the administrative assistant – who begrudged every hour she had to spend on their work – had shoved it to the bottom of the pile.

He was going to have to do something about that, and – when he did – it wasn't going to be pretty.

He gave up trying to decipher Tuck's writing, and lifted his gaze to peer at the man over the top of the frameless lenses.

Friar prided himself in being a good judge of character. His gut told him that Potter was nothing more that gutter trash dressed up to look classy. There was a saying that *clothes maketh the man*, but – in Potter's case – the smart suit and immaculate white button-down shirt did nothing to take the edge off his coarse vulgarity.

The man had absolutely no breeding or class. Being married, and using hookers, put paid to that concept.

Potter stared straight ahead, unblinking. If he was anxious about being interviewed, he didn't show it. He didn't fidget and he didn't try to fill the silence with inane banter. He was either cock-sure of himself, or too stupid to realise that he was about to be grilled on both sides. Friar wasn't sure which.

He cleared his throat and Potter's puffy eyes dropped, shifting his gaze from whatever spot on the wall he'd been staring at, to look him in the face.

"You have a question, detective, only I've been sitting here for a while now?"

"Actually, I have a few questions, Mister Potter."

"Go ahead, and ask them, then. No time like the present." He gave a humourless smile. "Time's a wasting."

*Smarmy bastard.*

Friar leaned back in his chair. "You don't seem perturbed about being asked to come here."

"Why would I be? I've done nothing wrong, and I'm only too happy to be of help with your investigation."

"Very civic-minded of you."

"That's me... a good citizen."

"Is that why you telephoned to report seeing the boy being abducted... just being a good citizen?"

"Of course."

"You didn't use your own phone to make the call."

He shrugged. "Battery was dead."

"You didn't attempt to intervene in any way?"

"That's how you get yourself knifed in the guts, detective. No – I did my civic duty by reporting it."

"Uh, huh, I see. So, tell me again... what were you doing on *that* street at *that* particular time of the evening."

Potter rolled his eyes. "Again? Haven't you heard it enough times already? It's written down there for all to see." He flapped a hand at the folder in Friar's hands. "Can't you read?"

"Humour me, Mister Potter. Pretend you've never been asked the question before now."

He dragged in an impatient sigh, then said, "I was on a date. We..."

"A date?" Friar hitched a brow. "Really?"

"Yes – *really*. I might've paid hard cash for my date, detective, but it *was* still a date."

"If you say so. Continue, please."

His expression turned mulish. Friar thought he might refuse to say any more. It was the first sign that he wasn't as comfortable as he appeared on the surface. He gave him a few seconds to think it over and then repeated, "Continue, please."

"My *date*, and I, just had dinner, and..."

"Do you often treat prostitutes to dinner?"

He flushed at that. "Natalie isn't a prostitute."

"Wasn't."

"What?"

"Natalie *wasn't* a prostitute. She's dead... remember?"

"I remember," he said.

"How do you feel about her being dead?"

He seemed to mull that over. "Devastated," he said. "Utterly bereft."

"Really? How well did you know her?"

"Well, I knew her in the biblical sense."

His attempt at flippancy caused a frown to darken Friar's face. His dislike of the man intensified.

"How long did you know her?"

He shrugged. "Six months... give or take."

"How often did you pay her to have sex with you?"

"A couple of times a week."

"That evening - what did you both have to eat?"

He shook his head, as if clearing it. "What does that have to do with anything?"

It was Friar's turn to shrug. "Probably nothing."

"Then, why ask it?"

"Just curious."

"You're wasting my time. Am I at liberty to leave?"

"I thought you wanted to be a good citizen?"

"I thought you wanted to ask me sensible questions?" he returned, bitingly.

"Now I come to think of it – it's really not simply out of curiosity. I really do need to know what you both ate that evening."

"I can't remember. Now, can I leave?"

"Not yet."

He sighed and shook his head. "This is becoming tedious." He made to stand, pushing back the chair with his legs, and pulling himself straight.

Friar didn't move. He didn't lift his head to look up at him. "Sit down," he said quietly. "I'm not finished."

"Well, I'm finished, detective. If you want to keep me here, then slap some cuffs on me and arrest me."

Friar allowed him to reach the door before saying, "I can always speak to your wife. Perhaps she can fill in some of the blanks for me? For example - what you like to eat when you're out to dinner?"

The door opened, and Friar turned. He expected to see Potter high-tail it out of there, but it was only Tuck entering. She almost crashed into the hovering Potter.

"You finished already?" she asked, flicking her gaze from Potter to Friar. "I'm not that late, am I?"

"Mister Potter was just about to sit back down... weren't you?"

Potter scowled and threw himself back around.

Tuck felt the tension in the air and saw Potter clench his fists at his sides before he seemed to visibly relax and walk back over to retake his seat.

"Detective Tuck has just entered the room," Friar said, for the benefit of the digital recording.

"Take a seat, Tuck. Mister Potter was just about to regale me with what he and Natalie Bridgman had for dinner the night Kevin Murphy went missing."

"And, I still don't see what the fuck that has to do with anything."

Tuck found herself agreeing with Potter and wondered what Friar was up to. She took the seat directly to Friar's right, and didn't voice her thoughts. She needed a minute to catch up on what was going on.

Potter dropped his eyes, and mumbled, "I already told you - I don't remember what we had to eat."

"You don't?" Friar hiked a brow. "Do you recall which restaurant you dined at? I think there are at least three close to where you witnessed the abduction."

"No."

Tuck leaned forward and placed her elbows on the table. It was suddenly getting interesting.

"I don't believe you," Friar said.

"Well, that's not my problem. I don't care if you believe me, or not."

"You should care."

"Oh, and why is that?"

"Because – if I think that you're a liar – it puts into question every single thing you've told me... and everything in the statement you made that evening becomes suspect." He handed the buff folder over to Tuck. "Detective Tuck – why don't you read out what Mister Potter said in his statement."

# FRIAR AND TUCK CASE NUMBER ONE: THE MISSING

Tuck opened the folder. Potter leaned back and stared up at the ceiling, making a show of disengaging. If it wasn't for the slight tremor in his jaw, he would have come across as completely relaxed.

Tuck cleared her throat. "I'll skip the preliminaries," she said. "We can take them as read." She cleared her throat a second time and then began to read aloud from the page.

"I didn't see much. We were just walking down the street minding our own business when Natalie yanked on my arm and pointed to a van across the intersection. I think the van was black, but I can't be sure. There were two men and a boy. The boy was struggling. One man lifted him off the ground and threw him into the van and then climbed in beside him and closed the door. It was one of those doors that slide, and I heard it roll and then clunk shut. The other man got in the front seat, behind the wheel, and the van sped off. I didn't see any more than that."

"You were asked to describe the two men," Friar put in. "You said you were unable to do that. You heard a van door roll and clunk shut. You were okay with that description, but not with the description of the men abducting the boy. I find that rather odd."

"I hear much better than I see," he returned, not taking his eyes from the ceiling.

"You saw that the van was most likely black. You saw that the door was a sliding one. You saw the boy lifted off the ground and thrown in, and one man climb in after him. You saw, and heard, the door close and then the other man get into the driver's seat. You saw the van speed away." A beat, then, "You actually saw quite a lot, Mister Potter."

Potter shrugged. Tuck saw him swallow back hard.

"But, not what the men looked like - how tall, or short; black or white; thin or fat."

"It was quite dark."

"The street and the intersection were well lit."

He didn't comment on that, merely rolled his shoulders.

"I think you lied on your statement, and I think you're lying now."

"Think what you like."

"Okay – so, tell me - what did Natalie see?"

"Same as me." He dropped his head and stared directly at Friar. "Her statement reads exactly the same as mine."

"It does," Tuck said, flicking through the folder. "Almost word for word."

Potter dragged his eyes around to her. "Well, it would... wouldn't it? We were both there. We both saw the same thing."

"Exactly the same thing?" She gave him a half-smile. "In exactly the same words?"

"So what? What are you getting at?"

Tuck answered his question with one of her own. "What do you think she wanted to tell us?"

"She wanted to tell you something? That's news to me."

"Yes, Mister Potter – she had something very important to say."

"I don't know anything about that."

"Whatever it was, it probably got her killed."

"Bullshit."

"Perhaps she recognized the men who took the boy?"

He shook his head violently. "No way."

"Let's assume, for the moment, that she *did* recognize them."

"I said... *no way*."

"Bear with me, Mister Potter." She glanced at Friar. He gave her a brief nod, and she turned back to Potter, saying, "It's a safe assumption to make. In her line of work, she probably came across any number of nefarious individuals."

"She would've told me."

"Perhaps she was too frightened to mention it?"

"Natalie ain't afraid of nothin'."

Friar noticed his change of diction. His working-class roots were beginning to show.

"She was afraid of something. I'm sure about that," Tuck insisted.

"Not Natalie," he returned, stubbornly.

"We were supposed to meet with her the morning she died."

That threw him. His eyed widened and he licked his lips nervously. "What for?"

"You tell us."

"I have no fucking idea."

"I think you do," Friar put in. "I think you knew exactly what she was afraid of, and exactly what information she withheld from us when she was questioned previously."

"This is all bullshit."

"So, you keep saying, but it's far from bullshit, Mister Potter." Friar shook his head. "I don't understand why you won't help us. A boy was grabbed off the street, a woman was brutally murdered, and you won't talk, and – when you do – you lie to us."

"I'm not lying. If you don't know why she wanted to talk to you, how do you expect me to know? She was a hooker, for fuck's sake. We weren't that close."

"You're contradicting yourself," Tuck said, levelly. "Earlier, you intimated that you were sure she would've told you if there was anyone, or anything she was frightened off."

"Well, she didn't... obviously."

"Have you wondered if, perhaps, your life is now in danger?" Friar put in. "Do you have any children?"

"Children?" His face blanched. "What are you getting at?"

Friar shrugged. "They go missing all the time."

"Now, just you wait a Goddamned minute." He got to his feet. "Don't you fucking threaten me with my children."

"I don't think it will be me making the threats. Natalie Bridgman is dead. Her head was almost cut off. If you have knowledge of what she was about to tell us, then, it might be *your* head... your *wife's*... your *children's* next."

He fell back into his chair, a look of horrified bewilderment on his face. "But, I don't know anything. Why won't you believe me?"

"Relax, Mister Potter," Tuck said gently. "Help us out here. Did she say *anything* to you?"

They could see his mind working behind his eyes. They both held their breaths.

He thought long and hard, and both Friar and Tuck recognized the exact moment he made up his mind to talk. Something shifted in his eyes. It looked very much like resignation.

"She knew the boy," he said, at last.

# 7

For long moments, no one spoke. Potter clamped his lips closed, and his expression suggested that he wasn't planning on opening them again anytime soon.

Both Friar and Tuck took the time to think about and digest what they'd just heard. It had been quite a revelation, and neither wanted to dive right in with questions – not before they were sure of what they wanted to ask.

Tuck didn't mind allowing the silence to stretch out. She was comfortable with silences. Instead of being weighty and anxiety-provoking, she found them soothing. She also acknowledged that, often, episodes of prolonged silence within an interview situation were strategic.

She allowed a couple of minutes to pass. She was the first one to speak, but she decided not to immediately focus on the elephant in the room. Potter would be expecting the questions to centre on what he'd just said about Natalie knowing the boy, and Tuck wanted to let that little nugget sit a while longer before she examined it.

Friar sat slouched in his seat. Tuck wasn't fooled by his nonchalant posture. She knew that his mind was racing. Like her, he was probably trying to work out what Natalie knowing the boy meant, and if it had anything to do with her death. She also knew that he wouldn't be as patient as she was. She had a sense that he was ready to steam in with direct questions on the matter.

So, she beat him to the punch.

She narrowed her eyes, and asked Potter, "Did you know that Natalie had a child?"

Friar threw her an astonished look. She hadn't told him that little piece of information. He wondered what the hell else she hadn't told him. He thought about asking her to step outside, so he could shake her until every piece of information was given over, but he realized that she was in full flow, and – if he interrupted - momentum would be lost.

Tuck felt her partner's angst. He now sat completely upright in his chair and his whole body was tense with frustration. She didn't dwell on his anger. He would get over it and, anyway, if he'd wanted the blow by blow outcomes of Natalie's autopsy, he should've been in attendance. It wasn't her fault that he was now having to play catch-up.

Potter's expression hadn't altered. She had no idea how her question had affected him.

"Did you know that, Mister Potter? Did you know that Natalie was a mother?"

He gave her a cold smile. "She never said, and I didn't ask. It's not exactly one of the topics of conversation we had when I was screwing her." His face took on a smug look. "In fact, we didn't talk much."

"What about when you were out having dinner?"

He shrugged. "We spoke about stupid things... the weather – things like that. I wasn't interested in her personal life."

She didn't believe him. "You never saw her with a child?"

He shook his head.

"Why do you think she would keep something like that a secret?"

"Who said it was a secret?"

"Well, you didn't know, so that makes it a secret, don't you think?"

"Hardly."

"Do you think she might've put the baby up for adoption?"

"How, the fuck, would I know?" His demeanour suddenly changed, and he shifted uncomfortably in his chair. "That's none of my business."

A beat, then, "Okay, let's move on. You said that Natalie knew the boy... did you recognize him?"

"Nope."

"Or either of the men?"

"I've already said that I didn't see them clearly. It was too dark."

"But, you saw the boy clearly enough to know that you didn't recognize him?"

His mouth worked. He rolled his eyes back to the ceiling. He had no answer to that.

"When did Natalie tell you that she knew him?"

"Later that night."

"Did she say *how* she knew him?"

He closed his eyes. He seemed distressed. Tuck glanced at Friar, and he took up the baton.

"You must've spoken to her about what you both witnessed?" he said. "You must've both wondered what had just gone down?"

He didn't reply. He kept his eyes closed and his mouth working silently. His arms were now folded across his chest and his posture was extremely defensive.

"There's a reason someone executed her," Tuck put in. "We think it has to do with the abduction of the boy. I told you that she wanted to speak to us about it, but someone stopped her. That someone might try to stop you, too."

Potter's whole body jerked forward. He unfolded his arms and slammed a fist on the table. As he turned his head from side to side – swinging his eyes from one to the other of them – his expression was furious.

"Stop threatening me with some fucking bogey-man. I know shit about the boy, and even less about Natalie's murder. You can keep me here all night, and I'll still say the same."

Friar removed his glasses, squeezed the bridge of his nose with finger and thumb, and sighed. They were getting nowhere with him.

"Okay, let's concentrate on how Natalie knew Kevin. Tell us what she said to you about it."

"She didn't say much."

Potter let out a slow breath. Friar was pleased to see him relax a little.

"All she said was that she'd seen him on the streets... talked to him sometimes... gave him money."

"Generous, was she?"

He shrugged. "She could be, I suppose."

"We haven't looked into her financial record yet, but she must've been pretty well off to live in that apartment, and to be giving money to street kids."

"She charged a lot of money for her services."

"Even so..."

"Her clients could be generous."

"Was there anyone particularly *generous*?"

"I wouldn't know."

He shifted the subject back to Kevin Murphy. "What else did she tell you about the boy?"

"Nothing."

"Didn't she wonder why he'd been taken? Surely, you must've spoken about it?"

"Shit happens. She knew that. What would've been the point in speculating?"

"Perhaps she knew something about it?"

"Why would she?"

"Oh, I don't know. You tell me."

"Nothing to tell."

Friar shook his head. "I think you're lying."

"Think what you fucking want."

"Now, I'm wondering – why would you lie to me? Perhaps because you know as much about the kid's abduction as Natalie did."

"Dream on, detective."

Friar glanced at Tuck. He wasn't sure where to go next with his questions.

"Why don't we take a break?" Tuck offered. "Grab some coffee? Would you like a coffee, Mister Potter?"

"Shove your coffee where the sun don't shine, lady."

"I'll take that as a *no*, then, shall I?"

"Take it any way you fucking want."

"That attitude really isn't helping," she said.

"Fuck you."

"Nice," Friar said. "Real nice."

"Fuck you, too, asshole."

Friar smiled. "I'll be back in five," he said to Tuck. "Gonna grab that coffee." He stood and turned to leave, giving her a knowing look before departing the room.

"Detective Friar is leaving the room," Tuck said, for the benefit of the recording.

When the door clicked closed behind him, Potter visibly relaxed. Tuck took it as a good sign.

With no hesitation, she said, "We can help you."

He narrowed his eyes. "Help me with what?"

"Help to protect you and your family."

He stared at her, then dragged his eyes the length and breadth of her face and body. A look of disgust flashed his face and he shook his head.

"You're as bad as him... making me out to be a liar."

"Everybody lies, so everybody is, by definition, a liar. You're surely not the exception to the rule?"

"Getting smart with me won't help you."

"What *would* help me?"

He shrugged, and didn't reply.

"Don't you realize the danger you're in? What about your children? Aren't you worried about them?"

"I warned you about threatening my kids."

"I'm not the one making the threats. That person is out there." She jerked her head to the side. "He's out there, just waiting to make you, your wife, and your children, his next victims."

"You don't know what you're talking about."

"I think you know that's not the case. I think you know, damned well, the danger you're in. What I don't know is why you're being so tight-lipped about an abduction and a murder."

"Change the record, will you. Get it into your thick skull that I'm saying nothing, because there's nothing *to* say."

"Okay."

"Okay?" His expression was suddenly comical.

"Sure." She nodded and shrugged. "If that's the case, then I give up... no more questions."

He was startled into silence.

"Only... I wonder," she mused aloud, her eyes narrowing. "I wonder what the word on the street will be?"

"What's that supposed to mean?"

"Nothing... just a thought, really."

She welcomed the silence that dropped between them. She knew that he was using it to try to work out what she meant. She hoped he would understand quite quickly. Friar would make an appearance pretty soon, and would be likely to interrupt what she believed was going to end up being a breakthrough.

"You think that someone will believe I ratted them out?"

She met his words without expression. "That's a possibility, especially if..."

"If, what?"

"If we dropped a word in the wrong ear... suggested that you helped us with our enquiries."

"You wouldn't do that." His voice was now a mere whisper.

"I might. What's to stop me?"

She wished she could zip-tie him to the chair, keep him in the room until she'd wrung every ounce of truth from him, sweat him until she'd emptied him, but the rules didn't allow for such treatment, so she had to adopt a more subtle approach. The implied threat to finger him as a rat was a ploy she knew other detectives used. She wasn't adverse to using it herself.

"Just out of curiosity," she asked rather absently. "Where were you this morning... around the time that Natalie was murdered?"

"You want my alibi?"

"It would help me to know. It would make me hesitate to whisper in certain ears."

"I really couldn't say, because how am I supposed to know what time she died?"

"That's a good point. How about between eight and ten-thirty?"

His lips peeled back from his teeth in a macabre grin. "I dropped the kids off at school, and then went to work."

"You usually do that... drop them off?"

He shrugged. "Sometimes."

"What time would that have been?"

"Around eight."

"And, you arrived at work, when?"

"Near nine."

"Are you sure?"

"As near as dammit."

"It took you an hour to drive from the school to your place of employment?"

His eyes darted to the side. She knew that a lie was coming.

"Yes," he said. "The traffic was horrendous."

"It usually is at rush hour."

"Frustrating, really."

"Had you far to go?"

He cleared his throat but didn't reply.

She waited. This was one of the times when she used her own silence strategically. He would answer, just to break it.

"Two miles," he said, clearing his voice once more.

"An hour to travel two miles?"

"I may have stopped off somewhere on the way."

She hiked a brow. "Where?"

Once more, his eyes darted to the side. "I don't want to say. You'll only jump to conclusions."

"I'd never do that," she replied, candidly.

He eyed the door and licked his lips.

"He won't be back for a while," she said. "It's just you and me, and I promise to believe everything you tell me. I know you'll tell me the truth, because – to do otherwise – could have dire consequences for you."

"This is nothing but blackmail."

She shrugged.

"Okay, but you have to hear me out... not think..."

"I promise," she put in. "I'll hear you out."

She could see him thinking about it, weighing up the risk of telling, as opposed to the risk of not.

On a sigh, he said, "I made a detour to Natalie's." He looked for a response, but none was forthcoming, so he went on, "I didn't go in. I just pulled up in front."

He ran a trembling hand through his hair. She could see how difficult the confession was for him, and encouraged him with a faint smile.

"I meant to go in. I was pretty mad at her. I'm sorry about that now... given what happened to her... but, I'd paid her good money and she was refusing to see me again. I wasn't having that. She had no right to refuse me."

"So... you drew up on the street?"

"Yeah." All the bravado had gone from his voice. "I knew she'd be there. I had every intention of going in and confronting her, but I changed my mind. I sat there for a while, working myself up, but I thought... she's just a fucking hooker... a whore. Plenty more where she came from."

"I see." Tuck felt a shiver pass through her body. The hairs on the back of her neck stood up.

The goalposts had suddenly shifted.

She had more questions, but he was on the cusp of incriminating himself. She now had no choice but to draw a halt to the interview, because - following the Miranda V Arizona Supreme Court decision in 1966 – she had to read him his rights and give him the opportunity to consult a lawyer.

She held up a hand, effectively shutting him up. He looked at her quizzically.

"I need to stop you there, Mister Potter," she said. "You've introduced new information... new evidence... and, to protect you, I need to inform you of your rights."

He immediately realized what that meant. "You're arresting me?"

"No, but I'm not prepared to allow you to incriminate yourself."

"I'm not," he returned, somewhat confused. "I didn't do anything. I told you – I didn't get out of the car."

"That's as may be, but..."

He threw his hands in the air. "I knew it... I knew you'd jump to conclusions. I should learn to keep my fat mouth shut."

"That's what I advise you to do now... just for a moment whilst I..."

"This is bullshit." He stood. "You're not pinning this on me."

"That's not my intention. Please, sit down."

"I'm sitting nowhere, lady. I'm outta here."

He barged past the table, causing it to skitter across the floor, and headed for the door.

Tuck sighed impatiently and pushed herself to her feet. Standing, she barely reached the height of his shoulder.

"What?" he sneered across at her. "You think you're gonna stop me?"

She took the necessary two steps required to get within arm's reach of him. She felt, as well as saw, his eyes rake the length of her. She knew what he was thinking. He didn't rate her one iota's worth of spit.

"Gonna pull your gun on me? Shoot me in cold blood?"

"No, Mister Potter. I'm going to put you on the floor."

His grin only reached half-way before his feet were swept out from under him and he was in flight.

He landed on his back. All the air whooshed from his lungs as he crashed exactly where she said she'd put him – on the floor.

With very little effort, she flipped him onto his belly and put a knee in the small of his back. He didn't even have a second to react before both arms felt as if they were being wrenched from their sockets, pinned, and zip-tied.

Tuck realized that he wouldn't immediately process what had just happened to him, so she gave him a moment before Mirandizing him.

# 8

"I'm impressed. He must have two hundred pounds on you."

"The bigger they are, the harder they fall," she returned, sensing a compliment and trying not to blush to the roots of her hair.

"Is that your attempt at flippancy?"

"Of course not. It's just a fact. It's easy to use a person's weight against them. You use their forward momentum to…"

"I *do* know that, Tuck. I've brought down my fair share of bad guys."

"Then, why point out that he's two hundred pound heavier than me?"

Friar sighed. "Just forget it."

Tuck replayed his words in her head, concluding that it was a definite attempt at a compliment.

"Thank you," she said.

"Why are you thanking me?" Friar bit into his sandwich, chewed several times and then washed it down with a mouthful of coffee.

Tuck watched him, fascinated. "You really ought to pay more attention to your diet. Your cholesterol must be through the roof."

"Nothing wrong with a bit of cholesterol."

"Are you being serious?"

"Nope." He finished the sandwich and drained his cup. "What were you thanking me for?"

"I think you were giving me a compliment on my ability to take Potter down."

"I was."

"I appreciate it."

"You don't get many compliments, do you?"

"I'm not sure. I don't think so."

"Well, you should. That was pretty slick in there... getting him to tell you all that shit, and then immobilizing him when he tried to do a runner."

Tuck brushed his words aside. She didn't want to hear them. They made her uncomfortable.

"What do you think... about what he told me?" she asked.

Instead of answering, Friar turned the question back on her. "What do you make of it?"

"Pretty dumb... to admit it."

"You think he's our killer?'

Tuck snorted. "He's big, but not strong enough - not to have killed Natalie that way."

"He's guilty of something, though."

She nodded. "I think you're right."

"When his lawyer gets here, we'll have another go at him. Meantime, I'm having another cup of coffee."

Tuck watched him stride over to the coffee machine. She grimaced when she saw him pick up a sugary doughnut. It would just be her luck to finally get a partner she could work with, only for him to drop down dead with a coronary because his arteries were fur-lined with fat.

Considering his appalling diet, Friar was in pretty good shape. He was also drop-dead gorgeous, but Tuck paid his looks no mind. She'd learned the hard way not to waste her time in admiring handsome men. They never saw her the way she saw them. Although their appraisal of her physical attributes wasn't in the least perfunctory, as soon as they realized what lay beneath, they ran for the hills..

Considering the fact that she was actually pretty easy on the eye, the lack of genuine male attention over the years surprised her parents. Despite their insight into her peculiar personality, they thought that her good looks and perfect curves should've provided sufficient compensation to have her married with a couple of kids by now.

Tuck hadn't even got close.

"You're covered in sugar," she said. "Why don't you use one of those paper plates?"

"What are you... my mother?" He flicked a hand down the front of his shirt. "What is it with women and plates?"

"It's always the woman doing the clearing up and the laundry. Plates help."

"Not in my house. My mom never lifted a finger. From the age of eight, I did all my own laundry." He licked the sugar off his fingers. "These doughnuts are good... you want one?"

She shook her head. "I'd rather swallow detergent."

"Your weirdness never ceases to amaze me, Tuck. What cop doesn't eat doughnuts?"

Tuck broke eye contact. She knew he meant no disrespect – not like the others – but she wished he would learn to choose his words more wisely.

"I've been thinking," he said, around a mouthful of masticated sugary dough. "About the motive for taking the boy."

"We should stop calling him *the boy*, *the Murphy boy*, or *the Murphy kid*. Let's just call him Kevin, okay?""

"Sure, but I don't suppose he cares what we call him, so long as we find him." He finished the doughnut. "Anyway, as I said... I've been thinking. It's unusual for two men to snatch a kid. So, why two this time? Do you think we have a pair of paedophiles working in tandem, willing to share?"

"Could be. It's not unheard of."

"But, pretty rare. Yes, they might pass a kid around their pals, but for two of them to go out on the prowl and abduct a child?" He shook his head. "I don't buy it."

"No, I guess I don't, either."

"We shouldn't rule it out, though."

"Not completely, but perhaps we should look at other motivations."

"That's what I was thinking."

"Any ideas?"

"Not yet."

"I think Natalie would've pointed us in the right direction."

Friar nodded.

"We need to find out how well she knew him... Kevin, that is. I don't accept that their relationship was as fleeting as Potter made out."

"Let's hope Potter can shine some more light on it."

Tuck looked at her watch. "His lawyer is taking his time in getting here."

"It won't do Potter any harm to sit a while longer and stew... get over the humiliation of being taken down by a girl."

"I'm far from a girl."

"I didn't mean it literally, Tuck."

"I know."

"Well, that's a step in the right direction. I actually think you're getting to know me."

"Enough to begin to differentiate between an insult and an inane exposition, I suppose."

"Well, that's something."

He sat behind his desk. They were alone in the large squad room, and several phones were jangling in their ears. Neither seemed perturbed by them, nor inclined to pick up. Both knew that the callers weren't looking for them. They had their own extensions and neither of those two phones were currently ringing.

"It's day three," he said.

She immediately knew what he referred to. She nodded.

"And, going on for twelve hours since we found Natalie."

She nodded once more.

"Why didn't you tell me about the baby?"

"I did. You heard me mention it to Potter."

"I meant before then. It kinda blindsided me."

"That wasn't my intention."

"I realize that, Tuck. That's why you're not wearing your tonsils as a necklace."

Her hand went automatically to her throat.

He rolled his eyes. Eye-rolling was beginning to become a habit around her.

"There was no opportunity to tell you anything. I came straight to the interview room from the autopsy."

"Next time... pull me out."

"Okay. But, perhaps next time, you could actually attend the autopsy?"

He ignored that. "Anything else you haven't told me... anything that would help?"

"Nothing specific."

He sighed. "So, we're nowhere?"

"We're here."

"Yes, Tuck – we're here."

They were still there an hour later, and five minutes after that, they both headed towards their cars, having given up on the lawyer.

"We'll have to either charge him, or let him go in the morning," Tuck said.

"I've been busy trying to think up a charge that'll stick."

"I'm sure you'll come up with something."

"It's a pity you didn't allow him to sneak in a punch to your face before you flattened him. Assaulting a police officer would've bought us some time."

"I'll be sure to remember that for next time."

They parted ways at their respective cars, but not before Tuck reminded Friar not to be late in the morning. She warned him that he couldn't eat into their limited time with Potter by rolling in at his usual ungodly hour.

Friar meant to head home. That was his intention. He pointed his car in the general direction, and put his foot down.

The rain had stopped, and - as the residual, airless heat of a New York summer night went to work drying up the puddles - the air grew sultry. The humidity was almost intolerable, and he was forced to turn on the air conditioning.

He hadn't got very far when his phone trilled. He pressed the button on his Bluetooth earpiece and accepted the call.

"Friar," he growled, already sorry he hadn't voided it.

It was Jerry, a long-time acquaintance from homicide at the $17^{th}$.

"Jerry...? It's been a long time since I've heard your dulcet tones. What's happening?"

He listened for a moment, his foot slowly easing off the gas as the meaning of the words began to penetrate his tired brain.

"You sure?" A beat, then, "Can you text me the address? Yes, I'm coming for a look. Any objections? Good." He ended the call and heard the rapid bleep in his ear that signalled the text message with the address being delivered to his phone.

He thought about calling Tuck. She'd be pissed if he didn't. He pulled over and took his mobile out of the docking station on his dashboard.

Tuck's phone went straight to voicemail. He left a message, urging her to call him as soon as possible, then pulled back onto the road.

Traffic was light, so he arrived at the address in under twenty minutes. The street was choked with police vehicles. He recognised the MEs van and the accompanying forensic vehicle that were pulled up in front of the large house standing in its own grounds yards from the sidewalk.

He flashed his badge and was allowed to duck under the yellow scene-of-crime tape. Before he ventured towards the house, he tried ringing Tuck again.

*Voicemail.*

He refrained from leaving another message.

There were the usual looky-loos gathered on either side of the street – quite a crowd for that time of night – and a few journalists stood amongst them.

"Why all the attention?" he asked Jerry, when the man walked to his side. "I didn't think it would be of interest to the newshounds."

"That's because of the kids. Word got out that they're on the missing list."

"The kids are missing? You didn't mention that on the phone."

Jerry shrugged.

"You got any idea what happened?"

"Well, one of the reasons I rang you was because of yours."

"Mine?"

"The hooker."

"Natalie Bridgman?"

Jerry nodded. "Seems mine is the same MO… or, that's what it looks like."

"You mean to tell me that my witness's wife has just been murdered by the same MO as *my* victim?"

"Single slash to the throat…near decapitation."

"How did you even know about my victim?"

"Simms is the ME on call. He's inside."

Friar's stared towards the door. His gaze was direct, but behind his eyes, his brain was already beginning to fog with confusion. He wondered what the fuck was going on. He was afraid that he actually knew.

"Some pretty weird shit, right?"

Friar nodded absently. It was weird, all right.

"Can I go in?" he asked, stepping through the gate. "Take a look and speak to Simms?"

Jerry nodded and they both stepped inside the house.

There was a greasy smell, like the odour of countless fried meals, and an immediate feeling of claustrophobia brought about by the piles of newspapers stacked against the walls and by the ceiling-high mounds of junk blocking the hallway.

"Hoarder," Jerry said. "Can you imagine three kids living in this? We're going to have to shift a ton of it to get the body out."

The space was just wide enough for a man to squeeze through, but their journey from the front door to the rear of the house wasn't an easy one. Nothing looked safe. The towers of stacked newspapers and magazines, and the rickety mounds of what was no more than rubbish, seemed precarious.

"Where was she found?" Friar asked, emerging into a small, square space with three doors off.

"The back yard. You get to it through the kitchen." He gestured towards the door straight ahead. "It's fenced in, and there's no back gate or side entrance."

"Was she the hoarder, or the husband?"

"Beats me. We haven't spoken to family or neighbours yet. I've got a couple of uniforms beginning a house to house as we speak, but haven't succeeded in reaching the husband."

"I've got him in custody."

"The husband?" Jerry hiked a brow. "What the fuck for?"

"He knew my victim... was in the vicinity at the time of her murder." His heart knocked against his ribs. He wondered if Potter was responsible for both women's deaths. "Who called it in?"

"Anonymous."

"And, the children?"

"Gone. We're assuming they were taken by the killer, but that's yet to be confirmed."

"How old?"

"Ten, eight and four."

"Jesus."

'Tell me about it. It's a right clusterfuck."

Just how much of a clusterfuck it actually was wouldn't become clear for quite some time.

Friar walked through the kitchen, out, and into the backyard, having no idea just what he was walking into; but what he already knew was that there were now two dead women and four missing kids, and only Potter being the link to all of them.

# 9

He was late... again. In anticipation of his early arrival, Tuck had stopped off at *Costa* and bought him a fresh coffee. It was now stone cold, as was her mood.

She was aware of her fixed stare and her clenched jaw and tried to force herself to relax. Potter wasn't going anywhere. They still had a little time to question him further before they either had to charge him or let him go. But, Friar had promised to be there no later than eight, and it was now after nine. Their small window of time was closing fast.

She felt anger at a visceral level. It was the only emotion she felt intensely. Over the years, it proved to her that there was something critical missing in the make-up of her psyche. She always knew how to compensate for her lack of empathy, and sometimes – like in the case of a missing child – she could actually hone her feelings into a semblance of actually giving a shit.

Her mother had once asked her, quite seriously, why she wanted to go into law enforcement. "It's not as if you care about people," she'd said. "I see you more in a laboratory coat with a pipette in your hand."

She'd ended up at odds with her mother over that statement. She couldn't understand her mother's blindness to the fact that she actually wanted to care, and that choosing law enforcement as a career was her way of striving towards what she hoped would be an epiphany of sorts. She hoped for the one great moment when her true nature – the one she fervently believed was there – to be revealed.

Now, the anger turned her blood to ice, and, once more, proved her mother right. She wasn't capable of working with people. To work alongside others, she needed the ability to not only tolerate their failings, but to accept and embrace them.

There was a great deal that she was beginning to respect about Friar. She appreciated the fact that he seemed to let her eccentric thinking and behaviour flow right over his head... most of the time, anyway. She believed that, given the chance, she could learn from him, but she feared that – if she didn't adjust to his tardiness, his inane sense of humour, and his peculiar way of working – she'd be the cause of the breakdown of their partnership.

She didn't blame herself for the other two detectives jumping ship. They hadn't stuck around long enough to get to know her properly. Granted, getting to know her was no guarantee that they'd be able to work with her – the opposite was more likely – but, at least she wouldn't have been left feeling as if she wasn't worth the effort.

Friar was making the effort, so the least she could do was to make some effort of her own.

She'd begin with her anger.

As a teenager, she'd attended anger management classes. No one had forced her to attend. She'd enrolled entirely of her own volition. Those classes had helped get her through puberty and helped her to cope with the bullying at school without resorting to gouging out a few eyes or breaking a few bones. Those classes literally ensured that she *had* a future.

She never liked the way that anger built inside and threatened to overtake any semblance she had of good judgement. There was always the potential for catastrophic loss of control. There was always the possibility that she would do, or say, something that she wouldn't be able to take back, so she knew, if she didn't use some of the techniques she'd learned in those classes, that - when Friar eventually showed up - she'd end up in such a state of heightened fury that she would end up being thrown into the cell right next to Potter.

To anyone else, the extent of her anger over something as trivial as being late would be entirely irrational. The thing was – to Tuck – it was a perfectly rational response to having the piss taken out of her. Because, that's what promising her one thing and then doing another was – it was one huge piss-take.

She glanced at her watch again, then walked the length of the room, ignoring the other detectives sitting at their desks, and stood at the window. With her back to the room, she was completely unaware of the eyes turned in her direction, or the heads shaking in paternalistic sufferance at her obvious impatience.

The window ran the length of the room. Each pane of glass was grubby and the long sill was smattered with dead flies. She eyed a crack in the corner, and flicked her gaze to the chipped paintwork on the frames and the tarnished handles. It was such a depressing place to be hemmed inside.

Outside, beyond the glass, it was overcast. She wondered if there would be a repeat of the previous evening's rain. She wondered if it would matter. She gave the sky a fleeting glance and then stood with her head bent, staring out through the glass and looking down to the street below at nothing in particular. She didn't expect or hope to see him hurrying towards the building. That's not why she was standing there and looking out. She was trying to focus on the knot of rage building in her belly and taking a few moments to silently remonstrate with it.

When the man taking the anger management class first told her to talk to her rage, she'd laughed at him. She'd said, "Everyone will think I'm barmy. I'm not doing that."

Then, he'd explained that she would only talk to it in her head, and that no one would ever know anything about it. She still thought that it sounded like something a lunatic would do, but she'd agreed to give it a go.

She no longer questioned the effectiveness of the one-sided conversations she'd had with her rage over the years. Talking to it really worked. She imagined that it was like talking to an errant child, or trying to talk someone down from jumping off a high ledge.

"Tuck?"

She lifted her head and turned on her heel. She saw him walking towards her – no, he was *hurrying* towards her.

*It's too late to rush now, mate.*

She thinned her lips and instructed her rage to stay where it was - not leap out and not take control of her next few words or moves.

Before deciding what level of hell to put him in, she decided to listen to his excuses. She half-hoped he would at least make them interesting.

Breathless, and gulping in huge mouthfuls of air, he looked as if he'd ran all the way from the car park. She stood back and watched as he bent forward, placed his hands on his knees and let out a hacking cough.

"Cover your mouth when you do that," she chided. "God knows how many germs your spraying everywhere."

"Give it... a rest... Tuck.... For fuck's sake," he spluttered and stammered. "I'm dying here."

A voice from the other side of the room called out, "You all right, Friar? Someone's husband been chasing you again?"

A titter circled the room, cut short when Friar reared up and panned a glower at all the smug and smiling faces.

"You okay?" Tuck asked, suddenly concerned.

"No, I'm fucking not."

"You should've left earlier then,' she said.

He gave her a level look. "Is your phone turned off?"

Taken aback by the question, she shook her head and frowned.

"Check it, will you?"

"It's not switched off, Friar." She reached into her pocket and pulled out her iPhone. The screen was black and didn't brighten when she tried to wake it up. "The battery must be dead," she intoned.

"I've been trying to call you."

"You could've tried the land-line."

"I couldn't be arsed, and I was a bit busy."

"Oh? Doing what?" She flapped a hand. "Never mind. I don't want to know. Let's just say that I'm pleased you finally turned up."

"I've been attending an autopsy."

She did a double-take.

"You heard me," he said. "Simms has cadavers coming out of his ears, but I persuaded him to put this new case to the front of the queue."

"New case?"

"The one I tried to phone you about... at least six times."

She glanced guiltily back at her phone. "So, we have a new case, is that what you're telling me... another death?"

"It's not our case... not yet, anyway. It should be, because of the connection, but the $17^{th}$ currently have jurisdiction. Fortunately, I know the homicide detective who picked it up. He agreed to hang fire before making his way over here and talking to Potter."

"What's Potter got to do with it?"

He dragged in a breath. 'It's his wife."

Moments later, hurrying to catch up with him as he strode down the corridor towards the elevator, she peppered his back with questions.

He ignored them all.

When the elevator doors closed on them, he finally looked at her and shared all the details.

She listened with mounting angst.

"What's being done to locate the children?"

"Everything possible."

"He'll go nuts."

"Who, Potter?" Friar's mouth turned down at the corners. "He's going to get an almighty fright, that's for sure."

"You tried to warn him."

"Frankly, Tuck – I was making that up as I went along. I wasn't convinced that his family *were* in any danger."

"And, you say that the wife was killed with the same MO?"

"Exactly the same. Simms is sure it's the same man... or as sure as he can be. Fibres taken from the clothing of the body look a match to those found on Natalie Bridgman. The blade looks to be the same, or similar, and everything else looks damned close. Everything has to be confirmed, of course, but I'll bet my next pay-check that we'll have a match for everything."

"Time of death?"

"Around the time Potter arrived at the precinct."

"I guess that rules him out."

"Looks that way."

The doors swished open and they stepped out.

"My buddy from the $17^{th}$ is arriving in an hour. *His* lieutenant is talking to *our* lieutenant, and it's hoped that the homicide and the three missing kids can be transferred to us."

"We'll need some help. We can't work this on our own."

They made their way along the corridor towards the suite of interview rooms.

"If we ask for help, I have a feeling that homicide will be asked to step in. We could end up working for them."

There were a row of six chairs along each wall and, on one of them, sat Potter's lawyer. His head was bent over a briefcase, open to show a sheaf of papers, and he was busy thumbing a message into the smartphone in his hands. He seemed oblivious to their arrival.

He was a dumpy man with a sallow complexion and a shock of white hair. Rimless glasses – not dissimilar to Friar's – were perched on the end of his nose. His suit was well-tailored and expensive, his shoes the best Italian leather.

"I thought he was a public defender?" Friar hissed at Tuck.

She shrugged. "That's what I was told."

"In those shoes, that suit?" He shook his head. "He's from one of the big firms... has to be."

When they were no more than a foot away, Friar cleared his throat and the dumpy lawyer held up a hand as if to say *wait*, and then finished texting his message. On a sigh, he sent it, and looked up.

Tuck noted that the owl-like eyes behind the glasses looked tired and puffy.

"About time," he said. "Do you know how long I've been waiting?"

Tuck looked at her watch, and said, "Seventy two minutes."

"That's seventy minutes too long, detectives. I'm a public defender... I'm not paid by the hour."

The incongruousness of the expensively attired man with his low-paying job struck Friar as more than a little odd, but he had more pressing matters to concern him, so pushed the thought to one side.

"We were expecting you last night," Tuck said. "We waited a lot longer than seventy two minutes for you."

Disregarding her words, he said, "I want to see my client."

"We'll have him brought to you in a minute," Friar said.

"Now, please. I've waited long enough."

"Another few minutes won't matter."

He looked at Friar with a certain disdain – the disdain most defence lawyers reserved for police officers – and shook his head. "I'll need at least an hour with him before I'll agree to allow you to question him."

"I don't think so."

"But, I insist."

Friar took the seat next to him, somewhat crowding him.

"Something happened last night," he said. "It changes things."

"Oh?" He pushed his glasses along the bridge of his nose with a pudgy finger. "And, what might that be?"

Friar glanced at Tuck. She could see the question in his eyes.

"It might be best to give him the details first," she said.

Friar considered it. He wasn't sure. He continued to believe – in fact, was now certain – that Potter knew exactly why Natalie Bridgman was killed, and probably had information as to the whereabouts of Kevin Murphy.

"Your client's wife was murdered last night." He waited a moment – until the lawyer's eyes unpopped themselves and settled back into their fatty folds - before continuing. "All three of his children are missing."

The lawyer swallowed back hard. Friar gave him another moment, then added, "So, that's two women your client was screwing who have had their throats cut."

# 10

Potter was wound tight. He felt vulnerable, afraid, confused. He'd made the mistake of talking – of telling that bitch of a detective that he'd gone to see Natalie. She obviously didn't believe that he hadn't entered her apartment, or killed her, and that was why he'd spent an uncomfortable and sleepless night in a cell. Well, he sure as hell wasn't going to do any more talking. He wouldn't be bumping his gums in response to any more of their dumb questions. Let them work it all out for themselves. They would get no help from him.

Now - as he viewed the taut expressions on all three faces in front of him – a burgeoning sense of trepidation overtook what was left of his equilibrium. Even his lawyer looked as if the truth of what was on his mind was so dark that the words to express them would be devastating.

Something had clearly happened overnight. He imagined that it was something quite terrible. He immediately thought of the man who'd commissioned Natalie's death and what he might have done to ensure his silence.

Friar watched the myriad of emotions sweep across Potter's face and tried not to feel sorry for him. He wasn't a man who evoked sympathy. He was too damned arrogant, too damned sure of himself, but he couldn't help but think that there would surely be a chink in his armour that would leak angst and sorrow at the devastating news he was about to hear? Surely, a husband and a father would crack and want to give up those who'd struck such awful blows?

He glanced away. He couldn't bear for Potter to catch even a glimpse of sympathy on his face. Whatever the circumstances of his wife's murder proved to be, one thing was for sure – Potter was in it up to his neck, just as he was with Natalie Bridgman's death. He'd stake his whole reputation on it.

As soon as he'd arrived at the scene, and seen the body, any doubts he'd had in Potter's innocence had been erased. That was one time when he definitely hadn't believed in coincidence. Just what part Potter had played in either death was yet to be determined, but, first, he had to observe his reaction to the news and try to draw some initial conclusions.

With the absence of any firm leads, Potter was all they had.

Steeling himself, he looked directly into Potter's face. It was time to tell him.

Potter swallowed and licked his lips. He was expecting a bombshell. The look on the detective's face told him that much.

"Spit it out," he said. then looked quickly from Friar to his lawyer. "Whatever it is, put me out of my fucking misery, for Christ's sake."

The lawyer dropped his eyes. He wasn't going to be the one to tell him, and he didn't want to be looking into his client's eyes when he heard the news.

Potter dragged his eyes across to Tuck. She stared back at him, unblinking. As much as she would love to sucker-punch the bastard with the news, she was going to leave it to Friar.

"Last night, I attended the scene of a homicide," Friar began.

Potter shifted in his seat. He had a sense of what was coming, but stiffened his spine and tilted his chin, as if preparing himself for it.

"So?" he said. "What's that got to do with me? You've had me banged up all night. Whoever was unlucky enough to get themselves killed, you can't pin it on me."

"No, Mister Potter – we're not looking at you as the killer and, in fact, it exonerates you from Natalie's murder."

"Oh, and why is that?" He had an awful feeling that he knew.

"Because the same person killed both women."

"It's a woman, then... your latest victim?" Hs voice had dropped an octave and carried more than a slight tremor. "Anyone I know?"

"I'm afraid so." Friar cleared his throat. "The victim is your wife."

Potter merely nodded. Friar watched him for a moment, waiting on the words to actually sink in. It wasn't unusual for such news to skate right over someone's consciousness. He would have to wait until his eyes glazed over, and for his chest to hitch with a giant heave, before he would know for certain that realization had struck. Only then would he speak again.

And, there it was – almost on cue – the eyes, and the chest, reacting exactly as he'd envisaged.

"Have you any idea who would want both Natalie Bridgman and your wife dead, Mister Potter?"

Potter's chest rose and fell far too quickly. Friar guessed that he was on the cusp of a panic attack. The lawyer had the same thought and reached over the table to pat his client's hand. It was an ineffectual gesture and, instead of steadying Potter, it seemed to electrify him. He shuddered and his whole body seemed to go into spasm. Jerking back in his chair, he almost toppled to the floor.

Tuck reacted quickly, placing herself behind him and putting both hands on his shoulders. Technically, she wasn't allowed to put her hands on anyone in custody. An unscrupulous lawyer could claim assault on his client, but Potter's lawyer actually appeared grateful for her intervention.

Friar didn't miss a beat. He asked the question again. "Who would want Natalie and your wife dead, Mister Potter? If you know, now is the time to tell us."

Potter's jaw worked. His eyes darted wildly in his head. Friar wasn't sure if he was struggling to find the words to rat out the killer, or if he was searching for a way to extricate himself from the whole sorry mess. Either way, nothing but a loud groan escaped his mouth.

Friar took a seat and clasped his hands on top of the table separating them. He gestured for the lawyer to take the seat next to his client, then, with cold eyes boring right into Potter's face, said, "You haven't asked about your children. I realize you're in shock, but – shock, or no shock - it would've been the first thing you should have enquired about."

"Fuck you," he ground out. "Don't use my kids, you bastard."

"Ask me about them," Friar said, blandly. "Go on... ask."

"Detective Friar," the lawyer interjected. "Perhaps we could have a short break? My client is obviously distressed."

"First, he has to ask me about his children." He cocked his head, but kept his eyes on Potter. "Well? Don't you want to know?"

"What? All right... what?" Spittle flew from Potter's mouth. He jerked out of Tuck's grip and leaned menacingly across the table. "Are they dead? Is that what you want me to ask?"

"It would be a start, I suppose." He took pity on him, and added, "They could be. We're not sure."

Another glance at his lawyer, then, "What's he on about?"

The lawyer opened his mouth to speak, but Friar held up a hand, effectively shutting him down before he could get a word out.

"They're missing and, unless you can tell me that they're spending the night with a relative, or a fiend, then the only conclusion I can draw is that they've been taken."

This time, there was no delayed reaction. Potter hauled himself quickly from his seat and made a beeline for the door.

"Where do you think you're off to?" Friar asked, standing to block his path.

"To find my fucking kids," he bit back sharply. "And, you're not going to stop me." He tried to push through the wall that was Friar. "Shift your arse," he snarled. "Shift it, or I'll put you on the floor."

Friar didn't budge. He said, "If you don't sit yourself back down, I'll have you escorted back to your cell. We'll carry on with our enquiries whilst you cool off, but – be warned – we might not have a chance to speak again for some time. Do you want that, Mister Potter? Do you want to be shut away whilst God knows what's happening to your children?"

Like a balloon with all the air being let out, Potter sagged and deflated. In an instant, all emotion drained from him. He suddenly looked like a man defeated. Meekly, he turned and walked back around the table to his chair.

"Is it true?" he asked his lawyer. "Is any of it true?"

The lawyer nodded dumbly.

"My wife... my kids?" In a daze, he shook his head.

"I'm so sorry, Mister Potter. It's a terrible way to hear the news."

Potter looked from the lawyer to Friar. "You said my wife died the same as Natalie?"

Friar nodded. "I think you know what that means, even more than we do," he said. "Don't you think it would be better if you told us what's going on, and what the Murphy boy's abduction has to do with the death of these two women?"

Jaws clenched, eyes narrowed to slits, Potter's mind finally began to turn over. The shock was wearing off, to be replaced by cunning. He had to take the time required to think things through. One wrong word, and either he would be dead, or maybe it would be his kids, or even all of them.

He let out a slow breath. His kids might be safe – for a while, at least. They were beautiful kids. He groaned.

*Oh, fuck.*

If he acted the rat, he knew exactly what would be in store for them. Even if he didn't – even if he kept his trap shut – the chances of him ever seeing them again were slim to none.

He'd warned that stupid bitch what would happen if she contacted the police. It was bad enough that she'd forced him to ring emergency services when the boy was taken, without then getting herself murdered because she couldn't stop her lips from flapping. Now, she'd got him tangled up in this mess, and he realized that, even if he succeeded in saving himself, his kids were gone. If Natalie Bridgman hadn't already been dead, he'd fucking kill her himself.

He shook his head slowly from side to side. Whatever way he cut it, he was fucked.

He ran a hand through his hair, knuckled his eyes, licked his lips. He did everything he could to distract himself from absorbing and ruminating on the shitstorm that was erupting all around him.

There was now a silence in the room. He focussed on that, gratefully drowning in it.

Tuck poured water into a plastic cup and pushed it across the table towards him. His eyes flicked down and fastened on it. It served to anchor him. It prevented his head from spinning.

Someone was talking. It was the woman. He tried to listen, but there was a buzzing in his ears that he recognized as the sound of mounting fury. He was becoming so angry that, if he remained seated, remained in that room, he feared he would self-combust.

The woman detective was asking him if he had any idea where his children had been taken. Oh, he had an idea, all right. He had more than an idea. He felt sick to his stomach and breathing was becoming increasingly difficult. He had to get the fuck out of there.

His mouth twisted into a scowl, a low snarl escaped his throat. For the second time, he pushed himself back up and out of his chair, his fists already swinging by the time he straightened his spine.

The lawyer immediately scooted to the side and got to his feet. Friar reacted immediately, exploding up and squaring off. Potter looked like a desperate man, and desperate men could be violent. He tried to talk him down, turning on a sympathetic, reassuring tone, but Potter was having none of it. He skirted around the table, his arms beginning to windmill as he pushed his way forward.

Friar put himself in his path. Avoiding his wildly swinging arms was an impossibility, and he accepted the violent punch to his shoulder with clenched teeth and as much good grace as he could muster. He barely rocked back on his heels. There had been little strength behind the punch. He blocked the second punch by raising a muscled arm and then deftly turned to the side, grabbed an arm, and wrenched it up Potter's back, pushing at him and flattening him against the wall.

Tuck had her work cut out holding the lawyer back. She was quite impressed that the tubby little man wanted to fly to his client's aid. It was more than a tad foolish. Didn't the man realize he could get hurt in the fray?

"Get back into your seat," she grated against his ear and taking his elbow none too gently. "He's not going to hurt him."

"He's already hurt him," he returned sharply, trying to shake loose from her firm grip. "I call that assault, detective."

"And, what do you call that punch to my partner... a lover's caress? Sit the fuck down, sir, before I charge you with obstruction."

The lawyer looked set to argue, thought better of it, and plonked his fat ass back into his chair.

Tuck went to Friar's aid and, between them, they manouvered Potter back into his seat. He didn't go quietly. Every raised word that spewed from his mouth was a curse. He damned them to hell and didn't let up until he ran out of breath. Friar did what Tuck had done earlier – he stood behind the chair, placed his meaty hands on Potter's shoulders, and pushed down.

Tuck picked up the cup of water and forced it into Potter's hand. "Take a drink," she said.

He pushed the cup away, splashing water across the table. It was a final act of bravado and there was relief all around when Friar finally felt him relax.

Tuck refilled the cup with water from the bottle on the table and placed it back in front of him. She then hunkered down at Potter's side whilst Friar continued to keep a firm hold on his shoulders.

"Do you understand what's happening here?" she asked him. "Do you understand that you need to help us find your children... that all this nonsense needs to stop?"

"Fuck you," he said, hawking in his throat and spitting at her.

Tuck deftly avoided the glob of mucous. His aim hadn't been particularly accurate. It landed with a wet plop on the floor.

Tuck hated any form of spit. She could tolerate filth, shit, and all sorts, but spit - particularly the thick yellow mucous that was formed in the back of the throat – she hated the most. If it had landed on her, she would've been a basket-case.

"Fuck you," he said, again, renewing his struggles to get up.

Friar flexed his fingers, digging in. Nothing was going well, and time was marching far too quickly onwards.

Potter was barely recognisable as the man who'd walked into the interview room the evening before. Gone was the calm demeanour and nonchalant bravado. Now, he presented as a man verging on a blistering meltdown.

Friar made a snap decision. He gestured at Tuck to stand and move away, and he then loosened his hold on Potter's shoulders and stepped back.

He was either going to calm down, or he wasn't. It was time to find out.

Released from Friar's iron grip, Potter pushed himself half out of the chair. He surveyed the room suspiciously. When no one moved towards him, he stretched to his full height.

Deep down – in the part of him that still had a modicum of sense – he knew that he wasn't going anywhere. Even if he managed to get out of the room, they'd stop him from leaving the building and from getting onto the street.

It was then that the tears came. They didn't arrive slowly. They came in a sudden flood and – accompanied by a grievous wail - they bubbled from his eyes, and his nose, and his mouth.

Tuck was taken by surprise. She had not expected the sudden tears. Friar was relieved. Tears were always good. He often found that they were the harbinger of acceptance.

They let him cry. No one intervened with soothing words or reassurances. No one reached out a hand to comfort.

The only sounds in the room were Potter's guttural sobs. Many minutes passed before they came to a shuddering stop and complete quiet then prevailed.

Then, a chair scraped across the floor as Friar sat down. Potter followed his lead, and, with resignation, retook his seat.

Friar's voice cut through the heavy layer of tension. "Are you ready to talk?"

Potter sniffed and wiped his nose on the sleeve of his jacket, but made no reply. He wasn't ready to talk. Despite the tears, and despite the remnants of shock, he remained fully aware of his predicament.

All the cunning required to keep himself out of the mess of Natalie's death, had – by the death of his wife - exploded into nothing. With her dead, and his children missing, he knew that he was caught in a vicious trap – cruelly caught between a rock and a hard place.

Whatever he decided to do, whatever he decided to say, he knew that he was fucked.

"It's time to tell us who killed your wife and who took your children." Friar spoke quietly, almost reverently. "Whatever message this was... whatever coded communication your wife's death was meant to convey to you... I want you to ignore it. I want you to trust us, Mister Potter, and not those guilty of her murder. I want you to help us to find Kevin Murphy and your children."

The lawyer suddenly seemed to remember that he had a job to do. He cleared his throat, and said, "I want a word with my client in private." He blinked at Friar and then at Tuck. "Will you excuse us?"

They ignored him.

Friar continued to focus his attention on Potter. His voice remained calm, soothing. "Things have got out of hand. You're now a liability to them. You know that, and I think it terrifies you. We won't let them get to you, but we don't want to risk the children's lives either... no more than they're already at risk."

"I insist that you give me a moment with my client." The lawyer forced a firm note into his voice. "He needs a break. You have to give him a little respite."

"There's no time for chit-chat," Tuck said. "And, no time to waste on a break. Once he's told us what we need to know, then you get to talk... only then will he get to catch his breath."

The lawyer gave a greasy smile. "That's not how it works, detective." He looked from Tuck and then directly at Friar. "Why don't you tell her that this isn't how it works? Explain to her how I get to talk to my client, and how you get to bugger off and twiddle your thumbs until I'm finished."

Tuck took in a gulp of air. Friar eyed her anxiously. She was about to blow.

He sighed. It was neither the time nor the place for a stand-up fight.

His tone lost all evidence of patient gentleness. He no longer wanted to soothe. "He's right, Tuck. We'll give them five minutes to concoct whatever the fuck they need to, and then we'll take Potter apart, piece by piece." He threw the lawyer a hard look. "And, as for you – four children's lives are at stake. If you don't convince your client to tell us everything he knows... and anything happens to those kids... I will personally remove your tonsils through the crack in your ass."

# 11

Outside the room, Tuck said, "Everything that went down in there was caught on the recording."

"At least it didn't catch the sound of the lawyer's nose breaking when you punched him on the face."

Their eyes locked.

"I wouldn't have done that," she said, aghast. "What do you take me for? I'm not a complete nutter." Something coiled in her belly. She had been so close to belting the prick, and the memory of how she felt only minutes before made her squirm.

He gave a wry smile. "You must admit, you were thinking about it."

"Maybe," she conceded, dropping her eyes. "But, I wouldn't have done it." *Liar.* Another word from him and he would've ended up bleeding on the floor.

He didn't fully believe her, but he let it pass. He led her along the corridor, talking as he walked.

"We'll go and see Mitchel... fill him in and see if we can persuade him to allow us to take on Potter's wife and kids."

"You think he will?"

He shrugged. "I doubt it, but we can ask."

Tuck had to jog to keep up with his long stride. By the time they reached Mitchel's office, she was panting.

They had to wait whilst the lieutenant finished talking on the phone. When he ended the call and waved them in, Friar wasted no time in explaining the current state of affairs.

"Yes," he said, nodding thoughtfully. "I've already had the necessary conversation with Butler over at the *17th*. We both agreed that it makes sense to combine all cases under one investigation."

"That's excellent news, sir. I'm presuming we'll take the lead on both homicides and the four missing kids." It was a statement, and not a question. Friar wanted Mitchel to realize, from the get-go, that they were up for it.

"I don't think so, Friar. That's not how I see it... not at all." Mitchel shook his head emphatically and his expression warned that he had no intention of brooking any argument. "It's simply not on," he continued. "The whole shitstorm sits right outside of your remit."

Friar paused to think before he replied. He waited for several beats, the frown on his face becoming more pronounced as the seconds ticked by. He knew that there would be no point whinging, and equally no point in attempting to ram down the lieutenant's throat that he and Tuck were the best people for the job. Mitchel considered himself the best judge of that, and he definitely didn't like sore losers.

"The Murphy boy's abduction started the whole thing," he finally got out, "and I can categorically say that the Bridgman homicide is linked. We've already made some headway in both cases."

He refused to catch Tuck's eye. He knew that he wouldn't like what he saw there. She wouldn't be best pleased with him embellishing the truth.

Mitchel was listening, so Friar carried on. "Potter is neck deep in all of this, sir. I think... no, I *more than think*... that he's fully aware of who killed Natalie Bridgman, and his wife, and I've no doubt that he knows where the children are. He'll talk to us. He'll tell us everything. He's scared shitless. He'll do anything to save his own skin." He cleared his throat, preparing himself for the next lie. "We've struck up quite a rapport. I've left him conferring with his lawyer, but we'll get right back in there pronto and get him to tell us everything."

He risked a glance at Tuck. She stood staring at him with her hands clasped around her waist and an incredulous look on her face.

"A rapport, eh?" Mitchel hiked a bushy eyebrow. "You have him eating out of your hands?"

Friar swung his eyes back around to the lieutenant. "Yes, sir."

"What do you say, Tuck?"

Tuck thinned her lips, but said nothing. Mitchel grinned.

"Bullshit... utter bullshit." His grin dropped to be replaced by a frown. "You've made little or no headway on the Murphy boy's abduction, have come up empty on the Bridgman homicide, and Potter won't talk. Is that a more accurate summing up?"

"But, we'd fingered Potter before his wife's murder," Tuck put in. "I'd say that was ample progress."

"Ample? Really?"

Tuck coloured under his mocking scrutiny. "I would say so, yes."

"He phoned in the abduction, didn't he?"

"Yes, sir, but..."

Mitchel held up a hand. He'd heard enough. He said, "I'm sure that the detectives taking over from you will be appreciative of your efforts, but it's time for you both to stand down."

"You're standing us down? You mean, you're taking us off everything?" Tuck was aghast. She looked at Friar who looked ready to blow a fuse.

"You can keep the Murphy boy. I'm not convinced his abduction has anything to do with either homicide."

"How can you think that?" Friar threw his arms in the air in frustration. "Natalie Bridgman was killed because of what she knew about Kevin Murphy being taken. Potter's wife was probably murdered by the same killer. It all started with Kevin Murphy, and it's ridiculous to think otherwise."

Mitchel met Friar's eyes. Their looks clashed.

"You're talking yourself out of keeping that case, Friar. Carry on, and you'll have nothing."

Friar had a fight on his hands. He'd never lost a fight in his life, and he wasn't about to lose one now. There was no point in emotional argument. Mitchel respected logic and he didn't mind any of his officers playing Devil's Advocate. Friar banked on him being willing to at least hear him out before shutting him down.

"You may as well pass the Murphy case over," he said. Tuck hitched in a breath, but he ignored her. "I mean - how can we work the missing Murphy kid without delving into both homicides and pursuing the missing Potter children? You say that you're not convinced that the Murphy case is tied in, but *I'm* sure, and I hope you have enough respect for my judgment to accept that it's a very real possibility."

"No one is doubting your opinion, Friar, but..."

"No, lieutenant – that's *exactly* what you're doing," he interjected. "And – to top it all - you believe we're not up to the job."

"I didn't say that. You know damned well what the boundaries of your roles are. Why the hell do we have a homicide division, if you're going to pick those cases up?"

"Only those pertinent to an ongoing investigation." Friar attempted to keep his voice level. "Look, lieutenant, I know you think this is a stretch, but Natalie Bridgman was killed because of what she was about to tell us about Kevin Murphy's abduction. Potter's wife was killed to prevent him from telling us what he knows, and his children were taken as insurance against him blabbing. Everything points to Kevin Murphy, and – as Kevin Murphy is our case – you should either allow us to work it properly, and follow up on every lead, or you should give it to homicide."

A full minute rolled past before Mitchel responded.

"Despite what you might think, I'm not shutting you, or Tuck, out of any loop."

"Well, it sure feels as if you are. Can't you just accept that we're the best people for the job?"

"Your job is finding those who've got themselves lost. That's your job, Friar... not working homicides."

"The Governor said..."

Mitchel jerked around and drew daggers in Tuck's direction. "I'll thank you to remember that I don't need chapter and verse rammed down my throat, Tuck. I know very well what the Governor dictated." He turned back to Friar. "This all goes way beyond a missing kid case. We've got homicides across two jurisdictions now."

Tuck's hands were clenched at her sides. Once again, the powers that be were placing the priority on the dead as opposed to on the living. Yes, it was imperative to solve the homicides, however her and Friar's emphasis would be on using the clues from the homicides to track the children. If they solved both murders along the way, then great, but that wouldn't be their motivation. Their motivation was finding those damned kids – all four of them, and that meant being given free rein to work all cases.

"I'm done discussing it,' Mitchel said with a firm finality. "It is what it is. Suck it up and go find that boy."

Friar rolled his head to the side and regarded Tuck with resignation. She stared back at him, the same look of resignation in her own eyes.

He was surprised by her calm countenance. He'd thought that he had begun to understand her, and to predict when she was about to lose her temper. She was no respecter of authority, and he'd half expected her to launch at least a verbal tirade at the hapless lieutenant.

Surprisingly, when he raised an eyebrow at her, she merely shrugged.

There was a tortured silence that Friar determined wasn't going to last any longer than it ought. In Mitchel's office, there was always a danger in silence. You never knew what the lieutenant would say to fill it, and Friar had – through bitter experience – learned not to give Mitchel the opportunity to say anything that would be to his detriment.

"I wish you'd reconsider, sir," he said, refusing to give up. He might be flogging a dead horse, but he couldn't simply walk away. "You have to at least consider that the Murphy case is linked. It makes sense, for the time being, to keep it within the main investigation."

"You're repeating yourself, Friar. It's becoming rather tedious."

"I had hoped…"

"That, by saying the same thing over and over, it would finally sink into my thick skull?" Mitchel wasn't amused. "I haven't the time for this. Just accept it for what it is, and bugger off."

Tuck turned, but Friar didn't budge. He wasn't done.

"Can't you give us twenty-four hours?"

"To do what?"

"Finish questioning Potter… find us a lead on the killer… get an idea of where the kids are."

"That's a tall order."

"It is, but we're getting close with him."

Mitchel tapped his bottom lip with a slender finger. He was thinking and mulling over Friar's words. His intelligent grey eyes never left Friar's face. He rated him as one of his best detectives, perhaps *the* best, and, because of that - and but for Tuck being in the mix - he would have been willing to go out on a bit of a limb and trust him to carry the load without compromising anything.

*Tuck*. It all came down to her. She was a hard worker – he'd give her that – but, where serious crimes were concerned, she was relatively untested. He worried that her inexperience and her strange personality would hinder Friar. Neither of those things mattered quite so much when they were both merely chasing after the elusive shadows of the missing. Even a straightforward, good old-fashioned, murder associated with a missing person case wouldn't normally be considered a problem for Friar - even with her as his partner - but these homicides weren't going to pan out that way. He had a nose for such things, and it was his judgement that counted, not Friar's, and certainly not Tuck's.

"You can't ignore the very real possibility of a link, sir."

"I'm ignoring nothing. I'm willing to concede that there might be a connection, but that doesn't alter the fact that we now have two brutal homicides and three... no, four... missing kids to get ahead of. You and Tuck have neither the resources nor the time to give to such high profile investigations." He sighed, not entirely unsympathetically. "How about a compromise?"

"Compromise?" Both Friar and Tuck spoke the word simultaneously, and both looked at one another with raised eyebrows.

"Yes – *compromise*. I'm sure that you understand the concept."

"Sure," Friar returned, "but, in this instance, what does it mean... exactly?"

"It *means*, Friar, that I'm going to allow you to keep your sticky beak inside the loop. It *means* that you can liaise with homicide, and follow up on any emerging leads you, or Tuck, stumble across. But..."

"But?" That from Tuck, who had moved closer to the desk and was hovering rather obtrusively at Friar's elbow.

"You're to focus on the missing kids, and not the homicides. I'll assume - for the moment, at least – that the same person has all four children."

"Thank you, sir."

"Don't thank me, yet, and don't misunderstand what it is that I'm saying. I'm saying that you and Tuck can work parallel to the homicide investigations, but I expect you to hand over anything you find that leads to either of the homicides. You are *not* to go off, half-cocked, on your own. You are not – under any circumstances – to go down any rabbit holes."

Friar reluctantly nodded. Tuck stood silent and immobile.

"Detective Henderson will pick up Bridgman and the Potter woman. You will both work under him on the missing kids and, together with the rest of Henderson's team, you'll contribute... *contribute*, mind you... to solving the whole kit and kaboodle."

"But..."

Mitchel flapped a hand. "Don't make me regret this - either of you. I've made my decision. It's best this way. To do otherwise would be a dereliction."

"You want us to work under Henderson? Not *with* him, but reporting to him?"

"He'll be in charge... yes."

Friar sucked in air through his teeth. He daren't look at Tuck. Seeing the horrified expression on her face would be the undoing of him, so he kept his eyes on Mitchel.

"Can we at least finish interviewing Potter?"

Mitchel shrugged. "That'll be up to Detective Henderson. He's going to be calling the shots."

They had no choice but to agree. Neither of them liked it, but it was either Mitchel's way, or no way.

"Bloody Hell," Friar said, once they were back out on the corridor. "That's not good."

"I can't believe you sucked that up."

"What choice did I have? It was either that, or lose the whole thing. At least, this way, we're still involved."

"*Henderson's* loop. You *do* know that he's an asshole, don't you?"

"At least he's *our* asshole."

Tuck folded her arms across her chest. "I'm not taking orders from the likes of him."

"Do either of us have a choice?"

"Too right, we do." Her eyes flashed with defiance, and then she seemed to wilt. "I guess we have our orders. It's just that it'll take Henderson ages to get up to speed."

"We could..." he began, then dropped his eyes, "No... just forget it."

"Forget what?"

He raised his eyes and gave her a sheepish look. "You won't like it."

She eyed him speculatively. "I might surprise you."

He shook his head, and said, "I doubt it. It would mean breaking the rules... going against the lieutenant's orders." He returned her speculative look. "That's not who you are, Tuck. You're not a rule-breaker."

"I break the rules," she returned, defensively. "I don't always follow orders."

"Yeah, right."

She felt herself flush. "Try me," she said. "Tell me what you're thinking."

"All right." He dragged in a breath. "I think we should go right back in with Potter. I think we should shake him until he rattles... get him to talk."

He couldn't believe it when she didn't immediately dismiss the idea. He couldn't believe that she was actually thinking about it.

"We could get into trouble," he said, belatedly attempting to back-track. "You can't afford another strike against you."

"What about you? You could lose your badge."

"I've earned a few brownie points over the years. I'll get a slap... no more, but, you..?" He shook his head. "I think the lieutenant is looking for any excuse to can you."

"You'd be slapped?"

"Figuratively speaking, Tuck. Jeeze..."

"And, I guess – me being canned means me getting fired?"

"You're learning."

She thought about it some more, then said, "Let's do it. Let's get back in there. There's no time to waste."

Neither of them needed to be reminded just how easily missing people – especially children – were so quickly lost in the ether. Throw a couple of dead bodies into the mix and those kids would be hidden so well that it would seem as if they'd never existed. Every sign of them would be erased. Interrogating Potter further was their only realistic hope of garnering the information necessary to set them off on the right path. Waiting for Henderson to either give them permission to speak to him again, or hanging back whilst he did the questioning himself, would waste too much time.

"Right." He rolled his shoulders. "Okay."

In absolute agreement, they moved off down the corridor.

# 12

Every community has an underbelly, and across New York there are many divergent communities, each with their own particular shade of nefarious factions. Scrape the surface, and - to the unsuspecting - the rancid stink of corruption is all-consuming. And, yet – in spite of the crime and the underlying culture of dog-eat-dog – Bolton Friar would never choose to live or work anywhere else but in Brooklyn.

He was New York born and bred, and – like most law-abiding Americans, and despite the many temptations to do otherwise – he had the tenacity and the gumption to live an honest life. That didn't mean he always walked a straight line. He wasn't a wholly righteous man, and he was far from perfect, so he wasn't completely averse to bending the rules, or the law, to the point where a break was imminent. He believed that, sometimes, the end justified the means.

In Tuck, he had inadvertently found a partner who wasn't shy about seeing how far she could go before smashing through what was actually right or legal. For someone who was such a stickler for protocol, he was shocked to realize that – when it mattered – she'd storm across any line.

The line they were now about to cross wasn't, in itself, illegal. It wasn't even immoral, but it *was* wrong. Their orders had been quite explicit. They had to back off from Potter and leave the decisions regarding further interrogation to Detective Henderson. They justified their decision to go back into the interview room on the fact that Mitchel had told them they could work all of the missing kid cases that were part of the overarching homicide investigations. That was enough to get them back in the room without the risk of receiving anything more than a bollocking.

Tuck preceded Friar through the door.

The lawyer, chin raised and eyes narrowed, watched her transverse the room before he transferred his gaze to Friar who appeared solidly behind her. Both Friar and Tuck had straight spines and solemn faces. He immediately knew that they meant business.

Potter's eyes were wide and glassy. Very little emotion was mirrored in their dark craters. Gone were the earlier tears and obvious anguish, to be replaced with an almost cold detachment. Whatever the lawyer had said to him, it had both calmed and reassured him.

"Don't waste your breath," he said, right off the bat. "I'm not talking." Despite his apparent nonchalance, his forehead beaded with perspiration. "My lawyer was pretty clear when he told me I had the right to remain silent."

Friar ignored him. He didn't even look at him as he crossed to the recording device, leaned over, and switched it back on.

"Detectives Friar and Tuck have re-entered the room," he said, for the benefit of the recording. "The time is eleven hundred hours."

"Did you hear what I said, ass-wipe?" Potter swivelled around in his chair. "There's no point turning that fucking thing on. I've got nothing to say... absolutely fucking nothing."

The legs of Friar's chair scraped noisily across the floor as he dragged it away from the table. He sat down and stretched out his long legs. Tuck chose to stand. She leaned against the wall, and folded her arms across her chest.

Friar addressed the lawyer, completely blanking Potter. "Did you have enough time to consult with your client?" he asked, pleasantly. "Only, time stops for no man, and it's marching ever forward."

"I did, thank you."

"And, you advised him to keep quiet... to keep his lying mouth shut?"

"For fear of incriminating himself... yes."

"What, I wonder, could he say that would do that?"

The lawyer gave a wry smile. "I'm not stupid enough to answer that."

"Hey!"

Everyone turned to Potter, who was rapping his knuckles on the table.

"Don't talk about me as if I wasn't here."

It was a no small thing for a man of Potter's ego to be ignored, so – when Friar merely gave him a condescending flick of his eyes, and then turned back to the lawyer – it was almost more than he could bear.

"Look at me when I'm fucking talking to you. Don't you look away from me."

He made to stand and the movement brought Tuck pushing off the wall. She took a step towards him, her eyes flashing a warning, and he flopped back down, shaking his head and mumbling obscenities.

"Is he going to sacrifice the children?" Friar asked the lawyer. "Is he going to allow them to die to save his own skin?"

"What's that supposed to mean?" Potter called out. "Talk to *me*. Ask *me* your damned questions."

Still, Friar ignored him.

The lawyer cleared his throat. "You know I can't speak for my client, Detective Friar."

"No? That's a pity. You might just save his life."

Potter said, "My life is safe enough, thank you very much."

Friar grinned at the lawyer. "For someone who was determined not to say anything, he's making plenty of noise."

The lawyer gave a wry smile and shook his head.

# FRIAR AND TUCK CASE NUMBER ONE: THE MISSING

Friar craned his neck to look up at Tuck. "Perhaps we should have a word with the lawyer outside... get away from this nutter's ramblings?"

Of course, that wasn't on the cards, but Friar banked on Potter not realizing it.

"We could do that," Tuck returned, playing along. "But I find his antics quite amusing. Let's stay here awhile."

The lawyer's eyebrows were in his hairline. He wasn't stupid. He knew exactly what their game plan was, but he had taken Friar's earlier words to heart. He didn't want to have the stain of three or four dead children on either his character or his conscience, so he made no comment and no objection to their banter. He would neither help nor hinder them in their quest to get at the truth. He would continue to do his best to protect his client's interests, but only to a certain point. He wouldn't go out of his way to sabotage the detective's attempts to find and save the children and, if that meant turning a blind eye, or keeping his mouth shut, then he wouldn't lose any sleep over it.

Friar saw the lawyer relax. He observed that he seemed somewhat resigned, and surmised that he'd scored a little bit of leeway with him.

The lawyer was thinking hard. He considered that Potter was a dirtbag, and further considered that dirtbags didn't deserve any undue consideration. However, he also had to consider the possibility that he could be disbarred. If it came to light that he'd sat back and watched as Potter was railroaded, his career would be over. He caught Friar's eye, held it, and then flicked his gaze quickly towards the recording device. Friar didn't seem to comprehend, so he made a subtle gesture with his head.

Friar didn't get it. He thought that the lawyer had developed a nervous tick. But, Tuck got it. She smiled, and said, "I don't think we'll bother with any more questions."

Friar hiked a brow. He had no idea what she was playing at. Now wasn't the time to draw a halt to the interview. He watched as she walked across to the recording device, said, "Interview suspended," and turned it off.

Her very serious expression told him she thought she knew what she was doing, so he decided to trust her, and made no objection.

Potter smirked. He thought he'd bested them. His glassy eyes now shone with triumph.

"You'll be letting me go, now," he said.

"Not yet," Tuck returned. "Just keep your ass in the chair and bear with us a while longer." She then spoke directly to the lawyer. "Did he tell you where the children are?"

Friar looked on, bemused, as the lawyer shook his head, and said, "You know perfectly well that I can't discuss what transpired between us."

Potter leaned forward. "Hey... no more questions. You said no more questions." He looked from Tuck to Friar. "Tell her, will you? No more fucking questions."

Friar merely shrugged.

"There's going to be a very serious complaint filed about all you jackasses. I'll sue this department into bankruptcy."

Friar yawned, making no attempt to hide his disdain.

Tuck asked the lawyer another question. "I don't suppose he admitted to knowing what happened to them?"

Again, the lawyer shook his head.

"I've had enough of this." Potter stood. Friar was on him immediately, pushing him back down.

Potter raised a fist to strike him, then thought better of it. He knew what would happen if he hit anyone. It would be a reason to charge him, and charging him meant that they could hold him longer.

He threw a watery grin around the room. "You can all relax," he said. "I'll be a good boy. Carry on with your parlour games."

"This is no game," Friar said. "It's very telling that you think that it is. It suggests that you have no real sense of just how much serious shit you're actually in."

"Dream on, detective. You know very well that I'll be walking out of here soon."

He was right. Unless they charged him, they would have to eventually let him go.

"Aren't you frightened?" Friar asked, seemingly genuinely interested in the answer. "I mean… who will be waiting on you out there?"

"I have no idea. Not my wife, obviously."

The flippant remark wasn't lost on his lawyer and he threw him a look of admonishment that Potter returned with a smirk. It was clearly apparent that the death of his wife no longer caused him any grief – if it ever actually had.

"Whoever it is, they may think that you've ratted them out."

It was Potter's turn to shrug. "That ruse has already been tried on me." He glanced across at Tuck. "Didn't work for her, and it's not gonna work for you."

Friar carried on as if he hadn't heard him. "I wouldn't like to be in your shoes when they confront you. Do you think you'll manage to convince them that you kept quiet?" Friar shook his head, sadly. "No. I'm afraid they'll think the worse.'

"Bullshit."

"I guess you think that, either way, your children are dead. You've already written them off, haven't you?"

"Fuck you."

"You're not keeping quiet in order to save them. You don't give a shit about them. You're keeping your cake-hole shut because you think it'll save *you*."

"I don't have to listen to this crap." He looked at the lawyer. "Say something, will you? Shut this fucker up."

"Perhaps you should listen to him?"

"Listen to him? Whose side are you on, you fucking snake?"

"I just think..."

"Well, don't think. I can do my own thinking."

"Let's just be frank with one another for a moment," Friar said, softening his tone. "We know you didn't kill either Natalie or your wife. We know you didn't have your children abducted. So far, you're not really in very much trouble... not with us, anyway."

"That's for damned sure... I didn't murder anyone – no way."

"But we suspect that you know the people who did."

Friar couldn't imagine the anguish a normal father would be feeling at that moment, wondering what atrocities their children were being subjected to. Potter should be a basket case. He should be spilling is guts, telling everything he knew, and not giving a shit about the danger he was putting himself in. He ought to be devastated over the death of his wife, insistent that the murderer be brought to justice. But, Potter was neither a normal father, not a grieving husband. He was a nihilistic son of a bitch. There was no point in appealing to his parental instincts, his outrage, or imagined grief. All he could do was to urge upon his sense of self-preservation.

"There's no need for you to be charged with anything." He went on, risking a glance at the lawyer. There was no way he should be making such a statement. He couldn't promise Potter anything, least of all that he wouldn't be charged with any crime. He was pleased to note the lawyer's total lack of interest.

"And, you need never see the inside of a prison cell. Whatever involvement you had in all of this, we can turn a blind eye." It was a blatant lie, and he was grateful for Tuck having turned off the recording.

Tuck shifted uneasily on her feet, making him wonder if he had gone too far. His promises to Potter could come back and take a chunk out of his ass. Did he care? Did he fuck. Anyway, nothing need ever be repeated outside of the room. It would be Potter's word against his. Tuck would back him up and, as for the lawyer, it seemed that he was content to turn a deaf ear.

"If you help us out, we'll put you and the children into witness protection."

"Yeah, right." Disbelief shone in Potter's eyes. He wasn't buying it. "Why would you do that?"

"Because there are four missing kids, and God knows how many more. Kevin Murphy is the tip of the iceberg, isn't he?" He was gambling on a hunch, and knew he'd hit pay dirt when Potter' sallow skin flushed with colour.

*Bingo*! Whatever nail he'd just hit on the head, it was enough to seriously unnerve Potter.

"What is it... a paedophile ring?" he asked, a tad nonchalantly, as if it didn't really matter.

"Fuck, no."

"What, then?"

Potter let out a bitter laugh. "You have no idea, do you? If you had the least fucking clue, you wouldn't be promising me something you'd never be able to deliver. Protect me? Put me into witness protection?" He shook his head. "You're outta your tiny mind."

"So, we're in agreement?"

He looked at Friar askance. "Agreement about what?"

"That there's something, or someone, you need protecting from."

"I didn't say that."

"No, but you intimated it. That's good enough for me."

A series of conflicting emotions fought with one another across Potter's features. His eyes had grown feverish. He licked his lips and struggled to find the words to counter what Friar had just stated.

"You're goading him," the lawyer said, finally rallying to his client's aid. He felt he had to at least make an effort to look as if he was doing his job. "Nothing is admissible. He's a man bereft at the loss of his wife and the abduction of his children. No court would..."

"I'm not interested in what a court would, or would not, accept." Friar stared fixedly into Potter's eyes, but spoke directly to the lawyer. "I'm only interested in the children. I know they were taken as assurance against him speaking to us. The thing is, Mister Potter knows that keeping quiet won't save them. As I mentioned before - he knows that they may already be dead. He doesn't care about that. Dead, or alive, he thinks he can still save his own skin. Talking to us poses a risk to him... a risk he won't take - not even on the small chance that he could save them. I've said we'll protect him, but it seems that he doesn't believe me. Well he'd best think on this... regardless if he talks or not, he's a dead man. He's a liability. They'll get to him in prison, or they'll get to him on the street. He'll end up sacrificing his children for nothing."

"My client doesn't know where the children are. I'm sure, if he knew, he would be only too willing to tell you."

Friar flicked his eyes across to the lawyer's face. "Don't tell me that you're stupid enough to believe that bullshit?"

"Looks like we have ourselves not one, but two imbeciles in the room," Tuck said, matter-of-fact.

The lawyer's face suffused with colour. He harrumphed in the back of his throat, then clenched his jaw, scattering the colour and turning his face ashen.

Impatient now, Friar said, "Let's wind this up." He tucked his legs under the chair beneath him and placed his elbows on the table. As he leaned forward, Potter drew back.

"Cut the crap, and tell us where to find the children. You don't have to give me any names... just a location."

# FRIAR AND TUCK CASE NUMBER ONE: THE MISSING

He wanted the names, desperately, but the location of the children was more urgent.

Tuck walked over and took the seat next to Friar. She was directly opposite the lawyer and she made a point of staring at him until – feeling her eyes on him - he lifted his head to look at her.

She said, "We'll charge your client with accessory to every crime we can think of related to the murder of Natalie Bridgman, the murder of his wife, the abduction of Kevin Murphy and the abduction of his three children. If any harm befalls any of the kids, he'll also be charged with accessory to that as well." She gave him a toothy grin. "Perhaps you'd like to explain how many years he would spend in prison for all those crimes... not that he'd live long enough to serve a single one of them."

"I hardly think..."

"She's bluffing," Potter interjected. "They both are." His expression clearly said that he wasn't sure if that was actually the case. As he looked from one to the other, his eyes were literally popping from his head. "Tell them to let me go. Tell them they can't hold me a minute longer."

The lawyer gave a curt nod, went to open his mouth to say just that, and closed it with a snap when Tuck slammed her fist on the table.

Friar hadn't been expecting it, and his heart lurched to his throat with shock. He tasted blood on his tongue from where he'd nipped it with his teeth.

He would have her for that.

"The location, Mister Potter," she said, now leaning over and rapping her knuckles directly in front of him. "You know where they've been taken... I *know* you do."

"I know fuck all about it. Go screw yourself, and your empty threats."

Tuck didn't let up. "What will happen to them, do you think? Will they be murdered, or sold as sex slaves?"

Potter thinned his lips, crossed his arms, and shook his head.

Friar chipped in. "What do you hope for them... death or gang rape?"

"You're sick, you are," he said to Friar, glowering.

"Not as sick as you," he returned. "In a moment, I'm rescinding my offer of immunity to prosecution, and my offer of protection."

The lawyer shook his head. He knew that Friar had no authority to offer either. He'd been winging it, and it was beginning to seem as if it had all been for nothing. Potter wasn't for shifting.

*Fuck it*, he thought. If he allowed Potter to remain quiet, without trying to persuade him to talk, he wouldn't be able to kiss his own children ever again.

"Tell them what you know," he said. "I'll do everything in my power to ensure that Detective Friar makes good on his promises."

"I've got nothing to say. It's about time all you assholes realized that."

"Just a location, Potter," Friar prompted. Give us that, and I'll let you walk right out of here."

"I..."

"No one need know."

"You're bullshitting me."

Friar shook his head. "I'm not. Cross my heart."

Potter wavered. Friar could see the indecision creep into his eyes. He held his breath.

"I..."

Friar leaned further forward.

"I..."

"Go on, Potter."

Potter's eyes swivelled towards the door as it was pushed open.

Detective Henderson walked in.

# FRIAR AND TUCK CASE NUMBER ONE: THE MISSING

It was game over.

# 13

All he wanted was five more minutes. It wasn't a lot to ask. The way Henderson reacted, anyone would think he'd requested the moon on a plate.

Seconds before he said something that would get him fired, he stomped from the room, trailed by Tuck.

"What now?" Tuck asked.

Friar massaged his temples, and rolled his shoulders. He felt as stiff as a board, wound up tight, and frustrated beyond all reason.

"Fucked if I know."

Following the events in the interview room, and without a whisper of a lead, he didn't know what else to say to her. A lump the size of a boulder was resting on his chest and he began to regret all the sugary doughnuts and gallons of coffee he'd recently consumed. He felt a heart attack looming.

"I think we need to revisit everything related to Kevin Murphy."

He threw himself into the chair at his desk in the squad room. He felt a pain radiate down his arm. *Here it comes*, he thought... *death*. He flexed his fingers, rubbed his biceps. He was more angry than frightened. He didn't want to keel over before finding the bastards who'd taken Kevin and the Potter children.

"Are you listening, Friar? I said..."

"I heard you." He burped, and the pain eased a little. "What do you think we missed?"

"Kevin's mother, for a start. We never did manage to locate her."

"She's a dead end."

"We don't know that... not for sure."

"So, how would we find her? We don't even know who her pimp is, and we couldn't find anyone who admitted to knowing her."

He heard his heart hammer in his ears and wondered if it was racing too quickly. He surreptitiously felt for the pulse at his wrist, and said, "We'd be wasting our time... time we don't have."

"Perhaps Natalie knew her? After all, they were both hookers."

"Natalie was a different class."

"It's a small world, Friar. Who's to say that they didn't bump into one another?"

Relief surged through him. The pain was almost gone. The boulder on his chest seemed lighter, less suffocating, and his pulse felt strong and steady.

"It's too much of a long shot and, anyway – Natalie's dead. If she knew her, she'll take that to her grave."

"I still think we should try and find her."

He sighed. She was like a dog with a bone. "Okay. Have it your way." He thought a moment, then said, "There's one thing that's been plaguing me. Why did Potter phone the police?"

"When he saw Kevin being taken?" A beat. "I never gave that a thought."

"If he was involved, then why would he speak to emergency services?"

"Perhaps Natalie made him?"

He sighed. "Perhaps, but it doesn't make any sense."

"It's certainly a puzzle. What about the Potter children? What are we going to do about finding them?"

"It stands to reason that, if we find Kevin, we'll find them."

"Should we pay a visit to their home... canvass the neighbours?"

"Henderson will have that in hand. No point in duplicating the work of his team. No..." He shook his head. "We concentrate on Kevin."

He stood and steadied himself before making for the door. "Let's see if we can run the mother to ground."

Tuck wondered if he was all right. Ever since they'd been turfed out of the interview room, he'd seemed ill at ease, out of sorts. She'd noticed him rubbing his temples and then his arm and – now that she looked at him closely – he seemed a little pale.

"Are you all right?"

"What?" He glanced at her over his shoulder. "I'm fine... why?"

She shrugged. "Never mind."

"You drive," he said, throwing her his car keys.

She snatched them out of the air and they both made their way down the stairs and out of the main entrance, onto the road and into the car that was parked illegally close-by.

"I'm surprised you didn't get a ticket," she said, buckling up and lowering the window.

"I never get a ticket around here. My car is well known, and I'm given a certain courtesy."

She started the engine. It purred gently until she pressed her foot on the gas and then it gave a growl.

"Why?" she asked.

"Why the courtesy of no parking tickets?" He shrugged. "I guess I'm too well liked, and I never cause an obstruction."

She turned to look out of the rear window and then pulled into the traffic.

"Where to?"

"Kevin's last known address."

"The mother moved out of there months ago."

"I know, but we ought to quiz the neighbours. Someone must have some idea where she went."

"Kevin left home long before his mother legged it. He'd been beaten up by one of her Johns once too often... that we *do* know."

"Out of the frying pan and into the fire."

"You think he was turning tricks, or dealing?"

"One, or the other, I suppose. How else was he to survive?"

"Thieving?"

Friar shrugged. "I hope we get the chance to ask him."

She took Atlantic Avenue and drove towards the Marcy Projects, the public housing complex in Bedford-Stuyvesant. It was less than a five mile trip, but took them close to thirty minutes to get there.

They were now within the jurisdiction of the $79^{th}$ precinct. The over seventeen hundred apartment housing project wasn't exactly a no-go area for the police, but both Friar and Tuck were nevertheless relieved not to be arriving in a squad car. Just like any officer or detective from the $79^{th}$, they wouldn't be welcome.

Tuck pulled the car to a stop and, for long moments, they both sat in silence. Eyes were already upon them. They might not be in an assigned police vehicle, but they were strangers, and easily identified as people on official business.

A group of four or five youths with blank faces stared across the blacktop at them. When Friar panned the street, he saw another group approach.

"I don't think the car will be here when we get back," he said.

"*If* we get back," she returned with a grimace.

"You think we're taking our lives in our hands venturing into this no man's land?"

"Undoubtedly." She opened her door and got out. "You coming?"

He didn't hesitate. Hesitation was for pansies.

Tuck strode straight over to the first group of boys. Her spine was straight and her head was high. Showing any sign of fear would make her an immediate target. Bravado was what was called for.

Friar was a step behind her. As soon as he drew to her side, she showed her badge. The tallest boy – Tuck gauged his age at around fourteen or fifteen years - looked at the gold shield with a sneer of contempt. He was lean and athletic. Adolescent acne smattered his cheeks and chin. *He should be in school*, she thought, glancing around and taking in the others, equally young, and equally contemptuous.

She took out her iPhone, set it to video, and held it out in front of her. She captured every one of their faces and swept around to take in the approaching second group.

"What are you doing?" the tall youth asked her.

"Yes," Friar whispered, leaning close. "What *are* you doing?"

She ignored them both, lowered the phone, and sent an email.

The space around them had grown cramped. At least twelve boys surrounded them.

"I have every one of you recorded," Tuck said. "I'm sure most, if not all of you, have arrest sheets as long as my arm. You'll be easily identified. If - when we return - I find anything has happened to our car, you'll be found, arrested, and hopefully it will be your third strike and you'll be locked up until you're too old to stand and take a piss straight."

"You let your bitch talk for you?" one of the smaller boys asked Friar. "Don't she know her place?"

"She knows it," Friar snapped back. "You'd be better off minding your own."

The tension was palpable. Even with the security of Tuck's emailed recording, it might not be the car they needed to worry about the most.

"We're not here looking for trouble," Tuck said.

"We're looking for Sadie Murphy," Friar put in. "She's not in any bother. We just want to talk to her about her boy, Kevin. Do any of you know Kevin?"

"You doughnuts need to do one."

Friar eyed the youth who'd just spoken. His hair was long and unkempt. Friar recognised his colours as belonging to one of the local gangs. He noticed that they were all wearing those same colours. He tried to recall the intricacies of that particular gang. Nothing came to mind. Although he was completely au-fait with the local gang culture – in his line of work, he had to be – those particular colours, and what they ought to have told him, evaded him for the moment.

"Do one?" he asked, quirking a brow.

"Get the fuck out of here. No one's gonna talk to you about no Sadie Murphy, and no Kevin."

"That's not very civic-minded of you."

The youth looked at him as if he'd just sprouted horns, and said, "Do you know where you are, doughnut?"

"I sure do."

"Then, you got a death wish?"

Tuck placed a hand on her gun, covertly releasing the safety, but not removing it from its holster.

Friar made no move towards his own gun. He kept direct eye contact with the boy and remained perfectly still. "Tell us where to find Sadie Murphy, and we'll leave."

"A'int gonna happen, but you should think about leaving, anyway."

A few of the youths shuffled from one foot to the other. A few put their hands on what Fitch imagined were concealed weapons inside their pockets.

"You think you can run us off?" Friar said, his own contempt now thick. "You bunch of punk kids think you can do that without a few of you dying in the attempt?" He drew his gun so quickly that even Tuck gave an involuntary gasp.

The youth backed off a step. Within a few seconds, several guns were drawn, and the confrontation had now become deadly serious.

Tuck intervened. She raised her hands, and said, "Kevin Murphy is missing... snatched off the street a few nights ago by two men. We just want to find him... hopefully still alive. His mother might be able to help us. That's the only reason we're looking for her."

Friar kept his gun trained on the mouthy one. He'd pegged him as the leader. "Tell your guys to lower their weapons. You don't want the heat. You don't want to see this whole place crawling with cops."

It was a true Mexican stand-off.

"Kevin Murphy means shit to us."

That meant he wasn't a member of their gang, but that didn't mean they were ignorant to who he was, or what had happened to him, and there was no reason to think that they didn't know his mother. Friar was sure that there wasn't anyone in the projects who they didn't know.

"Is she hereabouts?" Tuck asked. "Sadie Murphy?"

"That ho' made herself scarce." That from another member of the gang. "She a'int around here... not no more."

Friar nodded vaguely, and Tuck relaxed a little. The tension was still high, but it seemed to have eased a fraction.

"Anyone know who might've took the boy?"

"A'int our business, lady." There was a sneer in the word *lady*. It was definitely meant as an insult.

There was no point in either of them asking if anyone cared. It was obvious that no one did.

"Another three kids went missing last night. Any whispers about that on the streets?" She wasn't expecting a response to her question, but felt the need to ask. She was surprised, therefore, when the youth that Friar had singled out as the leader spoke.

He said, "If it gets you two doughnuts out of my face then, I'll tell you somethin'."

"We'll be gone as soon as you do," Friar returned, lowering his weapon, but not holstering it.

The leader made a gesture with his head, and every gun was lowered. He then chose his words carefully. He flicked his eyes from left to right, seriously contemplating whether he ought to follow-through. Finally, he squared his shoulders, and said, "It's not perv's. It's not kiddie fiddlers."

"Who, then?"

He narrowed his eyes and shrugged. "I got no names for you."

"Okay... no names, but give me something."

"Got nothing more to give."

"Can you at least tell us where we might find the mother?"

He glanced at Tuck. His eyes took her in from head to toe. "You sure are a pretty one for a filth. I could have you earning more in a night than you make in a month. How about a change of career?"

"How about you take yourself off to school, get an education?" she bit back, without missing a beat.

"I'm getting me an education, lady. No school can teach me what I need to know." He grinned, showing strong white teeth and a flashy diamond implant. "When you need a lesson or two, you come on back here and see me." He grabbed his crotch and made an obscene gesture. "Got me the teacher right here."

Friar threw out an arm and pushed him. Tuck grabbed him and yanked him back just as half a dozen guns were once again raised and then levelled at his head.

"We're leaving," she said, dragging Friar back towards the car.

The gang let them go. Tuck noticed that not a single gun was lowered until they were in the car and driving off.

"Little punk shithead."

"He had to do that," Tuck said. "He gave us something, and lost some face with the others."

"He gave us nothing."

"Not quite nothing."

"What? What did he give us, except something we could've worked out for ourselves? Neither of us were following the paedophile line."

"It's always good to have an opinion that reinforces our theory."

"*His* opinion... that gangsta?"

"We also had confirmation that Sadie Murphy is gone from the Projects."

"That could've been a lie."

"Well, what did you want to do, Friar... search seventeen hundred apartments?"

"No, because we knew which one she lived in. We were going to speak to her neighbours."

"We *did* speak to her neighbours. Who do you imagine those boys were?" She drew the car over to the side of the road and brought it to a standstill. Twisting around in her seat, she said, "We've got virtually no time, Friar, *and* we're on our own. Henderson, and that lot, aren't interested in Kevin Murphy, or what happened to him. You heard what Mitchel implied... what he said. He's not convinced that the homicides are anything to do with the Murphy kid, but we know different."

Friar dragged in a breath. "Do we? Let's face it, Tuck, we actually know very little."

"What about Potter."

"What about him?"

"He knows what happened to Natalie Bridgman. He knows what happened to his wife. Natalie wanted to talk to us about Kevin, and Potter knows what will happen if he talks to us about her. We might not be joining the dots up – not yet – but those dots *will* form the outline of a picture, so let's at least find out where the fucking dots are."

He grinned.

"What the fuck are you grinning at?"

"Have you listened to yourself? You're saying things like *joining the dots up*. The Tuck I know doesn't even understand what that means. Do you actually see little dots in your mind when you say that shit?"

She actually did, but denied it with a shake of her head.

"You see Sadie Murphy as being one of your little dots?"

She nodded. "Of course."

"Okay, so where do we look for her?"

Tuck thought a moment. "Nowhere yet. I think we need to wait until after dark."

"You think we'll find her plying her trade on the streets?"

"Where else? I don't think she'll be set up in a place like Natalie's, do you?"

"No."

"If we could find out who her pimp is..."

"If she has one."

"Oh, she'll have one."

"How many hookers do you know?"

Friar's eyebrows shot to his hairline. "Personally?"

Tuck rolled her eyes. "I'm not asking how many of them you pay to screw."

"None, actually." He didn't seem offended – rather, he was amused. "I don't pay for sex. No need."

"I wasn't suggesting..."

He smiled. "Yes, you were."

"Do you know any hookers, or not?"

"A couple have crossed my path."

"Let's start with them."

"And, do what?"

"Pay them a visit."

He shook his head. "At this time of day, they'll be in bed."

"Not for long," she said, taking the car back into the traffic.

# 14

"Mom!" Thirteen-year-old Jocelyn Bates shook her mother's shoulder roughly. She'd been shaking it for longer than five minutes, but rousing her was turning out to be impossible. The scorched foil, the bent teaspoon, and the syringe with the glistening needle laid out on the bedside cabinet clearly spoke as to why.

She gave up and walked back through to the living room where the two detectives stood, not daring to foul their clothes by sitting on either of the chairs or the sofa.

Jocelyn was small for her age with cropped yellow hair, knowing eyes, and an elfin face smudged with the previous night's cosmetics. She was dressed in nothing but a pair of panties and a torn T shirt. Her feet were bare and quite filthy. It was obvious that she wasn't ashamed of her home. She wasn't to know that it's rather sour stench and cluttered floors made it nothing more than a midden. She had two friends – Francine and Patty - and their homes smelled and looked exactly as hers did. What was normal to a child could never be considered odd or out of the ordinary. If she wondered why the detectives refused to take the proffered seats, she made nothing of it. If they preferred to stand, it was perfectly all right with her.

"I can't wake her," she said, bending down and lifting a pack of cigarettes from amongst a pile of take-away food cartons on the small coffee table. She lit up, dragging in the acrid smoke like a pro, and eyed Friar and Tuck through the haze.

"What you want her for, anyway? What's she been up to?"

"Shall I go in and have a go at waking her?" Tuck asked Friar.

"Won't do no good," the girl put in. "She's well under the needle."

"What did she take?" Friar asked.

"Brown."

"Brown?" Tuck enquired.

"Heroin," Friar returned.

"How old are you?" Tuck asked the girl.

"What's it to you?"

"You don't seem old enough to smoke."

Jocelyn looked at her sideways. No one had ever made such a comment to her before. No one gave a shit about how old she was, except when it came to pleasing the Johns. *They* liked to know *exactly* how old she was before they stuck their dicks in her. Sometimes, they preferred it when she said she was only eleven or twelve.

"I'll be fourteen in two months," she said, defiantly. "That's plenty old enough to smoke."

Friar passed along a look that told Tuck to drop it. They weren't there to lecture on the ills of nicotine. He'd be surprised if tobacco was the only thing that the girl smoked. He furtively checked her arms for tell-tale track-marks and was relieved to see nothing but grime and the faint marks of fingerprint bruising. She was obviously handled roughly, and he didn't need to guess what that meant.

A deep sadness overtook him. No one should have to live like that. It was a damned disgrace, but there was little he could do to affect the evils in society. All he could do was mop up the mess.

"You haven't said what you want my mom for. Police don't usually come knocking on our door."

"She isn't in any trouble," Friar said, breathing through his mouth to avoid the appalling stench of unwashed bodies, dirty clothes, and rancid food. "We just wanted to ask her if she knew where we might find someone, that's all."

"Well, sorry – you're out of luck. She won't rouse for hours yet."

"Perhaps you know her?" Tuck put in. "Sadie Murphy."

"Why? What's *she* done?"

"Do you know her?" That was Friar.

"Maybe." The girl narrowed her eyes, already calculating what the information might be worth.

"Twenty dollars," Friar said, as if having read her mind.

"For what?"

"Her whereabouts."

Jocelyn's face fell. She didn't know where she was. The twenty dollars evaporated before her eyes.

"Fifteen, if you point us in the right direction."

She brightened. She could do that.

"Well?"

She looked at Tuck for a few moments before nodding. "I know her. She's paired up with my mom a few times. Some men like a sandwich."

"A sandwich?" Tuck looked perplexed.

"One on top, one beneath, him in the middle." She turned to Friar. "Is she for real?"

He smiled. "Sheltered upbringing."

She nodded, as if getting it. She held out a grubby hand. "Fifteen dollars, and I'll put you on her scent."

He took the notes from his wallet. "If you send me on a wild goose chase, I'll come back and bust your ass."

"You can do what you like with my ass, detective, but it would cost you fifty bucks more." She licked her lips provocatively. She looked grotesque with her little girl face and her little girl eyes and the slutty, adult pose. "Sure you don't want to spend fifty now? Your friend can watch... learn a trick or two."

Friar suppressed a shudder. "I'll pass, but thanks all the same."

Tuck closed her eyes against the picture the girl's words conjured up in her mind. She might be nearly fourteen, but she didn't look much older than twelve. She felt sick to her stomach and wanted out of there, but her conscience wouldn't allow her to turn and flee.

"Does your mother know that you go around propositioning men?"

Jocelyn's look was shrewd and knowing. "Of course not. If she did, she'd get into trouble with Child and Family services."

Tuck didn't believe a word of it. "I don't believe you," she said.

"Believe what you want." She turned to Friar. "Do you want the information, or do you want to stand around pretending you give a shit about me?"

"Just tell me where I need to look."

Tuck threw him a look of disgust. She couldn't believe he was prepared to ignore what was going on with the child, because – despite her worldly ways, and smart mouth, she *was* a child.

Friar returned her hostile look with a cold stare. He knew what she was thinking, and she was way out of line. He would be straight onto social services as soon as they left the apartment. He knew it wouldn't do any good. There were far too many children being exploited by abusive or feckless parents, but he always reported a vulnerable child to the proper authorities. They'd pay Jocelyn's mother a visit, maybe take the child away, but he knew that – at the first opportunity - she'd run straight back to the squalor she called home. She was doomed to live out her mother's life. He had no doubt about that.

"I heard that she'd taken herself off to Hunts Point in the Bronx. I can't be sure if that's true, but it's all I've got."

"Where did you hear that?"

"Around and about."

"Did you hear about her son?"

"Kevin?" She shrugged. "Sure."

"Do you know anything about that?"

"Him being taken off in a van?" She waggled her head from side to side. "Just that."

"What do you think happened to him?"

"Probably a couple of pervs. Kevin is a skinny kid, but he has that look about him... you know that look, detective? The one that they all go for?"

"I'm not sure that I do."

"Innocent," she said. "He had an innocent look about him, and he looked awfully young. He's the same age as me, but even I look older than he does."

"We're not sure that it was pervs who took him," Tuck said.

"Well, they don't often go around in pairs... not the ones into boys, anyway, so you might be right about that."

"How well did you know him?" Tuck asked.

"Well enough to know he wasn't into any shit. He wouldn't take it up the ass willingly, and he wouldn't have gone into that van without a fight."

"He didn't sell himself, then?"

"Who, Kevin?" She laughed. It was almost an adult laugh and extremely stomach clenching. "I think he'd kill himself before he sucked anyone off, or let them fiddle with him."

"You don't seem worried about him."

"What's the point of worrying? Worrying don't help none."

That from a child. It was heart breaking. Even Tuck was moved by the whole shitty mess of her life.

They heard movement coming from behind the bedroom door. Jocelyn hastily stuffed the money into her panties. "Don't tell my mom," she said, a keening note in her voice. "About the money."

"We won't," Friar said, just as the door opened and something resembling a woman stood, tottering on her bare feet.

"Wha' the fu'?"

"It's the filth, mom," Jocelyn said, reaching out to steady her mother and leading her to the battered and soiled sofa before easing her down and sitting beside her. "They're looking for Sadie Murphy."

"Fag," she said, on a cough.

Jocelyn took a cigarette from the pack, lit it, and put it between her mother's lips.

She took a drag and then almost coughed her guts up.

Friar waited until she's stopped hacking, then said, "We heard she'd gone to work Hunts Point. You heard that?"

"Could be. Who the..." she pulled on the cigarette, this time holding the smoke in her lungs for a count of five before exhaling. "Who the fuck knows?"

"You got a phone number for her?"

"That bitch don't have no phone." She let out a throaty cackle. "You can get high for a week on the price of a phone." She gagged and hawked a clot of mucous onto the floor.

Tuck felt faint. She definitely had to get out of there.

"She got a pimp?" Friar asked, ignoring the swell of bile at the back of his throat.

"You think I'll tell you that? Fuck off."

*Who would have sex with that?* Tuck wondered. *What desperate fuck would stick his dick in her, and pay for the privelage?*

"When was the last time you saw her?"

"Dunno."

"Days? Weeks?"

"Yeah."

"Which one – days, or weeks?" Friar, despite his revulsion, hunkered down at the side of the sofa, at the woman's side. "Help us out here. You must know that her son's missing?"

"Kevin? He missing?"

"You know he is, mom. I told you about the men and the van."

"Oh, yeah. I remember." She sucked on the cigarette. The fingers holding it were brown to the knuckles. "He's long gone, poor little fucker."

"Your daughter should be in school," Tuck said.

Friar winced. It was completely the wrong thing to say. They'd now be lucky to get another word out of either of them.

Tuck's hand itched to form into a fist. She wanted to batter the filthy cow's face in. She switched her gaze to the girl. Tuck knew that she'd probably be dead before she was out of her twenties. Girls like her were mere fodder, and their lifespan wasn't much longer than a dogs.

"School's out," the girl said, blatantly lying. "Holiday, or something."

"Yeah," the mother said. 'A holiday."

"Dou *you* think Sadie went to the Bronx?" Friar asked the woman.

She shrugged. "It's possible, I s'pose."

"Running away from her pimp, perhaps?"

"Could be. He's a sadistic son of a bitch." Another hacking cough sent her doubling up and spitting.

Friar stood up, lest his shoes were splattered.

"You got a name?"

She wiped her mouth on the back of her hand. "Not one I'm prepared to give away."

"How much for it?"

"Fifty."

"Try again."

"Twenty."

"I'll give you ten." He removed the bill from his wallet.

She snatched it, quick as you like.

"The name," Friar prompted.

"D'Roy."

"Is that it?"

"All as I know."

"Where does he hang?"

"Park Slope."

They didn't linger. The urge to leave was so strong that they almost fought their way through the front door.

Out in the fresh air, they both took a moment to savour their escape from the stench indoors. Unfortunately, the odour had latched itself to their hair and their clothes – at least, it seemed that way.

"How do you know her?" Tuck asked.

"She didn't remember me, but I questioned her a couple of times last year on the murders of three hookers. I knew her beat, and I knew where she lived. Because they hung around on the same street corners, I thought she'd be our best bet for information on Sadie's whereabouts."

Tuck recovered her composure pretty quickly. Friar took a little longer. He gulped in a couple of mouthfuls of air and tried to clear his lungs of the last of the foul miasma.

"Are we going to the Bronx or to Park Slope?" Tuck asked, brushing herself off with her hands. She imagined that there were fleas, and God knew what other creatures, crawling all over her.

"That depends if you believe either of them."

Tuck considered, then nodded. "I believed the girl. I didn't get the sense that she was lying to us. Why would she?"

"For fifteen bucks, she'd tell us anything. So, you believed her over the mother?"

"Both could've been telling us the truth."

"And, both could've been lying through their rotten teeth."

They made their way back to the car. It began to rain and they were both glad of it. Unconsciously, rather than lengthening their stride, and getting to the car as quickly as possible, they dawdled. They appreciated the sharp, fresh sting of the water spitting down on them.

"She didn't want her mother to know about the money," Tuck said, opening the driver's side door and climbing in.

Friar threw himself into the passenger seat. "She probably takes all her earnings."

"What are we going to do about her?"

"The girl?" He shrugged. "What I always do... report the situation. It won't do any good. It never does."

"Then, why bother?"

"Because I live in hope that, one day, one child will be saved."

"I always knew that went on. I'm not naïve, but..."

"Seeing it, smelling it..?"

She nodded and started the engine. "I don't think I'm ever going to get rid of the smell from my nostrils, or the taste of it from the back of my throat."

"You will," he said. "You'll have to."

"Do you think..?" She chewed on her bottom lip. "Do you think that was the life that Kevin Murphy escaped from? Was that why living on the streets was preferable to being at home with his mother?"

"That, and the fact that he was used as a punch-bag by his mother's Johns."

The car pulled off. The wipers dragged across the windscreen. The rain was now pelting down, and visibility was poor.

"Popular opinion seems to be in favour of the abductors not being your run of the mill perverts."

"We guessed as much, Tuck. No, it's something organized."

"Still could be a paedophile ring snatching kids for their own particular meat market."

"I'm not ruling that out," Friar said.

"Sex *is* involved somewhere. Why else would Natalie Bridgman know something?"

"We should've asked if either of them knew her. If they *had* known one another, wouldn't that have been a turn up for the books?"

# FRIAR AND TUCK CASE NUMBER ONE: THE MISSING

"Well, I'm not going back. That's one question that'll remain unanswered."

Friar agreed. Nothing would get him back in that room.

"Head for Park Slope. We may as well try and find this D'Roy creep."

Tuck nodded and swept the car around in a wide arc.

# Natalie and Potter (the previous week)

# 15

NATALIE STOOD, COFFEE in hand, and stared out of her window at the houses across the street. Clouds, the colour of gunmetal, blocked out the morning sun, and the day was already as grey as her mood.

These days, her mood was always grey. She'd forgotten what it was to be happy.

*Had she ever been happy?* She'd certainly never been normal.

She often wondered what went on behind the closed doors of normal people. She'd never got anywhere close to whatever it was that made people ordinary. Well, maybe one time, but she'd well and truly fucked that up. The memory was suddenly sharp in her mind, and she closed her eyes against it.

No point in remembering. No point on dwelling on past mistakes. Her current, and ongoing, mistakes were quite enough to worry her, without dredging up old ones. There was only so much guilt a person could carry.

Her hand trembled and she nearly spilled her coffee. She wished he would hurry the fuck up. She hated waiting. It gave her too much opportunity to dwell.

The coffee was bitter. It was instant crap and, taken without cream, it was barely drinkable. But, it was warm, and she needed something warm in her belly. She couldn't face breakfast – she never could when *he* was expected to pay her a visit – and her stomach protested its emptiness with a growling rumble.

She noticed a woman on bended knees, scrubbing her doorstep, immediately opposite where she stood gazing out of the window. Who in their right mind did that these days, she wondered? Who gave a shit about a clean fucking doorstep? She shook her head in dismay. There was too much filth in the world to worry about muck on a step.

She stepped closer to the window and cast her eyes the length of the street. Her window gave her an excellent view of the road. She would see his car as it turned the corner.

He was late. He was always late. He actually made a point of never being on time. It was a clear statement that told her that *he* called the shots, that *he* dictated the rules.

*As if she didn't already know that, the prick.*

For a moment, she debated sneaking out and avoiding the meeting altogether. She could go to the shelter. Kevin might be there. She really would like to see Kevin, spend some time with him before... before...

*Shit.*

He probably only had a few days left, and that made the meeting imperative. How else was she to find out the details? How else was she to find out how much longer the boy actually had? Once she knew, she could work out what she was going to do.

Just what *was* she going to do? She didn't have that many options.

*Who was she trying to kid?* She didn't have *any* options.

But, this time, she couldn't simply nod and agree with the plan. This was *Kevin* they were talking about.

She really liked Kevin. It was always a mistake to become fond of the marks – the victims. It never ended well. But, you liked who you liked. It wasn't possible for her to make herself *not* like someone just because liking him could get her killed. There had been dozens of them – the marks – and Kevin was the only one she'd considered risking her life for. Funny how a thirteen-year old boy – a stranger up until a few weeks ago – elicited more emotion in her than her own baby had.

*Oh, God.*

She closed her eyes against the pain of the memory. She had done a terrible thing. She would burn in hell for what she'd done. She couldn't take it back, or reverse the clock. She probably wasn't the only one who wished they knew how to turn that trick - to be able to go back and right the wrongs, make different decisions, use hindsight to shape a new future – but, just like everyone else, she was already damned.

She refused to be double-damned. She couldn't change the past, but she could alter the future. She could save the kid.

If only she wasn't so afraid. The flames of hell's fire were already licking at her feet. Was she really brave enough to hasten her fall into those flames?

Opening her eyes, she blinked and panned the street. He would arrive in one of his fancy cars. She'd lost count of the number of different vehicles he'd arrived in over the months. Once, she'd been impressed. She'd loved riding up front, with him at her side, looking out at the envious eyes of other drivers and those pounding the sidewalks. Now, she would quite happily take a hammer to him and his fucking cars.

She shivered. She'd turned the heating up full blast, but she was still cold. Turning from the window, she grabbed the shawl draped over one of the plush sofas and threw it around her shoulders. It was cashmere, bought with blood money.

Everything she owned had been bought with the money she'd earned through procuring the children. The first payment had been for her own child, twelve months previously, and she'd used the cash to pay for the lease on the apartment. The sacrifice of her child had ensured the beginning of a life of luxury. She'd been greedy for it, didn't care what it cost her.

She cared now – when it was much too fucking late.

Sometimes, in the small hours of the morning, she thought she could hear her baby's cry. Every mother knows the sound of her own child. There's no mistaking it. A mother could distinguish that cry from a thousand others. Even she could – the woman who had no right to call herself a mother.

The sound of the cry was in her head. It wasn't, real, but it didn't prevent her from climbing out of bed, night after night, and searching every corner of the apartment in an effort to find and rescue her.

Up front, she'd known the fate of her baby. She'd been given full disclosure. She hadn't insisted on knowing, but *he* took pleasure in giving her all the sordid details. Looking back, she realized that he got off on the telling of it. In a way, he'd been mightily disappointed in her lack of emotion. He'd wanted tears, guilt, anguish. All he'd got was a dead-pan expression and a shrug of the shoulders.

Handing her little girl over – knowing everything that was about to befall her – had turned her into a monster, and made what came next easier to handle. After all, what did other people's children matter, when her own hadn't?

Her name had been Ruth. She hadn't wanted her. Being pregnant had been a nightmare and she'd felt absolutely nothing for the tiny bundle placed in her arms after a traumatic birth. It was only now – when it was much too late – that she felt something akin to love for that lost child.

Potter frequently told her that her feelings were nothing more than self-indulgent musings. He tried to force her to live in the present, and to look forward to a rich and rosy future. He was worried about her. She could tell that he was beginning to doubt her loyalty to the organization, and hiding her true intentions was becoming increasingly difficult. When it came right down to it, she knew that he would choose the organization over her. His loyalty to the man who was already on his way to see her was sacrosanct. His feelings for her didn't compare. And, he was afraid. He had every right to be. It was no secret what the organization did to those who betrayed it.

She had no feelings for Potter, and he found that hard to accept. He bought her, just like every other man in her life did, and – like those other men who she took to her bed – he was a means to an end.

There was no longer any need to sell her body, but – in a warped sense – by doing so, she felt she was meting out a just punishment. She took the men into her mouth and into every orifice, and allowed them every liberty. She gave the money her customers paid her to several deserving causes. She was gaining quite a reputation as a generous patron to those less fortunate than herself. All everyone ever saw was the whore with the big heart. They didn't see the rancid bitch beneath the flawless skin and immaculate figure.

She didn't donate any of the blood money. She didn't want anyone to be – however obscurely – tainted by it. She kept that all to herself and spent it on frivolous things – things she didn't really give a shit about. Things like the cashmere shawl and the silk dresses and the furnishings for her luxurious apartment. Things that, when she looked at them, she was reminded of what she'd had to do to earn them.

There had been girls as well as boys. Their ages ranged from newborn to sixteen years, but the majority of the victims had been in their early teens. All of them had one thing in common – they were innocents.

They wanted Kevin Murphy. He was a clean boy, in that he didn't do drugs and didn't take it up the ass. It was important that he was clean, and it had been one of her jobs to ensure that he stayed that way. She knew his mother – a depraved whore who cared for no one but herself. It was a marvel that the boy had managed to remain pure.

The fact that he hadn't been raped by one of the dirty shits his mother screwed was a miracle, or blind luck – one of the two. Now, Natalie wished that he had been buggered. It would've saved him.

Kevin Murphy was intelligent and kind-hearted. He stole to survive, and was an accomplished pick-pocket. He never hurt anyone, and always chose his marks with an eye to the affordability of their loss. He never took from those barely living above the bread-line.

When he caught the eye of the organization, it was the beginning of the end for him.

There were eyes everywhere. Those eyes could spot the perfect specimen from amongst a crowd of the thickest dross. He, or she, could be surrounded by dozens of other children, and they would still see that child's flawlessness, their absolute perfection. It was her job to isolate them, befriend them, set them up. It was her job to lead them into a cleverly laid trap.

She couldn't recall the last night she'd slept without the torment of nightmares. Even when her conscience hadn't pricked her, her unconscious mind threw up those awful dreams. When regret had finally set in, she thought those dreams would stop, but they didn't, and she woke each morning exhausted and weighed down with guilt.

No one else in the organization seemed troubled by what they did – not even Potter, who had three children of his own to worry about. He thought that his kids were safe. He often spoke about them as if they had bright futures ahead of them. She marvelled at his ability to see a future for his children and none for those he was instrumental in hurting. Of course, she knew better. She knew that no one's child was safe, not even his. She'd wanted to warn him to be careful, to take his wife and his kids and get the hell out of it, but she didn't trust him enough to express her anxieties. One wrong word from him in the right ear, and she'd be made to disappear without a trace. She wasn't ready for that. She wasn't ready to die. She was headed for the fires of hell, but wanted to delay that journey a little while longer.

Potter's complete absence of feeling, of shame, of guilt, repulsed her. She wasn't surprised by it – after all, she'd once been exactly the same. For the first few months after her baby was taken... no, she wouldn't use that word... her baby wasn't *taken*... she wouldn't excuse her culpability by lying to herself... not now. For the first few months after she'd *sold* her baby, she'd felt nothing but relief. With the baby gone, and with money in the bank, she was finally off the streets. She lived in a beautiful apartment. She'd been given a job that meant she no longer had to degrade herself. Life was suddenly good, and all it had cost her was a baby she didn't want, and then the lives of a dozen or so children who meant nothing to her.

It was only when she met Kevin that she began to look inwards, to examine the foulness within. It was then – when she discovered just how much she hated herself - that she began, once more, to sell her body.

The sound of the doorbell jarred through her ruminations. She glanced back out the window and saw the car parked just outside. It was a metallic blue Rolls Royce Phantom Drophead. She knew all about that car because he'd taken great pleasure in explaining every minute detail of it. He liked foreign cars best. It was more than a little out of place on her street, but he didn't worry about drawing attention to himself. He didn't care if someone took a note of his licence plate, or linked his car to anything nefarious. It would never matter because he was untouchable. Too many important people owed him. Too many important people protected him, and too many important people – whether it be high-ranking police officers, circuit and even supreme court justices, or billionaire movie stars - depended on him far too much to allow him to be indisposed or charged with any crimes.

# FRIAR AND TUCK CASE NUMBER ONE: THE MISSING

His name was Daniel King. She was sure that wasn't his real name. Potter was the only one high up in the whole shitty organization whose identity she was sure of. All the others hid behind false papers and construed personas. They weren't brave enough to show who they truly were.

She turned from the window. The doorbell rang again. He was becoming impatient. She moved gracefully and unhurriedly across the living room floor. She had no qualms about making him wait. He could've been buzzed through – not made to wait – but he didn't like that. He preferred her to open the door to him personally - invite him in as if she was a maid welcoming an esteemed visitor. Well, fuck him. She was done scurrying like a frightened rabbit. The worm was finally for turning.

Once, she'd been terribly afraid of him. His bulk alone was enough to put the fear of God into her, but it was his eyes that had been the most terrifying. There was nothing in them. They were deep pools of dark sludge, expressionless and completely dead. She'd read novels where a person's eyes had been described as dead. She'd never fully understood what that description meant - not until she'd looked up into King's face for the first time and saw them staring back down at her.

She'd just given birth. The child had been a girl and she'd been a mewling, scrawny little thing that evoked no maternal instinct in her whatsoever. He'd arrived, as expected, and spent a moment simply looking down at her before picking up the child, explaining in great detail what was about to happen to her, and then leaving. He'd only been in the room a matter of minutes, but they were the minutes that now comprised the majority of her nightmares. Those eyes were always present in her dreams. Those eyes were what forced her awake and left her a jittering, shuddering mess.

Now, on the doorstep, his stare was familiar, but much less frightening. She tried to smile, but her lips were frozen in a slash across her face. He grunted and pushed past her into the hallway. She had no choice but to follow him back to the apartment.

As usual, he was dressed immaculately. He always wore a suit – Armani, one of a kind – and he always walked with a swagger. She thought that – of all the men who had used and abused her in the whole of her life – she hated him the most.

He never visited without good reason. In the beginning, she thought he'd wanted sex. She'd never met a man who didn't. Although he terrified her, she'd been willing enough, but, when she'd made it clear that he could have her, he'd seemed almost disgusted at the mere thought of it.

He'd called her a filthy bitch... said he would rather die than put his dick anywhere near her. Instead of being relieved, she'd been mortally offended. If she'd had it in her, she'd now laugh at her stupidity. Imagine being offended because that sick fuck didn't want her. All she now felt was an intense feeling of having been reprieved.

She made him coffee, black, no sugar. He sat at the kitchen table and sipped it without uttering a word. As usual, she was expected to stand quietly and wait until he saw fit to speak.

He came to the point quickly. Two sips of coffee and he was already talking.

"Tell me about the boy," he said.

She really wished he hadn't asked about Kevin, that – by some miracle – he no longer wanted him. But, he *had* asked, and she wasn't foolish enough to answer with any lies. He had spies everywhere and already knew the answer to any question he might ask.

"He's fit and well. He keeps himself to himself and, as far as I'm aware, no one has touched him."

He looked over the rim of his cup. "As far as you are aware?"

"Well, there's always Marcus to consider. I don't trust him – not completely. God knows what he gets up to with those kids. You know what a sick fuck he is."

"Marcus wouldn't dare screw me over."

"No, I guess not."

She shuffled from one foot to the other, wishing she could sit down and hold herself better in check. It wouldn't take much for him to see right through her – see the concern beneath the surface. She tried to keep her hands still, not wring them or have them tremble.

"So, no one's been at him?"

"Not if Marcus has kept his cock behind his zipper."

"I'm sure that he has."

"Then, there's no problem. The boy is as pure as the driven snow."

"If I didn't know any better, I would think you were being facetious, Natalie."

She shook her head. "Just being truthful, Mister King."

He pondered her reply, measured it for truth, then nodded.

"I know you realize just how important it is, don't you, Natalie?"

She did – much to her disgust. She nodded.

"They can never be sullied."

"I know." She looked him straight in the face. "He's not." *More's the pity.*

A gleam in his eye. A small tilt to his mouth. King could read her like a book.

"You like him, huh?"

Fear spiralled up her spine. She shook her head.

"You can't fool me, Nat. You forget how well I know you."

"What's to like about the little punk?" Amazingly, her voice was steady. "Perhaps you don't know me as well as you think?"

His eyes narrowed. "Don't bet on it." He drained the last of his coffee. "Do you have the hospital report to hand?"

She turned and reached into a drawer beneath the granite worktop. The report was from a friendly doctor at the Maimonides Children's hospital. All the chosen children were taken there to undergo a variety of tests. They all believed it was simply another of her acts of kindness. They had no idea of the real purpose of all the needles, blood tests and scans. She'd taken Kevin there a couple of days before, and was disappointed that there was nothing in the report to prevent the next step from being taken.

King glanced perfunctorily through the documents. She knew that he didn't fully understand the contents of the report. It would be up to someone with a few more brain cells to determine if, what was stated, meant there would be a green light.

"You'll get a call later," he said, folding and tucking the documents into the inside pocket of his jacket. "If everything is in order, it'll be set up for Friday night."

It was soon – too soon. She felt her heart lurch to her throat.

His face stretched into a sneer. "You definitely like this kid, don't you?"

*Shit! Had she given herself away?*

She smoothed out her features. "He's a scrawny street kid with a junkie whore for a mother." She shook her head and shrugged. "He's a commodity – nothing more."

"That's more like it. That's the cold-hearted bitch we've come to love."

He stood up from the table, reached out and grabbed her arm. His hold was vice-like and unrelentingly painful, but she didn't attempt to pull away. That would earn her a slap.

"Don't ever think that it's all right to like them, Natalie. Liking them will get you your throat cut."

"You know me, Mister King," she said, with a bravado she didn't feel. "I don't give a shit about anyone." *Not even myself.*

He stared at her for long moments, sizing her up. Then, he smiled. It was a toothy smile, and didn't go anywhere near those black, soulless eyes.

"Glad to hear it," he said. "It wouldn't do to get sentimental."

# FRIAR AND TUCK CASE NUMBER ONE: THE MISSING

He left directly thereafter. As soon as he went through the door, the whole apartment seemed to breathe easier.

Natalie lit a cigarette with violently shaking hands. Two days was all the boy had.

Unless she could come up with a way to save him, the poor little fucker was doomed.

# 16

Potter wished that she would show a little more enthusiasm. Screwing her was like riding a docile pony. Even when he got between her legs with his mouth, she never showed the least sign of enjoyment or passion. Every other woman he'd fucked with his tongue had gone into raptures, but, not her – not Natalie fucking Bridgman.

*Fuck, these days, he barely got her wet.*

He'd try again later. There was no way he was leaving before he got her off. It was a pride thing. He never left any woman unsatisfied. If they didn't cum, he felt like a failure.

He rolled off and reached for his cigarettes. "I'd be just as well fucking my wife," he said. "I can't believe I pay good money for this."

Natalie ignored him, and pulled herself around and onto her side. She'd heard it all before. Unless she was climbing all over him, panting and moaning and telling him what a stud he was, he was never happy. She knew what he wanted from her, but sometimes she couldn't be arsed giving it to him.

She was a whore. She did it for the money. She offered him a hole to stick it in, so what else did he expect for his measly one hundred bucks?

The trouble was, the silly bastard thought that he was special, that he was her boyfriend, and - because of his misconstrued notion that he actually meant something to her - he would probably refuse to pay her. He usually made a big song and dance about handing over the bucks. It wasn't that he was mean. He could be pretty generous when the notion took him. No, he simply didn't like being treated like any other customer. It always took the threat of no more sex to make him cough up.

Potter insisted on a relationship. The truth of the matter was, they *did* have a relationship outside of the sex – a relationship forged on the destruction of children. They both worked for King, and they both knew too much about each other's sins to be really comfortable with the vulnerability that a real friendship would bring about. At least, that's how she saw it.

Potter wanted more, expected more, and often demanded more. He thought that it wouldn't interfere with business. She thought differently. Anyway, she didn't actually like him all that much.

She was conscious of him lying next to her, angrily puffing away at his cigarette. He definitely wasn't a happy bunny. She would give him a blow-job. That would put the smile back on his face.

She needed him smiling. She needed him to be in the right mood to listen to what she had to say.

Since King's visit earlier that day, she'd been preoccupied with thinking that she had to do something to extricate herself from her terrible existence. She wanted a fresh start. She didn't want to do this shit anymore.

Walking away wouldn't be easy. King would see her dead first and - God help her - Potter was her only hope. He wasn't much of a hope – after all, he was King's dog – but he felt something for her, and she believed she could build on that.

"I'm sorry she said," her back still to him. "You don't have to pay me."

Her apology meant shit to him. "I wasn't going to fucking pay you. I didn't even get to shoot my load. You're one big disappointment, Natalie."

"I know. You deserve better."

"Too right, I fucking do."

"I apologize for being a bitch. I'll make it up to you."

The cigarette stopped halfway to Potter's lips. He wondered what her game was. They were the softest words she'd ever spoken to him, and he was immediately suspicious. Regardless, his cock twitched.

She turned over onto her back, licked her luscious lips, and said, "Come here, big boy."

*Big boy*? His eyes widened a fraction. He liked the sound of that. His cock took on a renewed vigour.

If she wanted, she could have it, and – if he didn't bring her to orgasm this time – he'd be a monkey's uncle.

She smiled, spread her legs, and held out her arms, inviting him in. She was a dab-hand at faking it. He would be none the wiser.

The invitation was too good to pass up. He stubbed out his cigarette and climbed aboard.

Afterwards – when she'd drained him dry, and they were lying entwined beneath a sweat-soaked sheet - she said, "I want you to take me out to dinner on Friday night."

"Dinner?" There was a note of confusion in his voice. "Since when do we ever go out on a date?"

She bit her lip. She had to make him work for it, make him want it. The last thing she needed was for him to be suspicious. He wasn't a stupid man. It wouldn't take much for him to smell a rat.

"There's always a first time for everything, but... if you're not bothered..."

"I didn't say that."

"You could, at least, look pleased about it."

"I *am* pleased," he returned, confusion still shining in his eyes.

She gave a dramatic sigh, disengaged from his arms, and rolled onto her back. "Just forget I mentioned it. It's obvious you're not keen on the idea."

"It's not that," he said. "I'm just wondering what the catch is."

"No catch. I just wanted us to feel like a normal couple."

His expression was suddenly slack-mouthed. He wasn't sure that he'd heard right.

"A normal couple? Are you shitting me?"

"I'm being serious. For fuck's sake, Potter, can't you take a hint? I'm fed up with the way things are between us. I want more."

"But, why dinner? You don't eat enough to fill the belly of a sparrow. It would be a waste of money."

"You're worried about a hundred lousy bucks? That's all dinner would cost you. Jesus, Potter... you're such a dick."

She threw herself from the bed and marched, rather than padded, into the adjacent bathroom. She knew she was being overly dramatic, but she knew men, and she knew exactly how to press their buttons. Potter was no exception – he had to believe that he'd pissed her off. It was the only way to ensure he'd crawl on his belly over hot coals to appease her.

He watched her go and cursed himself for his stupidity. It was the first time she'd ever fucked him with abandon, the first time she'd shown any sign of thawing towards him, and he'd blown it. Dinner with her would've been absolutely wonderful.

He hadn't known her long – just four or five months - and he'd been fucking her for only two of those months. Theirs had been a professional relationship, and - despite his attempts to shift it to a more personal one – in many ways, it was still no more than that.

After that first shag, he'd been gutted when she'd asked for money. Although he knew that she sold herself on the side, he'd thought that he was different to all the others. He thought that she actually fancied him, really wanted him - just as much as he fancied and wanted her. One day, he'd hoped that she'd thrust the money back into his fist and tell him there was no longer any need to pay her. He'd lived for that day, and – at long last – it had arrived. Now, not only had he had a free fuck, but she wanted to go out with him. It was almost too good to be true. If he still wasn't so horny, he might've thought about it a little more, been wary, but he *was* horny, and he *did* want to show her off on his arm in public.

He heard the shower running. He couldn't get the image of her soaping her breasts, and standing beneath the spray, out of his mind. She was so fucking beautiful. She could have any man she wanted, and she wanted him.

Friday night was the next scheduled abduction. Remembering that put a damper on his mood because he suddenly wondered if Natalie's motive for suggesting that they go out was more to do with that, than craving his company. He knew that she liked the boy - had begun to regret her part in what was about to happen to him – and she, most likely, simply wanted to do something to take her mind off the inevitable.

Well, he'd take it any way he could. He wasn't proud. If a dinner date with him was a mere means to an end, then he could live with that.

He contemplated joining her in the shower. They'd never fucked anywhere but in her bed, and he grew excited at the thought of doing it all lathered up and slippery.

Before he could shift himself, she emerged from the bathroom with a sour look on her face. It didn't mar her beauty. She was the most exquisite woman he'd ever met and, no matter her mood, she was the only woman he craved.

"Okay," he said, propping himself onto one elbow and smiling across at her. "It's a date. Where would you like to go?"

She appeared to think about it, but she already knew exactly where she wanted to dine. There was a Greek restaurant immediately opposite where she would set Kevin up to meet with his abductors. It would be the first time she'd ever been close to the scene of the actual grab. She wasn't sure why she wanted to be there. She had no plans to interfere – at least, she wasn't conscious of having any – and thought she merely wanted the opportunity to see the boy one more time. Then, she would draw a line under her life, and – with Potter's help – escape.

Potter had no clue. He wasn't privy to her plans, or any of the details set up between her and King. He knew about Kevin. She'd spoken about him often enough, and King would've confided some of what was planned, but he would have no idea that they would be within spitting distance of the actual operation.

She sauntered over to the side of the bed and grabbed her robe. She felt his eyes on her the whole time and a flash of irritation pricked her. He was ruled by his cock, and that was a disappointment to her. It was just as well that she had plans to leave. He wanted too much from her. A doe-eyed puppy dog as a lover was not what she desired.

Truth be told, she didn't want anyone to have genuine feelings for her – even if they were sexually motivated. She didn't need the complication that pairing up with a lover would bring.

They had coffee before he left. He enjoyed those post-coital moments almost as much as the sex act itself. Seated at the kitchen table, with her pouring the coffee then sitting opposite, had always brought a sense of normalcy to their relationship. For a few precious minutes, he could fantasize that he was in his own kitchen, with a woman who loved and cherished him, and – when he left the money – he could force himself to believe that it was merely a gift between lovers. Well, there was no money changing hands now. Now, the fantasy was almost real.

"Will I see you tonight?" he asked, a hopeful note inflecting his voice.

She shook her head. "I have things I need to d0."

"For King?"

"Who else?"

He didn't bring up the Murphy boy. He didn't want to ruin the moment.

"What about tomorrow?"

"What about it?" She sipped her coffee and avoided looking at him. She feared the distaste would be all too evident in her eyes.

"Can I pop round?"

She shrugged. "Suit yourself, but not between seven and nine. I have a couple of clients."

The thought of fucking her, after two other dicks had been inside her, turned the coffee in his stomach sour. If he didn't know any better, he would've thought she'd shared that information with him in order to disgust him - put him off.

"I'll come round before six, then."

She pulled herself straighter in her chair and placed her coffee mug on the table. He would be gone in a minute. She could hardly contain her impatience. She wished that she liked him – even a little – but she didn't. Some days, she actually hated him.

She closed her eyes and sighed. "Just so long as you're gone by six."

His lips thinned with annoyance. *Why did she always have to ruin things?* They'd made their very first date, were having a leisurely coffee together, and she had to ram it down his throat that she was nothing more than a filthy hooker.

Sometimes, he actually hated her.

She saw that she'd gone too far. She'd inadvertently stopped playing the game. That had been short-sighted and foolish. She reached over the top of the table and took his hand.

"You know what I am," she said. "I'm sorry that what I do upsets you, but I'm not going to hide it, or apologize for it."

He stroked a thumb over the back of her hand, relishing the contact and the gesture. "I'm not asking you to do either," he said, gently, almost reverently. "It's just that I think you know how I feel about you, and you seem to get pleasure out of hurting me."

She wished that she did. Pleasure of any description would be a welcome distraction from her almost constant self-loathing and misery.

Forcing a smile, she reached over with her other hand and they sat for a time, holding on and staring at one another. She wold never know how she managed to keep that smile on her face and the softness in her eyes when, inside, she was a bubbling cauldron of repressed disgust.

"I'll have to get off in a minute," he said, regretfully. "But, before I go, I just want to say that today was... well, it was really something, and I'm looking forward to our date." He looked almost coy. "Thank you, Natalie."

*Jesus!* She felt the sudden need to prick a little of the air out of his bubble.

"Do you love your wife?" she asked, chewing on her lip as if concerned about the answer.

The question took him by surprise. He drew back, disengaging his hands, and dropped his eyes. A reply wasn't immediately forthcoming. Then, when he finally spoke, his voice was rough with emotion.

"I don't want to talk about my wife, Natalie. She has nothing to do with what we have."

"No?" She frowned. "I can't see how that's true. If you love her..."

"I don't love her. You don't have to worry on that score. She's the mother of my children, and I have a certain respect for her."

"Does she know about me?"

His head reared back. "Fuck, no."

"I'm your dirty little secret?"

"One of many... as you well know."

"If she found out – about me, about the other things – would she leave you?"

He didn't even have to think about that. "Absolutely... like a shot."

"And, you don't want that?"

For the briefest of moments, he allowed hope to surge through him. He wondered if her questions were her way of discovering if he'd leave his wife for her.

The hope quickly dissipated. Even if it were true – which he knew, deep down, that it wasn't – he realized that he'd never leave his wife. He liked being married, being a father. He wouldn't give that up – not even for her.

He cleared his throat and stood up. It was time to leave. For the first time, ever, he felt an urgency to get out of her apartment.

"You haven't finished your coffee," she said, a hint of amusement in her voice. "I guess talk of your wife has turned your stomach?"

"I'll see you tomorrow," he returned, ignoring her jibe. "And, we're still on for dinner Friday."

She didn't see him to the door. He knew the way well enough. When she was alone, she slumped in her chair and didn't move for a full hour.

# 17

Potter walked along the sidewalk with the gait of a jumped-up pimp. The arrogance of his swagger marked him as someone full of self-importance and arrogance, and people made wide swerves to avoid him as he passed them by.

He looked neither to the left nor the right. He wasn't interested in the other pedestrians. To him, they were nothing more than scrambling little ants, not worth his attention. His whole focus was on himself, and the meeting he was striding towards – a meeting with King, his boss.

Composing his features, he prepared himself for what he feared would be a confrontation. The face he always showed to King was very different to the one he showed to others. In fact, he was a man of many faces. He had a different face for everyone – Natalie, his wife, his kids, acquaintances, and – of course – his boss.

At a conscious level, he realized that he was a con-man. He didn't lose any sleep over it. He cut the cloth accordingly, and was pretty successful at making himself into whoever he was required to be. With King, he required to show a deferential expression. Mister King preferred his henchmen to be submissive. The bigger they were, the more they had to appear meek in his presence. To Potter, King's arrogance was quite staggering.

It was a windy afternoon, and his perfectly coiffed hair flapped across his forehead and – as he approached the apartment building – he couldn't resist glancing at his reflection in one of the shop windows as he walked past, and running a hand to flatten down his breeze-blown hair.

The meeting with King was an important one. He had to make a good impression. Promotion was on the cards, and he didn't want to fuck it up by arriving looking like something the cat had dragged in. There would be confrontation enough – there always was because that was simply the way of it with King – without giving him an excuse to berate him. King might prefer his lackeys big and burly, but he also liked them neat and tidy.

He'd worked for King, on and off, for two years. Introduced by a friend, he'd made the right impression and had soon been taken into the great man's confidence. The nature of the organization's business hadn't fazed him. Everyone had to make a buck, and who cared if it was a dishonest one? Some crooks – the ones with an edge of conscience – would be disgusted by what he got up to, but, to Potter, that didn't matter one jot. He was aligned to a business that was extremely lucrative, and that was all that mattered.

Up ahead was the Williamsburgh Savings Bank Tower. It was no longer the tallest building in Downtown Brooklyn, and was no longer a bank, but was still an imposing structure that caught the eye and - since its conversion into a number of luxurious condominium apartments - was *the* place to live.

King owned several apartments in the building. It was Potter's hope that, one day, he would be able to afford to move his family into one. It was probably a dream he would never realize, but it didn't stop him imagining the day when it could become a real possibility.

His wife would have to change her ways, though. There was no way she could carry on collecting all that shit if they lived in a swanky apartment. He would have to finally get around to talking to her about it. The place was so crammed with the things she couldn't bear to part with that it was getting so he could hardly squeeze from one room to the other.

Getting one of those apartments would mean sticking with King through thick and thin. King was where the money was. But, his future happiness wasn't simply about money, or a luxurious place to stay His happiness also depended on keeping Natalie sweet. She was an absolute necessity to him. She was also important to King. She was a Godsend – or had been before she'd began to develop a liking for the kids. He hadn't told King of his concerns about her. He believed that she would eventually come to her senses and revert back to type. Anyway, he liked her too much to drop her right in it with the boss.

He took the elevator to the top floor, adjusting his tie and brushing a hand over his jacket before stepping out. McGraw – one of King's personal bodyguards – held up a hand as he approached the door to the apartment.

"Is he expecting you?" he asked, his voice low and gruff.

Potter nodded.

"He's in the gym."

Potter was disappointed. He thought that, this time, he would be received within the walls of King's home. It would've been a great honour – one that very few were afforded – and it would've meant that the promotion he'd hoped for was likely to be forthcoming.

There was nothing else for it but to make his way back down in the elevator.

King wasn't alone, but none of the other people in the gym were fellow residents. When King was there, no one ventured in until he'd left. The other three people were best described as *heavies*, or *muscle*. Just like McGraw standing guard outside the apartment, they were bodyguards. King referred to them as his security detail. He thought it made him sound presidential.

Potter hovered in the doorway, awaiting the signal that gave him permission to enter.

The signal came after a full five minutes of watching King effortlessly bench-press more than double his body weight. It was a damn impressive feat of body strength and Potter believed he'd been shown it to make a point – the point being, fuck me over and I'm strong enough to kill you with my bare hands.

Not that he would ever dream of fucking him over. No one in their right mind would.

One of the heavies handed his boss a towel, and King stood up and swiped it across his sweat-glistened chest. Potter stood to the side and waited.

"I've got a special job for you," King eventually said. He took the bottle of high-end water handed to him and glugged it down his parched throat. "I don't trust anyone else to do it, so don't let me down."

Potter was inordinately pleased. His hoped-for promotion now looked firmly in the bag.

"Sure, boss. You know you can rely on me."

"You're not gonna like it," he said, throwing the towel on the bench and approaching the free weights on the floor by the door. "It's not your usual shit."

"I'm up for anything."

"Well, we'll see." He chose two humungous dumbbells and commenced a series of bicep curls. "It involves Natalie."

"Natalie?" His throat barely worked. "You want me to do a job with her?"

"Hardly," he sneered. "I want you to do a job *on* her."

He wasn't sure he knew what that meant. His expression spoke his confusion.

"I want her dead, Potter. She's on the verge of becoming a liability."

Potter had carried out many terrible crimes during his lifetime, but never murder. He'd hurt people, but never anyone he genuinely cared about. What was being asked of him filled him with horror.

"Leave it until after we take the Murphy boy. She still has one or two loose ends to tie up on that case."

# FRIAR AND TUCK CASE NUMBER ONE: THE MISSING

Potter shifted anxiously from one foot to the other. "Are you sure, boss? I mean... she's been good for the organization... earned you a great deal of money. No one else could've got you Kevin Murphy."

King ceased with the curls and stared at Potter through narrowed, feral eyes. "I told you that you wouldn't like it. You've got a soft spot for the bitch, and that's another reason I want her gone."

Potter rolled his shoulders, straightened his spine. He couldn't let that opinion stand. "What do you mean, boss? She's a dirty whore. I don't have anything like a soft spot for her."

King grunted. "I'll forgive that lie," he said. "Under the circumstances, I can find it in my heart to excuse it, but don't repeat it or you'll find yourself dressed in a concrete overcoat overhanging some deep water."

Potter gulped and nodded. The threat wasn't an idle one.

"I want it bloody, and I want the bitch to see it coming."

"Sure, boss." *No fucking way... no fucking way...* "Anything you say, boss."

He walked back out of the building in a daze, not knowing how he was going to extricate himself from the terrible thing expected of him. He knew he couldn't do it. Under no circumstances could he ever kill her. He could hurt her. If King had ordered him to rough her up, cut her, beat her to within an inch of his life, then that he could do, But, kill her? No way.

All the way back along the road to his car, he fretted. He was so preoccupied with his thoughts that he didn't once look at his reflection in any of the windows.

He went home. The familiar noise of an unruly threesome of kids, calmed him. He was brought back down to earth, and he savoured the relative ruckus of what was warm and familiar.

Making his way along the overstuffed and, frankly, dangerous hall from the front door was a feat in itself. There was even more stuff piled up the walls to the ceiling than there was the day before. His wife had a serious problem. In fact, she was a nut job. Why she had to keep hold of every newspaper, every magazine and – worse – every bit of rubbish, was beyond his understanding. If she carried on, they'd soon be buried in her shit.

"You're home early," she called from the kitchen.

For cover purposes, he worked a job downtown. That was where his wife expected him to be at two o'clock in the afternoon. Unbeknownst to her, he spent no more than a few hours a week toiling behind the sales desk at the Mercedes showroom. He got away with it because it was owned by King.

He pecked her absently on the cheek. She smelled of cheap perfume. He'd bought her some of the expensive stuff, but she much preferred knock-off scent from the flea market. That pissed him off no end. The least she could do was to smell nice for him.

"What are the kids doing out of school?"

"The teachers are having a training day."

"That shouldn't be allowed. Why can't they train in their own fucking time?"

"Don't curse, dear. Not in front of the children."

That was another thing that irked him about his wife – her holier-than-thou attitude to cursing in front of the children. Once – before she'd settled down to motherhood – her mouth had been filthy. Sometimes, when she'd really annoyed him, he reminded her about that and then sat back with a sense of satisfaction whilst she tried to justify herself.

Ignoring her, he pushed through a pile of junk in the middle of the floor to the refrigerator and removed a bottle of beer.

"It's a bit early for that," she said at his shoulder. "It's not like you to drink this early in the day." She frowned. "You haven't been fired from your job, have you? That's not why you're home?"

# FRIAR AND TUCK CASE NUMBER ONE: THE MISSING

"Oh, fuck off, Mona. Of course I haven't been fucking fired. Quit with the nagging. It's been a tough day."

"No tougher than having three squalling kids to cope with."

*She had no fucking clue.*

He threw himself around and flopped down into a chair at the kitchen table.

"Have you eaten?"

He shook his head. "I'm not hungry." He took a long pull at the beer.

"I don't mind making you a sandwich."

"For fuck's sake, Mona... didn't you hear me? I'm not hungry."

He didn't regret marrying Mona. He'd known her forever, and she was a safe partner to share that part of his life with. He didn't believe that he'd ever loved her. Before the kids came along, he'd enjoyed her body, but she was now a little too thick around the waist and a little too droopy in the tits department to spark his attention. He would never leave her – not even for the likes of Natalie – but that was more to do with the security of having a proper home – okay, not an ordinary home - to return to, than any feelings he had for her, or his children.

He was selfish. He had no qualms about admitting that to himself, but he didn't feel guilty about it. Mona had a good life. She wanted for nothing. His kids went to a good school – when the teachers deigned to turn up – and, if it wasn't for the new thing... the thing about killing Natalie, he wouldn't be snapping her head off.

He was now a worried man. He was about to move into the big league. Murder changed everything. It would catapult him into a whole different ball-park, and there would be no going back. If his wife would be horrified at the job he actually had, he shuddered to imagine what she'd make of him being a killer.

The alternative to committing the murder was unthinkable. King would neither understand nor forgive. He might actually find himself wearing that concrete overcoat.

Mona sensed his disquiet and placed a hand on his arm. He shrugged her off, stood up, and marched back out of the kitchen, the beer spilling from the bottle and soaking the carpet beneath his feet. He was relieved when she didn't follow. He wasn't in the mood for her company. She would just have to say the wrong thing and he'd be forced to give her a slap to shut her up. He wasn't in the mood for dishing out any violence to a woman... not at that moment in time.

He wandered into the small sitting room at the front of the house. As usual, it was a tip, but it was the one room in the house that he insisted was kept clear of her crap. There were toys, books, and a million pieces of Lego littering the floor, but that he could accept. His kids were untidy little bastards. He hated that they had no respect for the things he bought for them, and was furious that their mother allowed them to act as if they'd cost nothing to buy. It was his hard-earned money that lay like trash on the floor. But, what else could he expect when they had a mother that thought more of rubbish than she did of anything of value? He kicked a doll the length of the room and considered stomping and crushing everything else.

The kids were doing his head in. They were so fucking noisy. He tried ignoring them, then raised his voice in an almighty roar, warning them to shut the fuck up.

Blessed silence reigned for all of ten minutes. When the uproar began again, he walked out.

# 18

He knew where he would find her. He knew what loose ends she had to tie up with the Murphy boy, and he found himself in his car and heading to the place where she was sure to be.

Half-way there, he wished he'd mainlined some coffee before leaving the house. The beer he'd consumed had soured in his empty stomach and his head felt woozy. Just in case a cop felt inclined to stop him, he drove just under the legal limit and kept a close eye in the rear-view mirror. If he was pulled over and booked for a DUI, King would kill him.

Just for a moment, he thought that wouldn't be such a bad idea. Being dead would be the perfect excuse not to have to end the life of someone he cared so very much about. But – if he *was* dead - someone else would then have to do it, and he couldn't help but worry that the other killer – no doubt one of King's ruthless heavies – would inflict undue pain and suffering before executing her. The bastard might even rape her. At least, if he did it, it would be done humanely. King said that he wanted her death to be bloody – well, the blood could come after the deed. King would be none the wiser.

*Shit!* He really didn't want to do it. When it came right down to it, he didn't believe that he could.

He parked up and waited. The homeless shelter was well known to him. In the early days, one of his duties was to survey the place, keeping his eyes peeled for likely victims. The shelter had been known to him long before Natalie arrived on the scene, and, by the time it became her prescribed hunting ground, he'd already been promoted onto other duties.

It sat hunched between a gym and a rather run-down church. It was a squat, grey building with boarded-up windows to the front and a door that looked as if it had been kicked in on more than one occasion.

The neighbourhood was a poor one and culturally and racially diverse. If he sat too long, he'd attract unwelcome attention, but he was willing to risk it, so as to catch a glimpse of her.

He left the engine idling. He was between two parked cars and in a direct line of sight to the front of the building. He was pretty sure that, although he could clearly see every last coming and going, he wouldn't be easily spotted. Nevertheless, he slid down in the seat – just in case.

The minutes ticked passed and there was no sign of her. He didn't see her car in the small parking lot belonging to the shelter, but he knew that she often parked on the small road to the rear. He had no doubt that she was inside. He just had to be patient and wait. She would come out at some point and, as there was only one way in and out of the building, he knew that he wouldn't miss her.

The road he was parked up on was busier than he'd expected – much busier than he recalled it ever being. There was a steady stream of traffic blasting past and a sporadic flow of pedestrians on the sidewalks on either side. More than one set of curious eyes periodically peered in at him and he soon grew uncomfortable.

He couldn't afford to wait much longer. He was already sticking out like a sore thumb.

Why was he there, anyway, he wondered? Did he really plan on stalking her? Was he that much of a twat?

He shook his head and pulled himself upright in the seat. He would leave, go about his business, and then wait to see her as planned that evening. He'd made a fool of himself long enough.

Then, he caught sight of her, and his chest suddenly exploded in his chest. She was so fucking gorgeous. His eyes hurt just looking at her.

She was smiling down at the boy, talking to him animatedly. No wonder the fucking kid adored her. She radiated such warmth and human kindness that even the wariest of kids – and street kids were the wariest of them all - would've been fooled into believing she actually cared about them. The problem was – where the Murphy kid was concerned – Potter sensed that she *did* actually give a shit, and that was the ultimate sin. That was what was going to get her killed.

She'd been sloppy. He guessed that the bastard who ran the shelter had ratted her out to King. It was too late to warn her to be careful. The damage had already been done. She'd let her guard down, allowed her maternal instinct to kick in – which was ironic, considering what she'd done with her own child – and she'd let it be known that she felt something that she shouldn't. The price she was about to pay for her stupidity was tremendous.

A truck thundered past, rocking the car in its wake and blocking his view. When she was once more in his eyeline, he saw that she was looking directly across at him. Now that she'd spotted him, his head told him to leave, but his heart kept him from making a move. Inside, he was screaming for her to high-tail it and run. On the outside, despite the tension crackling in the air inside the car, he appeared resigned.

The boy was also looking across at him. He saw him say something to Natalie, her nod down at him, and then usher him back inside the building.

He wondered if she would approach him. He knew that she must be curious as to why he'd turned up at the shelter. He hadn't been there in months. Her first thought would be that something was wrong.

She would never know just how right that thought would turn out to be.

Against his better judgement, he turned off the engine and climbed out. He couldn't immediately think of a justifiable reason for being there, but – by the time he walked right up to her – he'd come up with a plausible excuse.

"I wasn't expecting to see you here," he said, lying through his teeth. "What a nice surprise."

She gave him a wary look. It wasn't easy to fool her.

"I guess you're wondering what brings me to this neck of the woods?" He hoped he wasn't flushing from the neck up. He wasn't good at subterfuge – not with her.

"You've been drinking," she said. "You stink of beer."

"I might've had a couple... so, what?"

"You shouldn't drink and drive."

"I'm hardly drunk, Natalie."

He wondered why she wasn't grilling him as to his reason for being there. The shelter was now her territory and he had no right muscling in. That, and not the fact that he'd had a beer or two, should've been the focus of her attention.

He finally heard the words he expected from her. "What *are* you doing here?"

He shrugged. "King's worried about Marcus."

"He never mentioned being worried about him to me. Why would he tell you?"

He shrugged a second time. The trouble with lying – and particularly lying to someone as astute as Natalie – was that you had to have the ability to think on your feet. He suddenly wished he'd simply been honest, and told her that he'd just wanted to see her... that he'd missed her, and couldn't wait.

# FRIAR AND TUCK CASE NUMBER ONE: THE MISSING

"Who knows with King?" he said. "He's fully aware of the fact that you can't stand the slimy bastard, and that he'd get a more honest opinion from me."

"He knows that I'm always honest, Potter."

*Was she*? She certainly hadn't been honest about her feelings for the boy.

"What's he worried about, anyway? Marcus is Marcus."

"He thinks he might be fiddling with the wrong kids... the ones we want you to earmark."

It was her turn to shrug. "He's kept his filthy hands off Kevin, and that's all that matters."

"He needs to leave them all alone." The disgust was thick on his tongue. "I'll never understand why King tolerates him."

"Because he's good at what he does. He keeps the tap turned on, and the flow of victims running. King doesn't care who he sticks his dick in."

"Unless they're one of the special ones."

"I haven't seen him mess with any of those," she returned.

"How would you know? There could be dozens of kids who are perfect for us, and he doesn't let on... simply pointing out the odd one or two."

"And, that's why I make a point of dropping in as often as I do. You need to tell King that I've got Marcus in hand. You need to tell him that I don't appreciate him sending you to check up on me."

"It's Marcus I'm checking up on, Natalie – not you. Stop being so fucking paranoid."

*Too late. She should've been paranoid a long time ago, and then she wouldn't be days away from annihilation.*

"Look, I'll tell him that he's got nothing to worry about. Just ignore that I've been here."

He forced his expression into a mask of nonchalance, and changed the subject. "You all set with the kid? Was that him... talking with you before?"

She nodded and dropped her eyes. "It's all set for Friday."

"I know. I guess that's why you chose that night to go out with me."

Her head snapped up. "Why do you assume that?"

"Because I'm not stupid."

But, he *was* stupid. He'd opened the door to warning her that he knew about how she felt, and that was an extremely dangerous thing to have done.

"Look, just forget I said anything."

She looked pointedly at him. She had a strong feeling that he was terribly worried about something. He never had a drink and then got behind the wheel of his car. He would never have turned up at the shelter without forewarning her first, and he was acting too squirrely not to be on tenterhooks over something.

"Spit it out, Potter," she said. "What's going on?"

"Nothing." He shook his head in denial and wished with all his soul that he'd stayed in the fucking car. He dragged in a sigh. "I've just had a fight with Mona... hence the two beers... and all this with King and Marcus – and King keeping you out of the loop about his concerns – it's all just one big piss-take. Truth be told, Natalie – I'm utterly fed up." He ran a hand over his face. "Sometimes, I feel like jacking it all in – marriage, kids, King and his fucking mood swings, and all."

She suddenly noticed the deep worry lines on his forehead, and the dark circles that weren't under his eyes the last time she saw him. Could he really look so much like shit in such a short time?

Something else was bugging him, and she was afraid it had something to do with Friday night.

"I'm going out to dinner with you for no other reason than I want to," she said. "Like you, I'm fed up. Friday night will mark the end of my latest job, and I want to enjoy a nice meal, a few drinks, and perhaps indulge in a fuck afterwards. The boy will be gone, and I deserve a little respite before the next one is put in my path."

He smiled at that. At least he would get one last fuck before he took her life.

"What you smiling at?"

"You. You make me smile, Natalie." In reality, he felt like crying.

"You going in, then?"

"In?"

"To see Marcus?"

"Nah." He shook his head. "If you say he's behaving himself, then that's good enough for me."

"What will you say to King?"

"You leave King to me."

He heard the door open and turned. His eyes widened a fraction when he saw the boy peek out.

It was his cue to leave.

# 19

"You look smart," she said to the boy, observing his freshly washed hair and almost new clothes. "You managed to get a shower, I see?"

He nodded and grinned. "Just a quick one. Marcus cleared them all out and gave me the whole shower block to myself. He's a good guy, that Marcus. He found me these clothes. My others stank to the heavens."

Marcus certainly wasn't a *good guy*, but she could see why Kevin thought that he was. He managed the shelter, and was instrumental in pointing out potential marks. He had a special way with the kids – an ability to take himself right down to their level – and they seemed to trust him implicitly. They all believed that he protected them – well all those who didn't suffer directly at his hands. For most, he was the only adult in their lives who seemed to care. But, she knew him for what he truly was – a predator and an integral cog in the organization's massive wheel. Almost every child she procured had passed through his hands. In some ways, they were the lucky ones, because – despite what Potter thought - he wouldn't dare touch them. The others – the ones already soiled – he could do what he liked with.

*The lucky ones...* she winced every time she thought of them. The others may have years of abuse and neglect ahead of them, but the kids that were protected had mere weeks left.

"I've got some news on that job I told you about," she said. "You're going to meet a Mister Yelsen. When you do, remember to pretend that you're sixteen. I've told him that you're small for your age, but that you're as smart as a whip."

Kevin bounced excitedly on the balls of his feet. "When am I gonna get to meet him?"

"Friday night." She forced a smile. "I'll meet you as arranged, and we'll head off to his restaurant."

"I can't wait. It's been getting pretty tough for me lately."

"I know, honey. I'm sorry I wasn't able to take you home with me. There's nothing I would've liked more than to make you part of my family, but..."

"I know, Natalie. There's no need to feel bad about it. I know your husband wouldn't let you. You've done enough for me... it's cool, honestly."

She hitched in a breath. He was such a good kid. *If only...*

"What are you up to today?"

His grin widened. "Marcus says I can hang around the shelter, have some food. He doesn't need to kick me out 'til later. Then, I might take a walk... see what I can pick up."

"No thieving, Kevin," she warned. "We can't run the risk of you being nabbed."

"I'm too quick to get caught."

If only that weren't true. An arrest might just save him, but – then again – he would risk getting hurt. Not every victim of his nimble fingers would call the police. Some of them would kick the shit out of him.

"It's not worth the risk," she said. "I can give you money. There's no need to steal."

His pale face flushed scarlet. The thought of taking money from her always embarrassed him.

He hunched against the cold breeze. Marcus hadn't given him a jacket, or a sweater, and the shirt was thin. He wanted to go back inside where it was warm, but he also didn't want to cut short his visit with Natalie. He lived for the times when she sought him out, chatted to him as if he was an adult, and made him feel good about himself. She didn't mind that his mother was a junkie hooker, or that he lived mostly on the streets and stole to survive. In her eyes, he wasn't a nothing, a nobody. He was special.

"Let's go inside," she said. "I want a word with Marcus."

Relieved to be out of the cold, Kevin headed straight for the electric fire in the corner of the large room. He hunkered down, rubbed friction into his cold arms, and soaked up the heat. Natalie followed him, skirting the rows of beds, and then walked through to the small office at the back. She knew that Kevin wouldn't follow her. He accepted that her chats with Marcus were private. He respected that.

She always felt a shiver of revulsion course through her body whenever she set eyes on the manager of the shelter. He was good enough to look at – being young, tall and extraordinarily handsome – but there was something completely rotten in his eyes. He might not look the part of the typical paedophile – or what people imagined such a creature looked like – but he definitely was one, through and through. In fact, he was one of the worst, with no preference to the gender of his victims. Boy, or girl, it made no odds to him.

Natalie hated him with a vengeance. What she was doing was bad enough, but – in her eyes – it wasn't anywhere close to the evil he perpetrated.

"Natalie!" he exclaimed, standing up and moving out from behind his desk. "I wasn't expecting to see you today. Is everything all right?"

There were all kinds of shit in the office – bundles of clothes, piles of documents, boxes of canned food – and no spare chair for her to sit on. She didn't mind. She never planned on spending more than a few minutes in the room. Five minutes was about her limit.

He was very animated. His whole face worked when he spoke. It was easy to see why the kids were drawn to him. There was nothing obvious in his expression, his speech, or his mannerisms to suggest that he was anything other than an amiable friend to them. They didn't see what she saw in the farthest recesses of his eyes. Of course, they eventually *did* see, but, by then, it was always too late.

"Everything is perfectly all right," she said. "I've just come to let you know that, as of Friday night, Kevin will be gone."

"So soon?" He seemed disappointed. "I'll miss that little man."

"And, I'm sure he'll miss you."

The sarcasm went right over his head. Like every other narcissist, Marcus was unaware that he drove people to hate him. He never dreamt that anyone would see him as less than the perfect specimen, and he always read respect in their tone of voice.

"I guess, pretty soon, you'll want me to look out for the next one?"

The question gave her pause for thought. King hadn't let her know the requirements for the next child. That was unusual. It was rather late in the day not to have been briefed. Usually, by the time one child was lined up to be taken, King was already imparting the requirements for the next one. Without fail, she was told whether it was to be a boy or a girl, roughly what age, and any other specifics considered relevant. Marcus, having mentioned it, forced her to wonder why she hadn't been given so much as a heads up. King should've told her something when he visited her. The fact that he hadn't now caused her some alarm.

There was a well-practiced procedure. King would tell her what they wanted, she would relay that information to Marcus and – once he'd identified a likely candidate – she did what she was really good at. She met with the child, befriended them, showed them that someone cared enough about them to take an interest in their wellbeing and their future. At first, they were always suspicious. Sometimes, it would take weeks, or even months, to gain sufficient trust to get them to agree to the battery of medical tests dictated by King. In the end, she always won out. Starved of love and attention, most were easy prey.

"I've not met with King, yet," she lied. There was no way she was going to let on that she was behind the curve ball. "I'm sure he'll be in touch with the details soon enough." She glanced down at the untidy desk. "How can you work in this mess? Just looking at it makes me want to set a match to it. If I were your boss, I'd fire you on the spot."

His face dropped into a scowl. For the first time, he felt the antipathy towards him coming off her in waves. It wasn't like her to act the bitch, and he wasn't sure how to react to it. He decided on a biting retort.

"Good job I don't answer to you, then, isn't it, Natalie?"

She brought up her eyes and stared at him. She said nothing in return. She wasn't in the mood for a fight with the likes of him. Potter was still on her mind. She couldn't shake the feeling that he was hiding something from her.

She knew him far better than he knew her. You couldn't fuck a man as often as she'd fucked him without getting to understand what made him tick. The same couldn't be said for any man getting to know the woman lying beneath him. No matter how regular they screwed their woman, there was no man on earth who had the ability to see past the length of their dicks. Yes, Potter had screwed her on a regular basis, but he'd never seen behind her eyes or known what was in her heart. Unlike women, men weren't as intuitive, or attuned to anything that didn't immediately affect them. So, knowing him as well as she did, she realized that he was a very worried an frightened man.

Her first thought was that, perhaps, the police were onto him… *them*, but, King would've squashed any undue interest in their activities. He had the money and the means to stop any errant cop looking to make his mark by bringing the organization down.

So, if not the police – then, who? What?

She didn't have the time to think about any of that. Marcus stood, as if waiting on something, and she really wanted to leave. She hoped he'd let her without any undue small talk getting in the way.

No such luck.

"I need to know pretty soon if it's a boy or a girl," he said, already forgiving of her earlier snarky comment about having him fired.

Resigned to at least a short exchange of words, she asked, "What's the rush?"

He smirked. God, she hated his oily, smarmy sneer.

"Well, there's a sweet little thing comes in here most evenings. She's one that I'd quite like a touch of, but I've hung back because she might be just what King is looking for – a virgin if ever there was one, and no track marks or the spaced-out look of the junkie. If it's a boy he wants..." He licked his lips. "Then, I can have the girl."

Her stomach roiled. He was one sick bastard. She decided to mark his card.

'Tough luck, Marcus. It'll probably be a girl this time around. Lately, it's been one boy after another." The sense of satisfaction she experienced on seeing his face drop, was gratifying in the extreme. "If I was you, I'd keep my filthy hands to myself... just in case."

"You enjoy doing that, don't you?"

"Doing what?" she asked in all innocence

"Spoiling things for me."

"Now, why would I want to do that?"

"Beats me, Natalie. I'm the good guy... remember? I'm the one who you can't do without, so a little sugar with your vinegar wouldn't go amiss."

"Give it a rest, will you? There are plenty more little tiddlers in the great sea of the unwashed to keep you happy. You have unfiltered access to every one of them, so the loss of one girl shouldn't make your balls ache."

"Ah, but she's a special one... little Miss Mattie Bloomer, nine years old and ripe for the plucking."

"Nine is a bit young to be on the streets. Who's looking out for her?"

"Her father. He's a bit of a wino... she doesn't know where he is half the time."

"And, the mother?"

He shrugged. "Long gone."

"How has the father managed to keep her safe?"

"Luck, I guess, but that is about to run out... one way or the other. She reminds me of Kevin. They've both got that particular *something*." He cast a knowing eye at her. "Know what I mean?"

Natalie ignored him. She knew his game. He wanted to rile her into being indiscreet. She never discussed any of the kids beyond outlining the most basic of information. She certainly never commented on what she thought of them. Until Kevin, she hadn't really thought *anything* of them. They were nothing more than mere commodities.

Now, she found herself worrying about the girl he'd mentioned. She might get him to point her out to her on some pretext or another. She might not be able to save Kevin, but perhaps she could save her?

"Don't you think Kevin has that special *something*, Natalie?"

It was obvious that he wanted some comment from her. She wasn't sure why. She worried that he sensed her close attachment to the boy and wanted to exploit her in some way. Marcus was good at that – reading between the lines and seeing beneath the surface. It was what made him so damned effective.

Rather than looking at him and making a reply, she turned for the door. She'd said all she'd come to say, and now all she wanted to do was get out of the claustrophobic office and have another word with the boy. She thought that it might be the last time she would ever see him. He expected to meet with her on Friday, but that was a ruse to lure him into the clutches of King's henchmen. Once they grabbed him, he would be gone from her life forever.

It amazed her just how much that hurt.

Marcus was speaking at her back. He said, "Next time you see him, tell King that I want paid pretty damned sharp. He's been a bit sloppy at getting me the cash. Tell him I won't put up with him dragging his heels."

Natalie actually felt her mouth drop open. She thought that he must have a death wish. No one spoke to King like that, and there was no way she was going to be shot as that stupid idiot's messenger. He could fire his own fucking bullets.

She turned to look over her shoulder, hiked a brow, and said, "Tell him yourself. I'd love to be a fly on the wall when you do."

Marcus' mouth twisted. It took away some of his good looks, and showed him for what he was. He didn't show that face very often, but – when he did – the vileness seeped from his expression.

"Oh, I forgot you were shit scared of him," he said. "Well, I'm not. He needs me far more than I need him."

*No way*, she thought. *You are ten a penny, mate.*

She found Kevin tidying away his things. He kept a few precious trinkets and a couple of books in a battered backpack with a broken zip. She had meant to buy him a new bag and she recalled promising him that she would take him to the used bookstore – Spoonbill and Sugartown on Bedford Avenue – to rummage for the adventure stories he so loved.

She suddenly wanted to make good on that promise.

She glanced at her watch. She had time to take him. The least she could do was to get him a new book to read. It would be the last story he would ever have the opportunity to get lost in.

When she mentioned it, his hazel eyes lit up with glee. Her heart broke at the thought of so little a thing filling him with such excitement. For a boy who had next to nothing, a book was everything.

She felt her eyes water, and had to blink rapidly to scatter the tears before they fell.

"Come on, then," she said. "The shop will be closing soon and, if you're good, I'll buy you a burger and fries when we're done."

He made a grab for her, clutching her arm and then throwing himself against her.

"Why are you so good to me, Natalie? I really don't deserve it."

Thank God, she didn't have to explain. He was too excited to notice her sharp intake of breath, or the fact that she avoided his question.

# 20

In the end, she bought him two books, knowing that he would be lucky if he had the time to finish even one of them. She also bought him a new bag and they then went to find the burger and fries she'd promised him.

They crossed Kent Avenue and sat on a bench near the edge of the East River whilst he ate and she watched. She loved to watch him eat. Unlike the other hungry street kids, he didn't swallow huge bites without chewing. He was slow and steady and it was always so very obvious just how much he savoured every mouthful.

She drank coffee but ate nothing. Despite having had no breakfast, or lunch, she had no appetite.

When he was finished, good boy that he was, he found a trash can to place the greasy paper, the used napkin and the packaging.

"Why don't you throw away that old bag of yours? she said. "You don't need it anymore."

"It's still a good bag," he replied. "Someone else can have it... someone who doesn't have one. Some of the kids I know have to use tatty plastic store bags to carry around their stuff."

That was true. She'd seen it often enough – not that there were that many kids with anything to carry in them.

"Do you have much to do with the other kids?"

He shrugged. "Mostly everyone keeps themselves to themselves. A lot of the kids have an adult who looks out for them. Those kids aren't supposed to get friendly with me."

Natalie knew that he was taking about a pimp. She shuddered.

"How have you managed to stay clear of those adults, Kevin?"

"Oh, they know that I'm friends with you. Because of that, they leave me alone."

"Really?" That surprised her. "How do they know that we're friends?"

"They just do."

"Did Marcus tell them?"

He looked up at her, askance. "Marcus doesn't know those people. He doesn't let them into the shelter, and hates it when they sneak in, or talk to any of us outside. I don't think he likes them."

*He wouldn't – not if they were poaching his prey – turning innocents into worthless shells that he could do nothing with.*

"I guess that they've maybe seen us together?"

She nodded. "Perhaps." It worried her that there were people out there who could link her to the boy, and possibly connect her to the other kids she had taken under her wing in the past.

She looked across the water, turning to watch a small boat as it bobbed its way to the other bank. There was probably someone normal on that little boat – someone with a life that didn't include destroying children's lives and denying them a future. The envy was like a stab to her heart and almost took her breath away. She had no relation to people on that boat, but she hated to think that she was anything like King or, God forbid, Marcus. Unfortunately, she had much more in common with them, than anyone she saw around her.

"What will I have to do for your friend?" Kevin asked, his question slicing through her morose thoughts. "Will I have to wash dishes, and stuff?"

"To begin with." She turned her eyes on him, drinking in his shining, animated face and silently cursing herself for her duplicity. "He's agreed to start you on as an apprentice. You'll learn to cook, and perhaps, one day, you'll be a famous chef."

"I like cooking. I had to do all the cooking at home. Mom never..." His bottom lip trembled. "She didn't have time to cook."

No, the slut was too busy screwing strangers and standing back as they knocked her son around.

"Do you miss her, Kevin… your mom?"

He shrugged. "Sometimes, I guess."

"Would you like me to take you to see her before you begin your new job?"

He looked up in alarm and shook his head. "She might want to keep me. She might not let me leave." He began to cry. "Please don't take me back to her."

"I won't." She put an arm around him and dragged him against her. "I'm sorry. I should never have mentioned it. I just thought…" She shook her head. "Never mind."

He snuffled against her shoulder. Many thirteen-year-old boys – especially those hardened by life on the Brooklyn streets – would rather die than shed a tear, especially in front of a woman, but not Kevin, and this wasn't the first time he'd sobbed in her arms.

She believed that she was probably the only person in his young life who'd been allowed to see beyond the stoic face he turned on the world. He was prepared to share his demons with her, cry out his despair, and seek solace in her motherly arms. It made her betrayal of him all the more poignant, and all the more bitter-tasting.

She tried to deflect her guilt by assuaging herself that she was saving him from a fate worse than death. Although Kevin believed himself to be a tough little guy, a few more weeks on the streets and he would undoubtedly be swallowed up and devoured whole. At least, this way, his suffering would be relatively short-lived.

In her quiet, introspective, moments, she really didn't believe that. She saw the pitiful excuse to justify her actions as abhorrent and it only served to increase the level of her self-loathing.

As she held him, she told herself, for about the hundredth time, that she wouldn't go through with it, or that she would go to the police. Both options were viable, but only one of them would give her and Kevin the hope of safety. If she took him and ran, there was a chance they would make it. If she went to the police, King would hunt her down and kill her, and then take Kevin anyway.

The fact that she hadn't done either – and, it was now the eleventh hour – gave her pause for thought. Despite her very real wish to save him, she wasn't quite at the point where she wanted to put herself at risk. She determined that she would decide before the deadline

She would be there, at the scene, with Potter. Potter had no clue, of course, but – if she decided to make a run for it with the boy – she was hopeful that he would help.

She pushed the thought away. It was nothing more than a fantasy – one she knew that she would never deliver on.

When he resurfaced and knuckled his eyes, she asked, "Shall we go find ourselves some ice-cream?"

It was a little chilly for ice cream, but if she knew one thing about the boy, it was that he could eat it quite happily in a blizzard.

He nodded, still caught up in his own thoughts. They moved off the bench and she took hold of his hand as they walked. To onlookers, they were mother and son. To Natalie, they were monster and victim.

The first time that Marcus had pointed him out to her, she'd barely paid him any heed. Although she'd been assured that he was fresh and untouched, his looks belied that. He had the bruised look of the victim, and there was no way that she could ever comprehend the notion that he'd survived, thus far, unscathed. She believed that Marcus was trying to get one over on her, and had all but decided to pass the boy over for someone else, when he'd approached her and asked if she minded if he sat with her a while. He'd confided in her that he was scared, that someone had tried to grab him off the streets the night before, and he wondered if she would have a word with

Marcus to see if he'd allow him to hide out at the shelter for a few days.

A few discreetly placed questions and she'd discovered that he was absolutely perfect for King. Now, weeks later, she'd come to know just how perfect he actually was.

There had been no other child as ideal as Kevin. The others had been perfect in varying degrees, but he was the whole package. Knowing why King wanted the kids – what he would use them for – meant that certain requirements were an absolute must. No individual child had to tick all of the boxes – just a particular few – but, to have one who surpassed all expectations was a once in a lifetime find.

After devouring his ice cream, she dropped him off at Bridge Park. It was his favourite haunt. With some reluctance, she watched him head away from the car. He was soon lost from her sight, disappearing from view as if dematerializing into thin air.

His disappearance off the face of the earth would be just as complete. No one would report him missing. No one would know of his fate. That's how it always was. Every previous abduction had gone without a hitch and, because they always chose the unloved and the unwanted, the police had never been involved. There were no bodies to discover and, as far as everyone knew, no crime had been committed.

There was a savage sadness about such a thing. Hundreds of children had passed through King's hands and each and every one of them had left no mark.

Kevin would leave a mark. It would stain her heart and her conscience forever.

# 21

*Jesus... it was the boy.* Potter looked down at Natalie with a look of horror on his face. The silly bitch was actually waving across at him, and the stupid little fucker was waving right back. He knew the score. Natalie always told the kids that she was meeting them. Of course, the only people to meet them were their abductors. Natalie knew not to be within a pile of the scene.

He saw the van and the two men. He dragged his eyes across the scene unfolding on the other side of the road. It was all going down right in front of their very eyes, *and she knew.* The bitch knew that, once they'd left the restaurant, they would walk right into it.

He was furious. The weight of his anger pressed heavily on his chest and squeezed all the air from his lungs. She'd blindsided him. The realization that he was on that particular spot, on that particular street, and at that particular time, had been preordained by Natalie fucking Bridgman was like a punch to the guts.

What he didn't know, was why.

He had to get them the fuck out of there, and quickly. He tried to yank her back along the sidewalk, but she was having none of it. She fought to stand her ground, and her antics were drawing curious stares from the people walking by.

With a hand firmly on her arm, he grated out, "What the fuck are you playing at?"

She tried to step out onto the road. Her foot hovered over the kerb. Her whole body was in forward motion. His grip tightened, and he hauled her back against his chest.

"Let me go," she hissed, struggling to free herself. "I can't let them take him."

A man approached, obviously concerned. Potter barked at him to *fuck off*. Others gave them a wide berth, not wishing to get involved in what was perceived as a lover's tiff gone wrong.

He clamped both arms around her waist and she kicked out, scraping a heel the length of his shin. He drew blood biting down on his bottom lip.

The two men approaching the boy momentarily glanced in their direction, but they were too preoccupied to take much notice, and Potter thanked fuck for that. If either of them were recognized, they'd be dead before the night was through.

Then, he saw that they had him. It had been a swift and subtle grab. He jerked his head from side to side, looking to see if anyone on the street had noticed.

No one had.

Natalie renewed her struggles.

"Have you gone stark, raving bonkers? You can't save him, so cut it out before I hurt you."

She wanted to scream at Kevin to run. She tried, but all that escaped her throat was an anguished croak. Then, he was in the van. The door was being pulled closed. It was almost too late.

She managed to get to her phone. It was an old-fashioned flip-phone. Potter always took the piss out of her for having such an antique as her only means of communication.

She relaxed and went floppy in Potter's arms, and then it was ringing in her ear.

*Nine-one-one, what is your emergency?*

"Jesus, Natalie." Potter grabbed the phone from her hand.

The call had been connected, so the phone number was already highlighted and recorded for prosperity. The stupid bitch had gone and done it now. He was screwed... they were both screwed.

He closed his eyes and put the phone to his ear.

*Nine-one-one, what is your emergency?*

Blinking, thinking, coming up with no way to extricate themselves from the situation, he said, "Police, please. I want to report an abduction."

Natalie was crying. He'd never witnessed her cry before, but there was no way he was going to be moved by her tears. She'd done a profoundly stupid and dangerous thing, and all he could think about was how he was going to save himself. He wouldn't be able to save her. She was already a dead woman, but – if he played his cards right – King might spare him.

The responding officers were both young and, much to Potter's relief, rather green. At first, they didn't seem unduly concerned. Neither he, nor Natalie told them much. Thankfully, she'd understood that it was much too late to save the boy, and heeded his warning to keep her trap shut. It was a bit like closing the stable door after the horse had bolted, but silence was still the best thing all around.

He played it down with the cops. He was vague with his responses to their questions and hoped they would toddle off, make a nondescript report, and then forget all about it.

Even when the other two turned up – the big guy with the designer stubble, and the blonde tart with the weird attitude – neither he, nor Natalie, gave anything away.

The questions were perfunctory. They weren't taken anywhere to be interviewed. They didn't give them the boy's name, because how were they supposed to know that? If it hadn't been for one of the young cops walking over with a backpack in his hands – a backpack with *Kevin Murphy* neatly stencilled inside – they would never have known who he was.

On catching sight of the backpack, Natalie inhaled a sharp breath. Potter squeezed her hand in warning and she released the breath slowly.

Potter thought that the backpack would be a gamechanger. It surely substantiated their claims, and proved that the boy had been grabbed off the street. He expected more questions, more interest to be shown in their eye-witness testimony, but – when it became absolutely obvious that they had nothing to add – after giving their addresses and contact details, they were sent on their way.

Out of sight, Potter heaved a sigh of relief. At his side, Natalie was rigid. What she'd done was only just beginning to sink in.

"I'm sorry," she repeated over and over again. "I'm so sorry."

He didn't trust himself to speak. He didn't trust himself to touch her, lest he batter her brains in. Instead, at the first opportunity, he called King.

When the telephone call ended, he was white with fear and trembling from head to toe. The jury was out and no decision had been reached as to the extent of his guilt in the whole debacle. King was, of course, both judge and jury. Natalie's sentence still stood, but the one thing that the night's events had changed was that he was no longer expected to carry out that sentence. He was now linked to her. Her death – bloody and gory as it was sure to be – would raise eyebrows, so King wanted him as far away from her as possible.

"When will I see you again?" she asked, before she made to get out of the car. "Tomorrow? Will you come see me tomorrow?"

He ground his teeth and clenched the steering wheel so tightly that his knuckles almost broke through the skin on the back of his hands.

"Are you having a laugh, Natalie? After what you just pulled, do you honestly think that we'll ever see one another again?"

Her throat worked. She swallowed back hard. "Is King really pissed?"

His look of incredulity made her blush to the roots of her hair. It had been a ridiculous question.

"What's he going to do?"

"Not forgive us, that's for sure."

"I'm glad, Potter, because I know that I can't do this anymore. If he cuts me loose, I won't be in the least upset."

*Cut her loose? Was she really that naïve? The only thing that King would cut was her throat.*

"Just fuck off inside, Natalie, and pray that you live to see another day. I'm going home to my wife and kids – somewhere I should've been all along."

Her expression hardened at his words. "Hark at you. Anyone would think that I had your arm twisted up your back." She shook her head – anger replacing the earlier fear and anxiety. "You make me fucking sick. You're just the same as all the rest. I can't believe that I actually thought you'd help me save Kevin."

"Save Kevin?" He almost choked on the words. "He was never going to be saved, you stupid whore. He'll be dead within days, and you'd better hope that we don't soon follow him to his grave."

That sobered her. "King wouldn't dare."

"Oh, wouldn't he? What planet do you inhabit, Natalie, because – here on Earth – King can dare anything."

He was right. Of course, he was right. "There's been no harm done. The police don't give a shit."

He blew out an exasperated breath. She really didn't have a clue.

"Just go," he said. "Get out of my sight."

Once inside her apartment, Natalie forced all thoughts about what was happening to Kevin out of her mind and tried to convince herself that everything was fine with him, and fine with her.

There was no rising tide of panic. She refused to believe that her actions had put her life in danger. She'd said nothing to the police. She hadn't compromised King or the organization in any way.

*Everything was fine.*

She contemplated the sense in attempting to contact King before she went to bed. She had a great deal of grovelling to do, and – having thought about it - she eventually concluded that it was better to do it sooner rather than later. Potter had already briefed him. He'd had the sense to get their side of the story in before King heard it from someone else – probably someone in the police.

She got as far as bringing up his name on the screen before chickening out. It could wait until morning.

She needed wine... no, something stronger. She walked through to the kitchen and took a bottle of JD from a cupboard. She swallowed half a glass without ice. It burned, but she knew that she would need a great deal more before she was anesthetized enough to be able to sleep.

She didn't sleep. She ended up sitting by the fire the whole night wondering what the fuck she was going to do.

# 22

Saturday morning greeted her with cold sunshine and the threat of rain. The apartment was cold and the air frigid. It took her a full hour, after showering and dressing, to get the place warmed up and to pluck up the courage to ring King. She couldn't put it off any longer. She had to apologize and beg forgiveness, and hope that he wasn't too angry at her for nearly fucking him over.

But, first – more coffee. She wished that she had the means to mainline the drink straight to her bloodstream. After the sleepless night she'd just endured, the dire need for a constant caffeine infusion was overwhelming.

She boiled the kettle and made do with a mug of instant. By the time she'd drank it, she was jittery and wired.

Sitting at the kitchen table, and mulling over what she would say to King, she worried that he wouldn't believe a word she had to say. That made her wonder what Potter's story had been. She hadn't overheard the telephone conversation he'd had with him. He'd made sure to be well out of earshot.

Now, it was important that they both sang from the same hymn sheet, so it made sense to ring him first to compare notes.

Potter didn't pick up. Potter *always* picked up when she called him.

It was only a little thing. It didn't necessarily mean that anything was wrong, so she wasn't going to jump to any conclusions. He was pissed at her... that's all it was. She'd try again later.

She tried to relax and let her mind play around with a variety of excuses for what she'd done. She wished she knew what Potter had told King. Had he put the blame firmly on her, or had he tried to protect her? Just how angry was King? What could she possibly say to make things right?

She was well aware of her boss's temper, and how quick he arrived at blinding fury. She was also well aware of the danger she was in. Calling the police had been stupid. Potter not hanging up, and then reporting the incident, went far beyond mere stupidity. It had bordered on utter madness.

There had never been any saving of Kevin. He'd been lost the moment he'd been targeted by Marcus and then chosen by her. She should never have allowed herself to feel something for the boy, but there was no point in regret. Regret wouldn't save her from King's wrath. Only Potter could save her.

She spent the morning pacing through every room in the apartment. She tried Potter's number a few times, and each time, the call went directly to voicemail. The messages she left became increasingly angry, but, still, he didn't call her back.

At two o'clock in the afternoon, she began to pack a suitcase. She had to get the hell out of there. Without Potter in her corner, she was in deep shit. Leaving seemed the safest thing to do.

Then, something that Marcus had said to her jumped to mind.

*The girl.*

The girl would be King's next victim.

She didn't feel ashamed of abandoning all thoughts and concerns about Kevin. He was the past. There was no saving him – not now that he was in their clutches. She'd left it too late with the boy, but could she leave, and abandon this next innocent child?

On a loud, drawn-out groan, she gave up on her hasty packing. She couldn't do it – she couldn't leave without trying to save her. It wasn't that she'd changed her mind about walking away, only that she had to delay her departure.

She felt overwhelmed with anxiety and, suddenly weak-kneed, plonked herself down onto the edge of the bed where she huffed in several breaths and tried to think.

It wouldn't be an easy thing – to save the girl. To save her, she had to convince King that she was still all-in. He had a bullshit detector that was second to none, and would find it near impossible to trust her again, so she knew she had to be clever.

By dinner-time, she still hadn't heard back from Potter. She needed him to get back into King's good books. Without his support, she wouldn't save herself, or the girl.

*Just what was his problem? He never left her hanging like that.* He must be really mad at her, so she had some serious sucking-up to do.

Left with no alternative, she tried to call King. Of course, he didn't pick up. She hadn't really expected him to. Unlike Potter, he never took her calls. He expected her to leave a message and then wait until he saw fit to call her back. So, she wasn't immediately worried.

The message she left was short and to the point. She admitted to fucking up, said she was sorry, and asked how she could make it up to him.

At midnight, with no return calls from either Potter or King, the niggling anxiety began to morph into genuine worry.

She didn't move immediately into full-blown panic mode. No, the panic uncurled in her stomach slowly. Instead of coffee, she drank vodka. In the circumstances, getting drunk seemed the sensible thing to do. At least it would mean there would be a chance she would sleep.

At two o'clock in the morning – when her body ran with sweat and her hands wouldn't stop shaking – she tried ringing Potter again. She was more than slightly sozzled. She hadn't eaten a thing since the meal at the restaurant, and the alcohol had made short work of her senses and equilibrium. It also made her paranoid. She now believed that King was going to have her killed.

Before calling Potter for the umpteenth time, she'd forced down a glass of water, and then another. The hydration did nothing to sober her, but she felt a little steadier in her mind.

With phone in hand, pressed tight against her ear, she prayed silently for him to accept her call. She promised herself that she wouldn't be waspish or sarcastic. She would be contrite and apologetic. She simply wanted to hear his voice, have him reassure her that nothing bad was about to happen to her. He would have the ability – with a few choice words – to take the rough edges off her mounting hysteria.

When he answered on the first ring, she was quite shocked. Really, she hadn't expected him to answer.

"What?" he said, groggily into the phone. "Do you know what the fucking time is?"

"Is that you?" She couldn't quite believe it. "I'm sorry... I know it's late." Her words were slurred. "I've been desperate to talk to you."

"I've been busy."

She closed her eyes, bit down on her lip. The temptation to let rip on him was almost overwhelming, but she managed to keep her shit together. "Too busy for me, Potter? That hurts."

"Bullshit, Natalie. What do you want?"

"I couldn't sleep."

"Well, I *was* sleeping. I've had a fucked-up day, and this is the last thing I need right now."

A beat, then, "Can you come round?"

"You, what?"

"Come round. I need to see you."

"You're kidding, right?"

"I miss you."

He laughed. He actually laughed. Her face flared. He was obviously *really* pissed at her.

"You must be really shitting yourself to say that to me," he said, the laughter still evident in his voice. "Just be honest, Natalie. Tell me what's really on your mind."

"He won't return my call," she said, rather frantically. "I'm scared."

"Who won't return your call?"

"King. Jesus, Potter... who else would I be talking about?" Her voice rose a notch. "He's going to kill me, isn't he?"

She didn't hear the lie in his voice, and sighed with relief when he told her not to be so fucking stupid – that, of course, he wasn't going to have her killed.

"Then, why won't he call me back? Have you spoken to him since... since that thing with the police?"

"Of course."

"So, the bastard took your call, but not mine?"

"I don't know anything about that. You know what he's like... a law unto himself."

"What did you tell him?"

"Nothing much. Nothing for you to worry about."

"But, I *am* worried. I know I was stupid. Did you tell him that I was sorry... that I didn't mean it?"

"He knows that you're sorry."

"He does?"

"Of course. He knows you inside out, Natalie. You made a mistake... got too close to the kid. You won't do that again."

"Have I caused any trouble for him?"

He laughed at that. This time, it was a quiet laugh. There was no humour in it whatsoever.

"What's funny?" she asked, peeved.

"You, Natalie… you're what's funny. How can you imagine that King would ever get in trouble with the police? He *owns* the fucking police."

There was more than a little truth in that, and she relaxed a little.

"So, will you come over?" she asked, a hint of desperation in her voice.

"What, now?" A beat. "Right this minute?"

"Yes."

"I can't do that."

"Why not?" She never thought to hear such words from him.

"Is your wife there?"

"Where else would she be? She's next to me in bed… dead to the world. Thank fuck she's a heavy sleeper, or… right now… she'd be flaying me alive."

"So, she won't notice if you sneak out, will she?"

"I can't do that… sorry."

She didn't like that one little bit. "You're punishing me, aren't you?"

"Don't be stupid."

"Why else won't you come?"

"Because, I'm tired… exhausted."

"I'm tired, too. I haven't slept a wink since… since they took Kevin."

"You need to stop thinking about him. What's done is done."

"I know that. I don't care about him anymore."

"Then, get to bed and go to sleep."

"I wish that I could. I want you here, Potter. I need you."

"And, I said… *I can't*."

He meant it. She knew that he meant it. Anger surged to displace her fear.

"Well, fuck you. If you don't come right now, then don't show your face here again. You got that?"

She heard him sigh. "Whatever," he breathed down the phone at her. "I'm well passed caring."

Every nerve in her body was jangling. Her anger swept ever upwards, completely overtaking her common sense. Later, she would blame the vodka.

"Has anyone ever told you that you're an asshole?" she screamed down the phone. "Well, you are, and I'll never forgive you for this."

"That's up to you.

"Then, go fuck yourself."

She ended the call, threw the phone down onto the bed, and let out a scream of frustrated rage.

*Now what?*

Her options were limited.

Without Potter backing her up, King would be less likely to forgive her. If he didn't forgive her, she would have no chance to save the girl, and would probably end up dead.

She was under no illusions that she was crucial to the organization's continued success. Even Marcus was more important than she was. King would find another woman to befriend the kids and get them to the hospital for the all-important tests. He didn't need her and – now that Potter had distanced himself from her – she only had her own wits to survive on.

Unfortunately, her wits were all shot to pieces. Exhaustion, fear and alcohol on an empty stomach saw to that.

She contemplated finishing packing up her suitcase. Running seemed her only salvation. King *would* kill her. She suddenly had no doubt about that.

But, there was another option. King might have influence within the police department, but she didn't believe that his reach stretched across every officer in every department. She could take a chance – find someone she could trust with her story.

She was willing to take that chance. She had to save the girl. It had become almost a quest – to save her. In doing so, she imagined that she would save her own soul.

*Tick, Tock... Tuck*!

The female detective – the weird one she met on the street when questioned about Kevin – came to mind. Her name was Tuck.

Feverishly, she made a grab for her phone and did an online search.

She was sure that finding reference to her wouldn't be difficult. How many *Tucks* could there be?

It was the early hours of Sunday morning, and there was no point in trying to contact her until a more reasonable hour. Now that she'd made up her mind to rat out King, she felt a little better.

Amazingly, she then slept.

On waking, she wasted no time in reaching out to the detective. She wasn't on duty, but she emphasized the urgency of the call, and the message was taken. Tuck rang her back, arrangements were made and Natalie prepared herself for a full confession the next morning.

# 23

After Natalie's phone call, Potter hadn't succeeded in getting back to sleep until thirty minutes before his alarm clock went off. He got up cranky and argumentative. It was Sunday – usually a day for doing nothing – but he wanted to spend some time doing something normal with the kids. He took them to the park, and then for ice-cream.

King rang him late in the afternoon with instructions to carry out a collection. The job was far beneath him, but Potter realized it was King's way of disciplining him. Potter was glad that the demeaning job seemed to be the extent of King's punishment.

Someone hadn't paid the organization their full fee. The person in question was a rich son-of-a-bitch, and there was no excuse to renege on the final payment. Potter's instructions were to extract – by fair means or foul – that final ten grand. He hoped that the man refused to pay. He needed someone to take his anger and frustration out on, and that particular asshole was as good a punchbag as any.

Yes, he really did hope that the rich asshole refused to pay.

A butler answered the door to his knock... *a fucking butler!* He showed him into a large room that was, to all intents and purposes, an impressive library. He was offered coffee, declined, and was left waiting a full twenty minutes before the asshole deigned to make an appearance. By the time he arrived, Potter's fury was boiling over.

The thing about mega-rich people was that they couldn't help looking down their aristocratic noses at the lesser mortals who had to work for a living, and they couldn't help thinking that – because someone didn't wear designer clothes or spoke as if they had a stick up their ass – they were unworthy of even a hint of good manners when being addressed.

That particular mega-rich dipstick was no exception. The first words out of his mouth, on greeting Potter, earned him a slap. A punch very nearly followed, but the man backed off and very sensibly apologized.

Potter couldn't recall the last time he was in the position of collecting a debt. Such a duty was now far beneath his status in the organization. He'd never really been employed as a heavy, and had very rarely been asked to use his fists on anyone. He'd felt a certain pride in being classed above those in King's employ who'd spent their days and nights brutalizing people. It wasn't a nice feeling to be seen as nothing more than someone to be feared for the threat they posed, however his current mood obliterated any shame he might've felt.

Brutalizing someone was exactly what he needed.

Unfortunately he left, mere minutes later, with ten grand in cash in his pocket, and without having the benefit of relieving the furious tension that caused his jaw and his teeth to ache.

He hoped King would have another collection lined up for him, and that it would prove more satisfying. He hoped the next one couldn't pay because he had a great need to punch a hole in someone.

---

MONDAY CAME AROUND, and it was supposed to be business as usual. Mona avoided him at breakfast, choosing to drink her coffee and eat her toast in bed rather than facing him over the kitchen table. She knew he was worried about something – or someone – but she had the sense not to question him about it. When he had that certain look in his eyes, she knew that he was best left to his own devices.

He couldn't stop thinking about Natalie. She only had a day or so left to live. King wouldn't leave it too long before ordering the hit – if he hadn't already done so. One of the reasons he had refused to go to her, when she'd virtually begged him to do so, was because of the very real fear that he would warn her of King's intention to have her whacked. It was too great a risk to his own life, and the lives of his family.

He had to forget about her. She was history. His loyalty was to King, and not to her.

So, why did he feel like crying, bawling his eyes out? Why did the thought of losing her hurt so damned much?

He was relieved when she hadn't tried to contact him all through that Sunday. She seemed to mean what she'd said about never wanting to see him again. So, it was with some surprise when – shortly after dropping the kids off at school - he found himself driving in the direction of her apartment.

# 24

The detective was very early. She wasn't expected for another hour. When the buzzer jarred her out of her usual morning routine, she halted what she was doing and automatically reached to press the release that opened the street door. She then rushed around - rinsing her coffee cup and clearing the newspapers off the kitchen table – before going to the door of her apartment to welcome her.

Although she hadn't experienced any second thoughts, a ball of anxiety unfurled in the pit of her stomach. It was all very well being sure that she was doing the right thing, and quite another to be comfortable with it.

For the part she'd played in procuring the children, a prison sentence was likely. She wasn't expecting any sympathy, or yet any understanding, from the detective. There was no doubt in her mind that she would receive censure and rebuke. Her story would evoke disgust and a certain disbelief, especially when she confessed to selling her baby to the very monsters she worked for.

Would she even be believed? On the whole, her story was quite fantastic. It would sound like the ravings of a deluded imbecile.

It was just as well that she had proof. That proof had been collected as insurance against King turning on her but she was quite content to now use it to back up her story. She would take the detective to the bank where the evidence was kept in a safety deposit box. She would hand it all over, and accept whatever punishment she deserved. She might remain in prison until she was an old woman, but she didn't care about that. All she cared about was saving the girl, and all the others who were doomed to follow her.

She reached the door just as a second gentle rap sounded in her ears. With trembling hands, she unlocked the deadbolt and pulled it open. The tentative smile on her face was poised to stretch wide. Her heart and her mind were open to whatever her words to the detective would catapult her into. Her mind was made up. She was ready.

It opened an inch and then the door exploded inwards. The force of it forced her to take several unsteady steps back. Then, a push on her chest from an unexpected hand caused her to stumble back on her heels and crash to the floor.

All the wind was knocked from her lungs. Confusion, but not yet fear, washed over her.

What, the fuck just happened?

Leaning back on her elbows, huffing in a ragged breath, she looked up. The face looming over her was one that she was familiar with, but it was not the face of the detective.

He stood staring down at her for a second, then turned and kicked the door closed.

She didn't immediately react. It took three or four seconds for her brain to sound the alarm and, when it did, she scrabbled back - her legs and feet pushing, her hands frantically working for purchase on the carpet beneath her - then, she threw herself around and onto her knees and tried to stand, to run, to escape.

Fear and panic all but stripped her of her equilibrium. Neither her arms, nor her legs did her bidding, and she flopped about on the floor like a puppet with its strings cut. Before she could even propel herself further than a few feet, he grabbed a handful of her hair in a meaty fist and yanked her back. Her scalp felt as if it was on fire. She fell back onto her ass.

"Please," she whimpered. "Please don't do this."

He said nothing in reply. He wasn't there to engage in conversation or negotiation. He had one job to do, and he intended on getting it done as quickly as possible, and with the least amount of fuss.

# FRIAR AND TUCK CASE NUMBER ONE: THE MISSING

He pulled on her hair and lifted her clean off her feet. Moving swiftly along the hallway, he hauled her, kicking and screaming, all the way through to the kitchen.

She didn't ask him why. There was no need. She knew exactly why he was there. An explanation wasn't necessary, but she did try begging. Before the words poured from her mouth, she already knew that they would fall on deaf ears. She knew, only too well, that he wasn't interested in reconsidering what he'd been sent there to do, but she continued to beg, nonetheless. She couldn't help herself.

When she felt herself pulled back against his chest, and felt the cold steel of the blade at her throat, she frantically considered her options. She could tell him about the insurance policy she kept locked in that safe deposit box. She could hurriedly tell him that he'd better contact King because – if he didn't – the evidence she'd collected would see them all in prison.

She thought about it for a brief few seconds, then closed her eyes and awaited the inevitable. She wouldn't give up that evidence, not even to save her own life.

Her last thought was of her baby. She wondered if she would be forgiven and be reunited with her in the afterlife.

# 25

He felt a savage tearing at his heart. His stomach clenched and unclenched painfully, and he felt sick. He knew that he shouldn't be there. It was the last place he should be. He'd dropped the children off at school and, instead of heading to work, he'd made his way to her street, to her apartment building... to her.

He left the engine running. He didn't switch it off and get out of the car. He simply sat there, like a deranged lunatic, and tried to talk himself into entering that apartment building and giving her fair warning.

Outside the car – street life carried on. It was all quite normal. People went about their business, completely oblivious to everything but their mundane little lives. They had no idea that the man sitting in the car wanted to prevent a murder. They had no idea of the pain he was in. If they had known, he doubted that they would've cared.

He wished that he didn't care. He wished that he hadn't allowed her to get under his skin. What was she, anyway? She was nothing more than a two-bit whore – certainly not worth all the angst he was feeling.

The noises of the street penetrated his thoughts – the sounds of the cars whooshing past, footsteps echoing on the sidewalk, chatter and laughter. Outside the car, it was ordinary - a world apart. He'd never lived an ordinary life. Being a husband and a father - whilst perpetuating a living hell on others, and keeping his dreadful secrets - made for an extraordinary existence. Sometimes, he longed for ordinary. At that precise moment, it was all he wanted.

He fidgeted. He ran an agitated hand through his hair. He thought of all the reasons why he ought to put the car in gear and get the hell off her street.

Still, he remained where he was. He couldn't compel himself to either get out of the car, or move off.

It would take courage to get out of the car, cross over the road, and ring the bell. If he managed to do those three simple things, he wondered if she would even let him in.

Why would she? She'd begged him to go over. He'd refused. He'd stayed in bed and went back to sleep, and then he'd spent all of the previous day trying not to think about her. He hadn't tried to contact her, and they hadn't spoken since her phone call in the early hours of Sunday morning. He hadn't cared enough, then, so why did he care enough now? Because, it sucked something awful. King's determination to kill Natalie simply stank to high heaven. The more he'd thought about it, and the more he'd succumbed to his doubts, the more he came to realize that he couldn't stand by and allow it to happen. He didn't know the when, the how, or the who. King hadn't deemed it necessary for him to know. Speaking to the police had well and truly blotted his copybook. Thankfully, King blamed Natalie far more than he blamed him, but a great deal of trust had been lost between them. He shuddered to think just how close he would be sailing to the wind, and - should he warn her – he no idea of just how little trust, if any, would remain.

A young couple, arm in arm, crossed the road and sidled around his car. He watched them with a certain envy as they swayed along the sidewalk. He'd never walked outside with his wife like that. They'd never even held hands, not even when they'd been courting. It was different with Natalie. He remembered how much he'd wanted to take her hand when they'd exited the restaurant the other night. He recalled reaching for it, and then she'd spied Kevin and stepped away, excited and apprehensive, and his hand had dropped to hang at his side.

She'd wanted to save the kid. He wasn't stupid. He'd realized her intentions as soon as he'd sussed out that being there at that precise moment wasn't a coincidence. It was too late for her to have a conscience. He'd been so angry with her, particularly over that stupid call to the police, that – for a time – he hadn't cared that King wanted her dead.

But, he cared now.

It wasn't just sex. He liked her... loved her, even. He couldn't allow King to have her butchered. He'd almost made up his mind to run away with her, to have a fresh start away from the pernicious influence of King and the organization. He wanted a chance to walk along some future sidewalk with his arm thrown lazily over her shoulder, and to feel the envious eyes on him. But, he wasn't quite there yet. He hadn't mustered the necessary courage, so he remained in the car.

He wrung the steering wheel with clenched fists. He blinked and swallowed the lump that had formed at the back of his throat. His chest tightened. As his eyes focussed on the door to the Brownstone, he began to waver.

Deep in his gut, he knew that he wasn't going to do it. He wasn't going to get out of the car. Any bravado he'd felt on the drive there, slowly dissipated as the reality of the situation began to sink in.

He couldn't... wouldn't... give it all up for her. There would be no running away together, no new life in some nondescript little town in the back of beyond where no one knew who, or what, they were. It had been a ridiculous notion. Natalie had sealed her own fate. Her conscience and her liking for the Murphy boy had seen to that. Her actions had almost brought him down with her. He might like her - love her, even – but it wasn't enough. Thank God he'd realized that in time.

# FRIAR AND TUCK CASE NUMBER ONE: THE MISSING

Shame surged through him. He ignored it. He'd come to terms with shame a long time ago. A little more, added to the rest, wasn't too heavy a burden to carry.

In the end, he sat there for perhaps half an hour before, on a deep sigh, he drove away.

He felt almost broken, bereft. He was leaving her to her fate and – although she'd brought it on herself – his sorrow was palpable. He wondered when it would happen – when the assassin would be called to action. How many minutes, hours, or days did she have left? In a way, he would be glad when King told him the news of her death. He thought it might put an end to his longing.

When he found out later that morning, he was relieved to finally know some peace.

# 26

His wife was oblivious. Early on in their marriage, she'd attempted to discover what he got up to whenever he wasn't at home or at work. At times, she'd accused him of cheating on her. He did – often - but he never admitted to it, and she never discovered the truth. When the children came along, one after the other, he saw a shift in her attitude. It was as if she no longer cared who he fucked, just so long as it wasn't her. When the police wanted to question him at home about the Murphy boy and, God forbid, Natalie's murder, he knew that would shift the dynamics. It was all very well for her to not give a shit if he screwed around with nameless, faceless women, but if the cops threw Natalie in her face, the shit would hit the fan.

So, he'd insisted on being interviewed at the precinct.

King knew. Potter planned on telling him, but King found out before he had a chance. He wondered just how many ears, and pairs of eyes, his boss had within the walls of every police station, in every precinct across New York. Enough, certainly, to always know what was going down.

"She's the whore that just keeps on giving," King said to him. "Fucking grief, that is," he added. "Even dead, she's a liability."

Potter made an effort to remain stone-faced. He would love to be brave enough to remind King that it was his hit on her that had drawn the eyes of the cops. If he'd left her alone – not sent that animal to cut her fucking throat from ear to ear – then everything would've quietened down. Ultimately, who the fuck would care about a missing street kid? All King had guaranteed was, at most, unnecessary scrutiny on something that should have been a three day wonder. Because of King, he was going to be grilled on both sides, and he knew only too well that it was going to be an extremely uncomfortable position when he was placed between a rock and a hard place.

King's beady little eyes were on him. He obviously expected some response to his glib comment about Natalie still being a liability. His boss's stare caused the sweat to gather under his armpits and run down the small of his back. He knew that the jury was still out regarding how much of a liability King saw *him* as. There was always the possibility that he would be seen as much less so, if he went the way of Natalie.

He swallowed back on the bitter taste of bile at the back of his throat. He momentarily closed his eyes and immediately pictured the bloody scene in Natalie's kitchen. There had been no need to almost hack her head off. When he'd been told, in graphic detail, how she'd died, he'd felt like crying. He still felt like crying. But, it could be him next. He had to remember that, and give King no reason to doubt his loyalty.

With a bravado he didn't feel, he said, "They'll be wasting their time with me. I'll stonewall them. I'll give them nothing."

King narrowed his eyes. Potter blinked.

"You just be sure that you do, Potter. I don't need the aggravation."

*Aggravation? What aggravation did King ever suffer?* It was minions – like him – who had to deal with every little bit of hassle that cropped up. King never dirtied his hands, or lost a minute's sleep.

"She can't be linked to me," King went on. "And, she can't be linked to Marcus, or the shelter."

He nodded. That much was fucking obvious.

"They mustn't find out that she knew the Murphy boy."

"No, boss. There's no way they'll find that out."

"Not unless you fuck up, Potter."

"I won't do that."

"Again, you mean? You won't fuck up *again*?"

The sigh almost escaped his mouth, but he caught it just in time.

"That was Natalie, boss. She called the cops... not me."

"No more fucking excuses. You should've scarpered. You should've ditched the phone, grabbed the bitch, and got the fuck out of there."

*And, then what, you bastard idiot?*

"They would've traced the phone call to her, boss. I thought it best just to play the innocent bystander scenario."

"Yes, well, I guess it's all water under the bridge now."

"Except for Natalie being killed." *Jesus, that was a dumb thing to have said.* "What I meant was..."

"I know what you meant, Potter. Pretty brave to say it, though."

He swallowed. Two of King's henchmen took a step towards him.

"She was going to rat me out." King sipped at a cup of coffee and then sat down on one of the plush sofas. The huge room had three such sofas, but he didn't invite Potter to sit.

They were in King's apartment. It was the first time that Potter had been inside it. Being there didn't feel like it was something that should make him feel privileged. It was actually quite ominous and intimidating. The underlying atmosphere was extremely threatening.

King placed his coffee cup on a small occasional table at his side and relaxed back. He said, "Did you know that the bitch made another one of her dumb-ass phone calls?"

He hadn't known that, and shook his head mutely.

"Seems like I had her taken out in the nick of time."

Potter's stomach dropped to his knees. "She phoned the police again?"

"She didn't tell you?" King eyed Potter with blatant suspicion. "I find that difficult to believe."

He scrabbled around for the words that would reassure him. "She wouldn't have dared tell me. She knew better than that."

"Because you're loyal to me?"

"Of course."

"There's no *of course* about it."

"I *am* loyal to you."

"That remains to be seen. You know what'll happen to you if you betray me."

It was a bald statement. It wasn't a question, so no reply was warranted, but Potter felt one was necessary.

He said, "I'll go the same way as Natalie, only I think I'd end up dying a little slower, and a little more painfully."

King smiled. "You're not as dumb as you look," he said. "I just might promote you, after all." He wiped the smile from his face. "She could've brought the whole organization crashing down. Our customers would've been compromised. Can you imagine the fallout from that?"

He certainly could. Although he wasn't privy to who most of those customers were, he knew them to be very powerful people – men mostly, but some women had an investment in the products King provided. The customers called the shots. Even King was afraid of them, and that was all the proof he needed about how precarious his position in the organization was.

"I'll stonewall them" he said, once more. "I'll keep my mouth shut."

King mulled that over. Potter could envisage the little cogs turning in his warped brain.

"I'll know everything that's said. Every word will be reported back to me."

Potter nodded.

"They may try to make a deal with you. Don't be fooled into thinking they can protect you."

"I won't."

Throughout the conversation, King's two heavies had remained stone-faced. They both had hands like huge hams and Potter involuntarily shuddered at the thought of them pounding on him, breaking his bones, beating him to death.

"I'll be in and out in an hour," he said, turning his gaze from the two brutes and back to King. "I promise that you have nothing to worry about."

King gave a cold smile. "Oh, I'm not worried. Did I say I was worried?"

Potter didn't know if King actually expected an answer, or if the question was rhetorical.

"Well, did I say I was worried?"

So, not rhetorical. "No, boss." *Then why go through all this bullshit?*

"I simply can't be bothered with having to clear up any mess you might make. That would inconvenience me. I don't like to be inconvenienced, Potter."

"No, boss."

"If you're in there with those turds for any more than four hours, then I'll know – without being told – that you've ratted me out."

"I won't... I..."

King held up a hand. "Save it until later. Save it until you can prove it."

Dismissed, he made his way from the apartment and out of the building. He walked on legs that felt like rubber. His heart hammered in his chest, and he was relieved to get back into his car. As he drove away – heading for the precinct - something niggled at the back of his mind. He almost called his wife and told her to take herself and the children to her sister's for a day or two. Later, he would bitterly regret not doing so.

# 27

He tried, he really did. Several times he made a run for the door, and several times he failed. They had him trapped in the interview room, and meeting King's four hour deadline increasingly became an impossibility.

He made it clear that he had no answers for them. Belligerent, his ego ruling what little common sense he possessed, and determined to stonewall them, he'd sat back and tried to demonstrate that he didn't take any of it seriously. When that failed, and when the hours ticked by, causing him to begin to panic, the need to get out of there intensified.

The interview had begun well. At first, it had been all about the kid. Even when Natalie's death was brought into the proceedings, he'd shrugged his way through most of what they'd asked. His confidence had been high, and then his anxiety began to overtake him and he'd lost his temper. When he had two detectives trying to punch holes in his story, it was impossible to remain calm, and impossible to hold back.

For the first few hours, he thought that he was giving nothing away. He had no notion that they actually suspected him of being complicit in the abduction of the boy, or in Natalie's death. He soon came to realize that he was kidding himself.

When he made the critical mistake of admitting he'd driven and sat outside Natalie's apartment building on the morning of her murder, he realized that he had played right into their hands and placed himself in the frame for killing her.

It was all they needed to hold him in a cell overnight.

King would know, and he would believe the worst.

Alone in the tiny, silent room, he'd found it impossible to sleep. When they sent for him in the morning, he felt shattered, exhausted and ready to concede at least some information about his relationship with Natalie. He remained adamant that he wouldn't rat out King. To give them anything – even a smidgen of information about him or the organization he represented – would have dire consequences similar to those that Natalie fatally endured, but he believed there would be no harm in demonstrating genuine grief over her death. If he did that – if he showed them that he'd cared about her, and that he was deeply saddened by her death - they would see that he had nothing to do with it.

Sometime in the small hours of the morning, he'd tried to convince himself that King would know that he hadn't talked. Yes, he'd been held overnight – far outside the four hours he'd been warned about – but King knew everything. He would know that he was still loyal, still holding out. At least, he prayed that was the case.

It wasn't.

When he met with the detectives in the morning, he was immediately struck by the expression on both of their faces. His lawyer couldn't look at him. It was apparent that a load of shit had hit the fan.

"Spit it out," he said, mentally preparing himself for some devastating news. "Whatever it is, put me out of my fucking misery."

And, they did.

He believed them. He had no doubt about the authenticity of what he'd been told.

He knew that he shouldn't be shocked, but he was. King had followed through on his threat. After the initial, brief instance of shock, he blubbered like a baby, then the only thing that ran through his mind was – *can I still save myself?*

He sat as still as a stone, staring straight ahead and shutting out everything but his thoughts. His wife was dead. There was fuck all he could do about that. King thought he'd sold him down the river, and – unless he could prove to him that he had remained silent and loyal - his own death would be on the cards.

They kept harping on about his kids. They wanted him to ask about them. He knew what had happened to them – that they weren't dead. King would never destroy such good commodities as three clean-living children.

He didn't want to react, to show any sign of being afraid. To do so would open a chink in his armour and make him vulnerable. More than ever, he had to be strong, and had to deflect any questions around Natalie's death, the boy's abduction, and ultimately thwart any reference to an underlying organizational hand in everything that had transpired. He certainly couldn't tell them where to find his children.

He could admit to knowing where his kids had been taken. He didn't have to guess. Every child grabbed off the streets were taken to the same safe house before being shifted to the place he'd always thought of as *Purgatory* – a specially adapted warehouse near Sheepshead Bay. Yes, he could admit to everything - perhaps save his children before they were hurt beyond repair - but he knew what that would mean for him. A raid on the warehouse would tell King everything he needed to know.

Staying calm and rational was easier said than done. He was disgusted to realize that he was much weaker than he'd thought. Mentally, he was slowly becoming a basket-case. Physically - his body was beginning to betray him. He was close to panic, and shaking like a leaf.

All his chickens had come home to roost. He was screwed. Even if he kept his trap shut, the chances of him surviving King's wrath, or seeing his children again, were slim to none.

*Fuck!* He really needed to get out of there.

He had no idea what he was going to do.

At last, he got a break. The detectives left him alone with his lawyer.

When they came back, they promised him protection. King had warned him that they'd try that little trick on him. But, was it a trick? Perhaps they *could* get him out from King's clutches... put him in witness protection... keep him safe? It would mean sacrificing the children, but – at least *he* would be kept alive. Under different circumstances, he would've laughed in their face, but, the circumstances were extraordinary, and he was running out of options.

He began to waver. Even if he was released from custody, there was always the danger that King wouldn't believe him when he insisted that he'd kept his mouth shut. If he couldn't convince him, he would be a dead man walking.

On the cusp of reluctantly grasping at the flimsy straw offered by the detectives, everything changed, and Friar and Tuck were no longer in the room.

# The Children
# 28

HE BLINKED BACK THE tears. Crying had never got him anywhere. Usually, they earned him a slap, a punch, or a kick. He'd learned a long time ago to be stoic, even when in great pain, or when his stomach cramped with hunger. Not many thirteen year olds could remember all the way back to standing in their crib, a wet nappy heavy and hanging to their knees, and crying for attention, only to be ignored or slapped. But, he could remember. He could remember as far back to when he was two years old. Sometimes, he even remembered a time before that. Not once did crying get him the attention he desired, so he'd stopped. From the age of two, he could count on the one hand the times he'd succumbed. If a two-year old Kevin could do it, then it stood to reason that a thirteen-year old certainly could.

They would get no tears out of him that, or any other day.

He had no idea where he was, or why he'd been brought there. He'd been asleep for huge chunks of time, so he wasn't able to determine how many days and nights had gone by. It was always bright. They never turned the lights off, and the disorienting effects of the humming fluorescent tubes set high on a steel-girded ceiling, made the passage of time all the more elusive. He didn't think it had been weeks – more like two or three days – but he couldn't be sure.

A man and a woman stood at the foot of the bed. They were talking in hushed tones and, to Kevin, their whispers sounded sinister. He tried to focus on what they were saying. Although they believed him to be asleep, they did their best not to be overheard and that made the words even more ominous.

What didn't they want him to hear?

He was a skilled listener. On more than one occasion in the past, understanding many a whisper had saved his bacon. More often than not, it was the whispered words that always drew his attention. Words spoken aloud and without any attempt to conceal their meaning, never frightened him. He was always on his guard, and more cautious of what he didn't know or couldn't hear.

His heart rose almost to his throat. His eyes jerked behind his closed lids, and he swallowed back hard. He thought he must have heard it wrong.

He felt his limbs go into spasm. The sheet covering him trembled. He tried to be still. He didn't want to draw their attention directly to him. That would be really bad.

Although the room was cold, and although the thin sheet offered very little heat, Kevin was sweating. He was frightened and the fear was quickly blossoming into terror. The more he listened, and the more he understood, the more he shook.

He didn't understand why they wanted his eyes, only that they did. They were making plans for the operation to remove them and the man – the doctor – was telling the woman that she had to put drops in them three times a day between now and the procedure.

*The procedure...* oh, God, he wanted to scream. He didn't. Instead, he bit down on his bottom lip, drawing blood. He wouldn't cry and he wouldn't scream – not like the others.

The others cried like babies, and boy did they scream.

There were two of them – a boy and a girl – held prisoner, just like him. Their cries, and their screams, changed nothing about their predicament. It would change nothing about his, so he remained quiet. He could scream until his throat was raw, or his lungs burst, and no one would care – it was the story of his life.

Maybe he'd got it wrong? Maybe they were talking about one of the others? Making the smallest of movements, he glanced to his left, where the boy – younger than he was by a couple of years – lay flat on his back. The boy was, for once, pretty quiet. The only sound that could be heard from him was a pitiful whimper. Kevin knew that he was in a great deal of pain. He'd had an operation the day before and the bandages covering his wounds were sopping wet with blood. He didn't think they'd given him any painkillers. He didn't think they'd given him so much as a sip of water all day.

Perhaps it was *his* eyes they were after? He felt an acute sense of shame for hoping that was truly the case. He quickly drew his gaze away.

He turned his head to the right. Thankfully the doctor and the woman didn't notice. The girl was asleep. To Kevin, it didn't seem like a natural sleep. She was much too still. Like the boy in the bed to his left, the girl had been operated upon, but – unlike the boy – they seemed to be caring for her much better. Her bandages were dry and clean. She wasn't in any pain. There was a glass of water with a bright pink straw in it on her bedside cabinet, and there was a tube in one of her arms that snaked all the way up to a bag hanging on a stand.

He couldn't work out why one was seemingly being well cared for, whilst the other was left to lie in agony. It was just one more thing he couldn't make any sense of.

He wasn't in a hospital. He knew that because it didn't smell like one, and, when he stared up at where the ceiling was, he saw steel girders and the inside of a rusty looking roof.

Although he hadn't been in many hospitals – just the times Natalie took him for tests, and the one time when his mother overdosed and he went with her to the emergency department – he knew what their ceilings were supposed to look like, and he knew how they smelled.

Although the man at the foot of his bed wore a white coat with a stethoscope hanging around his neck, and although the woman wore a nurse's uniform, he wasn't fooled. Rogue doctors, and rogue nurses, could work anywhere – not just in hospitals. His mind couldn't stretch far enough to work out how operations could be carried out in a place that wasn't a hospital.

The sour smell of his sweat made him screw up his nose. He always tried to keep himself clean. Living on the streets had never been an excuse to ignore his personal hygiene, but – since being strapped to the bed - he'd had no opportunity to wash.

It would take a miracle to get him out of there. He hoped that Natalie would come to rescue him. She'd tried to warn him – that night when the men took him. She'd tried to get to him, but, the man she was with, held her back. She'd tried, and he hoped that she would try again.

Sometime in the past hour or so, three additional beds had been wheeled into the room. Kevin knew what that meant. He felt terribly sorry for those kids who'd soon be joining him and the others. He wish he understood what it all meant. Understanding would be half the battle. If he understood, then he'd be able to work out what to do, how to escape. He'd escaped his mother, and the clutches of every pervert she'd allowed into their home. He'd survived for months on the streets. He was nothing if not wily. If Natalie didn't arrive to rescue him, he was confident that he would be able to rescue himself.

But, not if he didn't have any eyes.

He couldn't let them take them.

The woman in the nurse's uniform walked to the side of the bed. He didn't pretend to be asleep anymore. He turned to look up at her. She had a cruel face. He knew all about cruel faces. He'd seen enough of them in his thirteen years not to be fooled by a disingenuous smile, or a soft expression.

In a way, she reminded him of his mother. He couldn't recall his mother ever looking on him softly. In her often bloodshot eyes, there was only ever hatred. It was an expression he'd never questioned. Why would he have questioned it? It was an expression that had always been there – in her eyes and on her face – for as long as he could remember.

He knew what she was. He often heard the men she'd brought to the apartment call her a filthy whore. Despite knowing nothing but hatred from her, he'd wanted to defend her from that vile description. He would've done anything to protect her, but she never defended him against the attacks the men made when they battered down his bedroom door and tried to hurt him... *did* hurt him. Once, when one of the men he'd cut with the little knife he kept under his pillow threatened to call the police, his mother had slapped him so hard that his ears had rung for a full week.

She hadn't given him any food that week. She'd told him it was punishment for driving away a very good paying customer. That's when he'd begun to steal. He'd had to, or he would've starved. It was also the week when he'd begun to realize that there could be a life for him on the streets.

It was then that he planned his escape.

It ended up being a hard life, but no harder than trying to survive under the failed care of his mother.

The thought of being taken by those men so easily plagued him. He never let his guard down – not a single time since leaving home. That had been the first time. No matter how much he thought about it – tried to understand why he'd been so careless – he couldn't reconcile himself with his stupidity.

He felt the cool of the alcohol wipe on his arm, and then the sting of the needle. She hadn't been gentle when she'd stuck it in.

There was no point in asking what it was she'd injected him with. She wouldn't answer him. Apart from that one time – early on – they had never answered any of his questions.

The so-called doctor left and the so-called nurse moved to the bed of the other boy. She stripped back the sheet, exposing his nakedness. Kevin noticed that the boy had wet himself. The strong aroma of urine stung his eyes. He felt embarrassed for him.

"I should let you lie in it, you little turd," she said, slapping the boy hard on the face.

Kevin closed his eyes – feeling the boy's pain and humiliation.

*Just what was this place? Why was he there? Why was any of them there?*

Ignoring the fact that the boy was in a world of pain, the nurse rough-handled him, stripped off the offending sheet, and replaced it with a fresh one. By the time she'd finished, the doctor had re-entered the room.

"Catheterize him," he said. "We need to start monitoring his output, and it'll save on the laundry."

Kevin eyed him warily. He was one of the people in charge, and his orders were followed without question. The nurses all seemed a little afraid of him.

Kevin had come to know three nurses, but had only met the one doctor. There had been another man. The doctor had addressed him, rather deferentially, as Mister King. The nurses might all be a little afraid of the doctor, but they were terrified of this Mister King, and Kevin fully understood why. He was an evil son of a bitch.

"When is he due back in theatre, doctor?" the nurse asked.

"Tomorrow, most likely," he replied. "Get a dextrose infusion going. We need to flush out those precious kidneys."

"You want him linked up to dialysis afterwards?"

The doctor shook his head. "No need. We'll be finished with him after tomorrow's operation."

Kevin watched as a slow smile passed over the nurse's thin lips. It was obvious that she was pleased. No more pissy sheets to change. After tomorrow, no more having to put up with that particular boy's screams.

The doctor moved to the bottom of Kevin's bed. Kevin followed him with his eyes. He was a sharp-featured man, balding on top but with hair cropped to the skull at the sides and back. He stood tall and straight, no stooping or roundness at the shoulders. To Kevin, he seemed like a military man – like the pictures he'd seen in some of his comic books. All that was missing was the uniform.

He removed the chart hanging off the footboard. His fingers were long and bony. Kevin shivered as he recalled the last time those fingers had probed and prodded his body. They'd been cold. When Natalie had taken him to the hospital for tests, that doctor had warmed his hands before touching him. Not this one, though. He hadn't cared enough.

"Hello Kevin," he said, replacing the chart and peering up the length of the bed. "How are you doing? Has nurse Calder been taking good care of you?"

*No!*

He nodded, fearful of speaking the truth.

"Good. Good. Pleased to hear it." He turned and winked at the nurse. Kevin had the sense to realize that it was a conspiratorial wink. The doctor knew, full well, just how little care the nurse actually took. It was all a game, one huge pretence.

He turned his eyes back to Kevin and raked them over his face. "You look a little pale. Are you feeling well?"

His mouth was dry. He tried to swallow what little spit there was. The doctor expected an answer. If none was forthcoming, he wouldn't be pleased.

"I'm fine, sir," he said in a scratchy voice. "Just a little sleepy."

"That will be the injection taking effect. You'll soon be off in the land of nod."

A sudden terror gripped him. *Would he wake up without eyes?*

The doctor said, "When you wake up, I don't want you to be worried about any of the tubes."

He choked, blinked, said, "Tubes?"

The doctor smiled. His smile was dreadful. "You'll have one put in your little tiddler - just like Johnny next to you. We'll need to keep an eye on how much you piss. Do you understand why we need to do that... measure your piss?"

He shook his head. "No, sir."

He moved around to the side of the bed and sat down on the mattress. His weight made the mattress tilt, and Kevin rolled a little to the right.

"I think that it's only right that we keep you in the loop. After all – for a while – it's still your body."

*Still his body?* He shivered.

"In a few days, we have a little boy being flown in from Germany. Unfortunately, his kidneys don't work. We need to ensure that *your* kidneys work, Kevin and – to do that – we need to be sure that you piss out almost as much as we pump in."

His eyes flicked up to the bag of dextrose now hanging on Johnny's drip-stand. "You'll have one of those, too. We can't risk transplanting wonky kidneys into our little Kraut, now, can we?"

The doctor's flat, dark eyes crinkled at the corners. "No need to look so worried. We'll take good care of you."

Kevin gave Johnny a sidelong glance.

"Oh, don't you go paying him any heed," the doctor said. "Johnny isn't like you. There wasn't much pickings from him. You're different, Kevin... special."

"Special?" He didn't want to be special. "How am I special, sir?"

"Oh, in all kinds of ways, Kevin."

"Is that why you want my eyes... because I'm special?"

"Your eyes?" The doctor frowned, then his face brightened. "You know about your eyes?"

"I heard you talking."

He grinned. "I bet you did. There's nothing wrong with your hearing, is there, Kevin?"

He waited. He wanted an explanation, but had the sense not to push.

"All right, boy... I'll tell you all about it. I guess it's only fair." His grin widened. "Your eyes now belong to a little girl from South Africa. She's the daughter of one of my friends. Another friend is a pioneer... do you know what a pioneer is, Kevin?"

He nodded.

"Well, *this* pioneer is a famous eye surgeon. He can do wonders for blind little girls. All he needs are two healthy retinas."

His brain rejected every word. There was no way any of it could be true. *No fucking way*!

"You can't do that," he said. "It's not allowed."

"Not allowed?" The doctor's grin turned sinister. "Who says?"

"The... the police."

"Do you think that the police give a shit about the likes of you? We're the only people who care about you, Kevin. To us, you're precious. To everyone else – the police included – you don't even exist. Even your own mother won't miss you. We can do what we want with you, no questions asked."

His brain continued to refuse to accept what he was being told. None of it was true. He wouldn't believe it... couldn't believe it.

"Anyway..." The doctor got back to his feet. "There's no point in you worrying your little head about it."

He signalled to the nurse and she walked to his side, an expectant look on her face.

"Our other guests have arrived," he said. "They'll require sedation. To Kevin, he said, "You'll soon have new roomies. Won't that be fun?"

Kevin was oblivious to the arrival of the other children. Almost as soon as the doctor left with the nurse, he was asleep.

# 29

Mary Potter was brought in bound and gagged. Her younger siblings were led meekly by the hand. All three were terrified. Mary was a fighter, and a biter, and – having watched her mother being killed – she hadn't been taken easily, or quietly.

As a result of the killer's fist connecting with her face in retaliation to a particularly painful bite, she had a cut lip and a bruise on one cheekbone. Her wrists were chaffed from the nip of the zip-tie, and her whole body felt as if it had been pummelled – which, it had.

She prayed silently and feverishly for her dad. She moaned behind the gag, terrified that she was going to be sick and choke. Beneath the rushing sound in her ears, she heard her brother and sister crying, but there was nothing she could do to comfort them.

As her clothes were stripped from her body, she fought. They didn't release the zip-tie, so – to get the arms of her blouse over her wrists - it was torn from shoulders to cuffs.

The man who'd killed her mother grabbed her and threw her onto one of the beds. A strap secured her across the chest, and two others secured her ankles to the bed rails. Only then was the zip-tie binding her wrists cut, but the freeing up of her hands and arms was temporary. They, too, were strapped to the bedrails.

The gag remained in place. Above it, her eyes screamed out her fear and agony.

Within half an hour of their arrival, all three Potter children were drugged and unconscious.

For several hours, the only sound in the room was from the heavy breaths of six sleeping children. Even Johnny slept, which was a blessing because, asleep, he was free from pain.

Kevin woke to the sound of crying. He managed to lift his head from the pillow and look towards its source. He was extremely relieved to find that he could see. It meant that he still had his eyes.

The promised tubes were in place. The one in the back of his hand smarted where the needle entered the skin and then the vein. The one down below simply felt strange.

As he looked across the breadth of the room, his stomach felt as if it was somewhere north of his chest. His heart belted out a thunderous rhythm against his ribs, and he felt as sick as a dog. His shoulders sagged and he dropped back down onto the pillow, exhausted despite the time he'd spent asleep. He lay like that for a while, listening to the cries from across the room, and wondering what he would have to do to escape.

Summoning up some inner strength, and ignoring the churning feeling of nausea, he lifted his head once more. The room shifted and he had to blink a few times before he centred himself, and before he could make everything stop spinning.

The girl was younger than him. He guessed her ae to be about ten or eleven. She was one of the new ones and, by turning his head to the right, he could clearly see the other two – a much younger boy, and a girl who was no more than a toddler. They had a similar look about them, and he guessed that they were from the same family.

The younger two were asleep – drugged, most likely – but the older one was wide awake and clearly suffering.

He glanced to the left, ensuring that there were no nurses present, then called across to the girl.

"What's your name?" His tongue was still thick from the drug that had been used to enforce his slumber and the words came out sounding all slurred and funny.

She ignored him, but her cries became more pitiful.

"I'm Kevin," he said. "It's best that you stop that. You'll only get in trouble."

"Where am I?" she wailed. "Why am I here?"

He didn't want to tell her. He thought it best that she found that out from someone else. Anyway, how could he find the right words to explain that her body parts would be removed and given to someone else? She probably wouldn't even believe him. He hardly believed it himself.

"Try to be quiet," he said. "They don't like kids crying around here."

"I want my daddy. Where's my daddy?"

"I don't know where your dad is. He's not here. There's only the doctors and the nurses, and – if you don't stop that stupid crying – you'll bring them."

Johnny stirred and moaned and Kevin turned his head to the left. The piss bag hanging on his bedrail was full to bursting. It looked a bit bloody.

"Who's he?" the girl asked, sniffing back on her tears.

"His name is Johnny. He's had an operation and isn't too well."

"Have you had an operation?"

He shook his head. "Not yet."

"There's a girl over there." She jerked her head to the right. "What's her name?"

"I don't know. She's been asleep ever since I got here."

"They hurt me," she said. 'I bit the man, but I couldn't get away." She glanced at her sleeping siblings. "He killed my mom."

Kevin swallowed back painfully. There was nothing he could say to that. His eyelids quivered. He felt like crying, but knew that wouldn't set a good example to the girl. She needed to realize that it wasn't okay to cry.

"You haven't told me your name."

"Mary. Mary Potter."

"Is that your brother and sister?"

She nodded. "They're only little. When they wake up, they'll be really scared."

*Join the club.*

Mary tugged on her restraints. The bedframe rattled.

"Don't do that," Kevin hissed. "Lie still."

"I want out of here!" she screamed, yanking harder on the straps and now really making the bed shake.

Kevin lay back and closed his eyes. He'd warned her. There was nothing else he could do. Whatever happened now would be her own fault.

He heard rapid footsteps. He opened his eyes and a nurse he'd never seen before marched right up to Mary's bed. She spoke with an Irish accent, the words, though harsh and angry, had a melodious ring to them.

"Shut up," she said, taking a swipe at Mary's face with an open hand. "I don't mind slapping you senseless, girl."

Neither the slap, nor the words, had any effect on Mary. She simply screamed all the louder. Kevin thought she was either terribly brave, or terribly stupid. Either way, he knew that she'd be eventually beaten into silence.

It took at least half a dozen slaps before her screams were whittled down to quiet sobs. Satisfied, the nurse left, but not before giving the girl a final, dire warning not to disturb her peace with any more hysterics.

Johnny was awake. Kevin heard him muttering to himself. His quiet words were interspersed with gut-wrenching moans.

Every child in the room was living through their own nightmare, but Johnny was suffering the most. Kevin thought he heard him beg God to let him die.

He thought that Johnny was no more than nine years old.

# 30

Mary was screaming again. Kevin had dozed off and was woken by the air being rent with the noise. He couldn't understand how such a racket could erupt from such a small mouth.

This time, she was screaming because she needed to pee.

Good luck with that, he thought. They would leave her to piss the bed.

When the nurse entered the room and completely ignored Mary's wails - walking straight past her bed without so much as looking at her, or yelling at her to shut the fuck up – Kevin was surprised. He was more than surprised, he was gob-smacked. That particular nurse wasn't known for her forbearance – at least she hadn't been where Johnny was concerned. Kevin had witnessed the boy earning himself a few slaps, and even a punch with a closed fist, when *his* cries had rankled.

And, it was Johnny she was interested in – or, to be more specific, it was the bag holding his piss that drew her to the side of his bed.

She shook her head and tutted. Kevin heard her say, "The doc a'int gonna be pleased with that," before turning and waddling back the way she'd just come.

Minutes later, she returned, with the doctor who looked like a soldier in a white coat, following behind her.

They both peered at the piss-bag. It was more blood than piss.

"Could be his bladder," the doctor said. "Might not be the kidneys."

The nurse raised an eyebrow. "You want to take the risk?"

He shook his head. "I guess not." He thought a moment.

To Kevin, he looked worried.

*Good.*

"It's quite a lot of blood," the doctor said, scrubbing at his face with his hands. "That's all I need."

The nurse said nothing, simply looked up at him with a sympathetic expression on her face.

"I'll have to tell him. He's going to go mental."

"He'll know it's not your fault, doctor. These things happen."

"Not when the customer's son is already on the fucking plane."

"We could…"

He peered down at her. "What?"

"Test the others. You never know…"

He shook his head. "King won't hear of the new ones being touched… not yet, anyway."

"Why not?"

He shrugged. "Something to do with their father."

"What about Kevin's kidneys?"

"They're already earmarked and, anyway – wrong blood group."

She hadn't exhausted every possibility. "What about Alice?" She glanced over at the sleeping girl. "She's AB Positive."

Again, he shook his head. "Not Alice."

"Okay, so what do you want me to do with this one?" She poked at Johnny with a stubby finger. "Do you need him for anything else?"

"Not a damned thing." He turned and walked away, winking at Kevin as he strode past the bottom of his bed. As he reached the door, he turned and said over his shoulder to the nurse, "Shut that little bitch up. Double-dose her."

For someone more than a little fat, the nurse was pretty nimble on her feet. She was over at Mary's bedside in a flash, and her hand was soon lashing out mercilessly across the girl's face.

Mary couldn't defend herself. Her arms were still secured by straps to the bedframe, and all she could do was throw her head from side to side in attempt to avoid the blows.

"Leave her alone," Kevin screamed, earning himself a look that pretty much told him that he was next. He gulped, and tried to make himself look as small as possible, when – finished with Mary – she advanced on him.

"It's a good job you're off-limits," she hissed. "But, that won't always be the case. When it's your turn to piss blood, I'll break every bone in your fucking body."

Mary was sobbing now. Perhaps, next time, she'd listen when he told her to keep quiet – not that he'd taken his own advice when he'd screamed at the nurse.

It didn't take a genius to work out why he was *off-limits*. The doctor wouldn't want to risk an injury to his eyes. They belonged to a South African girl now, and he guessed payment would only be made for perfect retinas, and not those displaced by a hefty punch.

He felt sick. The fear was wearing down the last of his reserves, and now he had Mary and her brother and sister to worry about as well.

Because, he *did* worry about them. He couldn't help it. He must've got his caring nature from his father, because his mother didn't have a thoughtful bone in her body.

The nurse was tutting again. She was bent over, disconnecting the tube from Johnny's piss-bag, and then she was stretching up and disconnecting the other bag on the stand above his head.

All the while, the boy lay there gazing up at her, moaning quietly, and beseeching with his eyes to be finished off.

Mary was now quiet. When he glanced over at her, Kevin saw that she'd conked out, exhausted by all that screaming – either that or her mind had shut down and sent her to sleep to protect her from herself.

Surprisingly, the two younger children hadn't regained consciousness. Kevin worried that they'd been overdosed with whatever sedative had been used on them. He couldn't make up his mind whether a fatal overdose would, in the long run, be the kindest thing for them.

He watched as the nurse walked to the far corner of the long room and retrieved a trolley. It was a rickety old thing with a wheel that went north when it was supposed to go south. She pushed it, and it squeaked and weaved its way across the floor, the nurse cursing under her breath every time she had to haul it straight.

She parked it parallel to the bed and applied the brakes.

"Right," she said to Johnny. "Let's get you out of here."

When she hefted him up and onto the trolley, the boy's head lolled back. He was naked, and she didn't even have the decency to cover him once she'd plonked him down. Kevin couldn't tear his eyes away as she wheeled him away and straight out the door.

Kevin knew that he wasn't going to see Johnny again.

The nurse with the Irish accent appeared. She was humming an out of tune pop song, but didn't look too happy.

"Two more hours and I'm outta here," she said to Kevin. "It's been a fucker of a day, and I'll be glad to get off my feet." She began to strip Johnny's bed. "We don't usually have this many kids, and it's a fucking disgrace on what I'm paid."

Kevin didn't think that she was actually talking to him. She was just making noise and griping. He could've been anyone.

He risked a question. He asked, "If it's so bad why do you work here?"

"Struck off... can't work anywhere else."

That didn't come as a surprise.

He risked another question. "Why do you hate us so much?"

She seemed shocked by the question. She dropped the soiled linen onto the floor and leaned over the mattress. "Hate you?" She shook her head. "What makes you think I hate you?"

"You must do,'" he said.

She had a long face and a wide mouth, both stretched when she grinned.

"I suppose it seems that way, but – truth is – I don't hate any of you. I don't feel anything, one way or the other. It's not as if I know you. I'd have to know you to either like you or hate you. None of you are ever here long enough to grow on me... not that you would. Filthy street scum – that's what you are. I blame the parents. You wouldn't be here if you had proper parents."

She wheeled the drip stand to the bottom of the bed, picked up the discarded bedlinen, and dumped it in a huge basket by the door. She then went to check on Alice, adjusted her bedclothes and replaced the empty bag on her drip stand.

The child didn't stir. Her head lay on the pillow and she was as pale as alabaster. Her narrow chest rose and fell with each breath and it was the only thing that suggested she was alive.

She turned back to Kevin, and said, "I suppose you want something to eat?"

He nodded. He wasn't hungry, but had the sense to realize that his body needed fuel.

"I'll rustle you up a sandwich. Don't say I'm not good to you, you little fucker."

"Thank you," he said. "I appreciate it."

She eyed him suspiciously, trying to determine if he meant it, or if he was being sarcastic. "Got some manners, haven't you."

He shrugged. Throwing in the odd *thank you* never hurt anyone.

"Just for that, I'll butter the bread."

She had to undo one of the straps on his wrists to allow him to eat the sandwich. The strap was secured by a wide buckle and – distracted by a commotion going on outside the door - she left without ensuring the hand was securely strapped back down.

He couldn't believe it. He thought she'd be back – having realized her error. But, she didn't return.

*What to do?*

He could easily undo the buckle on his other wrist, and then free his legs. It wouldn't take but a minute, but he was scared.

*They're going to take your eyes, and your kidneys, and goodness knows what else. Move your fucking ass!*

He undid the other strap.

He was attached to a tube at both ends – one in his penis, and one leading from a needle on the back of his right hand. Taking the needle out was painful, but simple to do, but there was no way to take out the other tube.

And, he was naked.

How could he escape with a tube in his weeny and butt-naked into the bargain?

Blood leaked from his hand. He stripped off a pillowcase and wrapped it around it, pressing down to try and stop the flow.

He didn't think he had much time. Sometimes, they were left alone for long stretches, but he couldn't guarantee how long before one of the nurses, or the doctor showed their faces.

*What to do? What to do? What to do?*

Indecision paralyzed him.

He freed his legs and kicked them over the side of the bed. His head suddenly swam, and black spots appeared behind his eyes. He was terrified that he was going to faint.

The piss bag was hooked over the bottom of the bedframe. He unhooked it and sat it next to him on the mattress. No blood in it. That was good.

He glanced across at Mary. He didn't want her to wake and see him naked, so he pulled the sheet free and wrapped it around himself. He managed to make a pouch-cum pocket by folding it over, and he slipped the piss back inside and tied it up with two ends of the sheet. It held fairly firmly and the tube didn't pull.

Also good.

He slid down and placed his feet on the floor. Not so good. His legs felt like rubber.

The black spots were still there behind his eyes, but he didn't feel quite so woozy. He held onto the bed frame and hauled himself up.

The floor seemed to come up to meet him, but he refused to flop back down on the bed. He had no choice. He had to move.

His main dilemma was Mary. If he woke her and freed her, she would want to bring her brother and sister, but they were deep in the land of nod. He wasn't sure if they would be able to wake them and, if they did, how loud and troublesome would they be?

There was no waking Alice. All of Johnny's scrams, and then Mary's, hadn't even made her flinch. She was well gone.

He stood in the middle of the floor, neither moving towards Mary or towards the door.

If he got away on his own, he could send help back for the others. If he woke Mary, all hell could break loose.

It really was a no-brainer.

He made for the door.

# 31

It was much darker outside the room. The ceiling was boxed in with no girders in sight, and no fluorescent tubes to brighten his way. Everything felt make-shift – not like a true space - and the layout was very disorientating.

He was in a long, wide corridor with unpainted plywood walls. Ahead was an open space with light streaming through a huge window that acted like a beacon. To his left, another corridor – similar to the one he was in - branched off. Behind him was another door, next to the one he had just emerged from.

He stood still and listened. If anyone appeared, he'd be caught. There was nowhere to hide.

He heard nothing.

He didn't want to be caught like a rat in a trap, so he decided to head for the open space straight ahead.

Emotionally, he was a wreck. Physically, he felt weak and vulnerable. His heart beat in his chest like a pounding fist, and his legs could barely support him. The undigested sandwich sat like a stone in his stomach and bile built up at the back of his throat. He swallowed it back, but it kept bubbling back up his gullet and he gagged, then retched and spat mouthfuls of the burning acid on the floor.

He felt a little better, huffed in a breath, and took a moment to steady himself.

Moving forward, he winced. The floor was rough and small stones and pieces of rubble littered its length. His bare feet were going to be cut to ribbons, but he had no choice but to shift himself.

Keeping himself pressed tight against the wall, he made slow but steady headway. He thought he had a couple of hundred paces before he would reach the end of the corridor. Each of those paces were going to be torture on his poor feet, but rather that than staying to have his body dismantled.

He couldn't stop thinking of the kids he was leaving behind, or wondering what had happened to Johnny. He had a feeling that the boy was dead. He wished he could've escaped sooner and got help for him. A proper doctor would've been able to save him, he was sure of it.

He hadn't escaped yet, he told himself. He might not make it, and then they would all die.

He thought about Natalie. She would be worried sick about him. He wondered if she had the police out looking for him. He believed that she did. He wished that she'd been his mother. If he had been born to her, his life would've been so different. He had no idea what it would've felt like to grow up in a normal home with a mother who loved and cared for him, but he wasn't one for wishful thinking, or living in fantasy land, so he shook the thought from his mind.

He shivered inside the sheet. It was so cold that his breath plumed out in front of him with every breath. It shouldn't really be that cold. It wasn't winter and – even when it rained – it was never that bitter. He didn't give it any further thought. So, it was cold – so what? It was the least of his worries.

He kept his ears wide open for voices or footsteps. He had no idea what he would do if he heard any.

His knees buckled when a particularly sharp stone stabbed deep into the sole of one of his feet. He cried out, then rammed his fist into his mouth to stifle any further sound.

His eyes watered with pain. He held his breath before bending and pulling out the offending stone. There was blood on the floor. When he straightened up and took a tentative step forward, he noticed that he was leaving a bloody footprint behind him.

That wouldn't do. If he had to hide, they would be led straight to him.

Hunkering down, he grabbed up a handful of gritty dust and dirt and rubbed it into the puncture wound, effectively sealing the hole. It stung like hell and another cry almost escaped his lips. He snatched it back in time, closed his eyes and whimpered.

The pain made his head throb. His eyes flared in agony with every step, but he managed to hobble his way closer and closer and, when he was only a few paces away, he finally began to hope.

He wasn't sure what he'd expected, but it certainly wasn't the huge and empty space of what seemed like an industrial building.

Confused, he didn't know which way to turn. There were several doors, but none that appeared to lead to the outside. He turned full circle, squinting and trying to fathom out the right direction, to decide on the right door.

Behind him was the corridor. It was incongruent to the surroundings, looking as if it sat inside an enormous wooden box that filled three quarters of the building. It was actually a building inside a building, constructed to house the make-shift hospital.

There was no time to stand and make sense of anything. Others could work it all out and draw the necessary conclusions. He had to get out of there, and damned quick.

*Choose a door, numbskull.*

That was easier said than done. They all looked the same. There was no way to tell what one would be the right one.

The echo of voices reached his ears and the decision was made. He panicked and made a beeline straight for the nearest one.

The voices grew alarmed. The footsteps were now running, and running straight for him. He opened and closed the door and gasped when he saw what was directly in front of him.

Johnny, lying flat on his back on the trolley, a plastic bag over his head and secured at the neck.

The trolley was in front of a furnace. In fact, there were two furnaces – a large one and a much smaller one. The large one was lit and the heat coming off it was scorching. The door stood open like a huge mouth waiting to be fed, and Kevin was in no doubt what its next meal was going to be.

Poor Johnny. Beneath the plastic, his face was almost black. Kevin's stomach heaved at the sight of him.

They killed him. They hadn't simply left him until his body had given up. They'd put a bag over his head and deliberately suffocated him. That fact added a completely new dimension of terror to Kevin's psyche. He thought he'd known what evil was, but now realized that he'd not really had a clue.

The voices were now outside the door. His eyes darted around wildly. He turned in quick circles, frantically searching for somewhere to hide. He expected the door to be flung open at any moment and – as his panic grew – he began to hyperventilate.

He stopped turning and stared at the door. The handle was rattling and turning. He blinked and swallowed. His breathing slowed as a cold detachment swept over him, all panic suddenly evaporating.

He was resigned. It was all over.

---

MARY WOKE TO A COMMOTION. Her brother and sister were awake and both were raising the roof with their wailing. Two nurses were standing in the middle of the room arguing, their voices shrill and furious. Outside the door, footsteps moved at a run. It didn't take a genius to realize that something was up, and when Mary looked across and saw two empty beds – beds where there had once been two boys – her first thought was that they'd escaped.

Her second thought was that she'd been abandoned.

Maliciously, she hoped that they'd be caught. They had no right leaving without her, and Petey, and Molly. They could've all gone together and it was very mean of them to sneak out whilst she was asleep.

One of the nurses slapped the other one right across the face. The crack of the slap was so loud and so unexpected that Petey and Molly were shocked into silence.

It was a blessed silence and it gave Mary the opportunity to think a little more clearly.

She now hoped that the boys *wouldn't* be caught. If they got clean away, help would come – her daddy would come.

"You're a fucking nutjob," the nurse who'd been slapped said, a hand pressed against her stinging cheek.

"And, you're a liability," the other one spat back at her. "How could you be so fucking stupid?"

"It's no big deal. Why is everyone acting as if he can actually get out of here? It's a fucking fortress, for Christ's sake."

*He?* Mary frowned. Surely, she means *them*?

"*Mary, Mary, Mary,*" her brother cried, wailing once more. "I want mummy, Mary."

"Shut up, Petey," she rasped at him. "Lie still for a minute."

She glanced over at two-year-old Molly. The little girl's face was tear-streaked and she was violently sucking on her thumb.

"You okay, Molly-bear?" She twisted herself around as far as the restraints would allow. "I'm here, sweetie. It's gonna be okay."

The little girl's thumb plopped out of her mouth and she let out an ear-piercing scream that drew the attention of the nurses. One of them advanced on her and raised her hand.

Mary cried out, begging the nurse to leave her sister alone.

"Never mind the little bitch," the other nurse said, dragging on her colleague's arm. "We best get the fuck out of here before King arrives."

The very mention of King's name was enough to have the nurse nodding and dropping her hand.

"You really fucked up, Sarah."

Sarah – the nurse with the lilting Irish accent, nodded. *Fucked up* was an understatement. "They'll find him," she said. "They *have* to find him. If they don't..."

"We're both dead meat."

---

THE DOOR REMAIN CLOSED. Something, or someone, on the other side drew away whoever had been about to enter.

Kevin's relief would be short-lived. He still needed to find somewhere to hide. Galvanized by the temporary reprieve, he hurried over to see if there was a gap behind the largest of the two furnaces that he could squeeze into. It was his only option because – although the room was quite large - the space was almost completely taken up by the furnaces and the trolley. It was windowless, so that removed one possibility to escape to the outside. There was only the one door, and that pretty much snookered him.

The smaller of the furnaces was pressed tight against the brick wall, but the larger one seemed to jut out a little. Hope surged when he approached and spied the gap. Then, hope flattened and disintegrated when he saw just how small the gap actually was.

There was no way he could crush his body in there.

Voices again. This time, he knew that nothing would stop the door from opening.

He was going to get caught. When he was, and when they'd finished stripping his body of every vital organ, his remains would follow Johnny into the fire.

He made little yelping noises as he sucked in and exhaled air. Sheer terror gripped him and held him fast. He couldn't save himself. He was doomed.

Then, he suddenly knew what to do – where to hide. He hated the thought of it. It caused goose bumps to erupt all over his body, but he knew that he had no choice.

It was a small, cramped space, just large enough to allow him to hunker down. The ash inside was thick and filled his nose as it puffed up around him. It was dark, and it was eerily silent, but, thankfully – inside the small furnace – it was stone cold.

He tried not to think about what would happen to him if someone turned it on. He tried not to think about how much pain there would be, and how long it would take him to die. Mustering the last of his courage, he pulled the door closed behind him.

It was so dark that the air felt heavy and thick. He couldn't see his hand in front of his face, but he could hear perfectly well.

Less than a minute later, he heard the door to the room outside open. Two men were talking. One was very angry and his voice echoed in Kevin's ears – the inside of the furnace amplifying it considerably. He held his breath – didn't dare to breathe lest they heard him. The ash tickled his nose and he was terrified that he would sneeze, so he pinched his nostrils and buried his face in the crook of his elbow.

"Get rid of it," Kevin heard one man say. "And keep the fire going for when we find the other little fucker."

Footsteps, and it seemed that one man left.

Next, the familiar squeaking sound of the wheels on the trolley, then the clank as the lock on the large furnace was pulled.

Kevin didn't need to see anything to know what was happening.

Johnny was being put in the fire.

A small sob escaped him, but it was muffled by his arm. He heard the roar of the flames as it was fed, and then the thunk of the door closing and the clank of the lock being re engaged.

More footsteps, the sound of the door opening and closing, and Kevin let out a long breath, sneezed, and – for the first time in forever – sobbed.

A feeling of claustrophobia overtook him rather suddenly. He felt a desperate need to get out, but he waited on a silent count of one hundred before pushing at the door with his feet.

It didn't budge. He manouvered himself around, so he could feel around the door for a handle, or a lock. The inside of the door was flat and smooth.

He pictured the front of the furnace in his mind's eye. He remembered that the door looked different to the larger one. There was no locking bolt on the one he was in.

*So, how does it lock?*

He actually felt the blood drain all the way to his toes.

It locked automatically when it closed. It could only be opened from the outside.

He dragged in an unsteady breath and wondered just how many breaths he had left.

# 32

Mary recognized him. He was a friend of her daddy's. She'd only ever seen him the once, but she remembered him. She also remembered that her daddy had seemed a little afraid of him. Well, *she* wasn't afraid of him. For a start, he was smiling at her, and telling her that she was going to be all right.

She believed him, right up until the moment he put his hands around her throat and squeezed.

"Mister King?"

The pressure eased on her neck and she sucked in air, coughed and retched. Warm urine soaked the sheet.

King glanced down at the spreading wet stain, wrinkled his nose, and stepped back from the bed. He had an acute aversion to the body's waste products. He didn't mind blood, but couldn't stand piss or shit.

He turned to the source of the voice. "Have you found him?"

"Not yet," the doctor said. "We're on lockdown, so he's bound to be trapped somewhere in the building."

"I hope, for your sake, that he is. Do you have any understanding of how inconvenient this is?" His voice was low, reasonable, terrifying. "Do you understand how fucking angry I am right at this moment?"

The doctor dropped his eyes and nodded. He saw his life flash behind his eyes. He would be lucky to get out alive.

"Where is the bitch?"

He jerked in his shoes. "Outside... in the corridor."

"Well, fetch her in, numbskull."

"Right away, Mister King."

He was gone only a few seconds before returning with a significantly cowed nurse.

"Well, well," King said, sneeringly. "I should've guessed it was the thick Irish bitch's fault." He turned back to Mary, and said, "This is your lucky day, girl. It seems I have someone else to vent my anger on, so you get to breathe a while longer."

Mary wheezed and blinked. She had no idea what was happening, but one thing she was sure of – the man certainly wasn't a friend of her daddy.

Molly continued to scream at the top of her little lungs. Petey had gone quiet. Seeing his sister being choked had knocked the stuffing out of him, and he lay back with wide eyes, silently staring at nothing.

"Shut the brat up," King said to the doctor.

"She's... she's only just come... come around," he stammered. "I daren't..."

The look King gave him turned his blood to ice. He licked his lips and nodded, suddenly not giving a shit if the girl croaked through too much Propofol. It was, after all, no skin off his nose.

Twenty-eight-year old nurse Sarah Connolly knew that her life depended on how easily she could convince King that the boy's escape had nothing to do with her. There were two other nurses on duty and, as far as anyone was concerned, any one of them could've left the restraint accidentally undone. What she didn't know – couldn't know – was that King was more than prepared to blame and kill all three of them, just to be sure that he punished the right one.

She didn't see the punch coming. It floored her. Dazed and bleeding from the nose and mouth, she barely registered the first few kicks to her ribs.

When the pain set in, and when it finally dawned on her that she was about to be beaten and kicked to death, she tried to crawl back out through the door.

She didn't get very far.

Bending at the knees, and lifting himself a foot off the ground, King brought both his feet down onto her head. It made a popping, crunching sound, and splattered like a ripe melon.

He slithered in the blood, but caught himself before he went down.

Well satisfied, he gave her ribs a final kick with the toe of his shoe, rolled his shoulders, and then told the doctor to fetch the other two nurses.

The doctor was just about to administer the injection to the still squalling child. He'd purposefully avoided watching what was nothing more than a brutal execution, but he was now forced to turn his eyes towards King, and towards the body.

"I'll just give the girl…"

"Leave it, and do as I say. Go and fetch the other two. I'm hot to trot and impatient to get this over with."

Little Molly Potter was the luckiest person in the room. She'd been mere moments away from a lethal overdose – saved only by the blood-lust of one man.

"Shush my little Molly-bear," Mary rasped. "Petey, tell Molly to shush."

Petey either wouldn't, or couldn't hear her. He appeared almost catatonic. Nothing around him seemed to move or touch him.

Mary's throat was too painful to continue speaking, and she didn't want to divert the man's attention back to her, so she clamped her mouth shut and tried to block out the sounds of her sister's distress.

What the man had done to the nurse was awful, but not as awful as the memory of what another man had done to her mommy. Every time she closed her eyes, images of the flashing blade, the spurt of blood, and the horrible, awful gash across her mom's throat were vivid reminders that she would never see her again. Molly was crying out for her. She was too little to understand what Mary had witnessed and what it meant. Petey knew. He hadn't seen, but Mary knew that he was well aware of what happened. She wasn't surprized that he had zombied out. She wished that she could do the same.

*Daddy... please come, daddy... please come...*

She closed her eyes, muttering the words beneath her breath. Her daddy loved her. He loved all his children. She had no doubt that he would save them.

# Friar and Tuck

# 33

Considering that Park Slope was considered one of the most desirable places to live in Brooklyn - and, indeed, in New York - it was pretty incomprehensible that it once had one of the highest arrest rates for prostitution in the State. Much of the prostitution had now slithered behind closed doors, but pimps like D'Roy still ran a flourishing trade in flesh.

Tuck steered the car along Union Street. She had no idea where she was heading, and Friar wasn't offering her any direction.

"This is hopeless," she said. "It's like searching for a needle in a haystack."

Friar shook his head. "We'll find him."

She turned and gave him a brief look. "Really? How?"

"I'm thinking on that. Just give me a minute."

"You've already had an hour to think," she grumbled, her eyes back on the road. "At this rate, we're going to run out of gas. Why don't we forget about D'Roy, and head on over to The Bronx... find Kevin's mom?"

"We don't know that she's actually there. No... we need to find her pimp first."

"And then, what?"

"He'll tell us what we need to know."

"You seem awfully sure about that."

He shrugged. "I'll make it worth his while."

"Oh? How are you going to do that?"

"I won't arrest him."

"You *can't* arrest him."

"He won't know that."

Tuck started to shake her head, but then stopped and chewed on her lip.

Friar looked at her, and said, "Just tell me."

"Tell you?"

"What's eating at you."

Tuck said nothing.

"Suit yourself." He thought a moment, then said, "Head over to Seventh and Ninth."

She glanced at him. "What's at Seventh and Ninth?"

"A hang-out for wastrels and crooks."

"You know all the best places."

Her sarcasm wasn't lost on him, nor was her frustration. He knew she was beginning to think that looking for D'Roy was a waste of their precious time.

The car swept past Union Hall and crossed over Jon Cortese Way, after a few moments, Tuck swung a right onto Seventh Avenue. She slowed at the Junction with Ninth Street.

"Take a left and park up," Friar said.

She did as he bid without preamble, but didn't immediately switch off the car's engine.

"We'll walk from here," he said, opening his door and climbing out. "It's not far."

Tuck gave a weary sigh, switched off the engine, and climbed out. On the sidewalk, she followed him as he walked at pace towards goodness knew what.

That stretch on Ninth Street had no bars and no shops. There were buildings on their left, but no sign of anywhere appropriate to house those *wastrels and crooks* who Friar seemed hell-bent on finding.

She made no complaint, simply followed on his heels.

When they came upon the small, thin building – squeezed in between two apartment blocks – Friar abruptly halted mid-stride, and Tuck almost barrelled into his back.

"This is it," he said.

Tuck glanced up at the sign above the door. *The Resting Place.*

"What is this place?"

"I guess you could call it a private club of sorts." He shouldered his way through the door. "Keep your eyes peeled, and your hand close to your weapon."

After a moment's pause, she followed him through the door.

It was gloomy, and it didn't smell nice. The sourness in the air reminded her of a mix of pickled gherkins and stale beer. She wrinkled her nose in distaste, and said, "It stinks in here. Why are you getting into the habit of taking me to smelly places?"

Several hours later, the stench of the hooker's apartment was still in his nose, so he completely understood where she was coming from, and he had to agree – it *did* stink.

Immediately inside the door, there was a small bar area and a scattering of tables and chairs. Friar's eyes immediately latched onto the man seated at the table in the far corner of the room. He was nursing a beer and made no sign of noticing the arrival of the two detectives. The others in the room – two middle-aged men propping up the bar, and a woman who had obviously seen better days – fixed hostile eyes on them and barely blinked. The barman – a corpulent man of indefinable years, with a square jaw and massive ears – gave a wide grin and informed them that it was a members' only club, and then asked them to leave.

Friar ignored him, and strode the length of the room. Tuck bowed her head against the hostile looks and tripped after him.

The man in the corner looked up from his glass. Tuck winced at the sight of the scars deeply etched across his cheeks running jaggedly and diagonally from each corner of his mouth. She knew what those scars represented – punishment for being a rat.

The hand that held the glass seemed malformed and it took her a second or two to realize that he was missing two fingers. The sight of it sent a shudder through her whole body. She had heard tell of the violence meted out to informants, but it was the first time she'd seen the results. She was certainly gaining an education.

"Hello, John," Friar said.

Tuck averted her eyes and concentrated on keeping tabs on the people at her back, content enough to allow Friar to do all the talking, because - after all - she had no clue what they were doing there.

"Hello, Detective Friar," the man returned. "Fancy seeing you here. You *do* know that you're not welcome, don't you?"

Friar shrugged and pulled out a chair. He sat down with relaxed nonchalance, oblivious to the atmosphere growing heavy with menace in the room.

"I'm surprised that they allow you in here, John... not after what you did."

It was John's turn to shrug. "I still have a few friends who vouch for me, but not if they see me talking to you."

"They'll think you're my CI?"

"Something like that, yes." His eyes shifted uneasily. "I'm not doing that anymore. I've got nothing for you."

"I don't want much."

"You lot always say that. It's never true."

"Well, this time, it is."

He made a sound in the back of his throat and shook his head. "You don't believe me?"

"No matter... I've got nothing to tell you." He took a sip of his beer, his deformed hand trembling and causing a spill.

"No need to be so nervous. We can be gone in as little as a minute." He smiled. "Or, we can hang around... have a drink with you."

John dragged in a breath and raised his good hand to run a finger over his wet lips and then across one of the scars. He blinked, and then nodded, resigned to his fate.

"What do you want?"

"The whereabouts of a pimp named D'Roy."

"He in trouble?"

"Probably, but I'm not interested in that. I just want him to tell me about one of his women... Sadie Murphy."

"She the one in trouble?"

"I've no idea, but her boy is."

"Young Kevin?" His spine stiffened. "What's he got himself into?"

"You know him?" Friar couldn't keep the surprise from his voice. He glanced up at Tuck, whose eyes were now wide and fixed.

"I know him... skinny little runt... been on the streets a while." He looked around the room nervously. "Word is gonna get out that you're talking to me. Do you want to see me dead?"

"I don't care - not one way or the other."

"After all I did for you in the past... you'd see me dead?"

Friar shrugged and leaned back in his chair. "Tell me where to find D'Roy, and I'm outta here."

"Try prison. Last I heard, he's doing six to ten." The smirk he gave Friar was grotesque. "Suck on that, detective."

Friar didn't bat an eyelid. The news flummoxed him, but he kept his shit together admirably. "So, who's been running his women?" he asked. "Who owns Sadie Murphy?"

"That would be the cousin."

"You got a name?"

"Maybe."

# FRIAR AND TUCK CASE NUMBER ONE: THE MISSING

"Spit it out, John."

"First... tell me about Kevin. What trouble is he in?"

"What's it to you?" That was Tuck. She had grown tired of being a silent witness to Friar's verbal tennis match with the scummy turd with the awful scars. "Why are you interested in the boy?"

Jon looked up at her, appraised her with puffy, beer-sodden eyes, and said, "I like to know things about everyone, lady. I'm inclined to wonder why *you're* interested in the boy, and his bitch of a mother."

"That's none of your business," she returned.

Friar cleared his throat. The sound shut her up, and she turned away.

"He's missing," Friar said, placing his elbows on the table and leaning forward. "Taken, maybe dead already."

John swallowed. Friar was surprised to see shock on the other man's face. *Shit, the bastard seemed to care. Who would've thought it?*

"I guess you've lost your touch, John. Once upon a time, that wouldn't have been news to you."

"What can I say?" He shrugged and emptied the last of his beer down his throat, smacked his lips, and tapped the glass on the table.

"Get our friend another beer," Friar said to Tuck. "And, a glass of something hard."

Tuck opened her mouth to refuse, thought better off it, and walked huffily to the bar. She tried to make sense of what a glass of something hard meant.

"So," Friar went on, his voice dropping conspiratorially. "What do you know about Kevin Murphy?"

"I know fuck all about him being taken."

"Okay... I'll give you that, but..."

"I fucked his mother once or twice. I always wondered..."

"Jesus, John... do you think you might be the boy's father?"

"Nah." He shook his head. "I fire blanks, but – for a time – I might've wondered."

"You took an interest in him?"

"Not so you'd notice."

"You ever help him out?"

"That wouldn't have done him any favours."

"You didn't think it would be wise to befriend him... maybe have him tarred with the same brush as you?"

"Something like that, though I did point him towards a shelter that didn't turn away kids who were on their own. Most places report street kids to the authorities."

"Oh?"

"Not that one, though. I heard tell that he stayed there quite a bit."

He should've known that. Why, the fuck, hadn't he known that?

"What shelter?"

John's smirk turned into a full-blown grin. "That information will cost you more than a drink."

Friar reached into his pocket and drew out his wallet. He extracted two fifty dollar bills and placed them on the table. John licked his lips and reached for them, but Friar grabbed his wrist and stopped him grabbing them up.

"I want the address of the shelter, *and* I want the name of Sadie's new pimp," he said.

He gave up the information just as Tuck arrived with the drinks.

# 34

They walked back to the car, climbed in, and sat for a moment, neither of them speaking. They were both deep in thought, digesting the information, and individually determining what their next step should be.

After a few minutes of silent contemplation, Friar noticed that Tuck seemed jumpy. She was picking at the skin around her fingernails and drawing blood.

"You okay?" he asked, staring at the mess she was making of herself.

She noticed his stare and self-consciously balled her fists and stuck them under her armpits.

"I'm fine," she said.

"Do you make a habit of that?"

"What?"

"Picking holes in yourself."

"I'm hardly picking holes," she returned, defensively. "Anyway, it's none of your business."

"Okay. Sorry."

She sighed. "I do it when I'm thinking. It helps keep me focussed."

"Isn't it painful? Those fingers look raw."

"Can't say that I've noticed, and – no – it's not painful."

She wondered what he would think if she told him that she very rarely felt pain. That would really confirm her weirdness in his eyes, especially considering it wasn't anything physical that caused it. It wasn't an illness or a condition, merely mind over matter – like those people who could lie on beds of nails, or walk over hot coals.

"Well, I wish you wouldn't do it." He shuddered. "It gives me the creeps... makes my stomach clench."

"I'll bear that in mind, now..." she switched on the ignition. "Here are we off to now?"

"Well, we could carry on searching for Sadie Murphy, via her new pimp, or we could go and check out the homeless shelter. I vote for the homeless shelter."

"It gets my vote."

"I don't think Sadie could've told us anything, anyway," Friar said.

"Probably not."

"It wasn't a complete waste of time, was it?"

She shook her head. "We got a good lead from your friend."

"I wouldn't say that he was my friend, Tuck."

"You gave him money."

"Yes – for the information."

"Half that amount would've been plenty. You felt sorry for him."

"He's had a tough time of it."

"Because he was a CI?"

He nodded. "Turned out the *confidential* bit of CI wasn't so confidential, after all. He got found out. He's lucky he wasn't gutted."

"They would've removed his intestines?" She screwed up her face. "Gross."

"Not that sort of *gutted*, Tuck... although, nothing surprises me with the criminal fraternity... not when it comes to rats and snitches."

"Will he get into trouble for talking to us?"

He shrugged. "Probably."

"Then, why did you put him in that situation? You could've got him killed."

"He's learned to be nimble on his feet. He'll scarper and lie low for a while."

"What did he mean when he said he fired blanks?"

# FRIAR AND TUCK CASE NUMBER ONE: THE MISSING

"You never heard that saying?"

"Only when it pertains to guns, but I don't think he was talking about guns."

He didn't know if she was joshing him. She surely couldn't be that ill-informed.

She saw the question in his eyes. "I don't usually have the chance to explain myself," she said. "No one is ever interested enough to ask the reason why I seem stupid when it comes to some of the things they say."

"I'm interested."

"It's pretty boring, really."

"I don't mind boring. Do you really not know what a man means when he says he fires blanks?"

She shook her head. "It's amazing just how many sayings, metaphors, that sort of thing, I can't immediately associate a meaning to. It's just another one of my weird quirks." She looked at him rather earnestly, silently hoping he understood what she was trying to say. "My brain is a bit strange."

He thought her brain was pretty sharp, actually. So what if she took things far too literally?

She huffed in a breath. It was the first time she'd ever opened up about one of her issues to a work colleague. It made her anxious, but she carried on. "Everyone gets fed up of me slowing conversations down to get an explanation for ... well, like *-what does firing blanks mean?*" She smiled. "I stopped asking, and that made things worse. It's one of the reasons no one will work with me."

"Their loss."

She acknowledged his words with a nod. "Are you going to explain it, then?"

"Sure - it means that his sperm is useless. The millions of little fuckers won't make babies – hence, firing blanks."

"Ah, okay. That's a really succinct way of putting it."

He shifted in his seat and stared out of the window, suddenly uncomfortable. He wasn't sure if, deep down, he was any better than her previous partners. Up until recently, his opinion of her matched theirs, and he was on the verge of dumping her. He'd thought that she was simply too much effort.

He changed the subject. "I know about the shelter," he said. "I've never had a reason to pay it a visit, but it's on the precinct's radar. The guy running it - Marcus somebody – has been pulled in a couple of times on suspicion of one thing or another. Nothing stuck. He's a squirrely little shit, and I'm looking forward to squeezing his balls."

She frowned, shook her head, then smiled.

"You get what I mean?"

She nodded. "You're going to lean on him... hard."

He grinned. "You're learning."

She gunned the engine, and pulled out into the traffic. He gave her directions and they made the journey in silence.

It was late in the afternoon when Tuck stopped the car abruptly and stared blankly ahead.

Blue flashing lights, a line of police vehicles, yellow crime scene tape. Some shit had certainly hit the fan at the shelter. The road was jammed. She couldn't draw the car up any closer than a couple of hundred yards away and, even so, it was difficult to find somewhere safe to pull over.

"What the..?" Friar gave her a wary look. "Looks like we've arrived a little late to the party."

"Do you want to go over and find out what's going on, or shall I do it?"

"I'll go." He opened the door and climbed out.

The young uniformed officer standing guard spoke with a nasal voice and – not knowing who Friar was – put on a superior air and more or less told him to bugger off.

When Friar showed him his shield, he blushed to the roots of his hair and apologized.

"We've got looky-loos and reporters crawling all over the place, sir," he said. "I'm sick of running them off."

"What's gone on?"

"Nasty business. Some psycho was caught raping a young girl. Her daddy walked right in on the action... attacked the perv', and got stabbed for his trouble. The little girl ended up just as dead as her daddy. It's a bloodbath in there."

"You think me and my partner could go take a look? We're following another line of enquiry."

The officer looked abashed. "I'm afraid not, sir. I'm only allowed to let in the ME and CSI. It's pandemonium as it is... what with all the vagrants clogging up the place."

"Who's in charge?"

"Detective Cooper."

Friar frowned. "Sully Cooper?" He didn't get on terribly well with Sully. He was an asshole.

He nodded. "You know him?"

"Sure, I do."

"The medical examiner is on his way," he said to Tuck, once he was back in the car. "Double murder."

She jerked her head. "In there?"

He nodded. "Someone killed a kid and her father."

"That's all you know?"

He shrugged. "What else is there?"

"Don't you think it's one coincidence too many?"

He stared at her. "Shit like that goes down all the time. It's a homeless shelter, Tuck. Homeless shelters tend to have their fair share of nutters. What went on has probably nothing to do with Kevin Murphy."

"I wouldn't want to bet on it."

Neither would he, but he refrained from saying so. Instead, he said, "There's no use hanging around. Our man is off limits to us."

"Uh, uh." She shook her head. "I don't think so."

Unfastening her safety belt, she got out of the car.

"Where are you going?" he called after her.

She looked over her shoulder. "To do what you should have... get us in front of our man."

He watched her march across the road and head straight towards the officer. The officer was soon shaking his head, looking exasperated. Tuck was obviously haranguing him.

He sighed, thinking that he'd better go and rescue the poor schmuck.

He took his time getting out of the car. Having had no sleep the night before, he was exhausted. Every muscle in his body screamed at him for rest, and is eyes were scratchy with fatigue.

He wasn't in the mood for a stand-up fight with some young gun hell bent on following orders. He especially wasn't in the mood to tackle Tuck to the ground to prevent her barging in where she wasn't welcome. But, he had a feeling he was going to have to do both.

Some things you simply didn't do, and one of them was interfere with another detectives case. Tuck ought to know that, but – if he was being honest with himself – he wasn't sure what exactly she understood about unofficial protocol. She could quote the rule book verbatim, but – when it came to the intricacies of police politics – she hadn't much of a clue.

As he wandered over, he hoped that he would be able to talk her out of stepping on Sully's toes. He was one person she didn't want to make an enemy of. He was a mean bastard, and didn't have a high opinion of female detectives. He was just going to love Tuck... *not*. He needed to persuade her to let homicide do their stuff without interference. He doubted he would, thought. She was proving to be just as tenacious as he was – more so, even – and, despite how she worried him, he couldn't help feeling a little bit proud of her.

The officer was young, still green around the gills, but he held his ground. Neither of them were on the approved list, so there was no way they were being allowed past the scene of crime tape stretched across the sidewalk in front of the building.

"Leave it, Tuck," Friar said at her back. "We're not getting in there."

He saw her bristle. Small though she was, that bristle packed a punch. The officer took a step back and looked at Friar anxiously.

"It's more than my job's worth to let you through," he said, apologetically. "I've already told you I've had my orders, and It's just the ME and CSI allowed inside." He beseeched friar with his eyes. "Will you explain that to her, sir?"

"You heard what the officer said, Tuck. Let's get outta here."

Tuck turned and looked at him. Her face was set in a stubborn mask. "Where to, Friar? Back chasing hookers?" She shook her head. "No. We're going in, and we're going to talk to Marcus."

With no hesitation, she bent over and hunkered her way beneath the tape. The young officer moved to put his hands on her, but she slapped them away.

Friar felt immensely sorry for him. Obviously, there was no stopping her, and – obviously – he had no choice but to follow her. She was his partner and, for better or worse, where she went, he went. That's what it meant when you had someone's back.

"Sir? Please don't go in there, sir."

"Just add out names to your list," Friar told the officer. "Detective Friar and Detective Tuck. We have business here, and I'll take full responsibility for any crap that flies your way."

Before the officer could respond, Friar ducked below the tape and was hot on Tuck's heels.

There was a box of latex gloves, and a box of paper bootees on a table just inside the door. Tuck removed a pair of the gloves, snapped them on, and bent to cover her shoes with the bootees. Friar followed suit.

They entered a brightly lit corridor, that opened up into a wide reception area. The noisy melee of dozens of people being herded into a room at the far end took their attention for a few moments. With only two uniforms to take charge of such a large number, it appeared like they were herding cats.

"You'd better have a good reason for being here, Friar."

Friar turned and came face to face with Sully. "We do, Sully... we do."

Sully was a broad, florid looking man with a nest of ginger hair and a permanent sneer. He glanced with some derision at Tuck. "I know you," he said, screwing up his eyes. "Heard about you, too."

Tuck didn't respond, merely stood and stared up at him.

He turned back to Friar. "I suggest you turn the fuck around and high-tail it back out of here. You can't have a good enough reason for poking your nose into my business.""

"Ah, Sully, don't be a jerk. We won't get in your way."

Sully jerked his head at Tuck, who had moved away and was opening a door and peering inside.

"Tell *her* that." He turned to Tuck and hollered for her to *get the fuck away from the Goddamned door.*

Tuck ignored him, and pushed her way inside.

"Go fetch your side-kick, Friar, before I call the lieutenant and have her ass whopped."

"Look, Sully, we just want a work with the guy who runs this place. It's no big deal."

"Well, get in line, detective. There's a bunch of us with questions for that maniac. Now, get that stupid c..." Another breath, a beat, then, "Get, your partner outta here."

Friar put two and two together, and came up with, "He's your suspect?"

"Damned tooting, he is. Got him banged to rights."

"Marcus..?"

"Marcus Salzberg – the fucking animal."

Tuck reappeared from behind the door. "What's up?"

Friar turned a frown on her. "Seems the guy we want to question has got himself into a bit of bother." He turned back to the homicide detective. "What went down here, Sully?"

He sighed, thought it over, then said, "We have two bodies... a young girl – maybe seven or eight years old - and her daddy. Girl was strangled, daddy was stabbed. I'm betting the girl was raped before she was strangled, but the ME will have to verify that. If I was a guessing man, I'd say that the father walked in on his little girl being mauled over by the sick fuck who manages this place, and was stabbed to death when he tried to intervene. Again, if I was a guessing man, I'd reckon that there's more than forty stab wounds."

There was a long heavy pause as each of them mulled that over. No one had the words to fill the morbid silence.

Finally, Tuck said, "We'd still like to talk to him. Can you make that happen?"

Sully shook his head and flapped a hand in Friar's face. "Isn't gonna happen."

"It's a big ask," Friar said. "I know that, but it's important. I'll owe you big time, buddy."

"What can that little shit tell you that's so damned important?"

"Not sure, Sully – hence the need to question him."

"I dunno. He's pretty fucked-up. I can't even question him myself until I get a medical opinion on him."

"Our questions aren't related to your crime. The DA doesn't need to know."

"Have you hauled him away yet?" Tuck asked.

"What?" Sully threw his head around to look at her. "No. He's being bagged as we speak."

Tuck screwed up her eyes. "Bagged?"

"Baggies tied around his hands and feet... preserving any evidence. He's covered in blood – head to fucking toe - but I don't want him stripped here, so he's been wrapped up in a paper coverall."

"So, can we have five minutes with him?" Friar persisted.

"No, Friar, you fucking can't. Jesus... haven't I just explained what's gone down here?"

Friar gave him a long look, then said, "It's about those missing kids, Sully. Come on – give me a break."

"Well, I'm sorry for your trouble, and that of your missing kids, but the DA would have my balls on a string around her neck if I allowed you anywhere near him. Even if I said nought about it – she'd know. She knows fucking everything that goes on."

"I'll take the blame. Anyway, she likes me... she'll turn a blind eye."

Sully wavered. He licked his lips and was obviously thinking about it.

Just then, the ME arrived, bustling and shoving his way along the corridor. Tuck didn't recognize him, but both Friar and Sully nodded at him in acknowledgement.

"Thought you were off homicide?" he said to Friar.

"I am. I'm here on a different matter."

"Well out of my way." He elbowed passed them, then, to Sully – "Show the dog where the rabbits are."

Before Sully led the Medical Examiner away, he gave Friar a curt nod.

Tuck said, "What was that about rabbits?"

"Nothing. Just a turn of phrase." He turned full circle. "Let's see if we can find the perp."

# 35

They found him seated in a chair, bent double with his head on his knees. He was in a small, windowless room and guarded by two uniformed cops. He was handcuffed, the baggies underneath the cuffs bright red on the insides.

They gained entry to the room without any trouble. Friar's gold shield could actually get him through most doors without argument.

They both stood in the doorway and stared at the bent figure. He appeared slim – although the exact shape and size of his body was lost in the baggy coverall. There was no way to determine the colour of his hair. It was caked in blood. He had expensive sneakers on his feet, and Friar was surprised to note that he'd been allowed to keep them. If he'd been in charge, they would already have been bagged and tagged.

As they approached, the man didn't move, or otherwise acknowledge their presence. He was humming quietly to himself, which – under the circumstances – was an odd thing for him to be doing.

Friar cleared his throat, but the man didn't look up, or cease with the tuneless hum.

"Marcus," Friar said. "I have a few questions for you."

The humming stopped abruptly, but his head remained on his knees.

"Marcus?"

"Huh? What you say?" His voice sounded slurred. His eyes, when he lifted his head and peered up at Friar, looked loaded. "Who're you?"

"Detective Friar. This is Detective Tuck."

"Friar Tuck?" He grinned. His teeth were bloody, his lip was cut wide open, and his nose looked as if it was broken.

Someone had sure done a number on him, Friar thought.

He rolled his eyes. "Yeah, we've heard it before. Don't go all Robin Hood on me, Marcus."

Marcus sniggered and dropped his head once more, his shoulders shaking.

"Will you look at me when I'm talking to you, Marcus?"

"Sure." It came out sounding like *shoor*. He dragged his head back up. His face twitched.

"We want to talk to you about Kevin Murphy."

"Who?"

"Thirteen-year-old boy... one of your regulars."

"Don't know him."

"I think you do, Marcus. Don't you try lying to me. Your lies won't wash."

He groaned and squeezed his eyes tight shut. "I need a doctor. I don't feel so good."

Tuck looked to Friar. *Fat chance*, they both thought.

'Maybe, later," Friar lied, hunkering down so he could look the man square in the face. "You answer my questions, and I'll get you some medical attention."

"I don't know any Kevin. Leave me alone. Fetch me a doctor."

"You must hurt really bad," Friar said. "What are you climbing down from... Brown? Coke? Were you all coked up when you raped that little girl, Marcus?"

"Fuck off."

"I'll bet you're in need of something to level you out?"

His head jerked.

"Just tell me about Kevin, and I'll help you out."

"Kevin?" He shook his head and winced. "I've got nothing to say about him."

"So, you know Kevin?" Tuck asked.

"Out of bounds. Wasn't to touch the little prick."

Friar filed that piece of information away, then asked, "You know that he's missing?"

"Missing?" He grinned. "Don't think so."

"Someone took him off the street."

Marcus' expression turned suspicious. "You're not pinning that on me. I didn't grab the little shit."

"So, who did?"

They both witnessed the sudden shuttering of Marcus' eyes. It was as if a curtain had been drawn across them, and his expression was now one of stubborn obstruction.

His lips peeled back. His grin was now macabre. He winced again and raised a bagged hand to his torn lip.

"Nasty cut," Tuck said. "Did the girl bite your lip as you were raping her?"

"Fuck off, bitch. You don't know anything about squat."

Friar warned her with a look. Thankfully, she backed off.

Friar took a moment to study the man in front of him. He didn't look like a crazy son-of-a-bitch. Beneath the blood and the cuts and bruises, he looked pretty normal.

He thought that it's always the normal looking ones you have to watch out for. Bat-shit crazy is easily avoided, but the calm and lucid psychos are the most dangerous fuckers of all – especially when they were paedophiles into the bargain. And Marcus was certainly a perv'. He thought over what he'd said about Kevin being out of bounds.

"Who was protecting him?' he asked. "Who made sure that no one touched him?"

"Don't know."

"Come on, Marcus – smart guy like you? You know everything that goes on around here."

He perked up at that. He was nothing if not a narcissist. Any praise tasted like nectar.

'I might've heard a few things."

"What things?"

He shrugged. "This and that."

"Can you be more specific?" That question from Tuck.

"I'm not talking to you, bitch. I'm sick of being bossed around by bitches. That Natalie cunt for a start." He snorted and a plug of bloody snot landed on his knee. "She's not bossing me around anymore, that's for sure."

Both Friar and Tuck hitched in a breath, each holding them, and then letting them out slowly.

The motherload had just been struck.

Tuck nodded to Friar. She was letting him know that she wasn't going to risk another question. Alienating Marcus was now the last thing either of them wanted.

"Yeah, that Natalie sure was bossy," Friar said, sympathetically. "I'd heard that about her."

Marcus nodded. "Got what she deserved."

"Did she know Kevin?"

"Know him? I think she loved him... it's what got her sliced."

"Who did the slicing?" He held his breath for a count of five, then asked again, "Who did the slicing, Marcus? Was it you?" He didn't think so, but he had to ask.

"Nah, man... wasn't me. Wish it was, though. I'd 'a' loved that." He suddenly seemed to realize that he was allowing his mouth to flap a little too much. He said, "Where's that doctor. I need something for the pain."

Friar couldn't lose him now. He racked his brain for his next play.

"You need something strong, Marcus? How about some morphine?"

His eyes glittered. He prodded his damaged lip with his tongue. He nodded.

"First – a few more answers, okay?"

The shutters came down again. It was obvious that Marcus didn't want the morphine badly enough to fall foul of whoever made the hit on Natalie. It seemed that he knew when it was time to clamp his mouth shut.

His eyes shifted. It was subtle, but Friar noticed. He said, "Don't go all quiet on me, Marcus. Life's going to be bad enough without me making it a thousand times worse. I've got friends who work on Rikers Island. They just love little-girl- raping bastards like you."

Marcus tried to scratch his crotch. The handcuffs and the baggies prevented any satisfactory relief from whatever itch plagued him. He squirmed in his seat. His head swung low.

"You ever been inside Rikers, Marcus? You ever shared a cell with some other little girl's daddy – some murdering son-of-a-bitch that misses his little girl, and over the moon at having someone like you to pound on? Or, how about sharing a cell with someone with a two foot long prick whose just itching to use it to impale? Ever shared a cell with someone like that?"

Shockingly, Marcus laughed. "I'm going to no *Rikers fucking Island*. I'm a protected man."

"Is that right?"

"Sure is, dickhead."

"Tell me about Natalie and Kevin."

"Go screw yourself."

"Do yourself a favour."

"I've got friends in high places. They'll do *me* the favour."

"Tell me why you think that she loved him."

Marcus ignored the question. "My special friend… he's got judges in his pockets." He shook his head. "No, man – I'm not going to no *Rikers*."

Friar let out a slow breath. He stood and stretched his spine. "Thirty-five to life... that's my guess. You'll probably survive a month or so, but not much longer."

"A week, tops," Tuck put in. "Especially if we get the word out."

Marcus let out another laugh.

"What's so funny?" she asked, genuinely puzzled.

Marcus stared up at her. "You are bitch. You're what's funny. Haven't you been listening? I've got myself a real good friend. He knows people. I'm not doing any time for killing some little girl and her daddy."

"That friend got a name?"

He swung his eyes back to Friar. His gaze was stony. "None that I'm sharing with you."

Friar's brow furrowed. His voice hardened. "Don't piss around. I'm going to give you one last chance to co-operate, and then I'm out of here. When your friend doesn't come through for you – and he won't, I guarantee it – then it will be too late for any help I might've been able to give your sorry ass."

"Go fuck yourself, detective." His face contorted with contempt. "I don't need your help."

"Suit yourself."

He turned to leave. Tuck grabbed his arm, a look of confusion on her face. She couldn't believe he was giving up without more of a fight.

Just then, Sully poked his head around the door. "Times up," he said. "We're ready to ship him out."

Friar shrugged at Tuck and walked passed Sully and back out into the reception area where he knuckled his tired, scratchy eyes and sighed.

Tuck walked to his side.

"I've had it," he said to her. "I've got to get some sleep."

He did look like shit. "Sure," she said. "I'll drop you home."

# 36

"I'm so fucking exhausted. I could sleep for a week."

"You do look beat."

The clock on the dashboard said it was only twenty hundred hours. Eight pm. Although, it had been an exceptionally long day, Tuck wasn't in the least tired. She'd slept well the night before.

Friar lived in an apartment in Gravesend. She dropped him at the kerb with the arrangement that she'd drive his car back to the precinct, pick up her own, and call by in the morning to collect him

"Before he got out of the car, she asked, "Do you think we'll have a chance to speak to Potter again?"

"Potter will have walked by now."

She twisted around in her seat. "What do you mean... *walked*?"

"Henderson will have released him."

"Bullshit. No fucking way."

"What could he hold him on?"

"Plenty. The man's a crook."

"But, not the murderer Henderson is after."

"No, but..."

"That's all that matters to Henderson. Now – if you don't mind – I'm outta here."

He turned and waved at the bottom of the step, then entered the apartment building.

She didn't immediately drive off. She sat and tried to square everything away in her head. Natalie definitely knew Kevin and she also knew Marcus, which meant she probably frequented the homeless shelter. Why would she have done that? The homeless shelter wasn't exactly in her neighbourhood, and she'd have no reason to visit the place. Why befriend a street kid and – as Marcus put it – love him; and why hang around the likes of Marcus, bossing him about?

None of it made any sense – not without a bona fide reason.

Then, there was the abduction, right under Natalie and Potter's nose – the abduction of a child that Natalie seemed to have maternal feelings for.

*Curiouser and curiouser.*

Her phone rang. She fished it out of her pocket.

*Simms.*

"Hi, there, Tuck," he said. "I got some of that tea you like."

She rolled her eyes. "You shouldn't have."

"I wondered if you were free to pop around for a cup?"

"Not really."

"I'll make it worth your while."

She flushed. "Now, wait a minute..."

"No, no... sorry – I wasn't coming onto you."

She flushed deeper, more embarrassed for believing that was exactly what he was doing.

"I have something to give you," he said. "I think it might be important."

"What is it?"

"A key."

"Whose key? What's it for?"

"How about that cup of tea?" he wheedled.

She sighed. "Okay. I'm on my way."

"I'll put the kettle on"

Traffic was light, and she was in Simms' office, examining the key, and drinking camomile tea within thirty minutes of leaving Friar.

"Where did you find it?" she asked.

"I can't take the credit for that," he replied. "That was one of the forensic computer techs. Believe it, or not, it was hidden in that little drawer where you insert a compact disk... on the side of Natalie Bridgman's laptop."

She could see that it was small enough and thin enough to fit.

"How did you end up with it?"

"His wife is just about to pop out a baby, and he needed to dash off to the hospital. The key needed to get to Henderson as soon as, so he popped it in an evidence bag, and we did the chain of evidence stuff, and – here it is."

"It looks like a key to a safety deposit box."

"My thinking exactly."

"You should've given it to Henderson."

"You can give it to him. I'll sign it over to you, and you can sign it over to him. I just thought you might want to see if you could track down the bank and the box before relinquishing it."

"It's too late to do anything about it tonight." Her mind began to tick over. She could probably find out the name of the bank. The identifiable reference number on the key would tell her that much.

"Can I use your computer?" she asked, already pushing him out of the way and sitting behind his desk.

"Go right ahead," he said with a wry smile.

"Any more tea in the pot?"

He nodded, took her cup, and refilled it.

"Must be an important key to hide it as well as she did," he said.

'It's not the key that's the most important thing, it's what it unlocks. She wanted to tell me something, Simms. I'm hoping her safety deposit box tells me what that was."

"I hope so too. You deserve a break. You going to ring Friar?"

She shook her head, concentrating on scrolling down the computer screen. "He's exhausted. Probably asleep by now." She grinned. "Got it."

"Got what?"

They both swung their heads around in surprise.

Detective Henderson stood in the doorway. "Got what, Tuck?"

Without batting an eyelid, she said, "Just the answer to a question."

He stepped in, nodded to Simms, and took a seat.

"What brings you here at this late hour, Robert?"

"I was told you had something for me," he replied to Simms, then, to Tuck, "What question was that... the one you just got the answer to?"

She shrugged. "Nothing important."

"Okay. I guess it's none of my business."

Tuck waited. Henderson shifted in his chair, stretching his legs out and making himself comfortable.

"Is it none of my business?" He cleared his throat. "Only, I see that you have my key on the desk next to the computer. Was the question something to do with my key?"

"Your key?" Tuck hiked a brow. "It's evidence, isn't it?"

"Sure, but it's *my* evidence, therefore it's *my* key. I'm just wondering what the fuck you're doing with it."

"I have every right..."

He held up a hand. "I'm going to stop you right there, detective. I'm going to stop you dishing out your usual rude and pompous verbal diarrhea. I'm going to save you the embarrassment of having to apologize to me, in front of the lieutenant, for mouthing off a crap load of bullshit."

He leaned forward, bending his legs and placing his elbows on his knees. "You, see, Tuck you've overstepped the line... *again*. You're messing with my investigation. You're supposed to be looking for missing kids, not stealing my evidence."

"She didn't steal it, Henderson. I gave..."

"Shut up, Simms," he retorted mildly. "You're in enough trouble of your own without taking some of hers on board as well."

"It's not as if she wasn't going to hand it over to you," Simms said, not shutting up.

"After she had a peek at what's inside the safety deposit box?"

"How do you know that's what the key is for?"

"Well, Tuck, I guess it's because *I'm... a... fucking... detective*!"

She gave a slow blink. "I found the bank," she said. "We could go look together in the morning."

"I don't think so."

"Why not?"

"Because I'm in charge. Because I don't like you. Because it's none of your fucking business."

"Don't you give a shit that there's four kids missing?"

He shrugged. "You and Friar care. That's more than enough caring to go around. Now, hand the key over."

She thought about snatching it up and telling him to go fuck himself. She thought about telling him that, maybe, *she* would permit *him* to join *her* at the bank.

He had a half smile on his face. It was obvious that he was waiting on her to *really* overstep the line – overstep it so far so as to step right out of her job.

She picked up the evidence bag and lobbed it at him. He caught it in mid-air.

"Thank you," he said, standing and smiling. "You two have a good evening."

He left without a backward glance.

Once the door was closed behind the detective, Simms tried to inject a bit of levity into his voice, saying, "That's one less job for you to worry about."

The look she gave him was scorching. He flushed under its heat. He wished he could get a proper handle on her, then he'd know what *not* to say. She was hard work, that was for sure, but he wasn't going to be put off.

"More tea?" he asked.

# 37

Friar spent the whole morning trying to get a hold of Henderson. His phone went constantly to voicemail, and no one seemed to know where he was.

As soon as Tuck told him of the previous evening's shenanigans with the detective, and the story of the key, he'd ordered her to head straight for downtown and the bank she'd worked out was the one that provided the safety deposit box.

They had arrived twenty minutes after opening time, and Henderson had already been and gone, and – *no* – none of the bank staff could tell them a damned thing about what the detective might, or might not, have discovered.

For the umpteenth time, Friar berated Tuck for not calling him as soon as Simms had produced the key, and – for the umpteenth time – she told him to shut the fuck up about it, saying, *what's done is done, get fucking over it*.

Two other black clouds were on the horizon – Potter had been released, and had subsequently disappeared off the face of the earth, and Marcus Salzberg was awaiting a psych' evaluation and no one was allowed anywhere near him.

"We need three things," Friar said, sipping his fifth cup of coffee that morning. "We need to find Potter, we need to grill Marcus, and we need to find out what was in that box."

"Agreed."

"Any suggestions about where we start?"

"Well..." She thought a moment. "If Henderson found anything, he's obligated to book it into evidence, and forensics would need to go over it."

He shook his head. "I've already spoken to Charlie in evidence lock-up... nothing has been handed in."

"Yet."

"*Yet*... yes. He should've brought it to Charlie hours ago, but he might be following up on some leads, and simply hasn't got around to it."

"You're giving him the benefit of the doubt?"

"What doubt, Tuck? You think he's run off with it?" He gave a mirthless laugh. "That's pretty fucked-up thinking, even for you. Henderson might be a dick, but he's not bent."

"What if there were diamonds, or wads of money? You think he wouldn't be tempted to skip town?"

"You're being ridiculous." He shook his head. "Henderson is so rigidly straight that he'd snap if the wind blew on him."

"Then, why is his phone off?"

He shrugged. "A million reasons."

"A million?"

"You know what I mean. There could be dozens of reasons."

"Somebody should know where he is."

"You're right about that," he conceded. "He shouldn't have gone off the grid."

"Rules."

He nodded. "And, protocols."

"Are we going to look for him?"

"No," Friar replied. "I'd rather look for Potter. If Henderson shows his face at the lock-up with anything from that box, Charlie has promised to ring me."

"If we find Potter, what's the plan?"

"Fucked if I know. I just want to talk to him some more... find out what the score was with Natalie and the kid. He might know something about her interest in the homeless shelter."

"Where do we start looking?"

"I have an idea about that."

That *idea* turned out to be Potter's house. Friar believed that Potter would think it was the last place anyone would think of looking for him.

"Do you think he's hiding from whoever took his kids?" Tuck asked, as they turned into Potter's street.

"If he has any sense." He pointed to an empty space by the kerb. "Pull in over there. I want us to sit a while... get the lay of the land."

"We're not on the prairie, Friar. What's to see?"

"Comings and goings, the twitch of a curtain... anything and everything."

The front wheel bounced over the kerb, then dropped to settle on the road. She reversed to straighten the car, then turned off the engine.

At that very moment, Kevin Murphy was climbing inside a small furnace to hide, and Potter's children were just as much in fear of their lives as he was. Neither Friar nor Tuck – or, for that matter, Potter – were aware of that. All three realized that time wasn't on their side, but none of them understood just how critical its passing had become.

"It's pretty quiet around here," Tuck said. "Not much traffic."

"A nice place to live."

"Or, die."

"No place is a nice place to die, Tuck."

She didn't agree with that. She'd much rather die in a nice house, on a quiet street, than in some dank and foul-smelling alleyway, or in the middle of the ocean having been thrown overboard with a weight tied to her feet. She refrained from sharing that with him. She didn't think he'd understand.

"Why don't we simply go on up and knock on the door?"

He turned to look at her. "Are you serious? He'd bolt."

"Maybe not."

"Get real, Tuck. He'd be off like a shot."

"Maybe not," she said again. "He's had time to think. Perhaps he's ready to talk?"

"To us? He hates our guts."

"But, at least he knows we're prepared to help him."

"I'm not prepared to lift a finger to help that piece of shit."

"But, he *thinks* you are. Face it, Friar... we're all he's got."

He wasn't convinced. "Let's just sit and observe the house for a while. I'll think on what you said."

She began to absently pluck at her eyebrows, removing hairs and flicking them onto the floor of the car.

"Jesus, Tuck – stop doing that."

"Doing what?" She looked at him, surprised, not understanding what he was on about.

"Never mind, but keep your hands away from your eyes. You'll be ripping out your eyelashes next."

She flushed, suddenly realizing what she'd been doing. "Sorry," she said, folding her hands in her lap. "I'm bored."

"Haven't you done many stake-outs?"

She shook her head. "None."

"None?" His expression turned incredulous. "Are you *actually* a real detective?"

'Ha! Ha! Very amusing."

"Seriously, Tuck – you've never been on a stake-out?"

"*Seriously*, Friar – can you see anyone volunteering to have me join them in *their* stake-out?"

He grimaced. "Maybe not."

"I put myself forward for one or two... put my name on the roster, but..."

"Your name was skipped over?"

"Every time."

"Just as well, because that eyebrow plucking thing would've grossed your partner out."

"I said I was sorry."

He saw a movement in the corner of his eye and swung his head around.

"It's just the mailman," Tuck said. "He's not going near Potter's house."

"I guess the crime scene tape warned him off."

"The seal on the door seems intact."

"If he's in there, he probably got in through a window."

"I still think we should knock on the door."

"And, I still think we should wait."

So, they waited. It was Tuck's mutilation of her fingers that finally spurred him to get out of the car. He found that he couldn't sit there and watch her pick, pick, pick without saying something that would really upset her.

"You wait by the front door, and I'll go around back," Friar said." I'll have to climb over the fence as there's no gate. I'll check the seal on the back door, and take a peek through the windows. If he makes a break for it... scream. Try not to shoot him."

There was no point in a snarky reply. It would be water off a duck's back. She accepted his orders, and his sarcasm, far more stoically than she would've a mere few days before. She was losing some of her hyper-sensitivity – well, where Friar was concerned anyway – and she felt all the calmer for it.

It was beginning to rain. It was only spitting, but the sky suggested that it was ready to burst its clouds and dump a load at any moment.

"Hurry," she said. "I don't want to get soaked."

"You were the one that wanted to leave the car, so no complaints, all right?"

She pulled up the collar of her jacket, and nodded. He moved away, went a little way around the side of the house, and she heard him scramble over the fence.

She walked over to the large bay window to the left of the door, cupped her hands, and peered in. There was no movement behind the glass, and no shadows suggesting anyone was in the room. She scanned as much as she was able and, satisfied, she stepped back and craned her neck to look at the upstairs windows. Rain batted against her eyes. There were two windows, both closed. There were no twitches at any of the curtains.

Splatters of rain managed to get inside the collar of her jacket and she shivered. She moved to stand under the narrow overhang above the door and nearly jumped out of her skin when it was pulled open behind her.

"Back door was kicked in," Friar said, by means of explanation. "Not sure if that was Potter's handiwork, or someone else's." He stepped back. "Best come in out of the rain."

She was taken aback by the evidence of chronic hoarding. Friar wasn't surprised because he'd been in the house before.

"Quite a sight, huh?"

"How could they live like this... and, the children?" She wormed her way through the narrow tunnel between the ceiling-high piles of paper and junk. "It's so claustrophobic."

He sneezed. "And, dusty."

"Plenty of places to hide. It's a large house, and if every room is like this..."

"They pretty much are, except for the small sitting room at the front. In there, apart from a few toys, it's pretty clear."

She peered into the gloom ahead.

"Kitchen is up that way," he said. "I didn't see Potter skulking when I passed through." He closed the front door, throwing the hallway into a dark grey miasma.

# FRIAR AND TUCK CASE NUMBER ONE: THE MISSING

Tuck blinked and, when her eyes grew accustomed to the dim light, she carried on forward. She reached the bottom of the stairs and glanced up.

"Potter! You here, Potter?"

Friar jerked back. "Fuck's sake, Tuck. Next time, warn me if you're about to holler."

She smirked. He scowled. They both listened.

A small thud, barely loud enough to be noticed, pricked Friar's ears.

"Did you hear that?"

She nodded and they both turned their eyes to the ceiling.

"Someone is upstairs."

"That's what it sounds like," Friar said. He drew his gun. "I'll go first. You follow."

Newspapers were piled up each side of the stairs, rising two foot from every tread. It was impossible to get a clear view of the top, so they hunched over and crept up carefully and silently.

Five doors fed off the top landing. Clutter and mounds of dirty, musty clothes were a hazard to their feet, causing them to stumble and trip. They couldn't help but make noise.

It was brighter at the top of the stairs. A large skylight was directly above their heads and, although the sky outside was heavy and grey, enough light shone through to illuminate their way.

"This is a pigsty," Tuck rasped. "Why are you always bring me to filthy places like this?"

"I know how to show a girl a good time," he rasped back, smiling in spite of the smell.

"It smells like shit."

He nodded.

"No, Friar – it smells like *actual* shit."

He had to agree. The stink was unmistakably human excrement.

Another thud, coming from the door farthest to the right.

They were both immediately silent, each tilting their heads and cocking their ears

Friar nodded, and gestured towards the door. Tuck moved to his side, taking up an alert stance, her own gun drawn and held out in front of her.

Friar held up three fingers, counted down, then used the toe of his boot to push the door open. It swung inwards and bumped against something directly behind it.

"Police," he called out. "We're armed, and we're coming in."

Another thud, but no responding voice.

"Is that you, Potter? It's Detectives Friar and Tuck."

A pain-laden groan from within.

Friar shouldered past the door and went through, gun ready and every one of his senses on high alert. Tuck was quick on his heels.

It was a moment that neither of them believed they would ever forget. Nothing could've prepared them for what assaulted their eyes.

"Dear Lord," Tuck said.

"I second that," Friar replied, before holstering his gun and hurrying the length of the room to hunker down as close to the man on the floor as he dared.

# 38

His eyes were closed. His chest stuttered and wheezed. Blood bubbled pink on his lips, and there was gore everywhere, but it was what lay on his lap that had both Friar and Tuck heaving and covering their mouth with their hand.

An arm moved and a hand – surprisingly strong, considering the state he was in - thumped down on the bare floorboard. It was the sound they'd heard downstairs, and then again on the landing.

Irrationally, Friar felt sorry for Potter. He shouldn't, but he did. No man should die with their guts sitting on their lap like fat sausages waiting for the frying-pan.

He wrinkled his nose. The stench was overwhelmingly disgusting. It was like standing in an open sewer. It was acrid and eye-watering.

He didn't know what to do. Should he try and ram the man's guts back into his belly? Evisceration wasn't something he'd been taught how to deal with when he'd learned emergency first-aid. He couldn't recall a time when he'd felt so overwhelmed with helplessness.

He saw that there were two wounds – a long, cruel one from sternum to belly, and a horizontal slash above his pubis that spilled over with the eel-like coils of the intestines.

He closed his eyes against the sight, dragged in a breath, and steadied himself.

He leaned in. "Potter? Can you hear me, Potter?" How could the man still be alive? "It's detective Friar. Can you open your eyes?"

He turned to Tuck. "Call for..." He saw she was already on her phone. It was a waste of time, of course. Potter would be dead before the EMT's arrived. Friar thought that he was no more than a few seconds away from expiring.

The assailant could still be in the house, but he had no time to worry about that. He had to try and get Potter to talk. It was the only chance he had of finding the children, but getting anything out of the barely conscious Potter would be a miracle.

"Mister Potter... can you hear me, Mister Potter?" He leaned in further, the smell choking him and bringing bile to the back of his throat.

Potter opened his eyes a tiny slit. He moaned softly. Froth splashed from his mouth and his head lolled to the side.

"Your children, Potter... where are your children?" There was more than desperation in Friar's voice, there was also a note of hysteria.

*How many more fucking bodies?* He didn't want the next ones he'd stumble over to be that man's kids.

Tuck was at his back, bending over. "Ambulance is on its way," she said.

Friar swallowed and acknowledged her words with a curt nod.

Potter gave a tiny shake of his head. The effort almost finished him off and his eyes dropped closed once more. Friar shook him roughly by the shoulder, and Potter's intestines slithered to the floor.

"Jesus." Friar scrabbled backwards, avoiding having the vile things touch him. He hated autopsies, and that shit was one of the reasons why he never witnessed them.

"He's trying to say something." Tuck said, ignoring the gory entrails and kneeling down in the blood and goo. She dipped her head and pressed her ear as close to Potter's lips as she could.

"Sheepshead," she said. "I think he's trying to say Sheepshead."

"Anything else?"

She shook her head and pulled herself to her feet. "He's gone."

The finality of her statement caused Friar to turn and leave the room. He couldn't bear to be in it a moment longer. On the landing, he bent over, his head hanging almost to the floor, and dry-heaved.

"I'll clear the rest of the house," Tuck said. "Make sure no one else is here."

He shouldn't have allowed her to do the search alone, but he couldn't force himself to move and follow her.

"Be careful," he ground out.

He heard her move away. He concentrated his efforts on pulling himself together. He knew that, later, he'd be terribly embarrassed about his reaction to finding Potter, and his subsequent squeamish behaviour. Tuck had handled it much better, and that was the most embarrassing thing of all.

Minutes later, the EMT's rushed up the stairs. Friar told them not to bother. There was no point in messing up the crime scene any more than it already had been.

Tuck had determined that the assailant was long gone. There was no one else in the house.

"The ME is on his way," she said. "Why don't we go outside and wait for him... get some fresh air?"

It was a very welcome suggestion, and Friar almost tripped down the stairs in his haste to get out.

Tuck was looking at him funny. He was mortified.

"Sorry about that," he said.

"Sorry about what?"

"You know." He jerked his head back towards the house. "In there... my total wimp-out."

She shrugged. "It would take a strong stomach to cope with that."

"*You* coped, Tuck."

She had, but she wasn't proud of how little the scene had affected her. She would've much preferred to be spewing vomit everywhere and hyperventilating. That was how any normal person – a person as normal as Friar – would've reacted.

She didn't reply, instead, she asked, "What did he mean about Sheepshead?"

"It's a place – I know that much."

She nodded. "Sheepshead Bay. Do you think that's where the kids are?"

"Why else would he say it? He used his dying breath to say it. It must mean that."

"We have to save them, Friar."

"I know."

"It's not much to go on."

"I know that, too, Tuck. I'm not stupid."

She flushed. "I know... I'm sorry... I..."

He held up a hand. "No, *I'm* sorry. I'm being a jerk."

They stood in silence for a long moment, then Tuck said, "Someone is cleaning up pretty good – leaving no one who can shed a light on what's going on."

"This is a lot more than one kid being snatched off the street."

"We need to know why he was taken."

"We need to know what was in that safety deposit box."

She nodded. "Some reference to Sheepshead Bay, for instance?"

"That's what I'm hoping."

"We need to track down Henderson."

"I'll do that. You stay here and wait for the ME."

She didn't like that idea. "I think we should stick together," she said.

He was already walking away. "We'll meet up later."

In the car, Friar was disturbed enough by his feelings that he couldn't stop shaking. Most of it was self-disgust, but some of it was anger at the whole situation. They'd been going around in circles, stumbling across one body after another, and still no closer to finding

# FRIAR AND TUCK CASE NUMBER ONE: THE MISSING

Kevin Murphy. He more than suspected that an organized hand was orchestrating something quite terrible. It was much more than about a single kid. The Potter children notwithstanding, as they were mere innocent by-standers, it smacked of a substantial paedophile ring – one that had gone a step further than the usual hand-arounds and on-line debauchery. But, no one they'd spoken to supported that view. Word on the street was that it definitely wasn't anything to do with that sort of sick perversion.

No, it smelled like a completely different perversion altogether.

Natalie Bridgman continued to be the key to it all. He had to find out what she'd known. He wasn't about to get the Ouija board out, so that left Henderson, and – at a pinch – Marcus Salzberg.

He rang Charlie at the evidence lock-up. Still no sign of Henderson, or any evidence from the safety deposit box.

*What was the asshole playing at?*

He headed for the precinct. It was time to find out.

# King
# 39

THE DEMONIC POTENTIAL of a man like King wasn't lost on any of his subordinates. To most of them, he was the devil. They had sold their souls to him, but the money he paid them wasn't what kept them loyal, or kept them in line – it was fear. Even the biggest and ugliest of his henchmen trembled whenever he looked at them a certain way, or when he showed any sign of being pissed-off with them. He had the power of life and death over every one of them, and that fact ensured that his orders were followed without question.

King didn't give a rat's arse who he had killed. Loyalty was a one way street with him. He demanded it, but never returned it. Natalie and Potter found that out to their cost, and there wasn't a man currently in his employ who failed to realize that they were teetering on the very edge of a deep precipice.

King was fuming.

Kevin Murphy was still missing.

No one could find him, and the situation was quickly becoming untenable.

Heads were about to roll. Everyone knew it.

The nurse responsible for the kid escaping was dead. Under normal circumstances that would've been sufficient to assuage King's anger. but not this time, and everyone was looking around for another scapegoat.

The doctor was repeatedly licking his lips and jerking as if he was being assaulted with a cattle-prod. King's eyes were fixed on him. His stare turned the doctor's insides to molten lava.

"Explain to me again how you fucked-up," King said, his voice terrifyingly steady. "Not only did you manage to kill off a perfect set of kidneys in that Johnny boy, but you lost me a lovely pair of eyes, and every single organ in the Murphy kid's body." He cracked his oversized knuckles. They were still bloody from beating the nurse to death. "Do you realize how much money you've lost me... never mind the aggravation I'm going to have to suffer from the clients?"

The doctor was transfixed by King's eyes. He felt as if he was being pulled into them. He couldn't concentrate on what was being said to him, but felt it was important, so he tried to urge his consciousness to focus on the words.

They slithered over his mind. None of them made purchase. He hadn't a clue what King had just said, and, if he expected a reply to a question, then he was fucked.

King watched the doctor's face go slack. He lifted a hand and rapped his knuckles on his head.

"Anyone in there? Anyone at home? Jesus, doc, where the fuck have you gone?"

Someone sniggered at King's back. He swung around, and pierced the offender with a death-ray look. It was enough to have the man drop his head, chastised.

They were still in the room with the kids. The nurse's bloody corpse had been removed, but the floor still held the evidence of her brutal slaying. Everyone avoided looking at the blood. It was too much of a reminder of how close they all were to adding their own life's-blood to that huge puddle. King walked right through it - not caring that his immaculate Italian leather shoes were getting soiled – and did a round of the beds.

Four kids – three of them awake and at different levels of distress, one unconscious. He looked them all over, curled his lip, and shook his head.

They were a sorry lot. He had a decision to make – keep them, or kill them.

A man they all knew as *Blade* appeared in the doorway. He looked like his name implied – sharp, strong, and dangerous. In his mid-thirties, with shoulder-length hair tied back from his face in a ponytail, he was not your average guy. Next to King, he was the man everyone feared the most. He was King's ultimate weapon. He was the one he aimed and fired at those he wanted dead – well, those he didn't want the pleasure of killing himself. His presence in the room wasn't a good sign.

King sensed the temperature in the room drop a few degrees and turned to the door. He smiled. It was a warm smile, a welcoming smile. He was never irritated to see *his* Blade.

"Is it done?" he asked him, dragging his eyes over the man's face to determine if it would be good news, or bad.

Blade's expression gave nothing away, but he nodded.

"Any trouble?"

He shrugged. His whole body rippled with the small movement. "Those two cops showed up, but they didn't see me."

"Fractious Friar, and titillating Tuck?"

"The very ones."

"Those two have an uncanny sense of timing."

"Just lucky, I guess."

"How dead was Potter when they arrived?"

"As good as. I had to get out of there pretty damned sharp."

King's eyeballs quivered. He didn't like that. He repeated Blade's words back to him. "*As good as?*"

"There was a mere minute of life left in him."

"Was he in any fit state to talk... to rat?"

# FRIAR AND TUCK CASE NUMBER ONE: THE MISSING

"No way."

King relaxed. "I'm glad there's still someone I can trust to do their job." He swept his eyes around the room. "As for the rest of you – you all have shit for brains."

In all the years during which King had headed up the organization, he'd never found himself in a situation where he'd felt even a modicum of fear. No child had ever escaped his clutches before. Never had two of his most loyal employees had to be executed, and never had there been two tenacious cops on his trail.

At that moment, all those realities were sticking in his craw and causing his latent paranoia to surface.

*Who else was ready to betray him? What other kid was going to fuck him over?* He looked from one face to the other, calculating and measuring the extent to which this face, or that face was capable of treachery.

For the first time ever, King had his own fear to do battle with. He'd dealt quickly and effectively with Bridgman and Potter, and he knew that he could eventually deal with the two lousy cops, but it was a puny thirteen-year-old boy who had him cornered. If the boy succeeded in escaping the building, there was a very real chance that his whole empire would be put in jeopardy.

He couldn't allow that to happen. There were too many people waiting on the flimsiest excuse to see an end to him. Those people were strong and powerful. They didn't take too kindly to his years of blackmail and extortion, and he had no doubt that they'd all been biding their time, just waiting in the wings, to witness his downfall, and to take advantage of it.

They'd want revenge. He didn't blame them for that. He was known to be a vengeful man himself, so who was he to throw stones?

So, one thirteen-year-old boy held his life and his future in his hands. If those two bastard detectives got a hold of him, and heard everything he had to say, then King knew that he was done for, because those particular two detectives had the Governor on their side, and they were two straight arrows and couldn't be bought.

"Get this place packed up," he said to his lackeys. "We're leaving."

"What about Potter's kids?" the doctor asked, finally finding his tongue.

King thought about that for a moment. He could cut his losses by using them the way he'd used hundreds of other children before them. They hadn't been tested, but they were Potter's kids... they'd be clean. Potter hadn't been a kiddie fiddler, and he'd been known to abhor drugs, so – yes – his kids were probably as pure as the driven snow. He could pick the flesh off their bones and strip their insides, and perhaps be lucky enough to find matches for those clients he thought he'd have to disappoint.

"Bring them," he said. He looked over at the unconscious Alice. She'd been held in an induced coma for several days following a near-miss on the operating table, but she was still worth a pretty penny.

"Bring her as well," he said. "Her liver already has a sold label on it. Waste not, want not, as my dear old mom used to say."

Whilst everyone made busy, King pulled Blade to the side and whispered something in his ear. The man nodded and, without hesitation, walked up to the doctor, arced his arm in a narrow sweep, and opened the man's throat.

The doctor wasn't sure what had just happened. He hadn't felt anything more than a slight tug on his neck. He looked into Blade's flat eyes as blood spurted from his neck.

He looked down at the knife and his eyes bugged. One hand fluttered up to his neck to try and staunch the flow, but he was on his knees and dying before he could close his fingers.

All activity had stopped. All eyes were on the dying man. Every thought was the same – *thank fuck it wasn't me.*

# Kevin

## 40

HE COULD BREATHE. THE air was thick with ash, and it clogged up his nose and got right to the back of his throat, *but he could breathe.*

He didn't know a thing about furnaces. He didn't know how long the air inside would last, or if it was being replenished in some way. The one thing he *was* sure about was that he was trapped inside with no way of getting out unless he started kicking and screaming and drawing the attention of those who were searching for him.

He wasn't ready to do that. If he did, it would be out of the furnace and into the fire.

So he lay back and simply breathed, trying not to choke and cough. It was all he could do until he could think of some other way to get out of his prison, or until he suffocated.

He'd stopped hearing sounds quite some time ago. There were no voices, no footsteps, and no sign that anyone was out there. The silence wasn't reassuring.

Unlike the larger furnace, there was no window on the door. He wondered how the window on the large furnace didn't shatter from the heat. He thought about that for a while, trying to work it out. He also thought about Johnny and wondered if he'd already been burned to a crisp.

*Did bones burn? Would there be anything left of him when the fire was finished with him?*

*Poor Johnny.*

*Poor me.*

He sobbed quietly.

Natalie hadn't come. He'd been so sure that she would. He hoped nothing bad had happened to her. She was the first, and only, person he'd ever felt love for, and the thought of her being hurt caused him to sob harder.

He was making too much noise. He was terrified they would hear him, so he stifled his cries with his hand. He couldn't stop the racking shudders. His fear and his grief wouldn't be stilled.

After a short time – remarkably short considering the extent of his distress – he settled.

He stretched out his legs and pushed on the door again. He put as much of his weight as he could on his thighs, straining and pushing with all his might.

He wasn't particularly strong. He was wiry and fast, and that had held him to good stead on the streets. Muscle wasn't required to make a quick getaway, or to avoid the grasping hands of predators. Even if he had muscles, he didn't think they would do him any good against the locked door, but being small and wiry at least made the cramped conditions bearable.

He remembered being locked in the dark space under a set of stairs in some man's house once. He thought he had been only two or three years old at the time. His mother had locked him in there. It was the one and only time she'd ever tried to protect him from one of her Johns. The problem was, she'd got so high on drugs that she'd completely forgotten about him. She'd been so out of it that he was locked in that dark space for fifteen hours.

He remembered it. It wasn't something he'd ever been likely to forget, and the feelings he'd endured as that small child came back one hundred-fold.

He began to panic. It made breathing all the more difficult, causing his lungs to fill with ash. He coughed and spluttered and tried to scream. It suddenly didn't matter who heard him.

No one seemed to, because no one came to open the door.

Exhausted, choking, sobbing, his mind soon became fuzzy. He could no longer think of anything but hauling in tiny breaths of air.

As his disorientation and confusion grew, he no longer knew where he was

There was only the deep black of total darkness. He recognized nothing but the void that surrounded him. He didn't know it, but his brain was adjusting and taking over. It triggered something deep in his genes - a defence mechanism that was built into the nuclei of every cell in his body - and caused him to slump and sleep. He drifted off without even wondering if he would ever wake again.

# Friar

# 41

SOMETHING HINKY WAS definitely going on with Henderson. His partner – a far from bright detective called Quincey Malaware – hadn't seen him since they'd been at the bank hours before, and he couldn't shed any light on his whereabouts.

"I've been trying to get a hold of him myself," he told Friar with a frown. "I'm sat here scratching my balls and wondering what the fuck I'm supposed to be getting on with. He left me with no orders and no idea of what lines of enquiry he wants me following up on."

"He left you... just like that?"

"Yeah, just like that, Friar – I kid you not."

"Okay, so tell me what you found in the box at the bank."

"The box?"

Friar rolled his eyes. The guy really was a dumbass. "The safety deposit box belonging to Natalie Bridgman."

He shrugged. "I'm not sure what was in the box."

"You were there, weren't you – when it was opened?"

Malaware shook his head. "He had me go look at the Bank's CCTV. He said he wanted images of the Bridgman woman entering and leaving. I would've had to have searched through weeks of the fucking stuff before I could get even the slightest glimpse of her, so I said, *fuck that*, and went looking for him. I was gonna tell him I had better things to do, but I was told that he'd already left."

"Who told you that?"

"A clerk, I think."

"You didn't go check?"

"No. Why would I?"

"Because... oh, never mind." He flapped a hand and began to pace the squad room.

Malaware followed him with his eyes, wondering what all the fuss was about.

Friar's frustration was building. With fists clenched at his sides, and with an expression that seemed to fully charge his features with explosive energy, he was an intimidating sight. Not only Malaware's eyes were on him. Everyone in the squad room had ceased what they'd been doing to watch the animal-like prowl of the detective – all wondering what had got him so worked up.

If they'd seen what Friar had seen just a short time before, they wouldn't have wondered. Seeing a man's guts outside his body was quite something to behold and would make any half-way decent police officer want to turn over every rock until the person who'd carried out such a brutal act was caught. Factor in the possibility that one of your colleagues was in league with that person – or that person's boss – and they would think it no wonder that he was pacing the room like someone demented.

It became too much for Malaware. He stood and began to keep pace with Friar.

"What's all this about?" he asked. "What has Henderson done to get you so riled?"

Friar stopped in mid stride and turned to him. "You didn't think that it was weird... him walking out on you like that?"

He'd also stopped walking and was a few paces ahead of Friar. He shrugged. "Henderson always does his own thing... answers to no one."

Friar's eyes fixed on him.

The young detective came over all squirmy under his stare, and, the look in the other detective's eyes, couldn't help but make him think that he was the one who had done something wrong.

Malaware was what was known as a vanilla detective. He didn't mind that description. Vanilla detectives kept out of trouble and tended to fade into the shadows - neither making their mark, nor finding themselves under any scrutiny. That suited Malaware just fine. A quiet life, a steady income, and no hassle – what more could a lazy son-of-a-bitch hanker after? But, he had a feeling that Friar was going to drag him kicking and screaming out of the shadows, focus attention on him, and all because of that bastard Henderson.

He'd gone walkabout with evidence – evidence he, following protocol, should've had his eyes on.

He thought he might be in some deep shit.

"Have you tried ringing him?" Friar asked.

He nodded. "Keeps going to voicemail."

"Is that usual?"

"Sometimes." He dropped his eyes.

"What aren't you telling me, Malaware?"

"Well, he goes off the radar whenever... whenever..."

Friar took a step towards him, leaning in, brow furrowed. "Whenever what?"

Malaware swallowed. "I don't want to get him into any trouble."

*You don't want to get yourself into any trouble, more like.*

"Just spit it out, Malaware. I haven't time for any bullshit."

"I think he's got a woman on the side. He gets calls, and he disappears."

"When he's supposed to be on duty? And he turns his phone off?"

"Once or twice. I guessed that, maybe, he was with her."

"With an armful of important evidence?" Friar didn't buy it.

*Yes, it was definitely hinky.*

*Maybe...*

He shook his head. It couldn't possibly be *that* hinky.

Malaware said, "You think he's gone over to the dark side, don't you?"

Friar narrowed his eyes, but made no reply.

Malaware looked around the room. Everyone was watching and listening. There was no way he could dob Henderson in it – not with so many witnesses.

"Nothing would make me believe that of him," he said. "Henderson is poker-straight."

*All pokers are straight, until enough heat is applied to them*, Friar thought. Perhaps the errant detective had been held over a fire? He wouldn't be the first detective to be held over a barrel by some lowlife.

"He might go on the trot sometimes," Malaware went on, "but never with evidence. He's a stickler for dumping it in lock-up as soon as he can. He hates the responsibility of carrying it."

"You're suggesting that there wasn't any evidence in that box?"

"If there was, I think he would've given it to me, and sent me back with it before... before he took off."

"So, where does he meet up with this woman?"

"Jesus... I have no idea. I don't even know if there *is* a woman – I just surmised."

"He led you to believe that?"

"I guess."

Malaware was beginning to rankle. He might be vanilla, but he wasn't a pushover for some Neanderthal detective striving to burn his partner. He'd just about had enough.

Friar saw the shift in Malaware's eyes. The young detective was just about to grow a pair of balls. Any other time, he would've been proud of him for finding a spine, but not at that moment. At that moment, all he wanted was to find Henderson.

"You're just about to go rabbit on me, aren't you, Malaware?" he said, stepping forward another pace and getting right up and into his personal space.

Malaware tried to back off, but Friar grabbed his arm and dragged him back.

"Give me something. Point me in a direction... *any* direction."

Malaware tried to break free of his rip. "Take your hand off me, detective."

*So, he'd grown those balls.*

Friar dropped his hand. He said, "If I was you, I'd get all my ducks in a row, Malaware. I'd fess up to the lieutenant - get your side of the story told before hell's fire rains down on your head."

Malaware merely stared at him. Friar noted that his face was quite blank. He would get nothing out of him.

He headed for the door - the lieutenant's office his next port of call.

Unless – in the next five minutes - Henderson showed up at the precinct with the contents of Natalie Bridgman's box in his hands, Friar was going to hunt him down like a dog.

If there was one thing he despised, it was a corrupt cop. He hadn't quite tarred Henderson with that particular brush – not yet – but was getting pretty damned close to doing so. He couldn't think of a logical explanation for his behaviour and, when he ran everything past the lieutenant, was hard-pressed to come up with a plausible alternative for what Henderson had done.

"Perhaps he's off pursing whatever clues the contents of the box led him to," Mitchel said reasonably. "Didn't you think of that, Friar?"

"Without Malaware?" He shook his head. "Why would he do that, and without a word to him or to anyone else all day?"

"If you're worried about his safety..."

# FRIAR AND TUCK CASE NUMBER ONE: THE MISSING

"I'm not... at least, I don't think I am." He frowned. Perhaps he *should* be worried that something had happened to him.

"Henderson is a big boy. He can take care of himself. So, what exactly is on your mind, detective? What do you want from me?"

Friar huffed in a breath. It was going to be a hard sell. He said, "I want permission to locate him using his phone."

Mitchel laughed. "You're not serious?"

"Deadly serious, sir."

"Well, that's not asking much."

The sarcasm wasn't lost on Friar. "I need to find him."

"Well, I suggest you give him until his shift ends." He looked at his watch. "Unless he's pulling overtime, that will be in approximately three hours' time."

"I don't want to wait three fucking hours."

"Language, Friar. Remember who you're talking to."

"Sorry." He didn't look in the least bit sorry. "I'd rather not wait, if it's all the same to you... sir."

"I've got a view on all of this," Mitchel said. "I think it's a case of sour grapes. Henderson got the case, and you didn't. You want him to fuck up, and you want to be able to say that you were the best man for the job."

"You don't believe that crap," he returned, sharply."

"No, but others would. Do yourself a favour, Friar – drop all this horseshit.

Friar left the office determined not to drop a bloody thing.

# 42

Friar could obtain a real-time GPS location on Henderson's phone by requesting the cell company to *ping* it.

But, he needed the lieutenant's permission, and he needed a warrant.

It was all but impossible. The lieutenant had already refused. Without his permission, he wouldn't get a warrant. Without the warrant, the cell provider would tell him to go fuck himself.

He would have to lie. If he was caught, it would mean his badge, but - if he didn't do it - he knew in his bones that he would never find Kevin, and he would never find the fucker who'd made him face those guts on Potter's lap.

It was a no-brainer. He was not only going to lie, he was going to forge the lieutenant's signature on the warrant request.

He was glad that Tuck wasn't there to witness his blatant fraud – not because he was ashamed, but because she would probably try to stop him, and also because he didn't want to force her to be his accomplice.

*Shit. Was he really going to do it? Perhaps he should wait on Tuck's return – let her talk some sense into him?*

He practiced the lieutenant's signature on the back of an envelope. He'd seen Mitchel's scrawl so many times, and he had such a good hand, that getting it almost exact wasn't a problem.

He completed and printed off a request form and then sat staring at it. He knew he had to get a move on. He had to find a neutral judge to sign-off on the warrant and that would take time, and then he had to get in touch with the cell phone provider and wait for their bureaucracy to be waded through.

He signed the document, threw it on his desk, and blew out a long breath.

He could still back out. He could rip it up and think of some other way to find out where Henderson was and what he was up to.

*Fuck it.*

He picked up the paper, folded it neatly, and headed out. He wasn't going to fax it, or scan and email it. He was going to visit his favourite judge and get the ball rolling.

# Tuck

# 43

SIMMS OFFERED TO DRIVE her from Potter's house back to the precinct. She was without a vehicle – Friar having taken the car – but she didn't want to get a ride with him.

He'd been sweet to her, and had seemed quite pleased to find her without Friar at her side when he arrived at the scene. She thought that he was on the verge of asking her out on a date, and that was the last thing she wanted.

He was an okay guy, who didn't seem perturbed by her demeanour, and she was impressed by his knowledge and obvious skill, but he didn't float her boat. He sniffed too much, as if he had a perpetual runny nose, and she didn't like the way he smelled. It wasn't a nasty smell. He didn't smell of death, or of the morgue - it more of an underlying mustiness beneath a layer of sweet cologne. It was sickly, and a right turn-off.

He'd made the offer of the ride quite earnestly. His eyes had almost shone as he'd looked down on her, and she knew that refusing him would hurt.

She had never mastered the art of rejecting someone's advances – not that there had been many such overtures in her life - without bringing about a negative reaction. She had a feeling that, refusing the ride, would be tantamount to rejecting *him*.

"Thanks for the offer," she said, "but, I'm sure you have to get back with the body. I don't want to put you out."

"Nonsense," he returned, with a wide smile. "I don't need to play escort to a dead guy. It's no trouble to drop you back."

A little flustered, she said, "I wasn't planning on going straight back. There's something I want to check out first."

"Oh?" He seemed interested.

"Yeah, I want to take a look around Sheepshead Bay."

That made him jump in his skin. She was too preoccupied with brushing him off to notice.

"What's so interesting about Sheepshead Bay?" he asked, trying and failing for nonchalance.

She shrugged. "Probably nothing... just something Potter said before he croaked."

"He spoke to you?" His eyes were as wide as saucers. "He wasn't dead when you arrived?"

"Very nearly."

"Why didn't you say? It's important that I know that stuff."

"I thought I mentioned it when we were discussing time of death?"

"Did we?" He shook his head. "I would've remembered that."

She thought that she'd pissed him off. She wasn't sure whether it was because she'd refused his offer of a ride back to the precinct, mentioned Sheepshead Bay, or because he believed that she'd refrained from sharing a vital piece of information with him. She thought that it might be a combination of all three.

He was behaving all antsy.

"Look, Simms," she said, deciding not to pussy-foot around a moment longer. "I know you like me... I like you, but..."

"Of course, I like you. What are you getting at."

*Uh, oh... here comes the defensive stance.*

"I'm not getting at anything," she said.

"Then, hop in the car, and let's get you to Sheepshead." He narrowed his eyes. "Unless you *are* getting at something? Unless you think I'm coming onto you, and you're afraid to ride with me?"

She wasn't afraid of him. She was afraid of herself – afraid of completely alienating him as a potential friend. She didn't have many friends. In fact, she didn't have any, so losing the possibility of gaining one was just plain stupid.

She forced a smile. "If you have the time?".

"Sure... sure. I won't begin the autopsy until this evening. I quite fancy a trip out to Sheepshead."

She groaned inwardly, but kept the smile on her face. She hadn't really planned on going to Sheepshead. It had been no more than an excuse, but – now that she'd committed herself – she began to think it wasn't such a bad idea. Potter had used his dying breath to utter that one word. It must have meant something.

"What else did he say?" Simms asked, swinging the car out onto the road.

"Who, Potter?" She shook her head. "Nothing."

"But, he mentioned Sheepshead... just like that?"

"It was in response to me asking where his children were. He was seconds away from dying. He couldn't say any more. It took the last of his strength to say that one thing." She turned to look at him. "I really thought I'd mentioned it to you... that he was alive for a minute or so when we arrived."

"Maybe I wasn't paying enough attention?"

"Maybe." *Or, perhaps you were too busy ogling me?* It was a nasty thought, and she felt immediately ashamed.

"Let's just forget it," he said.

Grateful, she smiled.

He drove onto the Belt Parkway and turned off at ocean Avenue, which was a long stretch of road to the west of Sheepshead.

# FRIAR AND TUCK CASE NUMBER ONE: THE MISSING

Deep in thought, Simms drove without speaking. She was glad of the silence.

After a while, he said, "Sheepshead Bay covers a fair few miles."

"Does it? I've never been here before."

"Do you want me to just drive around?"

"I think so. Something might grab my attention."

"Like what?"

"I have no idea. It's probably a waste of time."

He made a right onto Avenue W, crossed over Bedford Avenue, and headed towards a Salvation Army Thrift Store.

"This is nice," he said.

"Nice?" She swallowed back anxiously, and began to pick at her fingers.

"Just the two of us, here, together, driving around." He cleared his throat. "I've been meaning to ask..."

"Don't, Simms."

He glanced to his right. "Don't what?"

"Ask me anything."

"You're pretty shy, huh?"

"No, not shy."

"Not interested?"

She shook her head, then jerked in her seat. "What's over there?" She pointed straight ahead.

"Just some warehouses."

"I thought I saw..." She screwed around in her seat, staring out the window and scrunching up her eyes.. "Can you drive over?"

"Sure. What did you think you saw?"

"Kids being loaded into a van."

"Outside a warehouse? Are you sure?"

"No, but..."

"No harm in checking it out, I don't suppose, but you're going to look pretty stupid when you discover it was some mannequin dummies, or something."

"I don't care about looking stupid," she said, irritated. "Hurry up, will you."

He floored the pedal and swerved to a stop opposite the warehouse.

"There's the van," she said, pointing.

"I don't see any kids."

Neither did she. "I want to go and take a look."

"Is that a good idea? Won't you be trespassing?"

"Hardly trespassing, Simms." She opened the door and stepped out onto the road. "You stay here," she said, throwing him a warning look. "Don't budge."

"Aye, aye, sir." He grinned and saluted.

As she approached the van, she heard a child's cry. She held her breath. Her mouth filled with saliva and the hairs stood to attention on the back of her neck. Glancing behind her, she checked that Simms had stayed put and was pissed to see him getting out of the car. She waved at him to get back inside, and unholstered her weapon.

Two cars were parked behind the van. The windows were heavily, and illegally, tinted, so she couldn't determine if there was anyone inside.

She studied the scene for a moment. She considered her best course of action. For all she knew, there could be dozens of people inside the warehouse and – if there really were children in the van – she needed back-up.

She pulled out her phone, speed-dialled Friar, and cursed when her call went straight to voicemail.

"Ten-thirteen," she said, stating that an officer required assistance. Then, looking hastily around for a street sign, added, "Warehouse... East twenty-ninth... Sheepshead. Hurry."

It could all be something and nothing. There was definitely a chance that she would end up looking foolish, but she was in Sheepshead, there was a van, and she was almost certain that she'd seen children being put into that van. Then, the cry. That cry had been unmistakably a child's.

A man with a shaved head and a stocky build walks around the van. He doesn't spot her, and she sidles stealthily into the shadow of a wall adjacent to one of the cars. No one gets out of either car, so she takes that as a good sign that they're empty of driver and passengers.

She used her phone to take photographs of all three licence plates – the van and the two cars. The man with the shaved head is still in view, so she took a photo of him as well.

Adrenaline is making her jumpy and she drags in deep breaths to calm and still herself. Every one of her senses is on high alert and, yet, Simms manages to creep up behind her without her noticing.

She smells him before she sees him – the cloying cologne an assault on her nose. She whirls around, grinds her teeth, and hauls him flat against the wall.

"Are you out of your fucking mind?" she hissed in his face. "I could've shot you, for Christ sake."

"I thought you might need some back up," he hissed back at her.

"Not from you, Simms... Jesus."

He wasn't insulted. "What are you doing here... exactly?" he asked. "Only, it all seems a little screwy."

"I heard a child cry."

"Children *do* cry, Tuck."

"I just have a feeling."

"A hunch?"

"You could say that."

"About?"

"Never fucking mind. Stay back, and don't get in my way."

She moved forward to get a better view of the warehouse door. The van obscured most of it, but she saw enough to know that there were at least another three men. One had a ponytail and looked a mean son-of-a-bitch.

"Shit," she said.

Simms moved to her shoulder. "What is it?"

"One of the men is getting into the van. I think he's about to take off with the children."

"What are you going to do?"

She stepped away from the wall, brought up her weapon, and advanced, head-on towards the van.

She knew exactly what she was going to do. She was going to stop the fucker.

Several pairs of eyes looked at her in shock, but no one raised their hands - despite her screaming at them to do so. They simply stood there, looking at her as if she was something akin to a slug.

They weren't worried. She'd identified herself, and was holding a gun on them, and they weren't worried.

That worried *her*.

She had no time to realize what was happening before she was driven to the ground, all the air being forced out of her. Her gun flew from her hand and skittered across the concrete paving.

A heavy weight pressed down on her back and pinned her flat. She tried to move, attempting to buck her assailant off, and received a blow to the side of her head for her efforts.

For a moment, the blow blinded and stunned her. She blinked and hauled in a breath, and her vision returned.

A pair of feet inside some pretty expensive shoes appeared in her periphery. She noticed splashes of blood on them.

"Detective Tuck, I presume?"

She didn't recognize the voice. Her ears were ringing, so she thought that – even if it had been familiar – her hearing was so distorted that she would be none the wiser.

"Who, the fuck, are you?" she ground out, her cheek losing skin as her head was held against the ground.

"Me?" the voice said. "I'm the man you've been working so hard at to find. You can call me Mister King."

Her assailant flipped her onto her back.

Before the punch landed between her eyes, she choked back a startled cry.

# Friar

# 44

HE'D SWITCHED OFF HIS phone. He knew that Mitchel would be baying for his blood, and he didn't want to be within screaming distance of his furious voice. No one could reach him, and that was just the way he wanted it.

He had the warrant. He had the phone provider working on pinging Henderson's phone. He was close to nailing the bastard.

Taking no chances, and wishing to be well out of the way of anyone who would try to stop him, he'd driven over the Brooklyn Bridge, and all the way to Lexington Avenue, New York city, where the registered office of the phone provider was housed.

And, there he waited.

It was a long wait, but he was finally rewarded with the current location of Henderson's phone.

He was momentarily confused. He couldn't understand what the detective was doing there. Apparently – according to what the record of the ping showed – he'd been there, or at least his phone had been there, for the past six hours.

*Six fucking hours?*

*Why?*

It would take him at least forty minutes to get there. Henderson had been there a long time, and he prayed that he would stay there those extra forty minutes.

He made his way to the lift, waited two full minutes for it to arrive, and then, losing patience, decided to take the stairs.

He needed to shift his ass. Placing the blue-light on the roof of his car, he made it back over the Brooklyn bridge in record time, and arrived at his destination in just under thirty four minutes.

Ignoring the receptionist, he barged trough the double doors that led to the morgue, calling out Henderson's name with an underlying snarl as he virtually threw himself along the corridor.

Doors opened to his left and to his right. Faces peered out, obviously alarmed. Friar flashed his badge, fired questions.

None of them were Henderson. None of them had seen Henderson.

Simms wasn't in his office. Potter's body had just arrived from the scene. He was in a body bag and being wheeled into the autopsy suite, just as Friar stepped through the door.

Friar enquired about the whereabouts of the ME.

One of the technicians said that Doctor Simms was giving Detective Friar a ride back to the precinct. He added that he wasn't sure when he was expected back to begin the autopsy, but, meantime, he'd been told to prep the body.

The stench emanating from the bag dragged Friar back to those hellish moments in Potter's bedroom. He covered his mouth with the back of his hand and turned away, forcing the images from behind his eyes.

Being in the autopsy suite gave him the heebie-jeebies. He hated the look of it – with its shiny steel tables, drains, and array of tools including, *of all fucking things*, a hacksaw. He knew he was a pussy. He was ashamed of his phobia, but Henderson was somewhere in the building and he knew he had to suck it up and swallow any feelings that being there induced.

As he continued his search, he began to wonder if Henderson's phone was there, but not Henderson himself. It wasn't beyond reason to assume that he'd forgotten to take his phone with him when he left, but Friar didn't buy that scenario. Cops were glued to their phones. They were their lifeline. There was no way that Henderson would leave without it.

He turned on his own phone to contact the cell phone provider and request an immediate ping. He wasn't shocked to hear his phone go mental as it fired off message after message. He had eight text messages, four WhatsApp messages, and a dozen voicemail messages. He ignored them all.

The ping showed that the phone, at least, was still in the building. Its whereabouts couldn't be narrowed down, so he shifted his search to desk drawers and tabletops. He still didn't believe that Henderson had left it behind, but he wasn't taking any chances.

When he came up empty, he was at a total loss. He'd searched the whole building. He'd looked into every nook and cranny. He'd questioned every man and woman in every office.

Still, no Henderson, and no Henderson's phone.

He considered his options, then slapped his head in frustration at his own stupidity. Because the phone could be pinged, it meant that it was switched on. He could simply ring it.

Feverishly, he fumbled with the screen and brought up Henderson's number.

It was faint, but he could hear it – the William Tell Overture, or, as he recognized it, the Lone Ranger tune.

It ceased, and he heard the familiar voicemail recording. He ended the call, and tried again, tilting his head to the side and homing in on the direction of the recognizable ringtone.

*Got you, you bastard.*

He wasn't sure at what point he finally knew where Henderson was. He wasn't sure because the confusion he felt overrode his senses. Disbelief fought with fact. Misperception and puzzlement warred with certainty. He shook his head.

It couldn't be.

He stood, transfixed, and searched the room, but his eyes kept being drawn back to that one spot. His brain refused to accept it, and then it simply did.

Pulling open the drawer, the body slid out atop a metal tray on coasters. Blood had pooled and congealed beneath his head. His skin was grey and waxy, and his eyes were open.

Henderson's phone lay on top of his broad chest – now silent.

It didn't make any sense. How could it? He'd suspected Henderson of being dirty, of stealing evidence. He'd thought... *Jesus Christ, he'd thought the worst of that man, and now he was dead.*

He stared long and hard at the body. Henderson had obviously met a violent end. Someone had killed him and stored him in the refrigerated drawer.

*But, who?*

That wasn't an easy question to answer. As far as he was aware, no murderers worked at the morgue. He knew most of the forensic pathologists – the medical examiners - and he couldn't bring himself to suspect a single one of them. He didn't really know the technicians, or the crime scene investigators that used the facilities in the building, so they automatically topped his list of suspects

It could be any one of a couple of dozen people.

The second question he asked himself was – *why*? *Why kill him?*

Because he'd discovered something. Was it something he'd found in the safety deposit box – something that brought him tearing across town to this place, looking for..? Back to the *who* again.

He let out a shuddering breath. He had to call Mitchel.

Holding the phone six inches from his ear, he withstood a full minute's angry tirade from the lieutenant. When Mitchel stopped to catch his breath, he explained the situation. The explanation was initially met with silence. Friar could hear the shock in that silence.

Then, "What, the fuck, Friar?"

"I don't know, sir. I haven't a bloody clue."

"Where's Tuck? Is she with you?"

"No. She should be back at the precinct by now. I left her with Potter, waiting on the ME."

"Well, she's not here. I'm in the squad room and no one has seen her."

Friar's brow furrowed. That didn't make any sense. Simms was... *Simms!*

"I've got to go," he said hurriedly.

"Wait, Friar... what's..?"

Friar ended the call and made for the door, where he suddenly stopped as if held there by an invisible hand.

He didn't know where he was heading to. There was no reason for her to still be at Potter's house. She wasn't at the precinct. So, where the hell was she?

He looked down at his phone. It was still in his hand. He tried ringing her, but couldn't get through. There wasn't even the option to leave a message.

*A message?*

He went straight to his voicemail. It was the third one.

*Ten-thirteen... Warehouse... East twenty-ninth... Sheepshead... Hurry.*

The message had been left nearly three hours ago.

He groaned and, ran an agitated hand through his hair. Everything still didn't make sense, but a few things were beginning to slot into place. The only thing that prevented him from pinning Henderson's murder on Simms was the fact that the ME had given Tuck the key to the safety deposit box. Why would he do that if he was somehow involved in whatever fucked-up thing was going on?

Then, there was the fact that Simms obviously had the hots for Tuck. It was feasible that they'd gone off together for a meal, or something. He closed his eyes against the image of them wiling away the day fucking in some sleazy motel.

He shook his head. Tuck wouldn't do that, particularly not with Simms. He'd noticed her reaction to him. It wasn't one that suggested that she wanted to fuck him. Actually, he couldn't imagine Tuck fucking anyone.

He could see her going to Sheepshead Bay. It was something she *would* do. Although three hours had passed since her hurried message, he would have to start there. Mitchel would see to Henderson.

*Henderson.*

He walked back over to the body, stared at it a moment, and then rolled it back into the huge drawer. He then sent the lieutenant a text message informing him what drawer the body was in, and telling him that he was going to find Tuck. That was all. He didn't elaborate.

He didn't rush, kept within the speed limit, and didn't use his blue light. He wanted time to think. The trouble was – he couldn't think. His brain was full of white noise, far too thick for any coherent thought to punch through. He gave up trying, and just drove.

There was only the one building on East twenty-ninth that looked anything like a warehouse. It wasn't shielded from the road by a wall, or trees, or even a fence, and from is car, he could see right onto the parking lot.

There were no vehicles, and the place looked locked-up tight.

Dusk was settling over the horizon. He glanced at his watch – seven-fifteen. Now three and a half hours since Tuck's message.

She could be dead. It was a sobering thought. He should never have left her at Potter's. They were partners. Partners never bailed on one another.

He knew that his only hope of finding her was in him staying cool. He couldn't allow the emotion of the situation to overwhelm him. It said a great deal about his fortitude in the face of the murder of a colleague, and the potential murder of his partner, that he didn't immediately get out of the car and rush the building. He was more prudent than that. He took his time surveying the scene – taking in the darkened windows, the empty lot, and – but for the traffic - the silence.

The sky was overcast. Rain was imminent. They'd had a great deal of rain that past week, and it was the threat of it, and the growing murky grey of early evening, that finally forced him to make a move. If there was something to be found on the parking lot, he needed to see it before it got too dark, or before it was washed away.

He knew what he was looking for – blood. He dreaded finding it, but his gut told him he was certainly going to.

It wasn't much – just a splash quite close to the main doors. He also found Tuck's cell phone, smashed to smithereens next to the step leading up to those doors.

The responsibility for Tuck's predicament – he refused to think of it as her death, not yet – rested heavily on his shoulders. It bowed him. His vision blurred and he had to blink rapidly to clear it.

He climbed the step to the wide metal doors and pulled on the broad handle. Of course, it was locked. Nevertheless, he yanked on it, refusing to believe that it wouldn't open.

He knew that there was no way that Tuck was in the building, but a clue or two might be found somewhere in its cavernous interior. He was determined to get in. Nothing was going to stop him – least of all a locked door.

He went back to his car and rummaged in the trunk for his flashlight. It was long and heavy. He also picked up his safety hammer. He had a feeling he was about to break some glass.

He found the perfect window at the rear. It had a single pane of glass, and it was large enough for him to climb through. He broke the glass as cleanly as he could, then smashed the jagged edges until he could climb through without injuring himself.

Once inside, he switched on his flashlight.

The powerful beam picked up on a very strange construction. There appeared to be a huge wooden erection with corridors and rooms leading off. It was certainly nothing he expected to see inside a warehouse. He thought that it took up at least three thousand square feet.

He swept the beam around the rest of the interior. There was a door standing ajar in front and to the left of him, and a series of tall shelves stacked with what looked like medical supplies. He thought he'd check out what was behind the open door before investigating what the strange construction housed.

As soon as he stepped over the threshold, he felt the heat. It came from fat pipes splayed along the walls and leading to a large furnace. He wasn't curious about the furnace. It was just a furnace. In fact, there were two of them, but only the larger one was throwing out heat.

He quickly searched the room and then turned to leave, his curiosity about the wooden erection taking precedence over any need to linger.

At the door, he turned. His ears might've been playing tricks on him, but he thought he heard something. He walked over to peer through the window of the larger of the two furnaces. Something had recently been burned inside it, and – when he saw something settle into the ash – he realized that was the sound he'd heard. Just the soft puff of settlement.

Satisfied, he turned once more for the door, then his brain clicked into gear and told him something of what his eyes had seen through the glass, but what his mind hadn't immediately registered – bones. The bones of a small hand.

The very foundations of his psyche shook. His body trembled, and his work-scarred heart lurched in his chest.

He feared – if his eyes and his brain hadn't totally deceived him –that he'd just spied what remained of the Murphy boy.

He took a tentative step forward, reached out, and opened the furnace door. Although the fire was out, the residual heat blasted his face. Blinking away the ash that had wafted into his eyes, he peered in.

It was definitely human bones, and definitely the bones of a child. Grief came like a punch to the belly.

He was too late, and guilt quickly followed on the back of the sorrow.

There was nothing he could do for the boy, and Tuck was out there somewhere – hurt, or possibly dead. His priority had to be finding her, so he closed the door and walked away.

He didn't think to look in the smaller furnace. Later, he would deeply regret that oversight.

# Simms

# 45

FOR HOWEVER LONG HE might have left with Tuck - before King got around to ordering her execution – Simms was determined to enjoy every wrung-out moment of it.

He genuinely liked her, although he quite understood the fact that she hated him with a vengeance. It was only natural, and he didn't hold it against her.

She looked a little bloody and bruised, and that was his fault. He'd hit her rather hard, right between the eyes.

He regretted the punch. He hadn't meant for it to knock her out, simply to stun her into submission, but he hadn't known his own strength, and he'd taken her completely by surprise, so - out she'd gone like a light.

As soon as she'd regained consciousness, he'd apologized profusely. The words didn't seem to touch her, except to make her angry, and she'd hawked in the back of her throat and sent a missile of phlegm straight at him. He'd laughed. It really had been quite amusing. He couldn't help but love her spirit.

He intended to have some fun with her. He was quite dizzy at the thought of it, but first, he offered her a cup of her favourite tea – the only tea she would drink – but, she refused. He didn't mind. Nothing she said, or did, bothered him.

He thought that he might actually be in love with her, and wondered if King would allow him to keep her. He never knew with King. Sometimes, he was really rather generous, and not just with money. In the past, he'd granted quite a few of his requests – mainly around being permitted to use the girls before they were put out of their misery. Those were the girls where only a single organ had been removed. He never wanted to fuck any of those who'd undergone multiple surgeries.

*Ugh, the very thought of it.* It was enough to turn his stomach.

It wasn't that he was really *into* little girls. He didn't consider himself a sicko – not like that stupid prick, Marcus. He wasn't the same as him. It was just sometimes convenient - with the girls being on tap, so to speak. If he had a choice, he'd always choose a woman over a girl, and he'd choose Tuck over *any* woman put in front of him.

He looked at her. Her eyes were beginning to blacken. There was blood crusted beneath her nose. She wasn't looking her best, but he thought she was delicious enough to eat. He licked his lips in anticipation, and sighed with satisfaction.

He still had a great deal to feel satisfied about. His career might be over, but not his work. He would no longer forensically examine dead bodies, but his other skills – those he applied in the make-shift theatres thrown up by King across the country – would still be very much in demand. Perhaps he could use that to bargain with? King might call it extortion, but Simms was sure he could persuade him that his ongoing support was worth the price of one skinny, weird as fuck, detective.

She was watching him from beneath lowered lashes. For the past thirty minutes, or so, she'd been quiet. He was quite glad about that.

He liked the sound of her voice, but not when it was raised to a shrill, and not when she was screaming obscenities at him. He thought it rather unbecoming, but - although the words hurt, and annoyed him to a certain extent - he didn't mind enough to chastise her. He still felt bad about that punch.

There was a chill in the room. He asked her if she was warm enough... should he fetch her a blanket?

She blatantly ignored him.

That was all right. He didn't mind. He smiled, and began to chatter earnestly about the future he hoped they would both share. He knew she was listening because, at one point, she stared straight at him and he saw her jaw clench.

"I guess you have questions," he said, winding down from his grandiose and exuberant ramblings. "I don't mind answering a few, and putting your mind at rest. There's things you have a right to know, and I'm just the man to fill you in. So, go on, Tuck... fire away. I'm all ears."

He saw her thinking. Her eyes lost focus and he could almost witness her brain turning over.

She said, "I just want to know why. Will you tell me why?"

He was shocked to hear her speak so quietly and so forlornly. He'd never heard that tone in her voice before, and he was intrigued enough by it to wonder if she was, at last, coming around to accepting her situation.

He loved the question. He couldn't wait to explain himself, knowing she would be sure to understand.

"Why do I do what I do? Because I know that I'm helping people, Tuck. I get to save a lot of lives."

She raised her head and looked at him in amazement. "Do you actually believe that self-deluded bullshit?"

"But, it's perfectly true... I've lost count of the kiddies who would've died if it hadn't been for me."

"More bullshit."

He gave her a wry smile. "Okay... okay... it's not just about saving lives. I'll give you that. It also about making me shit-loads of money."

"Blood money."

"Blood money spends just as well as the other sort. It buys all the same things... luxurious, wonderful things."

"You're despicable."

He made a tutting sound with his tongue. "Don't be so judgemental. So, what if it is about the money? I still do plenty of good. Do you know how many children I've saved? For every one of those guttersnipes that die, three, or even four children get to live. A kidney here, a liver there, a heart, lungs, eyes... Jesus, Tuck, think on that before you get on your high horse and condemn me."

He couldn't be mad at her. She was a principled person, and he allowed for that. She was also a police officer, and he accepted how that factored into how she looked at things.

"I forgive you," he said. "I forgive your narrow-thinking, and your judgement of me."

"I'm not asking for forgiveness. One day, I hope you go down on bended knee and beg for absolution."

"From who... God?" He gave a bitter laugh. "There is no heaven, and there is no hell, Tuck. Don't tell me you believe in all that crap... the balm to the masses... the big lie?"

She shook her head. She didn't know what she believed.

"What's going to happen to me?" she asked.

"Oh, don't you worry your little head about that."

"But, I *am* worried, Simms. I'm tied to a chair, surrounded by sociopaths, and that man over there with the ponytail is cleaning his fingernails with the knife I imagine he used to kill Natalie Bridgman, Potter and his wife."

Tuck makes eye contact with the man with the knife. Simms is suddenly uncomfortable. He doesn't like the look in the other man's eyes when he stares back at Tuck. It's almost as if he's contemplating whether to cut her throat or gut her.

He really had to have that word with King – certainly before *Blade* decided to take matters into his own hands.

"Where are we?" she asked, dragging her eyes back to Simms. "Are the children here?"

"Potter's brats?" His head jerked with a nod. "They're out for the count in the other room. As to where we are?" He shrugged. "Just somewhere off the beaten track."

"And, Kevin Murphy? Do you have him?"

"King did, but the little rascal escaped

She sighed with relief.

"That's why we came here. The warehouse is an absolute bust now. It's a pity, because it was well kitted out and well hidden in plain sight."

"You operated on the children there?"

"Quite a few."

"In a warehouse?" She was aghast.

"Sure. Why not?"

"Because... because..." With everything that had gone on, *was* going on, she wondered why she was so shocked about the place of all those children's execution. So what if it was in a make-shift operating room in a warehouse?

*So fucking what?*

"Any more questions?"

She shook her head. She actually had a great many questions for him, but she suddenly realized that knowing the answers would do her no good.

The room was illuminated by a single bare bulb in the middle of a cracked and dirty ceiling. Whenever any of the men moved, their shadows jerked and played out on the walls. There was an eerie atmosphere that made the air heavy and created a throbbing tension.

Counting Tuck, Simms, and the man with the knife, there were five people in the room. The room was big enough to take them all comfortably, but - although it was large enough to give a semblance of privacy to Simms and Tuck – it still felt claustrophobic.

Simms had been awaiting King's arrival for the best part of three hours and the wait was beginning to make him antsy. He didn't want Tuck to see him anxious, so he moved away, but kept himself between her and Blade. If the bastard wanted to kill her, he would have to go through him first.

*Where was King? What were his plans for them?* Simms knew that they couldn't remain at their current location for long, and wondered if they would head for one of the other warehouses in one of the other cities. There were fourteen other such sites, but none were as sophisticated as the warehouse adaption in Brooklyn.

He had to go and check on the children. The girl, Alice, was in a bad way. Keeping her comatose for so long had been a mistake, but one – thankfully – not made by him. The feckless doctor – now very dead at Blade's hand – was to blame. Simms thought he might suggest to King that it would be a good idea to euthanize her. He wouldn't be surprised if her liver had packed up. The last time he'd examined her, she'd looked a little yellow. They didn't want to transplant a defective liver – not good for business.

He took a quick look at his watch. He'd now been waiting on King for nearly four hours. He couldn't call him as their cell phones had all been confiscated and destroyed. King was smart. He knew the danger that cell phones posed.

Simms had asked for a burner phone, and King promised to bring him one. Well, he was still waiting on King, and he was still waiting on his phone, and the waiting was now shifting his anxiety to anger.

Who the fuck did King think he was dealing with? He wasn't just some lackey, some insignificant cog in the organization's mighty wheel. He was fucking important – too important to be left to stew alongside King's murderous henchmen. He would have strong words to say to him when he finally got there. He would make it clear that

# FRIAR AND TUCK CASE NUMBER ONE: THE MISSING

he wouldn't be treated like that in the future – not if King wanted to retain his services.

He never thought for a moment how such words would be received. The nihilist in him couldn't see any further than his own important nose.

He reminded himself that he needed to check on the brats. He'd been putting it off – not wanting to leave Tuck alone with Blade and the others. Fuck only knew what they would do to her if he wasn't there to offer his protection.

He turned to her, and asked, "Do you need to visit the little girl's room?"

She threw up her head. "What?"

"The little girl's room... the bathroom... I thought you might like to freshen up?"

Blade made a sound in the back of his throat, obviously displeased with Simms' suggestion.

Simms swung around and glared at him. "You got something to say about that, Blade? Did King leave you in charge, or did I hear him tell you to follow my orders?"

Blade smirked, but backed off.

"I thought so." Simms turned back to Tuck. "How about it? Do you want to go wash your face, use the toilet?"

She nodded.

He used a knife to cut through the zip ties on her wrists and ankles.

"I'm trusting you to behave," he said. "Don't give Blade over there an excuse to hurt you."

She nodded once more, not trusting herself to speak. She was free – sort of – and, for the first time in hours, felt a surge of hope. Tied to the chair, she had no options. Free of her restraints, she suddenly had a few.

"I'll take her along with me to check on the kids," he said to Blade. "Don't get all worried and think you need to send out a search party for us. I don't want to see your ugly mug behind us at any point."

Blade nodded. The smirk was still on his face, but his eyes sparked with fury. Simms, in his haste to get out of the room, either didn't notice that fury, or chose to ignore it.

The bathroom was filthy, but she washed up as well as she could. Her face hurt like hell, and her head throbbed. Simms' sucker-punch had been well aimed and well timed and she knew she would be feeling its effects for days.

When she wiped it clean, her nose started to bleed again. His punch hadn't landed on her nose, but the blow between her eyes had somehow ruptured a blood vessel in her nasal passage. She sniffed back and swallowed the blood gathering in her throat.

She didn't pee. She couldn't do it with him standing over her, watching.

The four children were lying on the floor in a room adjacent to the one they'd just left. There was no furniture and no beds. They were obviously drugged and Tuck was immediately fearful.

"Are they all right?" she asked, kneeling down and dragging the toddler into her arms. "They seem to be breathing all wrong."

"They're fine. Don't worry about them."

He began to rummage in a bag that had been left sitting in a corner. He withdrew a syringe and a single hypodermic needle. He rummaged some more and brought out a small bottle.

She hugged the child closer. "What are you doing?"

Simms attached the needle to the syringe, held the bottle upside down, and then stabbed the needle into the rubber bung, sucking up the milky fluid into the syringe until the bottle was empty.

"Simms?"

He flashed her a look. "They need to be kept under. It's for their own good."

She tried not to look at the knife on the floor by the bag. She really did try, but her eyes must've flickered to the side because he smiled, tutted, and bent down to pick it up.

"That's a lot of drug in that syringe," she said.

"It's for sharing. I'm not going to overdose any of the little shits."

"It's too dangerous, Simms. Look at the state of her. One more injection of that stuff, and it'll kill her."

"Don't be stupid. I know what I'm doing. I'm not going to kill her."

"Not yet, maybe, but what about when you attack her with your scalpel? How long will she live without her little kidneys?"

He looked at her in horror. "These are Potter's kids. They won't go under the knife."

"Says who?"

"King, of course. He's not a monster, Tuck."

She grated out a laugh. There was no humour in it whatsoever.

"Yeah, right," she said. "Not a monster? Okay."

"Honestly, Tuck," he said, in earnest. "He had their parents killed. He won't take their lives as well. He *does* have a grain or two of humanity."

"Then, let them wake up of their own accord. Let me get them out of here."

"I'm sorry. That's simply not possible. I can't let you go." He fixed her with a long stare. "I don't want to let you go."

She swallowed back hard. "Please, Simms."

He shook his head. "Isn't going to happen."

He hunkered down and made a grab for the child in her arms. Tuck held on tight and refused to release her to him.

"Come on, Tuck, let her go. Stop being silly."

"You're not having her," she said, through gritted teeth. "You'll have to kill me to take her."

There was that tutting sound again. To Tuck's ears, it really was quite a patronizing sound.

Simms kept a hold of the knife, but placed the syringe on the floor next to him. He waved the knife in front of Tuck's face.

"I'll cut you, Tuck," he said. "I don't want to, but I will."

"Go ahead, you bastard. Let's see if you have the balls."

"Just give me the girl and go and stand over by the door," he returned patiently. "I really don't want to hurt you."

She shook her head and scrabbled backwards on her knees. He followed, reaching out with his free hand to snag the sleeve of her jacket.

She was yanked forward. The weight of the child caused her forward momentum to be exaggerated and she toppled to the side, one hand slapping the floor as she tried to stop herself from falling flat on her face and crushing the girl beneath her.

Simms acted quickly, grabbing the girl and rocking back on his heels.

Tuck also acted quickly. Feeling the syringe at her fingertips, she grabbed it, swung herself up and around, and stabbed the needle into his neck.

A nanosecond later the syringe was depressed, and the drug was immediately coursing through his system.

He didn't make a sound. He merely stared at her, wide-eyed with shock. She stared back at him, equally shocked.

It had all happened so fast. She hadn't meant to do it.

"I think you've just killed me," he said, choking on the words.

She closed her gaping mouth with a snap. She thought that he was probably correct. She had killed him. The syringe had been full of whatever sedative he'd drawn up.

# FRIAR AND TUCK CASE NUMBER ONE: THE MISSING

She wrestled with her emotions. She knew that it would have been normal to feel guilt, but, she wasn't normal. The emotions that warred inside her mind were a mixture of anger, fear, and hate.

He deserved to die, but she needed him to live. She was angry at herself for injecting him with the full dose, frightened that he would die before she could extract any information from him, and full of hatred for everyone involved in the whole sordid, evil business.

"How long?" she grated out.

He grabbed the syringe, pulled it out, and shook his head.

"How long have you got, Simms?"

His eyelids fluttered.

She shook him. "Give me something. Don't die without giving me something."

He gave a soft groan. She shifted the unconscious child to safety and leaned in close.

"Something, Simms... *anything*... Help me, you bastard." She shook him until his teeth rattled.

He said, "Williams..."

"Someone called Williams?"

He shook his head and flopped back onto his elbows. He was deathly pale, as if all the blood had been sucked from him.

He took several shallow breaths, and managed to spit out, "Williamsburgh... Tower."

She had no idea what that meant, but it was all she was going to get from him, because – just then - he died quietly, without a murmur.

She huffed out a breath. She had just killed a man. Surely, she should feel something? He'd almost been her friend, but she felt nothing.

She heard a sound behind her. Before she could turn, she heard - "Well, well. What have we here?"

The blood ran ice-cold in her veins.

It was the man with the ponytail.
*Blade.*

# King
# 46

HE LOOKED AT THE CLOCK on the ornate mantle. It was a beautiful clock, a gift from one of his grateful clients. The time on the clock told him that his orders had most probably already been followed. All the unfortunate, but necessary, mopping up would have been done by Blade, and there would be no one left to compromise him. Once Blade reported in, he would finish his packing, and then he would be out of there.

Brooklyn had begun to put a sour taste in his mouth. There was too much attention being focussed on his business and, being a smart man, he knew when it was time to move on.

Over the years, he'd *moved on* numerous times. He always knew when the time was right, and he always acted on his intuition. He always left bodies behind. Those bodies never bothered him. Everyone was expendable – except, perhaps, Blade.

It wasn't common knowledge, but he'd grown up with Blade. Blade's real name was Norton Colgate, and they'd lived next door to one another as children. They were drawn to one another as only fellow sociopaths could be, and their affinity for the cruel and the macabre had made them the terror of the schoolyard, and a bane to both sets of parents.

Neither were into petty crime. Growing up, neither of them had ever shoplifted, or mugged any old ladies, and – although Norton became adept at killing – as a child, and unlike most sociopaths, he never mutilated any animals. The only things his knife was used for was the injuring and killing of human beings. – most at King's behest.

King liked to use his feet and his fists to kill, but – when any mopping up was ever required – it was Blade and his knife that were always up for the task.

King was the puppeteer and, over time, Blade had become his marionette. It wasn't an equal partnership, but it worked. Each was loyal to the other, but King realized that there would probably come a time when he would have to rid himself of his friend. He didn't look forward to that day, but he knew it would come.

He'd thought long and hard about where to go next. He quite fancied Florida. They only had a small operation running from the Sunshine State, but he had big plans. Both Florida and Texas were ideal places to fully expand the organization. The daily influx of illegal immigrants made for rich pickings in those two States.

Whilst he awaited Blade's phone call to tell him that he'd completed his mission, and that they were all dead, he decided to relax with a glass of fine cognac. He would only have the one, but he would make it a double. It was the end of an era in Brooklyn, and – what the hell – he could indulge just that once. It wasn't a celebration. The business run from Brooklyn had been very lucrative, and he'd developed a highly effective network of patsies in law enforcement and the judiciary – something he'd, as yet, to establish in what he considered his satellite locations.

It had all crumbled very quickly. Looking back, he wondered what he could've done differently. Choosing Natalie Bridgman as a trusted employee had turned out to be a grave error, but there had been no way to know that. She'd seemed perfect. She *had been* perfect, up until the Murphy boy had come on the scene, and up until she'd allowed Potter to fuck her. Those two things were the catalyst for what followed. But, how could he have known? He wasn't a fucking mind reader, or a fucking prophet. Then, there were the two cops.

# FRIAR AND TUCK CASE NUMBER ONE: THE MISSING

He would never have factored them into the equation. Cops weren't supposed to care about street brats going missing. He'd lucked out following the Governor's new initiative. Thank fuck, there was no such a scheme running elsewhere in the country. If there was, it would be the ruin of him.

The cognac slid down smoothly. It didn't burn, just warmed him nicely. He smacked his lips and sighed. Life would be good again, and all those wishing that everything would go tits up for him would be sorely disappointed.

Yes, it would definitely be Florida for him. He would be glad to get out of the rain.

# Tuck

# 47

THE BEAT OF HER HEART reverberated across every bone in her body, causing her limbs to jerk and her chest to stutter behind her ribs. Dread sucked out every bit of courage, and resignation sapped her strength.

Her life didn't flash before her eyes, but images of Friar pierced her consciousness and she feared for him much more than she feared for herself. If she was going to die – and, she didn't have much doubt about that – then, so was he.

Blade didn't seem perturbed about Simms' death. In fact, he seemed quite pleased. He told her that she'd saved him a job.

That didn't bode well.

The children were beginning to stir. Blade cast his eyes over them.

"Don't hurt them," she said.

"I won't," he replied. "I promise you that they won't feel a thing."

"You're going to kill them?" Her words sounded flat, even to her own ears. She couldn't muster a hint of emotion. Everything seemed trapped behind that wall of dread.

"I'm going to kill everybody," he said, matter-of-fact. "I'll leave you until last." He removed two sets of zip ties from his pocket and threw one at her. "Secure your feet at the ankles... nice and tight, mind."

She had no choice but to comply. She didn't think she would fare well against the knife he held almost casually in his hand.

When her feet were secure, he dropped to his knees and got at her back. He yanked her arms behind her and fastened her wrists. He was unnecessarily cruel in tightening the restraint. He then pushed her onto her side, and got back to his feet.

"How did you do it?" he asked. "How did you kill him?"

She refused to answer. Let him wonder.

He spotted the syringe with its glistening needle and smiled. "Ah," he said. "I see." He bent over and ran the sharp blade of his knife over Simms' throat, opening it up into a slick gash.

No blood pumped, it merely oozed.

Tuck blinked. That was going to be her fate, and that of the children – throats slashed, and bleeding to death. She had saved Simms from that. He'd died with much less pain and much less terror at her hands.

Blade seemed momentarily mesmerized by the blood. His eyes widened, his nostrils flared, and he licked his lips. He was savouring the sight, smell and the imagined taste of it.

Blade loved everything about blood. It was, after all, *life*. The one thing he craved above all other things was the taking of life, so, to watch someone bleed-out always evoked an orgasmic reaction – every single time.

This time, he felt very little. Simms' blood was already dead blood. He wasn't interested in dead blood, so he turned back to the woman and stared at the pulse pounding against the skin at her throat.

She could wait. He would get enough satisfaction from killing the two men in the other room to ensure that he could take his time with her.

Then there were the children. He was looking forward to the experience that their blood-letting would elicit. When it came time to take the woman, he would be in such a state of exalted arousal that – if he died at that moment – he would die happy and content.

He had no doubt that he was in for a very pleasant evening – no doubt at all.

Tuck didn't need to be a mind reader to know what he was thinking. From her position on the floor, she could see right into his eyes. He was staring at her throat. His gaze was otherworldly.

She swallowed, and he smiled. He liked what that swallow represented.

"You hang in there, girlie. I'll be back in two shakes of a lamb's tail."

When he disappeared back through the door, and when she heard the tread of his footsteps on the wooden floor, she began the struggle to free herself.

*How long did it take to murder two burly men? How much time did she have before he was back?*

Not enough.

The zip tie securing her wrists was so tight that she felt it biting into her skin almost to the bone. She tried to force her hands apart. She knew full well that there was no way she would snap the plastic, but trying to force that snap was an instinctive thing to do.

*Think, Tuck. Fucking think!*

*The bag… Simms bag. Perhaps there was a scalpel inside?* That was almost too much to hope for. Yes, in a movie, there would be a scalpel. There was always a piece of broken glass, or a knife lying just within reach. But, Tuck wasn't in a movie, and the chances of her finding something sharp enough to cut herself free before the psycho returned were slim to none.

Simms had cut up people for a living. He cut up the living to steal their organs. Chances were that there *would* be a scalpel in his bag. She hung onto that thought. Without it, there would be no hope, and no point in doing anything other than giving up.

The bag was sitting on a chair, several feet behind her. Getting to it would be difficult, but not impossible.

# FRIAR AND TUCK CASE NUMBER ONE: THE MISSING

One of the children – the oldest girl – suddenly woke up. She was groggy and, when she pulled herself into a sitting position on the floor, she swayed drunkenly from side to side.

Tuck looked at her through frenzied eyes. She didn't want her awake – not yet. Her being awake complicated things and would probably hasten all their deaths.

"Lie down," she hissed.

"Wha..?" the girl swung her head around and the movement caused her to flop over. She cried out, and Tuck shushed her.

She listened for the footsteps that would warn her of Blade's return. All she heard were muffled voices – none raised in alarm. It would take him time to take out the two men. He would have to surprise them. She would have to do something within the next five minutes – it was all the time she would allow.

"Girl," he hissed. "What's your name, girl?"

Mary Potter heard the question, but was too groggy to understand it. She was aware of very little, and she felt sick to her stomach.

"Girl! Look at me, girl."

With a concerted effort, Mary turned to the sound of the voice. Her stomach heaved, and she spewed out burning bile onto the floor.

Her groan was one of abject misery.

Sweat drips into Tuck's eyes. She can't wipe it away, so she blinks rapidly, trying to keep her vision clear.

The stench of vomit is acrid in the air. Tuck hopes that emptying her belly has made the girl more alert. She tries once more to ask her name.

"M...Mary," she stammers quietly.

"You're Mary Potter?"

She nods, then retches.

"There's a bad man here, Mary."

"There's always a bad man," she returns, amazingly clearly.

"I need your help. Can you help me?"

Mary reaches over and gently touches, first one, and then the other of her sleeping siblings. Her brother lets out a muffled snore. She sighs, relieved.

"They're all right, Mary, but the bad man will be back in a minute. He'll hurt us."

"I'm hurt already," the girl sniffed.

"He'll hurt you more, so I need you to listen up, be a big girl, and help me and your little brother and sister."

A beat, then, "Okay."

"Do you see that bag behind me... on the chair?"

"Yeah."

"Can you go get it and bring it to me?"

She shook her head. "I don't feel so good."

Tuck bit back on her frustration. The girl had been doped up to the eyeballs. She was still obviously woozy and sick. There was very little time to waste, but waste it she must. She had to give Mary Potter as many moments as she needed to steady herself.

"Can you see that I'm tied up, Mary?"

"Yeah."

"I need something to cut through the ties. I think there might be something in that bag... something sharp."

Her eyes were drawn to the bag. "Okay."

"I need you to bring me the bag, Mary, before the bad man comes back."

"I'll try."

She pulled herself around and got onto her hands and knees.

Tuck heard her drag in a few breaths and then saw her begin to crawl across the floor to where the bag sat waiting.

"That's it, Mary... keep going... hurry."

Tuck cocked her head to the side, listening. Still no footsteps. Still the muffled voices.

She thought she would have some warning before Blade returned. She expected a great deal of noise, commotion, chaos, to precede his appearance. It was often a noisy business – murder.

"I've got it," Mary said. "It's heavy."

"Drag it across the floor. Don't try to carry it."

It had already been much more than the five minutes she'd allotted, but there had been no change in the sounds from the other room. She would give herself five minutes more.

Mary arrived at her side with the bag.

"Tip the bag upside down," she told the girl. "Empty everything out onto the floor. Try to be really, really quiet."

Mary nodded, and did as she was bid. A few glass bottles clinked as they landed. If there was nothing else, Tuck new she could break one of the bottles and use the glass to free herself, but they were small bottles, and any shards of glass wouldn't be large enough to use as a weapon against Blade.

She needed a weapon.

She saw the set of scalpels and heaved in a huge sigh of relief. They were obviously treasured possessions, because they were placed within an expensive moleskin cover, the type with small pouches that you wrapped and tied.

She instructed the girl to remove the largest one by its handle and to take off the protective cover. She prayed that she wouldn't cut herself. That scalpel could quite easily take her finger off.

Tuck thought about asking her to place it between the palms of her hands, so she could cut through the tie herself, but that would take too long and – as she couldn't see behind her – she might injure herself. She couldn't afford to cut her hands. Before long, she was going to need them.

"Do you think you could cut the tie off, Mary... without touching me?"

She thought about it for a moment, then nodded.

Remarkably, Mary's hands were as steady as a rock. Seconds later, Tuck's hands were free.

The blood rushed to her fingers. They tingled and burned. Cutting through the tie at her ankles was difficult due to the severe tremor in her right hand.

Then, it was done. She was free.

She handed a second scalpel to Mary, and said, "I want you to lie back down pretend to be asleep. Use the knife on the bad man if he lays a finger on you."

A fierce look came into Mary's eyes. She nodded. She knew that – if she had to - she could certainly do that.

Tuck closed her hand around the large scalpel. She picked up another one, and armed with both, she moved across to the door. She looked back, frowned, and hurried back. She had to clear the contents of the bag out of sight. She kicked everything over to the side against the baseboard, then dashed back to the door.

Mary was lying curled up into a tight ball. All three children were quiet. The only sound in the room was the rasp of her own breathing.

The commotion started. It sounded as if furniture was being overturned, and there was a scream followed by shouts and curses. Then banging, then silence.

She hid behind the door. It was slightly ajar. When he pushed it open she would have a few seconds to prepare herself.

She had no real plan. He was a strong son-of-a-bitch – deceptively so – but she would have the element of surprise.

A surprise attack was her *only* plan.

She waited for what seemed an eternity. He was taking his time returning. She recalled how he'd stared at Simms' open throat and thought she knew what was keeping him. She felt her body relax and go limp and she silently admonished herself, and coiled herself once more.

She had to be ready. However long it took, she couldn't relax until it was all over.

# Friar

# 48

THE PLACE HAD BEEN ransacked. They'd obviously left in a hurry. Every room inside the strange wooden erection had been turned upside down. One room in particular shocked him to his core. It wasn't the long room with the beds and the puddles of blood on the floor. What really shook him was the room that looked like a miniature operating theatre. It was equipped with everything you would find in a hospital, and there was evidence of surgery having recently taken place.

He thought he now knew what part Simms had to play, but what he didn't know – couldn't immediately fathom – was why. Or, *what*, for that matter.

Even for someone like him – someone who thought he'd seen enough in his life as a detective not to be flummoxed – he was completely in the dark. As he stood and panned the room with unbelieving, confused eyes, he tried to piece it all together in his mind.

A dead woman who somehow knew the missing street kid – the kid who'd ended up in this place, possibly operated upon, then killed and burned. A murdered couple – the Potters, with Mister Potter connected to the dead woman. Three other kids abducted, possibly dead. Then, the murdered detective and the missing Tuck, and her abductor, the ME Simms. Where would Simms have taken her? He had no idea.

Then, factor in the homeless shelter and the scumbag, Marcus Salzberg, the operating theatres, and the link to Simms being a surgeon of sorts, and what did he get? Absolutely fucking nothing.

*Right. Think.*

He believed that Simms had killed Henderson because Henderson had found out something incriminating in Natalie Bridgman's safety deposit box – tick. But, he continued to be confused as to why Simms offered up the key. He put that to one side.

He didn't believe that Potter killed Natalie, or his wife – tick. So, who killed Potter? The same man who'd killed Natalie and his wife – tick. Who did that man work for? He filed that question away for the moment.

Kevin Murphy was a street kid. If Bridgman and Potter hadn't reported his abduction, then no one would ever have looked for him. There were several beds in the long room – he'd counted more than half a dozen. So, other kids had possibly been abducted and met with the same fate as Kevin – tick. Why were kids being abducted and brought here? What operations was Simms carrying out?

Organ retrieval?

*Yes.*

He wondered what a kidney went for on the black market, or – for that matter – a heart, or a pair of lungs?

He felt sick just thinking about it. It was the ultimate in blood money.

He re-examined the unanswered questions.

Where had Simms taken Tuck, and why – if he was up to his neck in everything - had he offered up the key? Who was Mister Big, and who was his hired assassin?

How many other kids were missing, or dead?

Simms would have all the answers. He had to find him, and he had to save Tuck.

He gave up a silent prayer that she was still alive.

He heard voices and realized that the crime scene officers had arrived.

He led them to the furnace room and then left them to it. He wasn't finished with his own search. He wasn't leaving the warehouse until he found something to point him to Simms' whereabouts.

He hadn't been searching long when his phone chirruped in his pocket.

"Yeah, I'm still here," he said in response to the question. "I'll be right along."

He made his way back to the furnace room. It had been one of the CSI guys who'd rung him. *They've found something.*

# Blade

# 49

BLADE WAS BREATHING hard. His heart was hammering a staccato in his chest. He was exhilarated, exhausted, but ready and eager for the next kill.

He'd taken the two men out without much effort. They hadn't been expecting him to attack and, when the attack came, they were so shocked that they wasted precious seconds failing to react. He'd waited until they were both reclining in their chairs, relaxed, smoking and drinking beer.

The knife wasn't his only weapon of choice. One day, a few years before, he'd discovered the wonderfully versatile collapsible telescopic baton. Once he'd discovered it, and the damage it could inflict, he'd wondered how he'd managed to survive without it all those years.

You had to get up really close with a knife. He'd never favoured guns – too impersonal – but, with the baton, which extended to twenty long inches, he could keep his distance and still have the pleasure of personally drawing blood and gore. It was most useful when tackling men. He could never be sure how a man was – especially if they were relative strangers. He hadn't needed to use it with Potter. When the chips had been laid down, Potter was a pussy.

He always used the knife to finish his victims. Nothing could beat *that* feeling.

He hammered the ball at the end of the baton directly onto the top of the first man's head. He'd been standing behind his chair, so was able to put the full force of his weight behind it. Bone crunched, blood flew. The other man screamed like a woman. One sweep of the baton across the second man's face soon shut *him* up. The zombified fool jumped up, overturned his chair and stood crying and moaning, and doing absolutely fuck all to defend himself.

The first man was stupefied, and didn't move.

He beat them both mercilessly, but stopped just short of killing them. That job waited for the knife.

Afterwards, he sat awhile, relishing, savouring, absorbing the bloodbath. Now, he was on his way to deal with the kids and, then...

He felt the throb of his erection. His knife wasn't the only thing capable of stabbing.

When he stepped through the door, his wide grin faltered. *Where was the bitch?* He threw a quick glance at the still unconscious kids and then panned the room. By the time he realized to turn to look behind the door, she was on him.

Clinging to his back, both legs wrapped around his waist, she wasn't much of a weight, but he found it awkward to get at her, or shake her off.

Something sliced into his cheek. He felt the skin pop and almost peel open. Pain erupted and he screamed.

Furious, punched-through with adrenaline, he reached up and back, grabbed a handful of her hair, and yanked.

She went head over heels, landing on her back on the floor at his feet.

He saw the scalpels in her hands. He kicked at one hand, knocking one of the blades away, and then put the heel of his boot on the second hand until she let loose on that blade.

Bending over her, he screamed obscenities directly into her face, then drew his knife from the sheaf at his waist. He was going to cut her, and cut her up good.

# FRIAR AND TUCK CASE NUMBER ONE: THE MISSING

He felt a punch on a buttock. He thought it was a punch, but when he touched the spot with his hand, there was blood. He felt a second punch, and then a third on his thigh. He looked down. The floor was awash with blood.

He immediately knew that his femoral artery had been ruptured. He'd ruptured a few of those in his time. He had particularly loved to watch the spurt of arterial blood drench everything in its path.

The girl was standing there, watching him. She was the oldest of the Potter brats. Before his legs buckled, he saw the blade in her hand.

The little bitch had fucking done for him.

Tuck scooted backwards through the blood. She wasn't sure if she could trust what she'd just witnessed. It took her many moments to conclude that Blade was, indeed, mortally wounded.

He died on a wail of rage.

He didn't have a phone. Tuck knew that there had to be one somewhere.

Dripping with his blood, she searched the other room, searched the pockets of the two brutalized and very dead men, and then staggered outside to search the van.

She found it on the floor beneath the driver's seat. She used it to ring Friar.

# The King is dead
# 50

"IS HE DEAD?"

The boy, wrapped in the filthy sheet, and held in the arms of one of the uniformed police officers, looked dead to Friar. He wasn't moving, didn't seem to be breathing, and Friar was finding it difficult to swallow back on his horror and on his guilt.

He would never forgive himself for leaving him in that furnace. He couldn't believe that he hadn't checked the smaller one. If, all those hours before, he'd opened the door and found him, perhaps he would still be alive.

"Is he dead?" he asked again, knowing and dreading the answer.

It was as if the police officer either didn't hear him, or was, himself, too shocked to speak.

Friar wanted to reach out a hand to make contact with the body. He wanted his touch to be a kind of profound apology, but – just as he reached out - two EMT's rushed into the room, jostling him out of the way.

On instructions from one of the EMT's, the police officer laid the boy gently on the floor. They worked on him. Friar knew it was routine. The EMT's often worked on a dead body, not giving up until every last procedure had been attempted.

The uniformed officer moved to Friar's side. He said, "He's alive, sir."

Friar looked at him in confusion.

# FRIAR AND TUCK CASE NUMBER ONE: THE MISSING

The officer gave a curt nod of his head. "It's true. You might not know it – unless you know about furnaces – but that particular furnace has an outside air inlet. It would surprise you just how many aren't actually airtight. Fire dies without oxygen, so it makes sense, doesn't it, sir... to have air feeding in."

Friar nodded foolishly.

"I think the poor mite's lungs are fucked... what with inhaling all that ash... but he's alive... that's something."

Friar's phone rang. He considered ignoring it. He didn't think he would be able to utter a single word.

He looked at the screen, didn't recognize the number, and was just about to reject it, when he thought better of it.

He heard the familiar voice. It sounded hysterical, but there was no doubting who it belonged to.

It was Tuck. By all the saints, it was Tuck.

He gave a single sob. She was alive, and not only her. The Murphy boy was alive. Potter's kids were alive.

The frosting on the cake was that all the other fuckers were dead – all except one.

Friar soon remedied that.

Tuck, once such a stickler for protocol, a straight arrow who, when it came to doing what was right, stood by and watched as Friar shot King dead-centre between the eyes.

There had been no doubt about his guilt. When they confronted him at his apartment, his guilt was clear to see in his eyes and in his actions. He goaded them, laughed at them, told them that their superiors would have something to say about them arresting him. He said they wouldn't be pleased, would nullify any arrest warrant, put them on desk duty until they pulled their pensions. He boasted of the judges he had in his pocket, and then he pulled a gun on them.

Later, Tuck would swear that King went for his gun first, but no one knew if that had been true. Only Friar and Tuck knew.

They never spoke of it. Justice had been served, and that was all that mattered.

---

THANK YOU FOR READING *Friar and Tuck, The Missing*. The author would be grateful if you would consider leaving a review or a rating. Reviews and ratings are appreciated by the author as is the time that readers take to give them.

Why not take a look at the author's UK crime series –

***The Superintendent Lorrie Sullivan series.***

**The series titles are:**

Maelstrom of White

A Murder of Clowns

A Flock of Innocents

A Bouquet of Brides

A Rhapsody of Rage

A Brace of Fiends

**Sci-Fi/Fantasy by the author**

Beyond the Bloodline – Book One: The Empty Throne

Beyond the Bloodline – Book Two: The Rise of the Witch

Beyond the Bloodline – Book Three: Kulku

Tomorrow – an apocalyptic dystopian thriller

**Writing as Annie Gordon:**

The English Prince and the American

An English Prince Comes to Dinner

The English Prince and the Reluctant Bride

The English Prince and the Bad Girl

Made in the USA
Middletown, DE
17 July 2021